IN THE COMPANY

OF *Women*

BY

KATE CHRISTIE

Bella
BOOKS

2015

Bella Books, Inc.
P.O. Box 10543
Tallahassee, FL 32302

Printed in the United States of America on acid-free paper.

First Bella Books Edition 2015

Editor: Medora MacDougall
Cover Designer: Judith Fellows

ISBN: 978-1-59493-446-9

Other Bella Books by Kate Christie

Beautiful Game
Leaving L.A.
Solstice

Dedication

This book is dedicated to the nearly 400,000 American women who served in uniform from 1939 to 1945 in the Women's Army Corps (WAC), Navy (WAVES), Army and Navy Nurse Corps, Coast Guard (SPARs), Marine Corps Women's Reserves, and Women Airforce Service Pilots (WASPs).

It is also dedicated to the memory of Betty M. and Pauline R., "life partners for infinity" in the words of their granddaughter. Betty and Pauline met in the Women's Army Corps during World War II, fell in love, and managed to spend most of the next sixty years together. Their quiet bravery—and that of the tens of thousands of women and men like them who have led happy lives in plain sight of a disapproving government and culture—deserves special commendation.

Acknowledgments

As ever, I extend my love and gratitude to my wife and daughters for holding down the fort and for giving me the time and space to write—a space that now consists of a backyard structure otherwise known as "Mimi's office shed."

I'd also like to thank Medora MacDougall, editor and proofreader extraordinaire, for both the big picture and nitpicky assistance. This was only the first of what I hope will be many creative collaborations.

CHAPTER ONE

October 1943

Caroline Jamieson stood at the back of the train, watching the tracks recede into dusky brown hills that stretched as far as she could see. She'd left Chicago two days earlier and crossed through four states in the first twenty-four hours: Illinois, Missouri, Arkansas and the northwest corner of Louisiana. Sometime during the second night, while she failed to sleep in her upright seat—*not* the Pullman overnighters they'd been promised, the GIs around her griped—the train had crossed into Texas, another state she'd only ever visited on maps and in history books, a vast, sprawling landscape that made her native Michigan feel puny, insubstantial. Now each mile that slipped away beneath her represented the farthest she'd ever been from home.

"We're not in Kansas anymore, Toto," she murmured, drawing on her cigarette as sunrise lightened the browns and tans of the surrounding desert.

Not Iowa, either, where she'd completed a month of basic training, nor Illinois where she'd spent a dozen weeks learning how to be an airplane mechanic for the Army Air Forces. Definitely not California, where her initial orders had placed her along with a sizable contingent of her training class. Shari and Denise and the others were on their way home for two weeks of leave before they would journey west to work at airfields affiliated with the Douglas, Martin or Boeing factories, spending their days off at the Pacific Ocean and the Presidio, their nights out in Chinatown and on Market Street. Meanwhile CJ, chosen to serve as a replacement soldier at Fort Bliss in El Paso, had seen her leave revoked. Still smarting from the sudden change in assignment, she'd been hustled onto the train in Chicago and shuttled off to the farthest western edge of Texas. Lucky her.

Would there be cowboys and sagebrush, Indians and prong-armed cacti? She couldn't imagine what waited at the end of the line, but at least her real life in the Women's Army Corps was about to begin. She was tired of training, weary of temporary friendships and tenuous homes. She was ready to put down roots and dig into GI life. Even if that meant living in Texas.

Grinding out her cigarette, she pocketed the butt and returned to the car where she'd settled in with a handful of civilians and a larger group of servicemen. The boys were playing cards again, but Edith, the middle-aged Arkansan on her way to meet her new baby granddaughter in San Diego, looked up and waved her over.

"Pound cake?" she asked, holding out yet another tin lined with wax paper.

CJ helped herself to the cake she had a feeling would be delicious despite current shortages in sugar and butter. "At this rate, I'm not going to fit into my uniform."

"Don't be silly. You're built like my older boy, Chet. I'll bet you have to work to put on weight."

A bite of cake saved her from the need to respond. In 1943, curves were all the rage—curves she most certainly had not been blessed with. Or cursed with, as the case may be. Unlike some of her fellow WAC AAF trainees, she had managed to avoid anything more than passing interest from the men stationed at Chanute Field. Likewise, the boys on the train had treated her more like a little sister than a "dame." The big brother attitude didn't bother her. Since her recent split with her college boyfriend, she had resolved to keep her head down on the dating front. Besides, the WAC had strict rules about fraternization, probably for good reason.

The boys in the seat across the aisle batted their eyes at Edith, and she sighed good-naturedly. "Take it. I've got more."

The one nicknamed Dorsey, presumably for his musical talents, winked at CJ as he held the tin out to his buddies. "Let them eat cake!"

He, like the others, seemed to flirt almost automatically. But more than once she'd caught him staring at a girl's photo when he thought no one was looking. They were all from somewhere—hayseeds straight from the Kansas plains; Polish kids from Chicago; Jersey boys with tough accents; Mainers who'd joined the Army because they were tired of the sea; 'Bama boys riled up about the War Between the States. They each had a home and family and girl they had left behind, thanks to the draft or their sense of duty. The sheer number of young men—and women—who now found themselves in Uncle Sam's service was staggering. In her own family, the three who were of an age to do so had joined up, and they were hardly uncommon among their friends and neighbors.

She trained her gaze again on the landscape beyond the train's window. Still flat, still brown, still utterly foreign. Her family's farm would be beautiful right about now. But then, it was always beautiful, except maybe in the heart of summer when the black flies would rather die than leave you in peace. She loved autumn in Southwest Michigan—the cool, dewy mornings, the rattling bugle cries of sandhill cranes, the rose-cheeked apples that all but begged to be picked with a twist and flick of the wrist. Soon cooler nights would settle over the farm, and the leaves would begin to color and dry out, the horses' coats would thicken, and the furrowed fields would lay empty, waiting for snow. But for now, the land and forests would be green, pumpkins plumping on the vine, potato leaves plentiful.

The thought of home was like a missing tooth—she couldn't help but poke the gaping hole with her tongue, testing the raw emptiness of the space left behind. But at the same time, she knew she was fortunate to live where she did. Protected on either coast by the world's largest oceans, America's cities and its people had remained largely untouched, except for those who had volunteered—or been chosen—to "do their part."

As she was doing now. Soon the train would reach El Paso, and then it would be time to say more goodbyes, to greet a new set of pals whose company may or may not prove to be brief. Why did the military see fit to keep its constituents in constant flux? Although, she supposed she could see the value in teaching soldiers not to grow too attached to a place or to individual people. They were insignificant parts of a great machine erected to defeat the fascist forces currently clawing their way across the planet, blackening each nation, state, city and village they touched.

Ours is not to reason why; ours is but to do and die. She shivered at the thought.

Beside her, the clack of Edith's knitting needles paused. "Goose walk over your grave?"

"If by goose you mean the German Army, then yes."

Edith's gaze sharpened. "Don't give them the satisfaction. Now that our boys are over there, those Nasties will be running home with their tails between their legs, you mark my words."

CJ nodded politely. But she doubted that battle-hardened Wehrmacht soldiers would find much reason to run from green American boys like the ones across the aisle, bickering over whose mother made the best chocolate chip cookies.

* * *

The train arrived at El Paso's Union Depot shortly before nine that night. CJ had barely retrieved her GI rucksack from an overhead rack near the car's entrance when one of the boys liberated her of its heft.

"I've got it, Private," he said. "Lead away."

She could fix a 2,500 horsepower engine but she couldn't carry her own luggage? She faked a gracious nod. "Thank you, Sergeant."

His friends whistled, but he ignored them. "Are you riding out to Bliss with us?"

"I don't know."

She'd checked in at the Dallas USO to let the Fort Bliss WAC command know her arrival plans, but she had no way of knowing if they'd received her communique. As they stepped onto the platform, she noticed a WAC sergeant and private watching passengers stream from the train. Message received, obviously. She freed her bag from the helpful non-com and made her way to the two women in uniform.

"Private Jamieson?" the sergeant asked, her sweet voice an odd match for her military bearing and slightly squarer than average jaw.

"Yes, Sergeant."

"Welcome to Bliss," the private said, smiling as she reached for CJ's rucksack. "Let me. You must be tired after your trip."

Giving up her bag to a Wac didn't have nearly the same connotations as to a GI, especially when the woman in question was nearly a half foot shorter.

They introduced themselves on the way out to the Jeep—Toby Peterson, the private, hailed from New York City, while Staff Sergeant Velta Welch was an Okie, which explained the twang. That was as far as they got before Welch turned the ignition and put the Jeep in gear. Open cars weren't conducive to conversation.

The autumn night was cold and dark, and CJ barely got an impression of brick buildings and arched streetlights before they were pulling up to the post gate. El Paso didn't seem to be much of an urban center, that was for sure. But Fort Bliss was an antiaircraft artillery, or AA, training post. Probably it was better not to have your ack-ack guns and tow target planes careening close to human population centers. Soon they passed through another gate into a separate compound signed "WAC Personnel Only" and guarded by MPs and barbed wire. The exaggerated security might have alarmed her if the WAC compound at Chanute hadn't been similarly circumscribed from the rest of the airfield.

Friday night was GI night the country over, CJ realized as the sarge went off to park the Jeep and Toby led her to an empty bunk in her new barracks. The other women in her assigned squad room paused to introduce themselves, mostly young women like her with hair pinned up off their shoulders and the same shade of red lipstick fading after a long work day. Then they returned to scrubbing floors, untangling the contents of lockers and trunks and disposing of clothes, civilian suitcases and shoes piled every which way. In the morning, company officers would stroll through the barracks opening this locker, checking that bunk, examining the latrine, day room and orderly room for even the minutest speck of dust. Friday night detail and Saturday morning inspection always reminded CJ of the saying she'd learned in basic training: "If it moves, salute it. If it doesn't, clean it."

Her new barracks were a step up from her previous GI accommodations. Here each Wac had her own cot, an individual wall locker and a private trunk, and every two girls shared a dressing table that doubled as a desk. The latrine impressed as well: two bathtubs, six showers and actual doors on the stalls, for a change. Beside it lay a large laundry room with multiple sinks, indoor drying lines and wood clothing pins. But best of all was the day room, decked out in comfortable, early American furniture and decorated with painted murals of famous women warriors: Boadicea, Joan of Arc, Deborah Sampson, Molly Pitcher, a nameless Amazon and the WAC patron saint Pallas Athene.

Once Toby had given her the barracks tour, there wasn't much for CJ to do but unpack, shine her shoes and iron her travel-wrinkled clothes in the laundry room before stowing them away. No latrine detail yet, and no chance to socialize with the women who whirl-wound past in their hurry to get the squad room as clean as was soldierly possible.

Soon three nights of train travel caught up, and she dropped off without intending to in the brightly lit barracks, women murmuring and laughing around her.

* * *

The next morning CJ stood at attention in front of her bunk as three WAC officers paraded through the barracks. She wondered what they were like—rigid and by-the-book like the officers at Chanute Field or intelligent leaders like the non-coms at Fort Des Moines, where she'd completed basic?

Lieutenant Fiona Kelly paused before her. "How are you settling in, Private Jamieson?"

"Fine, ma'am." She was careful not to meet the lieutenant's gaze.

"Good. Let me know if you have any questions or concerns, soldier."

"Thank you, ma'am."

She risked a glance at the lieutenant's face as she moved on to the next bunk. With gray streaks showing in neat auburn hair cut above the collar of her "A" uniform, she was older than most of the other women in the company and exuded a confidence borne not solely of age and rank. Gym teacher? College administrator? The WAC officer ranks were filled with executive secretaries and university instructors and even a dean and college president, if the rumors were correct.

Inspection didn't last long, and by the end of it she had her answer—the enlisted women had worked hard the night before to put their barracks in order, and the officers recognized their efforts. No gigs on Company D, which meant no restrictions for the week ahead. Intelligent leaders by the look of it.

After inspection she went outside to survey the multitude of white wooden and adobe buildings that made up the WAC area, the brown, rocky mountains that hulked in the near distance. Somehow she doubted California would have felt quite so alien. Lit cigarette in hand, she sat on the front steps of the barracks and watched women hang laundry on lines that stretched between low-slung buildings. The coolness of the desert night had faded soon after morning mess, and now the Texas sun was strong in the cloudless sky. Another regional quirk—she wasn't used to such warmth in mid-October.

"Mind if I join you?" Toby, the private who had met her at the train station the night before, paused beside the steps.

"Not at all."

Toby, CJ noted, had changed from her formal "A" uniform into the same one-piece coveralls the WAC trainees at Chanute Field had worn on duty. Both uniforms bore the blue and yellow Army Air Forces shoulder sleeve insignia.

"So, Jamieson, do you like sports?" she asked, lighting a cigarette.

"Absolutely."

"Good. There's a basketball hoop in back of the officers' quarters, and a group of us get together on the weekends for softball. We're playing today, in fact, after noon mess. You're welcome to join us."

"Thanks. I will."

She'd played softball, basketball and tennis on the weekends in Illinois too. Sports were second nature to her. She'd grown up shadowing her two older brothers around the farm and assorted playing fields. Only now Joe, a Marine officer in the Pacific, and Alec, a B-17 flight engineer in Italy, probably didn't get much opportunity to play games.

"Lieutenant Kelly's our ump." Toby blew a cloud of smoke into the air and watched it dissipate. "I thought you looked like the sporting type."

Just then another Wac dropped onto the steps. "Hiya, girls."

"Hi yourself," Toby said, smiling at the newcomer. "Kate, this is CJ, our newest grease monkey. CJ, this is Kate Delaney. She's with Personnel."

"Welcome to Bliss," Kate said, proffering the same greeting Toby and the staff sergeant had given the night before.

Other than the greeting, however, she seemed to have little in common with Toby or the sarge, both of whom were short-haired, narrow-hipped women who looked more natural in coveralls than in the WAC summer uniform that Kate filled out so well. Unlike them, she managed to look curvy and pretty even in a shirt and tie.

"Hiya, kids," another woman said, snagging Toby's cigarette and taking a deep draw.

"Antonelli," Toby mock-growled, "you better watch it."

"Gee, I'm shaking in my GI shoes," the dark-haired newcomer returned as she handed back the smoke. Like Toby, she was wearing coveralls.

Between them, Kate rolled her eyes. "Reggie, have you met CJ?"

"Sure did, last night." Reggie offered CJ a nod. "Hey."

"Hey." CJ waved a little and tapped ash from the end of her cigarette. Was being a replacement soldier always this awkward? No doubt it was worse trying to join a tight-knit combat team during an offensive.

Count your lucky stars, she reminded herself for the umpteenth time since joining up.

"We should probably get going," Kate said. Without warning she grabbed Toby's cigarette and leaped down the steps.

"Come back here," Toby said good-naturedly.

"You'll have to come and get me."

Toby laughed and took off after the smaller woman, who held the cigarette over her head as she trotted away.

"Duty calls," Reggie told CJ. "The general has us working half-days on Saturdays."

She rose quickly. "Am I supposed to report too?"

"Nope. Sarge says you're on limited duty until Monday."

Whew.

"Feel like a walk anyway?" Reggie added.

"Why not?"

As they marched down the dusty road that led through the WAC compound, CJ exchanged pertinent details with the others. Kate was from Wisconsin—practically neighbors, they agreed—so the conversation skewed briefly toward the Midwest, Wisconsin cheese and the Great Lakes. Toby and Reggie, both from the Northeast, refused to believe that Lake Michigan was too wide to see across.

"I'll take you there someday," Kate said, bumping Toby's hip with her own.

"That's a promise I plan to hold you to."

At the edge of the compound a pair of military police guards nodded politely, their eyes friendliest, CJ noted, as they rested on Kate's face. The two men returned to their conversation—they seemed to be ranking their favorite desserts—before the women were out of earshot. CJ didn't envy them, but then again, being an MP was better than being an infantryman in a foxhole on the Italian front. Besides, they probably weren't alone much. Back in Illinois, despite the rules against fraternization, sympathetic Wacs had often stopped to chat with the MPs on duty.

CJ accompanied the others along the main road toward the center of the post, examining her surroundings curiously. She had passed through the night before but had been too tired to take much notice. Like in the WAC area, the buildings here were mostly whitewashed wood or adobe that reflected the bright sunlight. The landscape, a mixture of tan and brown, stretched toward nearby mountains and the outer reaches of El Paso like a colorless sea.

Ah, the ocean. She tried not to curse the girl she'd replaced, a married Wac who had apparently gotten pregnant while on furlough with her husband, a Navy pilot home on rotation from the Pacific. Maybe she'd wanted out of the Army without the shame of quitting, or perhaps she'd merely longed to have a child with her husband before it was too late. Couldn't begrudge her that, could she?

At the PX, Toby and the others said their farewells and strode off to their respective assignments. CJ ducked inside and glanced around, wondering if she should pick up an extra pair of sunglasses. As she wandered the aisles, she trailed her fingers over the metal shelf edges. The post general store at Chanute, with its postcards, candy bars and other non-GI items, had felt like a direct link to the outside world. Would this new PX offer the same reassuring connection to a life she had previously taken for granted?

Lost in thought, she turned a corner near a display of stationary and nearly collided with another khaki-clad woman.

"Sorry," she said quickly, reaching out to steady the Wac. At five-nine, she was used to looking down, literally, on other women. But the private first class before her, trim and attractive in what must be a specially tailored summer uniform, met her gaze nearly square on.

"It's my fault," she said, her hands on CJ's. "I was moving too quickly, as usual."

Her hair was the color of honey, her eyes pale blue with a tawny starburst about the pupil—but only in her right eye, CJ noted, intrigued.

The other woman's brow rose slightly. "I don't think we've met, have we?"

CJ realized she was still holding the stranger's arms. "No," she agreed, relinquishing her grip. "I arrived last night."

"From?"

"Chanute Field."

"Ah," the Wac said. And then, with a slightly ironic smile, "Welcome to Bliss."

"And is it blissful here?"

"If you happen to love all things GI."

CJ tilted her head. "Do you?"

"As a third-generation Army enlistee, I should probably toe the party line. But let's just say I'd rather be here than back at home, wishing I'd taken the leap. I'm Brady, by the way."

She offered her hand, and CJ squeezed it.

"CJ. Where's home for you?"

"Southern California. You?"

"Michigan. Kalamazoo, actually."

Brady smiled again. "'I Got a Gal'—bet you never heard that one."

"Hardly ever." CJ returned the smile. Glenn Miller's hit song had launched her hometown into the national spotlight a year earlier. As Brady continued to gaze at her, she felt a blush creeping up her neck. "Well, it was nice meeting you."

"I don't suppose you'd fancy a tour of the base? I have a Jeep waiting outside."

Even if Brady had been the peskiest of GIs, CJ would have had a hard time refusing the offer. Like her father and her brother Alec, she loved motorized conveyances of any kind, which was how she'd ended up with a Military Occupational Specialty (MOS) in Maintenance.

"Sounds like fun."

"Swell. Let me pay for these," Brady added as she moved away, brandishing a box of red pens and a stack of typing paper.

CJ waited near the front of the PX, watching Brady interact with the civilian cashier. Not as friendly, definitely cooler—which meant she probably didn't invite everyone she met for a Jeep ride.

Outside, the promised vehicle sat parked illegally at the curb, two GIs chattering away in its front seat.

Brady held the door open for CJ. "Hop in," she said, her words more of a dare than an invitation.

CJ maneuvered into the back seat, keeping her skirt down and her shoulders squared as the two men up front did a double-take.

"Hang on," said the driver, a lanky youth with smooth cheeks and sharp brown eyes. "Did I miss something?"

"This is CJ," Brady said, sliding in beside her. "She's new. I thought we could give her a tour of Bliss."

"Why didn't you say so?" the front-seat passenger quipped. He was almost as blonde as Brady. "Carry on, Jeeves."

The driver punched him and put the Jeep in gear. "Your wish is my command, my queen," he slung at Brady as he pulled out onto the main post road.

"That's Charlie," she said, nodding regally in his direction.

"And I'm O'Neil," put in the passenger. "But you can call me Mick. Everyone else does."

Charmed by his open face and laughing eyes, CJ liked him immediately. The driver she wasn't so sure about.

"I suppose you're wondering why we have a Jeep," Brady said.

"Uh, sure."

In reality, she'd been noticing again how well Brady's uniform fit. More than a year after its inception, the Women's Army Corps was still working out supply issues.

"We work at Administration," Mick helpfully put in.

That meant this ride probably wouldn't be repeated once she was on active duty. CJ had noted at Chanute that there seemed to be an invisible barrier between the administrative and maintenance ranks, a division that reminded her of the farm girl versus city girl split at her high school.

"What's your rating?" Charlie asked, taking his eyes off the road long enough to give her an appraising stare.

"Seven forty-seven."

Mick chewed his lip. "Maintenance, but what specialty?"

"Airplane engine mechanic," CJ clarified.

The boys up front were silent, perhaps aware that her military occupation required more brawn than theirs. This disparity could create an awkwardness that many men did not appreciate, she had learned. On the train to Bliss, she'd avoided mentioning her rating to the GIs who'd tried to pick her up in the dining car or followed her back to her seat.

But now she was on the base that could, for all she knew, be home for the duration of the war plus six months she'd signed up for. No avoiding reality here.

Brady said, "You must be skilled. There can't be many Wacs rated as airplane mechanics."

"I guess not," she said, smiling at Brady. "What do you do?"

"I work for the Public Relations Office doing news releases and soldier profiles for the *Fort Bliss Monitor*. Oh, and I write a bimonthly column, 'Wacs on Parade.'"

"You actually get to use your brain?"

"Shocking, isn't it?"

From what CJ had heard, a majority of Wacs were underemployed or assigned to positions that didn't match their skills or stated interests. Bliss, in direct proportion to its sprawling size, had a fairly large contingent of women soldiers. On the walk in, her new squad mates had informed her that in addition to Biggs Airfield, women in their battalion were assigned to the Transportation Corps, Personnel, Materials Management and other administrative offices. There were four companies of Wacs at Bliss, close to four hundred female soldiers in all. And more than eight thousand men on any given day, including armored and artillery units and Army Air cadets.

Charlie slowed the Jeep as they neared headquarters, where the post, state of Texas and US flags all waved languidly in the breeze.

"There's the Grinder," he said, jerking his chin at the wide parade grounds that seemed to go right up to the mountains in the distance.

"Those are the Franklins," Brady said, following her gaze. "Some of us like to go hiking up there on weekends."

"Are you one of those outdoor types too?" Mick asked CJ, aversion evident in his tone.

"Don't listen to him," Brady said. "He grew up in New York City. Claims to be allergic to trees."

"Then this is a good place for you, Mick, isn't it?" CJ commented.

"What do you call those?" Charlie nodded at the low, scruffy deciduous trees ringing the parade ground.

"Pathetic, mainly."

Michigan trees—elms, maples, oaks, evergreens—were majestic life forms her parents had taught her to respect. These, on the other hand, were barely more than shrubs.

Brady laughed. "Are you a tree snob?"

"Apparently," she said, smiling back.

"I suppose there are worse things to be."

Charlie careened the Jeep around a corner, throwing Brady into her. CJ held out a steadying hand. This close, Brady's eyes were more cornflower than ice, she decided.

"I have to stop running into you." Brady slid back to her side of the seat. "Otherwise you won't be any good for PT."

I don't mind. But CJ didn't say the words. Just because she felt an immediate connection to Brady didn't mean the sentiment was mutual. Still, as they continued the tour of Bliss, she thought that despite a noticeable lack of stately hardwoods, West Texas might not be so bad after all.

CHAPTER TWO

During the next half hour, CJ learned the layout of the post and nearby town while exchanging GI pedigrees with her guides—where they were from, where they'd done basic, how long they'd been at Bliss. Then Brady and the two men agreed that they should probably get back to work before their officers sent a search party after them.

"Where are you headed?" Brady asked as they parked beside the building that housed the Public Relations and *Monitor* offices.

"No idea. It feels like I'm the only one who doesn't have to work this morning."

"The post library is down the hall from us," Brady said. "You could pick up some reading material, and then maybe we could walk back to the compound together for mess."

"Works for me."

Brady, it seemed, didn't want to get rid of her yet. Funny how quickly someone in the Army could become a friend. The instant camaraderie reminded her of the teams she'd played on in high school and college—shared hardship could bond you in a very short time. Not that she and Brady had experienced any hardship this morning. There was still noon mess to get through, though. No doubt the cooks here were, like all Army cooks, fond of serving chipped beef on toast—SOS in soldier parlance, short for "shit on a shingle."

In the fluorescent lamp-lit library, Brady introduced CJ to the WAC librarian, Marjory from Albany. Then she headed back to work, promising to retrieve CJ shortly before noon for the slog back to the WAC area, where women soldiers cooked, dined and performed KP in their own mess halls. Marjory went back to the book she was reading, a beat-up copy of what looked like a mystery novel. CJ paced the stacks, curious what the collection had to offer. Mysteries, westerns, military biographies, a few classics like Shakespeare and Dickens, and piles of old issues of *Life*, *Yank* and *Stars and Stripes*. The walls bore the usual propaganda posters: "Buy War Bonds," "Loose Lips Sink Ships" and the library favorite, "Books Cannot Be Killed by Fire," which showed oafish German soldiers burning books by the armful.

In the periodicals section, she found what she was looking for: the *Fort Bliss Monitor*. She picked up the latest edition of the base weekly, sat down at a reading table and turned on a lamp. The library was a windowless interior room; without the clock on the wall, she wouldn't have known whether it was morning or evening. Soon she was skimming the paper, looking for a particular byline. She found it on page two: Brady Buchanan. Had to be her, didn't it? She read the article carefully, a profile of the 203rd, an artillery company about to ship overseas. The story was good, she realized—writing crisp, details sharply drawn, tone of the piece a good balance between patriotism, humor and human interest. For once the Army had gotten a Wac's MOS right.

As she stared at the smiling faces of a handful of the soldiers Brady had profiled, CJ felt a familiar knot in her stomach. These boys were all someone's son, brother, sweetheart, friend. Each of their lives touched a hundred others, lives that would be permanently altered if something happened to them. Her family would certainly never be the same if one of her brothers were to go missing or—God forbid—be killed in action.

For the past year her family, like so many others, had lived in fear of receiving a War Department telegram. Alec had been with the Northwest African Air Forces originally. Now that the mission in Africa had ended, he had been transferred to Southern Europe. Being on a bomber crew was one of the most dangerous jobs in the ETO, and Alec's tour wouldn't be over for months assuming he—she stopped the thought. Dark-haired, light-eyed and barely a year older, he looked so much like her that people used to mistake them for twins. She couldn't conceive of a world without him.

In the Pacific, meanwhile, where Joe was stationed, American forces were moving from one fortified island to another on the march to the Philippines, taking substantial losses as they attempted to expel the dug-in Japanese. "Substantial losses"—CJ closed her eyes as her eldest brother's face flashed before her, the candid image of him in his Cubs uniform from the front page of the *Chicago Tribune* the week after he joined up. "Jamieson Swaps the Majors for the Marines," read the headline. Her mother had cut out the article and placed it in the scrapbook she had started keeping for him when he made the leap from farm team to major leagues.

The last photo in the book was from Fort Lewis in Washington state, an official Marine portrait Joe had sent home before he shipped overseas. Occasionally CJ remembered that scrapbook, tucked onto a bookshelf in the family room. Joe wanted to come home and go back to his baseball career, she knew, but in a recent rare missive, he'd told her that he hadn't thrown a ball in months. What was worse, he couldn't seem to bring himself to care.

"Whatcha reading?" a low voice enquired at her shoulder.

CJ jumped. "Nothing," she said, folding the newspaper quickly.

"Funny, it looked like you were reading one of my articles."

"I might have skimmed it," she said as she returned the *Monitor* to its rack.

"And?" Brady prodded.

"Not bad. For a Californian."

"Hey, now." Brady whacked her shoulder.

"Ow. You have brothers, don't you?"

"How did you know?"

"Lucky guess."

They waved to the librarian and headed down the long, low-ceilinged hall to the outdoors, chatting about family as they went. CJ described growing up on a working farm outside the Kalamazoo city limits with a school teacher mother, two older brothers, a younger brother and a little sister. In turn, Brady described her upbringing in the hills of Los Angeles—businessman father who was rarely home, mother who kept busy with community work, one older brother, one younger, nannies, private schools and later, a Seven Sisters women's college on the East Coast.

"Which one?" CJ asked.

"Smith, in western Massachusetts."

"My grandmother and aunts went to Wellesley."

"Really?"

CJ read the surprise in her glance. "My mother comes from old Detroit money, but she left it all behind to attend teachers college and marry my dad. My grandmother wanted me to apply to Wellesley, but I picked U of M instead."

"Good thing you didn't go to Wellesley, or I wouldn't be able to be friends with you."

"Good thing then," CJ said, her arm brushing Brady's as they walked toward the still-distant WAC compound, low-heeled GI shoes crunching audibly on the gravel road.

"Speaking of Smith," Brady added, "did you know a woman at Chanute named Adele Talbot? She would have been in Admin."

"Sounds familiar," CJ hedged.

Adele, a wealthy Manhattanite, had seemed to derive untoward pleasure from complaining about the Midwest, military bureaucracy and anything else that caught her attention. She had further endeared herself by proclaiming that WAC mechanics and drivers were social anathema. Why she had joined the Army was anyone's guess.

"I couldn't stand her," Brady said.

"Neither could I," CJ confessed, laughing. "So what did you study?"

"English, of course. You?"

"History. Who's your favorite writer?"

"Depends. For fiction, the Brontë sisters and Jane Austen. Poetry, I'm a Byron girl all the way."

"Sounds like you're a romantic."

"It would seem so. Who's your favorite writer?"

"Mary Wollstonecraft. And Mark Twain. Frederick Douglass too. Did you know that slave narratives are considered the only uniquely American literary form?"

"I did know that. But I'm surprised a Michigan farm girl would."

"Hey, now," CJ said, laughing again.

They walked on, discussing books and classes they had loved until finally Brady paused.

"You know what?" She glanced sideways at CJ. "I haven't had a conversation like this since I joined the Army."

"Same here. When did you graduate?"

"'42. You?"

"In May."

She didn't mention her decision to defer graduate school. She wasn't sure why except that maybe she felt inexcusably naïve for the way everything had gone down, as if she should have seen it coming.

At the gate to the women's compound, they passed MPs who tugged on their caps, eyes glued to Brady.

"Friends of yours?" CJ asked.

"Not that I know of."

In the mess hall, they had just joined the line when a pretty brunette PFC approached.

"Where did you run off to, Brady?" she asked in a polished New England accent. "I didn't see you in the usual spot."

"Sorry, couldn't wait for my turn at a little SOS. By the way, this is CJ. She transferred in last night. CJ, this is Janice. She works in Personnel."

CJ nodded. "Nice to meet you."

"You too," Janice said as they moved forward with the rest of the line. "What company are you in?"

"D." CJ glanced down the line. Lunch didn't look too bad—soup, sandwiches and chocolate chip cookies. Lucky for them, soldiers weren't impacted by home front rationing nearly as much as civilians were.

"D?" Janice frowned slightly. "Isn't that a maintenance company?"

"CJ's an airplane mechanic," Brady said with what CJ found to be undue enthusiasm.

Apparently so did Janice: "Oh," she said coolly, and looked away.

CJ resisted the urge to wrinkle her nose at Janice's cold shoulder. Across the mess, she noticed Toby and Reggie waving.

"Friends of yours?" Brady asked.

"Squad mates. They're mechanics too."

"Naturally."

Did she sound a tiny bit disappointed? Was it possible the Army's pecking order frustrated her too?

At the end of the line, Janice edged between them, gazing expectantly at Brady.

"Well, it was nice meeting you," CJ offered, pausing with tray in hand.

"You too," Brady said. "We should meet for a drink at the club sometime. What do you think?"

CJ felt Janice watching her with a stare reminiscent of Charlie, the jealous Jeep driver.

"Sure," she said casually. "Why not?"

"Good." Brady smiled, her blue eyes warm. "I'll see you soon, then."

CJ hoped so, but once again she held back the words that would give away her interest in their fledgling friendship. Was it that Brady Buchanan, Smith College graduate and Admin Wac, seemed out of her league? But that was silly. Brady was the one who had invited her on the Jeep ride, the one who had suggested they go for a drink.

She nodded and turned away, wondering at herself as she crossed the mess to the table Toby, Kate and Reggie occupied with a group of familiar-looking women. It wasn't like she believed social divisions had real merit. Her parents had raised her and her siblings to value all people equally, no matter their race, class or sex. At least in theory.

"How do you know Brady Buchanan?" Reggie asked as she slid in beside CJ.

"I met her at the PX this morning."

"Half the boys on base are in love with her," Toby said. "She's engaged to a soldier, though, so one wave of the ring and they back off. Usually."

Brady was attractive and already out of college, so it wasn't surprising she would be engaged. But why hadn't she mentioned something as significant as a fiancé?

Toby interrupted CJ's thoughts. "You still planning to join us for softball?"

"I wouldn't miss it."

She was stiff from her cross-country train adventure, but it would be fun to get hot and dusty and then clean up and maybe take a nap before evening mess. And after supper, rehash the game over drinks and smokes at the enlisted women's club.

As CJ ate, she recognized a familiar surge of guilt. Her stint in the Army so far had offered significantly more R&R than her brothers and their buddies had, and as an American, she already knew she was luckier than most people. Sure, she had signed over her personal freedom to the Army, which could move her anywhere it wanted without warning and assign her any work it deemed necessary. But she didn't have to worry about her family or hometown being destroyed by bombing or, worse, occupation forces. She was learning new skills, exploring parts of the country she had only ever read about, and meeting new people with different outlooks. The war was a disruption to her previously comfortable life, but the interruption wasn't necessarily unwelcome.

She tamped down the guilt, as she always did, and finished her lunch quickly, looking forward to the afternoon ahead. She wouldn't have thought it possible even a few days earlier, but she was already settling into life at Bliss. Was it possible this place might actually manage to live up to its name?

CHAPTER THREE

Back at the barracks after lunch, Toby called CJ over to her bunk, where she pulled a folded piece of khaki from her locker. The lockers here were full-sized closets instead of the footlocker she'd had at Chanute. Which meant it would be easier to hide contraband—like non-GI clothing, for example.

"I managed to get hold of these before lunch," Toby said. "Welcome to the Fort Bliss Sporting Club, as we like to call ourselves."

CJ unfolded the cloth. It was a pair of GI pants, cut off below the knees. "These are swell. In Illinois, we played in our PT kits. Talk about raspberries."

"You should still wear your PT kit," Toby said. "But wear the pants instead of the bloomers. That way you won't be gigged for being out of uniform."

All WAC recruits were issued knee-length, seersucker dresses with matching khaki bloomers to wear during the physical training component of the Army regimen. With short sleeves, a belt and buttons down the front, the dresses covered more real estate than CJ's high school and college basketball uniforms had. The PT dress was intended to be worn during KP, latrine duty and garbage detail too, but with a skirt cut above the knees, it was deemed inappropriate for wear outside the WAC area.

"By the way, what position do you play?"

"Catcher."

"That's jake." Toby walloped her on the back. "You may have just made yourself the most popular replacement soldier at Bliss."

A little while later, they headed across the compound to the baseball diamond that former cavalry soldiers had staked out behind the officers' quarters, located not far from the basketball court with its lone hoop. The WAC compound at Bliss had previously been home to a cavalry division, as had Fort Oglethorpe in Georgia, an important WAC training post. A captain CJ knew at Chanute used to say, "Are we being trained to replace men or horses?"

Sitting on the ground next to Toby and Reggie, CJ stretched her legs and watched women from various companies assemble on the playing field. Everyone wore PT dresses except Lieutenant Kelly, who wore her summer uniform minus the jacket and tie. Like the others, CJ wore her WAC fatigue hat to keep the sun—and her hair, cut above her collar according to regulation—out of her eyes.

"Hey, stranger."

CJ squinted up at the Wac who loomed over her, blocking the sun. Then Brady dropped to the ground.

"Are you following me?" CJ asked.

"I could ask you the same question."

"Smith girls play sports? I thought maybe all you did was drink tea and eat crumpets."

"A Smith gym teacher invented women's basketball. But I should have known you would play. Not much else to do out in the country, is there?"

"We'll see who's better," CJ said, bending forward to grab her toes.

"You betcha."

The lieutenant and a couple of sergeants disappeared into the garage behind the officers' house and reappeared with bases, mitts, bats and balls. CJ looked the catcher's equipment over. She'd played behind the plate ever since she started playing baseball with her brothers and their friends in the field behind the feed barn. At first they had made her play the position because no one else wanted to, but after a while, she started choosing it. For nearly a decade, she and her brothers had spent their summer evenings playing ball. Joe had always outshone everyone else, of course, even when they were little. A high school prep star in Kalamazoo, he hadn't even finished a year at the University of Michigan when the Cubs signed him to their farm team.

Unlike her eldest brother, CJ hadn't had a professional sports career to disrupt her undergraduate education. Now here she was, six months out of college, getting ready to play ball with a bunch of ill-clad Army women on a lazy Saturday afternoon in West Texas. Sometimes, secretly, she could almost appreciate the social mores that kept women out of combat. If things had been different, she would have taken up arms alongside her brothers. She was relieved she wouldn't have to, though. She wasn't sure she would be able to kill a fellow human being—or live with herself afterward if she somehow managed it.

Maintenance had enough people to field their own team. The stragglers, including Brady and a couple of other Admin Wacs, organized themselves into an opposing side, and the gathered women began to warm up. CJ's team batted first. From the bench, CJ watched Brady warm up at catcher, impressed by her quickness and arm strength.

Toby followed her gaze. "Normally she pitches, but Susie from the post office is away this weekend."

When it was her turn, CJ grabbed a bat and walked toward home plate. Ignoring Brady, she set her feet and took a few practice swings. A little rusty, but it would take more than a cross-country train journey to make her lose her swing.

"Ready to strike out, Private?" Brady drawled as CJ squared up for the pitch.

She glanced back at Brady, whose face was hidden by the catcher's mask. "Strike out in slow pitch? That'll be the day."

"Let's see you put your money where your mouth is." Brady pounded her glove.

CJ squared up for the pitch again, leaning over the plate. The pitcher wound up and sent the ball hurtling through the air. CJ swung, muscles in her arms and back contracting—and missed the ball. Not even a tip.

"Striiike," the lieutenant announced.

"Nice swing." Brady snickered.

CJ ground her teeth and planted her feet again. She was out of practice, that was all. On the next pitch, she shut Brady's presence out of her mind and sent the ball sailing into left field for a stand-up double. Not bad for a farm girl.

The next batter popped the ball up in foul territory, and Brady made a dramatic diving catch for the final out. CJ jogged in from second.

"Show-off," she said, watching Brady shed the bulky pads.

"You're just jealous."

"Hardly." CJ picked up the discarded mitt.

"You're playing catcher?"

"Yep. Now we get to see if you can hit, Buchanan."

Brady batted third. CJ waited until she'd faced up for the first pitch before murmuring, "Don't strike out, crumpet girl."

Brady swung and missed, and then glared over her shoulder at CJ. "Nice swing."

On the next pitch, Brady hit a triple. Perhaps getting her riled was not the best strategy.

The innings marched along. CJ and Brady razzed each other good-naturedly, talking tough and elbowing one another as they traded the catcher's gear back and forth. In the end, CJ's team won by three. Afterward, CJ helped Reggie and Toby collect the equipment and store it back in the garage.

Brady was waiting for them when they emerged. "Hey," she said, eyes fixed on CJ. "Good game, even if you did try to break my ankle on that one slide."

"Get out of the kitchen if you can't stand the heat."

"What a quaint saying." Brady arched an eyebrow. "Did you pick that up on the farm?"

Laughing, CJ held out her hand. "Good game, seriously."

Brady squeezed her hand, smiling back. "You too."

"Were the two of you in basic together, by any chance?" Toby asked.

CJ shook her head. "No. But do you know each other? Brady, this is Toby and Reggie."

They nodded at one another and then stood awkwardly for a moment.

"I'm going back to the barracks," Brady volunteered. "If you're walking that way."

Toby slid her arm around CJ's neck. "We are definitely walking that way."

"Where did you learn to play ball?" CJ asked Brady as they fell into step together.

"My brothers. It was either learn to love what they did or spend a lot of time alone. I wasn't an indoors kind of girl, anyway."

"Neither was I," Reggie said, smiling at Brady and then ducking her head.

Was she shy? This seemed an unexpected development in the previously brash Italian American servicewoman.

Brady probed like the skilled reporter she apparently was, and soon Reggie was sharing her story. She was the oldest of four girls. Her father had been invited to training camp with the Yankees, but he had busted up his knee in a motorcycle wreck one week before he was supposed to report. He'd wanted a son to take over where he left off, but he settled for Reggie, the most athletic of his daughters.

CJ thought about volunteering that her brother was Joe Jamieson—*yes, that Joe Jamieson*—but swallowed the words before they could emerge into the Texas daylight. She wanted to be liked for herself, not for her well-known, eminently likable brother.

"Have you heard about the professional women's baseball league that started up over the summer?" Brady asked.

"It'll probably be a bust after the war," Toby said.

"After the war"—this was another favorite soldier conversation piece. Like everyone else, CJ wanted her brothers and the other boys back safely and prayed that the conflict would end sooner rather than later. Hundreds of thousands of civilians had been killed in bomb strikes, artillery strikes, illegal executions, village massacres, slave labor camps. It went without saying that she wanted an end to the horror; that was why she had joined the military rather than take a job in a war factory or pursue some other method of contributing to the war effort. By becoming a soldier, she released a man to fight and therefore (in theory) directly helped the war effort. Or so the Army recruiter had assured her.

And yet, there were certain changes the war had forced that she wished would endure. When the stock market crashed in '29, American women were forced out of the workplace because, they were told, men needed a paycheck to support their families. Now, thanks to the war, women were back at work in record numbers and in a variety of positions traditionally denied the "lesser" sex. For those like her, whose dreams involved challenges other than marriage and raising a family, the war had engendered a level of freedom she doubted many had known before. So while of course she wanted the war to end, it was complicated—for the return of men like her brothers would signal an end to her relative freedom as a single woman in a world that preferred to define women as wives and mothers.

"Anyway," Brady said, linking her arm through CJ's, "I think it would be fun to go see an all-girls baseball game sometime."

"Me too," CJ agreed, smiling over at her.

Brady's face was pink from exertion, her fatigue hat tilted over her forehead, blue eyes shining. As she leaned into CJ's shoulder,

CJ thought she saw Toby elbow Reggie. But she didn't care if they regarded her friendship with an Admin Wac unfavorably. Right then, the cliques that governed Fort Bliss society seemed unimportant.

Brady dropped them at their barracks, where CJ flopped face first onto her neatly made bed. The train ride and afternoon of activity were catching up to her. She needed a massage like the kind her mother offered at the end of a long day throwing hay.

"What are you, an old lady?" Toby teased.

"If I'm old, then you two are ancient."

Reggie laughed, and Toby slapped CJ on the back.

"Sweet dreams, farm girl."

She closed her eyes and snuggled into her cot. Fort Bliss was growing on her, no doubt about it.

* * *

At Bliss, as at Chanute, Sunday was the one day of the week that most GIs were off-duty. From experience, CJ knew that while you could be gloriously unscheduled on Sundays, you also had to take advantage of the rare period of unregimented time to complete a hundred varied tasks—laundry, mending, shoe-polishing, letters and trips to the PX for any necessary items. But she hadn't been on base long enough for the chores to pile up, so she spent her first Sunday in Texas napping, writing letters and shooting baskets in the mid-day sun.

Honestly, the officers' quarters felt more like home than her own barracks. On Saturday night she had accompanied Reggie, Toby and Kate to the PX for ice cream sandwiches, and then they'd made their way back to the WAC compound where they sat on the rear steps of the officers' house watching a pick-up game of basketball. Some of the women from the softball match were present, including their squad mates Sarah from Montana and Mary from New Orleans. The evening air was warm, the chatter was friendly, and CJ relaxed beside her new friends, her belly full and her heart as content as it could be with the world at war.

Now Sunday evening stretched ahead, the hours as yet unspoken for. Maybe she'd see if Brady wanted to stop by the service club later—assuming she hadn't changed her mind about going for a drink. At breakfast and noon mess, they'd only managed to nod at each other in passing. Admin and Maintenance were like foreign territories.

At supper she checked for Brady in the crowded mess, but there was no sign of her.

"Looking for someone?" Toby asked after the tenth time CJ had craned her head.

There was something about her tone that seemed off, but CJ couldn't quite put her finger on it.

"I think I'll head back early," she said, rising with her tray. "I have some letters to catch up on."

As she turned away she could have sworn she heard Reggie murmur something, but when she glanced back her squad mate gazed up at her innocently.

"See ya," Reggie said cheerfully.

Five minutes later, CJ detoured past Brady's barracks and found her sitting on the front steps, frowning down at a V-mail letter.

She glanced up as CJ approached. "Hey, soldier."

"Hey." CJ stopped beside the steps. "I didn't see you at supper."

"I wasn't feeling very social."

The sun was setting over El Paso, and the fading light brought out golden highlights in Brady's hair. CJ nodded at the letter. "Bad news?"

"Not exactly. I didn't tell you I was engaged, did I?"

And there it was—Brady was going to be married. Would she end up quitting the Army too, like the soldier CJ had replaced? It didn't seem like her style, but then, CJ didn't really know her. "Congratulations."

"Thanks." But Brady didn't smile or blush or otherwise appear the picture of the glowing bride-to-be. She folded the letter in half. "What are you up to tonight?"

"No plans yet."

"Feel like a movie? *Stage Door Canteen* is playing at the post theater."

"I've seen it."

"So have I. It starts in an hour. What do you say?"

CJ hesitated. "Give me a minute, will you?"

"I'll be here."

Back at her barracks, CJ brushed her teeth, examining her mirrored reflection. Her cheeks were flushed, or maybe she was sunburned. But she never burned. She'd grown up outdoors, playing in the woods and streams near her family's farm. She spat out the toothpaste, still studying her face in the mirror. Why did she feel so different here? What had changed between the time she left Illinois and now? Whatever it was, she couldn't detect any outward sign of a shift. Maybe she needed more time to get used to the move. A few days ago she hadn't even known about Fort Bliss, and now it was her home for the near—and possibly far—future.

A little while later she and Brady headed away from the WAC compound, dressed in their "A" uniforms. While they wore matching

Hobby hats, collared shirts, ties, straight khaki skirts that fell below their knees, and sensible brown shoes, CJ thought she probably resembled a gawky teenager while Brady looked like she belonged on a recruiting poster. The sun crept closer to the mountains lining the horizon as they walked, and CJ watched the sky change colors, keeping quiet. Brady didn't say much either as they walked down the road toward the center of base life, lamps flicking on as the sky darkened.

"You're not engaged, are you?" Brady said suddenly.

"No." Sean's eyes, hurt and angry, flickered before her, but she blinked away the unwelcome image. "I don't want to get married yet."

"Neither do I."

"Then why are you engaged?"

Brady squinted at the sun where it lingered at the edge of the horizon. "Because Nate asked me the day before he shipped out and I didn't know how to say no."

"I know a lot of people who got engaged or even married right before their boyfriends shipped."

"So do I. I can't quite believe I'm one of them."

They walked on quietly toward the theater, a hundred yards down the road from the men's enlisted and non-com service clubs. Jeeps passed them, boys in uniform hanging out the sides whistling and offering rides, among other things. They ignored their would-be suitors and walked on through the cooling air together.

As they passed the enlisted club, a buck private did a literal double-take, gawking at them. CJ, assuming the look was for Brady, kept walking. Men could be such idiots, falling all over themselves for a girl they didn't even know.

"Hey! CJ!"

She turned back as the soldier left his friends and jogged toward her. Jack Sawyer. A year younger, he had been part of the same crowd she and Sean were in at Michigan.

"What are you doing here?" she asked, smiling at him.

"I should ask you that." He gave her a quick hug. "I heard you'd run off and joined the Wackos, but I didn't think we'd cross paths."

"I guess it really is a small army." She glanced at Brady, who was watching the exchange with apparent interest. "Brady, meet Jack. We were at school together."

He took Brady's hand and gave a half-bow. "The pleasure is all mine."

"Behave," CJ chided. "She's a Seven Sisters woman, well above your pay grade."

"Now I'm really impressed," he said, still holding Brady's hand.

"Don't be," she said, and took it back.

"We're on our way to a movie," CJ added, "so maybe you and I can catch up later. What unit are you in?"

He recited his assigned antiaircraft regiment, battalion and company, adding, "I can't believe you're stationed at Bliss! Maybe we could grab a drink later in the week."

"It's a date." CJ started to turn away.

"Say, how's Sean?" Jack asked.

Dang it—the question she'd been hoping to avoid.

"He got into the PhD program at Michigan," she said, feeling Brady's gaze on her again. "But that's all I know. We're not in touch anymore."

"No kidding?" Jack shoved his cap back. "I'm sorry. I always assumed you two would get married."

"Wasn't meant to be, I guess. We should get going. I'll track you down soon, okay?"

He nodded. "Sure. Nice meeting you, Brady."

"You too."

CJ chewed her lip as they continued toward the theater. Seeing someone from her old life was not part of the plan tonight. At least he hadn't pressed for details about the breakup. But what must Brady think? Even after she had confessed her uncertainty about being engaged, CJ had continued to pretend Sean didn't exist. Then again, to her he didn't anymore. He'd made it clear that if she joined the service, they were through, not seeming to realize that from her perspective they already were.

"Michigan, hmm?" Brady commented.

CJ glanced at her. "Yeah. It's strange running into people in the Army you know from real life."

"Like you're both playing dress-up?"

"Exactly."

A few minutes later, popcorn and Cokes in hand, they entered the theater as the news reel was starting. Brady led the way past a dozen cat-calling GIs to open seats beside two boys who barely glanced their way. As CJ waited for the movie to begin, the war news washed over her, failing to find purchase in her crowded mind. Jack had always been more Sean's friend than hers. How had he not known about their breakup? And what had Brady thought about her now apparent lie of omission? She would have mentioned Sean eventually, but it was still difficult to talk about his betrayal without feeling foolish. For some reason, Brady's good opinion mattered more than it ought to, strictly speaking.

Even after the feature started, she had a hard time concentrating until Katharine Hepburn's scenes. She loved Hepburn, loved the characters she played, wild young women who refused to be tamed. One of her favorite movies was *The Philadelphia Story*, released back in 1940 when war was only a threat and her brothers were where they ought to be. Katharine Hepburn, Jimmy Stewart and Cary Grant in one film. What more could you ask for? Other than world peace, of course.

When they got to the scene where Hepburn comforted the USO girl whose fiancé shipped out the day they were supposed to be married, CJ watched Brady out of the corner of her eye. All through Hepburn's speech about the life the girl's fiancé was fighting for— to live and love and raise a family in a free country—Brady's fingers drummed against the side of the popcorn container. Only after the girl kissed Hepburn's cheek and walked off, shoulders squared resolutely, did Brady stop fidgeting.

After the show, they lingered outside in the rapidly cooling evening, talking with a couple of GIs Brady knew from the PRO. CJ couldn't miss the way the men looked at Brady. One even tried flirting with her, but not very seriously. Mostly she felt sorry for boys in uniform. The majority had been drafted and would be sent off God-knew-where as soon as they completed training. Other than the rare, gung-ho hero types, most male soldiers she'd met hoped to get through the war without having to kill or risk being killed. Overseas assignments in the WAC, on the other hand, were a hot commodity. More women had already applied for overseas duty than would ever be required. Same with officers. The chances of being promoted or sent overseas were low for Wacs like her who'd joined "late."

One of the GIs invited them to the enlisted men's club. Expression neutral, Brady glanced at CJ. "Feel like a drink?"

The idea of being a third wheel did not excite her. "I think I'll go for a walk. But you go ahead."

"Don't be silly. It isn't safe to wander the post alone," Brady said, linking her arm through CJ's.

They made their farewells and meandered away from the theater. Overhead, stars poked tiny holes through the pitch sky, and a nearly full moon hung suspended over the horizon.

As they passed the men's service club, CJ said, "You can go in if you want."

"It's too nice to go indoors. Besides, I'm not going to abandon you on your first weekend at Bliss."

"Does that mean you asked me out tonight because you felt sorry for me?" CJ asked, smiling a little. "And here I thought we were getting to be friends, crumpet girl."

Brady elbowed her. "We are getting to be friends. Assuming you lose the nickname."

"I suppose that could be arranged. Where are we going, anyway?"

"You'll see."

Brady led her between buildings, along narrow sidewalks and behind bored MPs who somehow didn't seem to notice a couple of giggling Wacs slipping past in the night. By the time they reached a sprawling parking lot filled with Jeeps and bordered by an airplane hangar, CJ was thoroughly lost. Her sole hope at finding her way back would be to judge directions based on the stars. But the West Texas night sky was different from the one she'd grown up with. Apparently she would have to depend on Brady to lead her back to the WAC compound.

Brady hopped into the back seat of an empty Jeep at the edge of the lot. "Come on, Private," she said. "You're not chicken, are you?"

"Chicken? Not a chance." CJ climbed in next to her. How much trouble would they be in if they got caught? Actually, she didn't want to know. "So, sweetheart, do you come here often?" she asked in her best Humphrey Bogart impression.

"Nah, I don't usually skulk around this much. I just wasn't in the mood to be around all those people tonight."

"It's almost impossible to escape in the Army, isn't it?"

"You have to leave the post to truly get away. Fortunately, the command here is pretty free with weekend passes." Brady paused. "I've also heard rumors about Wacs making deals with MPs and taking Jeeps off base without a pass. Taking hops, too."

"Hops?"

"Rides on ferry planes or whatnot. You should ask your friends about it. Maintenance as a company seems to get away with more than the rest of us."

CJ leaned her head against the seat and looked up at the wide Texas sky awash with starlight. Would she be up there soon, getting a "hop" on a giant C-47 or, even better, a B-17? She'd always wanted to go up in a Flying Fortress, mostly to see what Alec's war experiences were like firsthand. Not that a training flight in West Texas compared to a combat mission over Axis-controlled Africa or Europe, of course.

"I'm surprised they accepted you so quickly," Brady added. "Your buddies don't welcome strangers into their midst, except the WASPs. Women pilots seem to be kosher with your crew."

"Are there WASPs here?" CJ asked. The Women's Airforce Service Pilots was an auxiliary organization without military authorization or oversight, like the Women's Army Auxiliary Corps had been before Congress had voted to remove the "Auxiliary" and grant the corps full military status earlier in the year.

"A small contingent. But like everything else related to the military, the situation changes weekly. Rumor has it a much larger group is due to arrive any day."

"You must have access to a lot of information, working for the PRO."

"I do. And some of it is classified, so don't try to make me talk."

"I'll keep that in mind."

And then, because Brady was staring at her somehow a little too intently as they sat on the Jeep's back seat in the middle of the deserted parking lot, surrounded by thousands of male officers and soldiers and cadets they couldn't see, CJ went back to tracing the constellations overhead, learning the layout of the southwestern heavens.

"So who's Sean?" Brady asked. "If you don't mind my asking."

CJ sat up straighter, khaki skirt sliding noiselessly across the smooth seat. "A friend from school."

"Only a friend?"

"Well, no. We dated for almost a year." She frowned, wishing she had pockets to shove her hands into. Men's pants had wonderfully deep pockets, she knew from wearing her brother's hand-me-downs around the farm.

"What happened?"

She hesitated. "He wanted to marry me, but I wasn't ready. So we broke up."

It was more complicated than that, of course. She'd thought they would, in fact, probably be married someday. That was why she'd deferred her acceptance to the graduate history program at the University of North Carolina, which boasted the largest collection of slave narratives in the country. Sean was in a master's program at Michigan and had agreed that as soon as he finished his degree in the spring, they would pack up and move to Chapel Hill together. But then his thesis advisor had suggested he stay on in the doctorate program, and he had come to her jubilant that his dreams were coming true, expecting her to be elated for him.

She leaned her head against the Jeep seat, remembering the night she'd pulled him up from his knees and told him that she couldn't marry him. He'd stared at her there on her parents' driveway, lit by the nearly full moon, as if some strange creature inhabited her body.

"What do you mean you can't marry me?" he had demanded. "I told you, they'll let you stay on at Michigan. We can both get our doctorates right here, close to our families."

"I don't want to stay here. You know that. You can't change the plan without asking me, Sean."

He drew a breath, and then he took her hand and said in a tone he typically reserved for the greenest undergraduates, "But you have to see that your chances of completing a doctorate at UNC—or even at Michigan—aren't all that high."

She had stared at him. "And why is that?"

"Because you won't be able to stay in school once the children come. If we went to UNC, we would end up back here anyway. This way makes infinitely more sense. I'll be able to find a permanent position while the children are still young."

She'd yanked her hand back, realizing how narrowly she'd dodged the bullet of his love. He had always seemed to love her more, to need more from her than she did from him, but she had thought that was how love worked. She knew she cared about him. True, she didn't daydream about him the way other girls did with the men they were dating. But she liked him better than any other man she knew, and liked kissing him too. He'd seemed to respect her mind and her goals for the future. Surely all those factors represented a healthy basis for marriage.

And yet, all along, he'd been thinking of her as his future wife and the mother of his children. The problem was, she wasn't ready to be a historian's wife, not when she wanted to be a historian herself.

"That must have been a difficult decision," Brady said.

"It was. He was my best friend. But in the end, we didn't want the same things."

"And you haven't heard from him since you broke up?"

CJ shook her head, looking back up at the sky again. "My mother told me he rang once while I was in basic, but he didn't leave a message."

"I'm sorry. Is it difficult not to have him in your life anymore?"

"Not nearly as bad as I expected." She barely thought about him now, another indication that what she had felt for him couldn't have been true love, could it?

"I probably should have turned Nate down too," Brady said, "but I couldn't. We've been friends since first grade. He ended up at Yale and was one of the few people I knew on the East Coast. It was so easy—I always had a date for formals, but we didn't have to see each other all the time. Then he got drafted right after we graduated, and his orders came through for North Africa. What was I supposed to do? There didn't seem to be any other choice."

"I don't think I could have refused Sean if he had proposed right before shipping out."

Instead, he had come to her in early summer when she was working long hours at the farm trying to make up for Alec's absence. He had appeared at the house with his graduate deferment secure, his plans for their future complete.

She'd tried before to picture him in a uniform. He would have hated the Army—the regulations, the restrictions, the drab uniform. The Navy would have suited him better, but either way, he would have mourned the loss of his beautifully thick, curly black hair. Sean always looked well put together. Senior year, she had taken more pains with her appearance than ever before so that she would look good beside him. Like her mother, he came from a wealthy East Detroit family. While he never called her, say, "farm girl," she had always been distinctly aware of the differences in their backgrounds.

"But why would you say no?" her mother had asked the night Sean stormed away, car tires kicking up gravel on their long driveway.

"Because I don't think he's the right person for me."

"It's not too late," her mother had said as they sat on the swing on the screened-in back porch listening to the summer night music of crickets and peepers. "You could always change your mind. You could go to him tomorrow. I'll pay the train fare, or you could borrow the car. I'm sure your father wouldn't mind."

"Mom, I'm not going to change my mind. I'm not going to marry him."

"He's a good man, Caroline, and would make a wonderful husband and father. He loves you, I know he does."

CJ stood abruptly, jolting the swing chains. "But I don't love him, not like I should. Why are you acting like this? You've always told us to do what makes us happy. Why are you trying to talk me into marrying someone I don't want to?"

Her mother had lifted a hand to her mouth and said slowly, "I'm not, honey. I'm sorry. I'm sure you know what's best for you."

Shortly after that she had joined the WAC, and though her mother offered outward support, CJ could read the doubt in her eyes. Since when had her mother stopped believing in her? She and her older brothers had always agreed they were lucky when it came to parents. Apparently her mother didn't quite feel the same way about her.

Reaching into her jacket pocket, Brady pulled out a pack of cigarettes. "Want one?"

"Sure."

They smoked in the back of the Jeep while the night sky shifted overhead, new paths through the stars revealed as the Earth spun on its axis. *Like the Axis Powers*, CJ thought, and shivered.

"Are you cold?" Brady asked.

"No, I was thinking about the Axis. Do they honestly think they can win?"

"Until we joined the fight, it looked like they might." Brady exhaled a cloud of smoke. "Sometimes I try to imagine how they could devalue human life to such a degree, but I simply can't comprehend it."

"It's inconceivable, some of the things they've done: the destruction in Nanking, the massacres in Brest-Litovsk, the civilian dead in Stalingrad. Have you heard the rumors about the camps in Poland where they're supposedly gassing Jews and political prisoners?"

"I have, but do you think they exist?" Brady asked. "Could anyone actually do such a thing?"

"I hope not. There's so much propaganda on both sides, it's hard to know what's real."

"There was a rumor that the slander campaign against the WAC— you know, the one claiming that we're all prostitutes?—was German propaganda, but it turns out it was Regular Army officers trying to 'protect their legacy,' to hear them tell."

"What legacy? And protect it from whom?"

"Seems some of the old boys were upset about the attention being given the higher recruiting standards in the WAAC, so they fed lies to the newspapers about how we were all a bunch of drunken good-time girls. That's partly why so many WAACs took a discharge rather than sign on with the Regular Army."

"I almost joined the WAVES because of those rumors," CJ confessed.

"Why didn't you? The WAVES tend to have more traction with the college crowd."

"They recruited hard at Michigan. But their pitch included bad-mouthing the WAAC, so when it came time to join up, I crossed the street and signed up with the Army instead."

The WAVES recruiter had reminded her of her Detroit aunts and cousins, who didn't bother to hide their contempt for her mother's chosen lifestyle. Not a chance she wanted to share this part of her life with women like them.

"That's so nonconformist of you," Brady remarked.

"I thought it was me being bullheaded. Why didn't *you* join the WAVES? Don't they train at Seven Sisters schools?"

"Smith and Mount Holyoke," Brady confirmed. "But my great-grandfather, grandfather, uncle and older brother are all Army men. Seemed like a foregone conclusion."

"Was your family supportive when you told them you were joining up?"

"Not especially. Was yours?"

"Mostly. My father bragged to all the neighbors, and my mother sewed another blue star flag before I even left for basic. My grandmother, on the other hand, claimed she needed smelling salts when she heard the news."

"Your Wellesley grandmother?"

CJ nodded.

"Typical." Brady snorted.

"So where's your brother stationed?"

"New Guinea. When the Army found out Chris studied theater at UCLA, they sent him to Fort Meade to become a recreation officer, one of those boys tasked with keeping up morale in the face of malaria and monsoons. My little brother Josh, meanwhile, is still in school."

CJ heard the disapproval in Brady's voice. "It's different for them. You and I won't be made to fight, but the boys know there's always a chance they'll be shipped off to the front."

Brady regarded her unwaveringly. "Both of your brothers are in, and I bet you'd join up if you were a man, wouldn't you?"

"Probably. You would too, wouldn't you?"

She nodded. "I don't know why he doesn't."

Usually she didn't like to admit it, but CJ had felt the same way about Sean. Some part of her had considered him cowardly for wanting to study history rather than participate in the war, despite the fact she didn't want to be ordered to shoot the enemy or drop bombs on civilians any more than he did. It was a double standard, she knew, but there it was.

The air cooled appreciably as night deepened, and after a while they rose from their seats, stretched stiff muscles and climbed down from the Jeep. With one last look at the peaceful parking lot, CJ followed Brady back to the heart of the post and from there to the WAC compound.

They stopped at Brady's barracks, lingering on the steps talking about nothing until finally CJ took a step back.

"I should probably get back for bed check," she said. "But thanks for tonight. I had a really good time."

"Same here," Brady said, smiling at her. "I'm glad you ended up at Bliss, CJ."

"So am I." And, surprisingly, she was. The beacon of Northern California no longer shone quite as brightly.

"See you tomorrow?" Brady asked, hand on the door.

"Definitely."

CJ turned away, heading toward her own barracks. It had been a long day, but she wasn't tired. As she walked, she even sang a ditty from basic set to the tune of "The Man on the Flying Trapeze."

Once we were civilians, but now we are Wacs,
Dressed in our khaki, discarding our slacks,
Marching, saluting, with pains in our backs,
And our loves they are far, far away.

We'll be good soldiers if it takes us years,
We'll stiffen our spines and we'll pin back our ears,
We'll flatten abdomens and tuck in our rears,
If that's what it takes to be Wacs!

CHAPTER FOUR

When reveille sounded across the WAC compound on Monday morning, CJ yawned, rolled out of bed and climbed into her waiting clothes. She was accustomed to rising early on the farm to get a start on the day's work. Basic training, when reveille had sounded at five fifteen every morning, hadn't seemed as god-awful to her as it had to some of her fellow recruits.

The sun hadn't risen yet as she joined her company in the courtyard for PT and morning drill. They exercised and marched by platoon every weekday morning from six fifteen to seven. Up ahead she glimpsed Brady marching under the lights with Company A, looking sleepy as she went through the motions of the drill. CJ shook her head, thinking of their adventure the night before. Usually disobeying orders made her stomach hurt, but Brady had managed to make unlawful trespassing seem downright enjoyable. Her Detroit cousins were similar and termed their own willful disregard of rules as "hijinks" or "shenanigans." How did the wealthy get away with treating the law as mere suggestion?

After drill, CJ got cleaned up and went to breakfast with the rest of her platoon. They had to report for duty at eight, so they didn't linger. At quarter to eight, she left the WAC compound with Toby,

Reggie and Sarah and walked the mile to the Army Air Corps Division headquarters, located not far from Brady's Jeep parking lot.

Much of the walk was spent in a discussion of favorite cars and airplanes. The other three were, like her, motor vehicle enthusiasts. Sarah, a tall, lean girl who had grown up on a ranch near Missoula, had even flown an airplane a few times, though she didn't have a license. Her ex-boyfriend had taught her.

"We work at the Transient Hangar," Toby said as they neared the airfield. "Planes visiting from other airfields come to us for repairs. Along with B-24 replacement and antiaircraft artillery training, Biggs is one of the main stops for the ferry command, so we see a lot of different types of aircraft."

"What's the flight line like here?" CJ asked.

The others exchanged grins. "You'll see."

And she did—the Biggs flight line occupied two wide runways laid out parallel, each with a row of airplanes parked wingtip to wingtip. As far as CJ could see were airplanes and more airplanes of stunning variety, a few of which she easily recognized—P-51 Mustangs, P-47 Thunderbolts, C-47 Skytrains, B-17 Flying Fortresses, B-24 Liberators and the Biggs specialty, B-29 Superfortresses. She shook her head in awe. This was one American airfield of many. No wonder the general consensus was that they couldn't lose—in a war that depended in large part on air power, manufacturing supremacy translated directly into military might.

As they stared down the line, CJ asked Sarah, "Is it true we get to go on hops sometimes?"

Sarah nodded. "It's true. Where did you hear that?"

"Around," CJ said vaguely, remembering Toby and Reggie's reaction to her friendship with Brady.

Before they reached the hangar, Sarah said, "By the way, the higher-ups have been having a tantrum lately over our work attire."

"What's the problem?"

"They caught a few of us rolling up our pant legs and shirt sleeves. Now we're supposed to be buttoned and covered head to toe. At least the hangars are cooler than out on the line."

Like the others, CJ had dressed this morning in her HBTs, standard WAC-issue herringbone twill fatigues that served as one-piece khaki coveralls. Already she could tell the material would be stifling during the warmer months. Maybe by spring the WAC supply officers would have figured out an alternative.

As they rounded the corner into the Transient Hangar, CJ swallowed hard. After months of specialized training, her life as an Army Air Corps mechanic was finally about to begin.

Roll call came first and involved the four of them and fifty other Wacs, GIs and civilians who worked in assorted positions. When her turn came, she answered, "Here," mildly surprised when her voice didn't shake. Then again, she'd had plenty of time to prepare.

After roll call, everyone split up into their work groups. Flight C, their crew, was made up of five Wacs, a dozen GIs and a few civilians, and included a hangar chief, armorers, radio operators, interior and exterior mechanics and a handful of other specialists. Until a couple of years before, pilots had supervised the maintenance of their own airplanes, but this responsibility was now assumed by a nonflying squadron officer. Flight C's crew chief was Master Sergeant Griggs, whom the others had described as a tough twenty-year man. Griggs gave her the once-over, then grunted and turned away.

"Tripp," he barked at Sarah, "you're Jamieson's babysitter until I tell you otherwise. Got it?"

"Yes, sir," Sarah said smartly, and flashed a smile at CJ.

The first order of business was a hundred-hour check on a B-29. Sarah and Jill, a Wac from another company, maneuvered a hard stand over to the left wing, and soon mechanics, armorers and radiomen were swarming around the massive bomber like yellow jackets on a Coke bottle.

From advanced training, CJ knew that military aircraft were brought in for inspection after twenty-five, fifty and one hundred hours in the sky. At each check point, specific inspections were required as well as any repair work that might be needed. Any engine that had accumulated five hundred hours of flight time had to be removed and completely overhauled. Such overhauls were usually completed at civilian production facilities that contracted their services out to the Army.

Jill and Sarah had been at Biggs for six months and had completed a short course on the B-29 over the summer, they told her as they worked. CJ's multi-engine rating was on the B-24, so at first she observed, helping out when asked. Her extended training course at Chanute had prepared her mainly for squadron repairs of the first- and second-echelon variety: regular servicing of aircraft, routine inspections and adjustments and minor repairs. For more difficult jobs, maintenance squadrons on the home front were expected to defer to highly trained civilian mechanics for what was officially designated third- and fourth-echelon maintenance. But at Biggs, Jill and Sarah explained, the AAF command believed strongly in on-the-job training.

They worked hard all morning, going over the massive bomber from the nose of its windowed cockpit to the tip of its pressurized tail gunner's compartment. The B-29's Wright Duplex Cyclone engines were a headache, Sarah told her, due to a troubling tendency to overheat and catch fire. As a result, some of the boys were reluctant to fly them.

"Sometimes the Wright engines are actually the wrong engines," Jill quipped.

Sarah ignored what CJ guessed to be a very old joke and waved her closer on the hard stand platform. "After every twenty-five hours, the flight crew replaces these, the uppermost five cylinders. And at seventy-five hours, we replace the entire engine."

"Seventy-five hours? But isn't that expensive?"

"The Army considers the flight crew's lives more valuable than the money it takes to keep them safe," Sarah said.

"Besides, it's less expensive than training a replacement crew," Jill added.

As they worked, the two Wacs showed CJ a few tricks to keep the B-29's four radial engines cool: cuffs on propeller blades, baffles on intakes and rubber fittings, and increased oil flow to the valves.

"We do everything we can to help and nothing, we hope, to harm," Sarah told her.

"I'll try to remember that," CJ promised.

It was hard to hear over the sound of jacks, lifts and other noisy tools, but a radio in one corner of the hangar was tuned to the base radio station. At ten, when the news came on, CJ stopped in mid-twist of a wrench. She knew that voice. She glanced at Sarah, who was chatting with the jack operator.

"Is that Brady Buchanan on the radio?"

Sarah nodded. "She usually reads the morning news."

CJ tried to listen, but after a few minutes she gave up. She would see Brady later anyway—after supper if not before. Time enough then to tell her about the B-29. It wasn't a hop, but taking apart four radial engines wasn't bad for her first day.

At noon mess, CJ and Sarah caught a ride back to the WAC compound in a Jeep with Toby and Reggie, who were airplane instrument specialists. That meant they worked mainly on the interior of planes in the Transient Hangar. Their work environment could either be "nice and cool" or like "burning in Hades," but rarely in between.

At the mess hall, the four women took over a table and chatted as they ate. Kate joined them, and with the others soon filled CJ in on platoon and company gossip, relating who was friends with whom and which women had "special" friends. CJ knew they were talking about homosexual relationships, but the word went unspoken.

Back at Michigan, she had known a handful of women in "Boston marriages," mostly older professors or graduate students who kept their relationships private. Love between adult women—or men, for that matter—was hardly a new concept, particularly in academia. The only thing new was the increasing fixation with uncovering and eliminating such relationships. Some higher-ups in the WAC were bent on ridding the corps of queer women, she knew, like some male officers were obsessed with ridding the Army ranks of homosexual men. As a result, even heterosexual soldiers avoided mention of the situation that clearly existed, afraid of receiving a discharge that didn't qualify as honorable *or* dishonorable—a blue ticket, in GI parlance, reserved for those deemed "unfit" for military service.

During the First World War, CJ knew, any soldier found to be involved in a homosexual relationship was arrested, court-martialed and dishonorably discharged. This process took valuable time and resources, so in the early stages of the second "great" war, blue ticket discharges became an administrative stopgap for dealing with military misconduct. Along with homosexuals, blue tickets were routinely issued to Wacs who engaged in fraternization with superiors, GIs with a history of problems with alcohol, soldiers who developed a personality conflict with a commanding officer, and those who couldn't perform their duties adequately for myriad other reasons.

Kate and Toby exchanged a look, and instantly CJ understood. They were more than friends; of course they were. Momentarily she worried about guilt by association, but then she pushed the fear away. Why the Army cared was beyond her, but then, so many aspects of the military defied logic that this was one more gripe to add to the list.

After lunch, she piled into the Jeep with the others for the return trip to the airfield. As they neared the hangar, Reggie asked, "Anyone interested in getting a drink at the club tonight?"

"Always," Toby said.

"Count me in," CJ agreed.

"And me," Sarah said.

It was unanimous. CJ wondered if she might talk Brady into coming too. They'd waved at each other across the mess hall again at both breakfast and lunch, but each sat with her own buddies. Brady hadn't minded being seen with her, a lowly Maintenance Wac, in the darkened theater or in the shadows at the far end of the post, but the enlisted women's club was a different matter.

One way to find out how far Brady's daring streak extended.

* * *

CJ, Sarah and Jill worked on the B-29's engines throughout the afternoon, running through a checklist that Jill carried around on a clipboard. CJ had always enjoyed getting grimy around the farm in the name of accomplishment. This work, as far as she was concerned, was not much different, though the stakes were admittedly higher.

At break time, she and the other Wacs strolled out to the flight line and chatted with nearby crews. Most of the men were friendly, but a few spit tobacco juice in their general direction and pointedly looked away.

"Get used to it," Sarah said as they returned to the hangar. "The combat returnees are the worst. I had one non-com, his chest covered in ribbons, nearly knock me over on the sidewalk a few weeks ago."

"What? Why?"

"I don't know. He didn't say."

Their squad was relieved at six p.m. by the all-male night crew. A staff sergeant who doubled as a propeller specialist gave everyone a ride home in a GI truck. Back at the WAC compound, CJ stopped at her barracks to get cleaned up before mess, using the homemade lye soap her parents had sent her in Illinois. The scrub-down took so long that the mess crowd had dwindled by the time she arrived. There was still food, though. There always seemed to be more than enough food, even with items that had long been on the ration list.

As a WAC cook handed her a food-filled tray, CJ felt a tap on her shoulder: Brady, holding a cup of coffee and smiling at her. It felt like ages since they'd seen each other.

"I thought maybe you were boycotting Army food," Brady said.

"Me? Never."

"Good. Come and tell me all about your first day."

"It was amazing," CJ enthused, following her to an empty table. "There were hundreds of planes on the flight line, and we got to work on a B-29 all day."

"A B-29?" She whistled. "Talk about starting in the deep end."

"Did you know their engines overheat at the slightest encouragement?"

"I didn't, in fact."

CJ shoveled turkey, mashed potatoes and black-eyed peas into her mouth and tried at the same time to describe her first day in the hangar. Finally, her mother's voice sounded in her head, reminding her to mind her manners.

"Anyway," she added, "I heard you on the radio. Didn't you say you were a writer?"

Brady described her role in the PRO in more detail while CJ demolished her supper. The previous winter, she had begun her office stint filing and typing. Then her male CO found out she had edited her college newspaper and done some writing for an L.A. paper, and he had broadened her duties. The PRO was responsible for all publicity on the post, maintaining relations with the townspeople of El Paso, censoring news and correspondence, publishing the eight-page *Monitor*, releasing stories to the two El Paso newspapers and running a daily fifteen-minute radio broadcast. In addition to assorted news stories, Brady was responsible for editing the radio scripts.

"How do you get everything done?" CJ asked.

"I don't always," Brady admitted, tracing a gouge in the wooden table with a fingertip. "Sometimes it gets so overwhelming that I need a break, like on Saturday. We see things almost no one else on base does. The casualty lists, for example. I used to look, wondering what I'd do if I found my brother's name or Nate's."

"That sounds traumatic," CJ said, setting her fork down. Her plate was empty, her stomach was full and, despite the mention of casualty lists, she felt unaccountably happy being with Brady.

"It can be. We're a pretty tight group, though. That helps."

"Too bad your company can't field a decent softball team," CJ said, shaking her head in mock regret.

Brady narrowed her eyes. "You got lucky last weekend, Jamieson."

"I think I speak for Maintenance when I say we're up for a rematch anytime."

They lingered over coffee, arguing good-naturedly about whose company was better. A Wac on KP finally asked them to bring their dishes to the window, and they complied, smiling sheepishly at each other as they left the mess hall.

Back at Brady's barracks, they paused outside chatting until CJ finally steeled herself and asked, "What are you doing tonight?"

"Writing letters, probably. Why?"

"A bunch of us are going to the club later. Want to come?"

"Does 'the bunch' know I'm invited?"

"Not exactly."

"Huh." Brady chewed her lip briefly. Then: "What the heck. Come get me on your way."

"Swell."

CJ gave her smile full rein as she jogged back to her own barracks. It was only a drink. Why did it seem like more, then?

* * *

An hour later, CJ and her buddies commandeered a table near the bar in the enlisted women's service club. A WAC band played recent hits in a corner that functioned as a stage. The music was too loud to talk over, so they nursed their beers, smoked cigarettes and people-watched. Occasionally a boy would come by and ask one of them to dance. More often than not, the invitee politely declined.

All the EW clubs CJ had visited were the same—bright and gaily decorated, jukebox off to one side, ping pong and billiards tables crowded into a side room, and a handful of servicemen laughing it up with their WAC friends at the bar, which looked more like it belonged in a soda fountain. A handful of couples danced, including two pairs of Wacs. For a change in an enlisted service club, there weren't enough men to go around.

CJ was at the bar waiting for refills when Jack Sawyer appeared beside her.

"Hiya, soldier," he said, leaning close to be heard over the music.

She grinned, genuinely glad to see him. "Hi yourself. How did you weasel your way in here?"

"I have friends in the right places. Can I buy you a drink?" he asked, pulling a wad of bills from his pocket and catching the bartender's eye.

"Sure, but I'm buying for my table."

He relayed the order and glanced back at the table in question, his gaze resting on Brady.

"Join us," CJ said, taking pity on him. "But go easy on the Romeo act, okay? These are friends of mine."

"I won't embarrass you," he promised.

The band finished their set, and someone dropped a quarter in the jukebox. Popular tunes rolled on, Glenn Miller and the Andrew Sisters and Tommy Dorsey. At CJ's table, Jack surveyed the group of women, smiling like the proverbial cat. She resisted the urge to smack him.

"CJ and Jack go way back," Brady told the others.

"Then you must have some good stories." Toby eyed him encouragingly.

Before CJ knew it, he was telling her new friends all about their Michigan days. Over her protests, he described in overly generous detail the time someone spiked the punch at a Homecoming Dance and she decided, uninvited, to perform with the band.

"It's not like I can't sing," she said, kicking him under the table.

She retaliated by sharing how Jack and Sean had been picked up by university security while skinny-dipping in a campus pond. Their punishment had been to spend a dozen hours a week the rest of the semester working with the grounds crew. Neither had ever mowed a lawn before, let alone cleaned a fountain or painted a fence.

"Just a couple of city boys," CJ said.

"We can't all hail from the sticks," he retorted.

"Where do you hail from?" Sarah asked. While the rest of the group was well on their way to getting drunk, she had barely started in on her second glass.

"Evanston, Illinois."

"Really? I went to school near Evanston," she said, and named a small, private college.

Jack knew it. In fact, he had a friend whose mother had taught there; maybe Sarah knew her? She did, and they were off on a tangential conversation.

Brady leaned closer, one hand on her glass and the other on the table close to CJ's. "So," she said, "why do you think they call it the sticks?"

"I never thought about it." This close, Brady smelled of strawberries. Her hair brushed against CJ's neck, tickling her, but she didn't move away. "Your hair smells good."

"Thanks." She leaned back, and the intimacy enfolding them faded. "How do you feel about road trips?"

"Generally positive. Why?"

"A lot of people at Bliss go exploring on the weekends. You'll be eligible for a pass in a few weeks, and I know someone with a car and gas coupons to spare. Interested?"

"Of course."

"We could even go camping once it gets warmer."

"*You* like camping?"

"Don't sound so shocked. My grandparents used to take my brothers and me up to the Redwoods for a couple of weeks every summer."

"Huh. I wouldn't have guessed."

Brady leaned close again and let her arm rest on the back of CJ's chair. "There's plenty you don't know about me."

"I don't doubt it."

CJ looked away, remembering the odd moment in the Jeep the night before. It was almost as if—but no. Brady was an intense person, that was all.

They stayed until the attendants kicked them out—they'd overstayed their welcome twice in one night, Brady pointed out to CJ. Then they said goodnight to Jack and hurried back to their barracks to make bed check, running into other groups of women like themselves, tipsy and giggling.

CJ stopped outside Brady's barracks. "I thought you said you could hold your liquor, Buchanan."

"I can," she said, slurring the words slightly. "See you tomorrow, Caroline."

"Don't call me that."

"It's a term of affection." Brady tried to slap her on the shoulder but misjudged the distance between them and nearly fell over.

CJ caught her and pointed her toward the barracks door. "Goodnight, Brady."

"Goodnight, CJ." She saluted smartly even though she was the one with stripes on her sleeve, and went inside.

CJ jogged to catch up with her buddies.

"I like Brady," Sarah said, holding their barracks door open.

"Me too," Toby said.

This surprised CJ. She'd caught more looks passing between Toby and Reggie at the club and had assumed they were still leery of allowing "outsiders" into their midst.

Then again, what wasn't to like about Brady?

"Me three," she said, and followed Reggie inside.

CHAPTER FIVE

Over the next few weeks, life at Bliss settled into a comfortable pattern. During the day, CJ worked on bombers and transport planes, mostly in the Transient Hangar but occasionally out on the flight line. She got her "wings" the first week—Air Corps patches to sew onto her uniforms and HBTs. Surprisingly, she actually teared up a little when Master Sergeant Griggs handed them over, but she was careful to hide her emotions. She may have been a "penguin"—an Air Force service member who didn't fly—but it sure beat being at home, as Brady had pointed out.

Off-duty, she hung around with the usual crowd, which sometimes included Brady and sometimes didn't. They played softball and basketball, sunbathed, watched movies at the post theater, played endless rounds of ping pong, listened to music at the enlisted club and played cards in the barracks until lights out. Sometimes they joined Jack and his buddies for drinks or dinner on base or in nearby El Paso. As Jack and Sarah started spending more time together, he stopped making teasing remarks about farming and country life. A wise move, CJ thought, given that Sarah's family owned a cattle ranch in Montana.

On her third weekend at Bliss, CJ joined Brady and a handful of other Admin Wacs on a hike in the nearby Franklin Mountains. She had a good time—other than the hot, dry conditions and the cold, supercilious looks from Janice and one of her friends, neither of whom, it turned out, were impressed with stories of the Biggs Airfield flight line.

Brady held back with CJ as they descended from the summit of the Aztec Cave Trail, a short steep climb down a talus slope from a collection of cool, spooky alcoves that had nothing to do with Aztecs and everything to do with the region's geology. CJ had taken an introductory geology course and struggled now to recall the meaning of terms like *stromatolite*, *rhyolite* and *quartzite*. Why did rock formations always end in -*ite*? She was pretty sure she had once known that too.

"Don't hold it against her," Brady said in a low voice as Janice cast them another brooding look.

"Why shouldn't I?"

"Because before you got here, she had me all to herself. Besides, she's had a rough year. Her fiancé was killed in Sicily."

"Oh." CJ paused. "You know, Brady, it's fine if you want to spend more time with your other friends. I know we don't run in the same circles."

Brady caught her hand. "That's not what I meant."

CJ glanced down at their clasped fingers. Brady's skin was pale and freckled, while her own coloring was more brown than white. Growing up on a farm would do that.

"What did you mean then?"

Brady gazed at her, frowning slightly. "I don't know. I guess I want you two to get along. You're my closest friends, even if I *am* the one thing you have in common."

At that moment, the subject of their conversation turned back to wait for them, and Brady dropped her hand as if it had suddenly grown as hot as a Duplex Cyclone engine.

Drama. CJ pulled her fatigue hat lower to block out the blinding Texas sky. She had never been a fan of drama. Probably, then, she shouldn't have joined the Army, pressure cooker that it was with masses of soldiers jammed into chronically small spaces.

Currently, though, there was plenty of space to enjoy, unfamiliar as it was. She was still getting used to the Southwest. Unlike Michigan, where fields of green and gray, their color dependent on the time of year, abutted green and gray forests or blue-gray bodies of water, the land in this corner of the country was brown and bounded by rocky outcrops that exposed millions of years of geologic history to passersby. The earth was revealed in a way here that she wasn't used to, sediment layers permanently visible to sun and wind and human observation. Where she came from, you only saw the earth's skeleton during planting and harvest, brief seasons delineated by winter's drifting snow and summer's riotous greenery.

So different, she thought again, watching Brady cast her high-wattage smile at Janice, who beamed up at her in return.

* * *

Her first hop came sooner than she'd expected. Two days after the hike to Aztec Caves, a staff sergeant CJ hadn't seen before stood talking to Sarah and Jill during the two-thirty break. Work was slack that afternoon. Their crew had already completed a fifty-hour check on an AT-10 trainer, nicknamed the "Flying Coffin" by Air Corps cadets because of the frequency with which it crashed, and they were basically sitting around on their tool chests waiting for a new assignment when the sergeant dropped by. CJ saw Sarah gesture toward her, and the next thing she knew, Jill and Sarah were telling her to come to the supply room to get fitted for a parachute. A pilot they knew had invited them along on a test flight of a recently repaired trainer.

"That is, assuming you want to come with us?" Jill asked, smiling.

"Yes!" CJ grinned back. "Please!"

In the supply room, the GIs fitted them with the smallest parachutes available. Even so, the packs were nearly as heavy as a pile of wet hay and almost as difficult to maneuver. The Wacs had plenty of volunteers to carry them out to the plane—the boys they worked with seemed almost as excited as CJ felt. Everyone in the hangar waved and yelled goodbye, and CJ tried to forget the stories her squad mates had told her about airfield crashes. What were the odds that her first flight would end in flames? It wasn't like they would be facing down Messerschmitts or Zeroes.

The plane was waiting for them, hitched to a tug that would tow it out to the line. At first sight, CJ fell in love. The AT-21 Gunner, a bomber trainer prototype, was like no other plane she'd ever seen, with gull-like wings and a tail so high you had to use a ladder to board her. After the crew chief dumped the parachutes in the tail under the gunner's seat, CJ clambered up behind Jill and Sarah. The pilot and copilot were already in their seats running their preflight checks, and introductions were made quickly as the three women donned headsets.

Soon CJ was watching the land roll past as Captain Fitzgerald and the control tower discussed the passenger load and intended flight path. Then the tow plane pulled away, and the pilot started the plane's engines. He pointed the AT-21's nose down the runway and eased the throttle forward. CJ checked her watch. It wasn't even three yet. Everything had happened so quickly. Was she really on a military aircraft racing down the runway? Her stomach fluttered crazily, and she hoped she wouldn't be sick. Then they were in the air, the ground dropping away faster than she had anticipated. Below them was Texas—the post and houses and cars on the roads, all very distinct. For a second she was dizzy looking down.

"Focus on the horizon."

The pilot's voice sounded in her headset, and CJ saw Sarah and Jill lift their gazes to the flat desert arcing away to the northeast as they flew parallel to the Franklin Mountains. The day was clear, not a cloud in sight. As soon as they leveled off, the three Wacs took off their seat belts and walked around, seeking the best view out. The pilot turned the plane north, and in a short time they were flying close to the Organ Mountains near Las Cruces. From the air, the mountains loomed impossibly high above the desert floor. The copilot pointed out Organ Needle, the highest peak in the range, its rocky surface dusted with snow.

To the east, the valley floor shone white as well. Sarah caught CJ staring and said, "It isn't snow. It's White Sands National Monument. Those are sand dunes."

CJ gazed in wonder at the vast field of dunes that stretched north and east of the Organ Mountains. What a fascinating region. Why had she ever believed the desert would be boring?

At the northern end of the mountain range, the pilot turned the plane west and brought them low over Las Cruces. Downtown looked a bit like a giant grid with several main roads crisscrossing. CJ looked down upon the houses and schools and churches and factories with their adobe walls and tile roofs, and she knew that down on the ground there were men and women and children looking up at them, hands shielding eyes from the afternoon sunlight glinting off the plane's metal and glass exterior. She tried to imagine operating controls that would open payload doors and unleash tons of explosives on those people and the buildings around them, but she couldn't. The American Southwest was too far from Schweinfurt and New Guinea for her to possibly conceive of what the conditions there must be like.

She couldn't picture the war, no matter how many photos she saw or firsthand accounts she read.

The return trip took less than a half hour. Soon the pilot was requesting permission to land. The airplane touched down more smoothly than CJ would have expected. They taxied back to the Transient Hangar, and then they were climbing down from the craft and waiting for their parachutes to be dropped down to them. Her first hop was over. It had lasted nearly an hour and yet had seemed to go by too fast.

"What do you think?" Sarah asked as they strolled back to the hangar, weighted down by their parachutes. "Do you like flying, or are you a landlubber?"

"I love it," CJ said. "I absolutely love it!" And she raced ahead of her squad mate, adrenaline easily besting the weight of the parachute.

That night, CJ looked for Brady as soon as she reached the mess hall. She was in her usual spot with Janice, Marjory and their other Admin friends. CJ strode over, still in her coveralls, and clapped Brady on the shoulder.

"I flew," she said, smiling so broadly it almost hurt her face. "I went up on a hop today."

Brady smiled in return. "I don't suppose I have to ask how you liked it, do I?"

"It was amazing. I wish you could have seen it."

Janice gave her an almost pained look of condescension and then glanced back at the other women arrayed about the table, muttering something low that CJ didn't hear. They tittered unkindly, reminding her of a flock of starlings.

They probably considered her naïve for showing such enthusiasm over something as commonplace to them as an airplane flight. The farm girl on a plane—not exactly the stuff of fairytales. Or maybe it was like a fairytale, and she was the poor peasant girl who, in the end, would win the prince away from the snooty ladies of the court. Except there didn't seem to be a prince in this scenario, did there?

She took a step back. "Anyway, I'll see you later," she told Brady, and turned away.

Some part of her hoped Brady would follow her to the mess line and declare there in front of everyone that what Janice and the other Admin Wacs thought didn't matter. But Brady stayed where she was, and CJ stood alone in line, trying not to let her disappointment take root. Closing her eyes, she pictured the horizon where blue sky met brown earth, the Organ Mountains rising from the surface like a strange creature, a dinosaur perhaps, armor-plated and spiny against the desert backdrop. From the air, Fort Bliss had appeared immense. It had been easy then to remember that she was one of thousands of military and civilian personnel at the sprawling post working together for a common cause. In the way that mattered most, even she and Janice were on the same side.

A little while later, Brady brought an after-dinner cup of coffee over to CJ's table. Toby and Reggie made room for her, and she slid in beside CJ.

"Hey." Brady nudged her.

"What?" CJ focused on her food, spearing an overly soft piece of broccoli with her fork.

"Hey," Brady repeated, nudging her again.

"I said what." CJ looked up this time.

"I'm sorry about before."

Instead of making things better, the apology made CJ feel worse. Cheeks warm, she stood up, tray in hand. "Fine."

"Wait." Brady followed her to the mess window. "Come on, CJ."

CJ ignored her, smiling tightly at the Wac on KP as she handed over her tray and utensils.

Brady followed her out of the stuffy mess hall into the cooling evening. "Look, I said I was sorry."

"I heard you."

Brady grabbed her arm. "Then what is your problem?"

CJ shook her arm free. "I'm not the one with the problem, am I? Careful, Brady. Your friends might see you talking to me." And she turned and stalked back to her barracks.

By the time she got there, she already regretted the outburst. Snide comments weren't her style, which was one of the reasons she actively disliked Janice. Except that wasn't the main reason, was it? She couldn't deny that she was jealous of Janice, embarrassing as that may be. They were adults, not school girls; Brady shouldn't have to choose between them. But somehow it felt like her sophomore year of high school all over again, when Carol Getz had befriended her and, for weeks, Carol's cousin and another friend had taken every available opportunity to snub her. Then one night they'd all shared a fifth of Earl Baker's moonshine during a Kalamazoo Central football game, and after that, the foursome had been more united than divided.

Seemed unlikely a bottle of hooch would have the same effect on Janice, unfortunately.

CJ shook her head, trying to empty it of company drama. She had flown in an airplane today, and here she was worrying about petty inter-squad dynamics. There were more important things in the world to dwell on, that much was certain.

Back at the barracks, she set about washing her HBTs, relying on the desert air to do its usual magic and dry them in time for duty tomorrow. In the day room, she found an empty couch corner and started in on her mail as women laughed and chatted around her and popular tunes played on the wireless set. She owed her parents several letters, not to mention both of her brothers. The V-mail letters would probably reach Alec and Joe not long after the regular first-class mail reached Michigan, given the microfilm technology used to reduce the letters to thumbnail size and transport them overseas. Then again, if a supply ship was torpedoed or otherwise destroyed, the V-mail would be lost. That wasn't the only way to lose a letter, either. She'd heard that the Fort Bliss post office had burned down the previous spring with most of the mail still inside. You could never be sure a letter to or from a soldier would reach its destination.

She was finishing a cheery update to her parents, long on hop details and short on interpersonal conflict, when the Wac in charge of quarters stuck her head into the day room and said, "Jamieson, visitor for you."

Brady, CJ thought, unable to hold back the flare of hope. It might not even be her, she told herself as she left the day room trailed by the Andrews Sisters crooning, "Don't sit under the apple tree with anyone else but me."

But it was her, waiting in a pool of lamp light. And she wasn't alone—Janice stood at her side, arms crossed tightly against the front of her uniform.

CJ paused on the front stoop, aware of Sarah and Reggie nearby hanging laundry on the line outside their barracks.

"Hi," Brady said.

"This is a surprise. Not that it isn't good to see you." She bit her lip. "Do you want to come in?"

"No, thank you. We can't stay." She nudged Janice unsubtly, much as she had CJ earlier.

"I'm sorry," Janice said, her eyes fixed over CJ's shoulder. "I was terribly rude at supper. I hope you can forgive me."

"Of course," CJ said, blinking. How had Brady gotten her to offer an apology? And more importantly, why had she gone to such trouble?

"Are we okay?" Brady asked, eyes anxious on CJ.

"We always were."

And yet, she thought, rubbing her bare arms in the cool desert air, something had shifted. Brady seemed to have made a decision, and CJ couldn't pretend the outcome didn't matter.

"Good." Brady smiled up at her. "See you tomorrow?"

"Yes, all right."

They turned away, and CJ watched them walk back to their own barracks. *Before you got here, she had me all to herself*, she heard Brady say again.

For a second she almost felt sorry for Janice. Then the moment slipped away, and she returned to the day room where her unfinished letters waited under the watchful eyes of Boadicea and Joan of Arc, who, she was fairly certain, had never had to worry about such matters.

* * *

After thirty days on base, Wacs at Fort Bliss were eligible for weekend passes. Kate had an in with one of the officers who handled leave requests, so their group of friends could usually get passes together. The first weekend CJ would be eligible they were planning to see the Andrews Sisters at a USO concert in El Paso, with an overnight stay in a downtown hotel afterward.

"You interested?" Toby asked as they smoked a cigarette on the front stoop of the barracks, bracing themselves for GI night festivities. "It's still a week away. I bet we could scrounge up an extra ticket."

"Thanks," CJ said, "but I already told Brady I would go to White Sands with her."

"Really?" Toby glanced over at her. "Just the two of you out in the middle of nowhere together?"

"Well, yes."

"Huh."

CJ was getting tired of the looks that passed between her Maintenance buddies whenever Brady was around. "What's that supposed to mean?"

"Beware of things that go bump in the night." Toby ground out her cigarette and rose, holding the butt between her fingers. "Unfortunately, latrine detail is calling my name. Better not keep those duckboards waiting."

Toby retreated but CJ stayed where she was, gazing out across the crowded compound with its barbed wire enclosure and armed guards at the gates. Four buildings away was Company A, where Brady would be recovering from KP duty—assuming she'd finished at the mess hall by now. She might still be scrubbing pots and pans or lugging garbage, exhausted from a day in the hot kitchen at the beck and call of the cooks. Or worse, emptying the grease traps.

Kitchen Police was the scourge of every soldier's life. She and Brady had gone to a show recently in which the Russians captured a German soldier and were discussing what to do with him when a GI at the back of the theater called out, "Give him KP!" The movie-goers groaned approvingly—even the mention of the horrid duty every private pulled once a month no matter their MOS was enough to send a spasm of disgust through the crowd.

During basic training, she and her fellow recruits had often sung the WAC version of a popular GI ditty, "The KPs are Scrubbing Away," to the tune of "The Caissons Go Rolling Along":

Over sinks, over pails
With the sergeant on our tails
All the KPs are scrubbing away
Shining pots, shining pans,
Cleaning out the garbage cans
All the KPs are scrubbing away!

Oh it's hi, hi, hee in the kitchen scullery
Sixteen long hours of the day
And wher'er we go,
By the smell you'll always know,
That the KPs are scrubbing away
(Keep 'em scrubbing)
That the KPs are scrubbing away!

CJ pictured Brady with her sleeves rolled up above her elbows, hands red from hot water and GI soap, face flushed, skin shiny. Even all sweaty from KP, she would be beautiful. Sometimes when they played basketball, CJ missed an easy shot or dribbled the ball out of bounds because she was distracted by the way Brady flipped her hair off her face or by the color of her eyes, which reminded CJ of a hazy summer sky. It wasn't just the way she looked or moved, either. There was something else about Brady that drew people to her, a quality CJ couldn't quite put into words.

Brady herself often seemed oblivious to the effect she had on other people, though.

"Are you sure you don't want to go to the concert in El Paso instead?" she asked CJ at supper mess a week later.

"Hmm. Now that you mention it, maybe I will."

Brady bit her lip and looked down at the battered wooden table.

"I'm kidding," CJ added. "Don't worry. I'm not going to change my mind."

"But you know you can go with them if you want, right?"

"For one thing, it would take a miracle to find a ticket at this point. And for another, I'd much rather spend the night with you than with hundreds of screaming GIs."

"When you put it that way…"

Brady smiled at her, and CJ smiled back. How could Brady have thought she would want to be anywhere else? She was looking forward to their getaway weekend so much that she hadn't slept well in days. Finally, a break from regimentation, from duty, from Army life. Compared to the squad of women she normally shared her quarters with, having Brady as her lone roommate Saturday night was going to seem like a luxury.

They went over their list of supplies again, mostly hiking gear, extra food and a camera Brady was planning to check out from work. One of the officers from the PRO was loaning them his car for the weekend, so they didn't have to worry about traveling light.

"We're skipping inspection and parade, right?" Brady asked later as they walked back to their barracks. They hadn't stayed long at the service club—their pass officially began at midnight and they wanted to get an early start in the morning.

"Right."

"I wonder if we'll even want to come back Sunday, or if we'll be tempted to keep driving."

CJ stared at her. "Of course we're coming back."

Brady shook her head, clearly trying to hold back a smile. "Not much for breaking rules, are you?"

"I'm as rebellious as the next person." As Brady eyed her, she conceded, "Okay, maybe not. It's possible I don't like to upset people."

"Apparently I don't have the same qualms."

"That's because all you have to do is smile and everything magically goes your way."

Brady snorted. "That's a load of crap."

"No, it isn't. People fall all over themselves to please you."

"They do not!"

"Yes, they do."

"You don't."

CJ paused. "Well, someone has to keep you honest."

A few minutes later, they said goodnight at Brady's barracks. CJ walked on alone, wondering if she was immune to Brady's appeal or if she simply hid her feelings better than the majority of Bliss personnel. She had a feeling their weekend away would answer that question, one way or another.

CHAPTER SIX

In the morning, they met at the mess hall to finagle food for the trip from the WAC cooks. Then, PBJ sandwiches, fruit, cookies and barracks bags in hand, they said goodbye to their friends and headed for the officers' quarters. Lieutenant Kelly had given them permission to park behind the WAC officers' house the night before.

"Nice car," CJ said, sliding into the passenger seat. It was a 1938 LaSalle, the same model her brother Joe owned. His was back in Michigan now, up on blocks behind the feed barn where they used to play summer ball.

"She's a beauty." Brady started the engine and checked the dash, then smiled at CJ across the narrow front seat. "Full tank, like Brent said, with gas coupons in the glove box. I think we're ready."

"Let's go then," CJ said, grinning back. They were free. Almost.

They drove across base, windows down, music from an El Paso radio station playing on the car radio. At the main entrance to the post, they showed the MP on duty their leave papers. He waved them through.

It wasn't quite nine yet. They should have been at work, but instead they were in a car speeding toward Las Cruces and the Organ

Mountains beyond. CJ had enthused so much about her recent hop that Brady had proposed they take a road trip to White Sands National Monument and the town of Cloudcroft, New Mexico, both popular tourist spots among Fort Bliss GIs. Their route via Las Cruces would take them in a triangle of sorts around the Organ Mountains, which they would be able to view from every angle possible.

She glanced at Brady in the driver's seat, bare arm hanging out the open window. They were both in shirt-sleeves and skirts, hastily shed summer uniform jackets and ties in the back seat along with their barracks bags. Brady's eyes were hidden behind sunglasses, her blonde curls swept up off her forehead like Rita Hayworth. She truly was beautiful.

"What?" Brady asked, glancing at her quizzically. "Do I have egg on my face?"

"Of course not. I was wondering… You haven't said much about your first trip to White Sands."

"It was last spring right after we arrived."

"Did you go with Janice?"

"Among others."

"Oh." CJ tried to keep her tone disinterested.

"You know, she's all right when you get to know her."

"I'll take your word for it."

Brady frowned. "I thought you were trying to get along better."

"We are. I'm just being a brat. Ignore me, okay?"

Brady lifted her hand from the wheel and captured CJ's, giving it a squeeze. At the same time, she flashed one of her mercurial smiles. "I could never ignore you." Then she let go of CJ's hand and turned her attention back to the road, humming with the music as she guided the car along the southwest edge of the Franklin Mountains.

"Anyway," CJ said, trying to pretend Brady's words didn't affect her, "are you still up for brunch in Las Cruces?"

As they followed the two-lane highway along the Rio Grande past ranches and historic adobe settlements, they discussed the plan for their New Mexican getaway: brunch and shopping in Las Cruces, hiking in White Sands National Monument, an overnight stay in Cloudcroft and a hike in the Sacramento Mountains before hitting the road back to Bliss. Another time they would visit Carlsbad Caverns, they agreed.

"Too bad we're not camping," Brady said. "I could go for s'mores."

"Were you a Girl Scout?"

"Naturally. Wasn't it a prerequisite for joining the Wackos?"

CJ would have bet Molly, her childhood horse, that Janice had never seen the inside of a Girl Scout uniform. But she kept the churlish thought to herself.

Twenty-five miles in, they crossed the border into New Mexico. By the time they reached Las Cruces forty-five minutes later, they were ready for their first stop: hot cakes and hash browns at the least mess hall-like restaurant they could find.

Main Street was dusty and wide, with a view of the nearby mountains and the occasional hitching post for those who preferred a more traditional mode of travel. With automobile companies contracted out to the government to build war materials and "new" cars from the 1942 government stockpile only available to specially designated "essential drivers," cars were increasingly difficult to come by. Gasoline and tires were rationed, and the national speed limit of thirty-five miles per hour was intended to preserve both—though CJ was pretty sure Brady had reached nearly double that limit during the drive from El Paso.

"It looks like a movie set," CJ said, looking up the long street with its brick and sandstone buildings standing shoulder to shoulder, awnings brightly colored, paint on the windows fresh.

Brady parked the car on an angle between an ancient Ford truck and a shiny recent model Chrysler.

"You know," she said as she shut off the engine, "cold s'mores are pretty good too. Do you think they have marshmallows at Woolworth's?"

"I doubt it. But fortunately, it turns out the PX really does have almost everything."

Brady lifted her, eyes wide. "You brought marshmallows?"

"And graham crackers and Hershey's bars. You know the Girl Scout motto: Always—"

"Be prepared." Brady reached across the front seat and hugged her. "I knew I brought you along for a reason."

Eyes closed, CJ inhaled the scent of strawberries and lavender that seemed to follow Brady. If she'd known all it would take was a few marshmallows to get Brady to hug her... Wait. Where had that come from?

"And here I thought it was for my conversational skills," she said, slipping from Brady's grasp.

The café they settled on had wide windows open to the sun and sky. A grandmotherly waitress took their order, insisting on giving them the serviceman's discount.

"You girls are in uniform," she said, patting CJ's shoulder. "You deserve it. Thank you for what you're doing to bring our boys home sooner."

"You're welcome," CJ and Brady said together, exchanging a look.

The men at Bliss more often than not gave them grief for daring to "impersonate" soldiers, while many El Paso residents seemed tired of soldiers in general, possibly because GIs had the unappealing habit of drinking too much at downtown bars and getting sick in bushes and trash cans. But the people of Las Cruces didn't appear to be fed up with soldiers. Far from it. Everywhere CJ and Brady went, men and women and even children smiled and thanked them for their service.

Shortly before noon, they headed back to the car, weighed down by gifts for their families and far-flung friends: pottery from a local artist for their mothers, a Mexican blanket for CJ's father and postcards for college friends. Brady, CJ noted, hadn't picked out anything for her fiancé.

"Apparently the good people of Las Cruces haven't heard the rumor about two hundred Wacs being sent home from Tunisia pregnant with illegitimate children," Brady commented.

"Or the story about Wacs in Des Moines buying up all the diapers in town before shipping out," CJ added.

"Even I haven't heard that one."

"Sadly, it happened—the women were told there wouldn't be any sanitary supplies where they were going overseas, so…"

"Well done, US Army. I can imagine the genius who came up with that helpful tip."

When they reached the car, Brady unlocked the passenger door and held it open with a slight bow.

"Thanks," CJ said, smiling at her as she climbed in. When Sean had held doors for her, it seemed patronizing. With Brady, the gesture simply felt friendly.

They drove in silence for a little while, the mostly empty highway taking them east toward the northern tip of the Organ Mountains, whose rocky spires rose high above the desert floor. In mid-November, the landscape was a nearly uniform dull brown and yet a tad less barren than West Texas. *Another state*, CJ thought, counting them up in her head. So far she had visited twenty-nine. She hoped someday to make it to all forty-eight.

"Did you know that New Mexico and Arizona were the last states admitted to the Union?" she asked.

"In nineteen twelve, right?"

"Right." CJ paused. "Why do you know that?"

"Because I'm from California," Brady said, as if she were stating the obvious.

They rode on in silence again, CJ trying to gauge Brady's mood. At brunch she had seemed happy to be away from base, tackling her stack of hot cakes with gusto and trying on hats afterward at Woolworth's: ladies' sailor caps, shakos, pillboxes, feathered homburgs and CJ's favorite, an ostrich feather-veil combination of the sort that Brady claimed several of her classmates' mothers had worn to graduation. But somewhere between the shops and the car she had gone all quiet, and CJ wasn't sure now how to cajole her back into her former good mood.

Soon the road began the ascent to a pass between the Organ Range and the San Andres Mountains. After climbing more than fifteen hundred feet, they neared a sign that read, "San Augustin Pass, Elev. 5719 feet."

"Look behind us," Brady said, nodding at the rearview mirror.

CJ turned, her eyes widening—to the west lay the Rio Grande Valley with Las Cruces in the foreground and layers of mountains receding into the distance.

"I still can't get used to seeing mountains," she said.

"You mean there aren't any in Kalamazoo? What a surprise."

"The closest range is in the Upper Peninsula. What about you?"

"L.A. is surrounded by mountains. So is Smith. Every autumn the Smith president gives the college the day off for Mountain Day. We usually went hiking on Mount Tom or Mount Holyoke. They're small, maybe a couple of thousand feet high, but they're beautiful, especially in the fall when the leaves turn."

"You sound like you miss it."

"I do. It's funny, but when I was there I missed California. Then after college I went home, and I missed western Massachusetts. It's as if my heart is permanently divided between two places that feel like home."

CJ couldn't imagine what having more than one home would feel like. Despite her grandmother's influence, she had never seriously considered leaving Michigan for higher education. Not many of her high school friends had even gone on to college, mostly boys who had ended up in Ann Arbor, at State in East Lansing or at Kalamazoo College. No one she knew from home had gone away to the East Coast. At Michigan, however, several of her classmates had hailed from New York and Massachusetts. Even after a few years in the Midwest, her Eastern friends got Missouri, Mississippi and Minnesota confused. "Those darned *M* states," they would say, shrugging helplessly.

How different might her life have been if she had gone to Wellesley, after all, or even Smith? Would she and Brady have met in Massachusetts? Would they have become instant friends like they had at Bliss, or had Brady cleaved to a different crowd there, one that could never accept a girl who liked cars and slave narratives and vegetable gardens? Fortunately, or perhaps not, there was no redoing the past.

A verse from a Robert Frost poem that had experienced a recent resurgence crept into her mind:

…The same
Grim giving to do over for them both.
She dared no more than ask him with her eyes
How was it with him for a second trial.
And with his eyes he asked her not to ask.
They had given him back to her, but not to keep.

She closed her eyes. The poem was from the first war, the so-called Great War, but the sentiment was as apt now as it had been then.

"Okay?" Brady asked, interrupting her bleak musing.

"Of course. Do you mind if I turn on the radio?" she added, even though the odds of finding a station this far from civilization seemed slim.

"Of course not," Brady said, smiling at her across the gap between them. The expression seemed tentative somehow.

Without thinking, CJ covered her hand on the steering wheel. "Are you okay driving? I wouldn't mind taking over if you're tired."

"I'm fine right now, but maybe after the next stop." She hesitated and then focused on the road again. "I'm glad you're here."

"So am I."

CJ felt warmth seeping through her, chasing away the melancholy induced by Frost's poem. Reluctantly, she let go of Brady's hand and reached for the radio dial, stumbling eventually across a faint Alamogordo station playing popular big band tunes.

On the east side of the pass, the road curved to reveal a long, smooth valley that stretched as far as she could see. In the distance, low on the horizon, there was snow. No, sand. White Sands. Soon they would get a closer look at the unusual geological formation that Hoover had set aside as a national monument during the last days of his presidency.

The dunes came closer and closer, sometimes in sight and sometimes not, sometimes drifting right up to the edge of the highway only to recede again. Then, all at once it seemed, they reached the signed turnoff to the park. Brady almost drove past it and hit the brakes, laughing.

"Some navigator you are," she said, turning the car onto the park road.

"I can't help it if you like to speed."

"Are you saying you don't?"

She had a point.

The visitor center, a low, brown adobe building that blended into the desert landscape, sat just inside the park's entrance.

"Want to visit the museum?" CJ asked.

"Of course," Brady said, peering at her as if she suspected CJ had perhaps gotten too much sun. "We'll need a map too."

A stop at the visitor center wasn't necessarily a given, CJ thought as they exited the car. Toby and Reggie, if they were along, would probably want to drive out into the middle of the dunes and pelt each other with handfuls of sand crystals. Not that there was anything wrong with that. If they had been along, she would have joined them. Still, it was nice to be with someone whose approach matched hers.

Inside, the building was surprisingly cool, its thick walls ably blocking the sun. An older woman greeted them, her gray hair pulled back in a neat bun.

"Welcome," she said, smiling at them from behind a nearby counter. "Are you gals up from Texas?"

"Yes, we are." Brady returned her smile.

"We do see a lot of you up here," the woman said. "But you two picked the perfect time of year, not too hot and not too busy."

The attendant—Marge, according to her nametag—gave them a quick rundown. The entry fee was waived for active military, given they were government employees, and maps were free to all visitors. The museum cases in the other room focused on three topics: the origins of the dunes, the ecology of White Sands and the ethnology of the Mescalero Apache and Spanish explorers.

At the first case they stood shoulder to shoulder reading about the history and ecology of the Tularosa Basin, home to the 275-square-mile sand dune field—the largest in the world.

"Listen to this," Brady said. "'During the last ice age of the Pleistocene era, a large lake known as Lake Otero covered the basin. When the lake dried out, it left behind large gypsum deposits in the

San Andres and Sacramento Mountains.' Amazing to think this area was covered by a freshwater lake, isn't it?"

"I know." CJ skipped ahead. "'Unlike quartz-based sand crystals, gypsum does not easily convert the sun's energy into heat. This means that the dunes at White Sands can be walked on safely with bare feet even in the hottest summer months.' That's right. I remember learning that in my geology course in college."

"You took geo?"

"I may have been a tad obsessed. My friends called me RH for a while—you know, for rock hound?"

Brady laughed. "That's nothing. *My* friends started a 'rock jar'— every time I tried to share what I found to be a fascinating geological fact about the Holyoke Range or the impact of the ice age on the Connecticut River Valley, I had to add a nickel."

Laughing too, CJ moved on to the next display case. Though she'd already known of Brady's cerebral tendencies, she couldn't help but enjoy digging deeper into Brady's intellectual interests, especially when the passion was something they shared. Back in Michigan, she had loved the duality of her life as a laborer on her family's farm, getting her hands dirty and watching the literal fruits of her labor bloom and ripen, balanced against the work of a student, losing herself in the letters and diary entries of those who had come before. She missed that duality now, but less somehow when she was with Brady.

As she leaned over the display dedicated to area flora and fauna, she felt Brady's gaze on her.

"What?"

"I don't think I've ever met anyone like you."

CJ narrowed her eyes teasingly. "Which, of course, you mean in a good way."

"I mean it in the best possible way," Brady said, her words accompanied by a penetrating look.

"I haven't met anyone like you either," she admitted. Then, aware of Marge's presence in the next room, she turned her attention back to the hearty shrubs, grasses, birds and other critters that called White Sands home.

After a moment, Brady came and stood close to her again, peering through the glass. Soon they were giggling over the strange names of the many different varieties of lizard in the park, from the little striped whiptail and common side-botched to the greater earless and bleached earless.

"Did you read this part?" Brady asked, pointing.

"How brown lizards evolved into white lizards in order to blend into their environment?"

"Isn't that incredible? I love biology," Brady said, her eyes glowing as she peered into the case where rodent skeletons, molted snake skins and insect cadavers shared the shelves.

"You do?"

"I minored in it. I'd like to become a science writer someday, if anyone would hire me."

"Why *someday*?" she asked. "Why not now?"

"Well, there's this little thing called the Army."

"You know what I mean."

Brady shrugged and looked down at her hand, spinning her engagement ring around. "I haven't figured it all out yet."

Usually CJ could forget about Nate and the domestic future awaiting Brady at war's end, assuming Nate made it home safely. There was no reason to expect otherwise—Brady had told her that he was an officer in the AFHQ Signal Section, where he was tasked with trouble-shooting communications switchboards first in North Africa and now in Italy. In both places he'd been stationed well behind the front lines and had yet to come under fire. Mostly he wrote to her about parties at the officers' club and meetings with members of the British communications command, who'd reminded him of Harvard men, he said: supercilious and full of themselves.

CJ didn't want to think about him, didn't want to picture Brady playing house with a bright Yale alumnus she had known nearly all her life. She couldn't see this Brady, *her* Brady, settling into such a life.

"Fortunately," she said, reminding herself as well as Brady, "you have plenty of time to figure out what you want."

Brady stopped fidgeting. "You're right. Speaking of time, I'm hungry again. What do you say to a picnic on the dunes?"

"I say lead away."

Marge offered directions to a parking area at the end of the loop road where WPA workers had built picnic tables from lumber harvested from nearby Sacramento peaks. She also gave them a map of the area and directions to Cloudcroft, where they were planning to stay the night.

"Anything else I can do for you girls?" she asked.

"Actually," Brady said, holding out her camera, "would you mind?"

They posed in front of the museum case. CJ was aware of Brady's body close against her, of Brady's arm about her waist, and all at once her lungs seemed tight, as if she couldn't get enough air. What was wrong with her? *Get it together, Jamieson*, she chided herself, forcing a smile for the photos.

Marge took a few different shots before handing back the camera. "Now, get on out there and enjoy yourselves," she said.

They thanked her, filled up their canteens from the drinking fountain and returned to the car.

"Ready?" Brady asked, pulling on the black cowboy hat she'd bought at the Las Cruces Woolworth's.

"Ready," CJ said, and tugged on the brown cowboy hat she'd picked out for herself.

Brady watched her across the car seat. "I like you in that hat."

"I like you in yours too."

They gazed at each other, and CJ thought Brady was looking at her as if she wanted to say something momentous, possibly even earth-shattering. But was she ready for the Earth to be shattered?

"You promised me a picnic, remember?" she said quickly.

Brady nodded and looked away. "I remember."

And then the car began to move again, waves of bright, white dunes rising and falling into the distance on one side, the flat, brown, sagebrush-strewn desert stretching off on the other. CJ wished there was some way to forget about the past and the future and focus instead on this lovely moment that found her in a place she had read about in college but never imagined she would visit. But with the world upended, it was difficult to focus on a single point in time, knowing as you did that events in far-flung locales were happening—may have already happened—that could change forever the way you viewed your present, your past, your future.

For those left behind on the home front, the questions were always there: Would a brother, friend, husband, fiancé come home, or would his broken body be left behind on a forgotten beach or mountainside? Was he alive still, or had he left this world minutes, hours, days, even weeks before? How could anyone plan for the future, not knowing who would be left at war's end—assuming the war ever ended?

It had to, of course. The war would end, and she would go to North Carolina and study the largest trove of slave narratives in the nation. Talk about primary sources—she likely wouldn't get through even a quarter of the narratives in the UNC collection before she finished her PhD. Normally that thought put a smile on her face. But today, she found herself thinking how far North Carolina was from everything and everyone she loved.

That was another aspect of war: the appreciation of the things and people in your life. In a way, wasn't that sentiment almost as much of a threat to civilization as violence was? Content people tended to remain exactly as they were. They didn't seek change, didn't evolve. Or perhaps the opposite was true—maybe those who had risked their lives once were more likely to stand up for what they knew to be right, whatever the stakes.

As the road curved into the park's interior, dunes appearing on both sides now and gypsum crystals stacked on the shoulders like snow drifts, Brady fiddled with the radio dial. A scratchy version of Artie Shaw's "Begin the Beguine" floated into the car's interior.

"I love this song," Brady said, her eyes warm as she smiled at CJ.

"So do I."

As they sang aloud to the familiar tune, their borrowed car skimming along the gypsum-dusted pavement, CJ couldn't help wishing that the war would remain as it was then—far, far away.

CHAPTER SEVEN

"What was your favorite part today?" CJ asked, sitting back in the Victorian loveseat as firelight flickered against the blue and white pin-striped wallpaper of their room.

When they'd pulled into the forested mountain village of Cloudcroft a few hours earlier, Brady had insisted on splurging first for supper and then a suite at the Cloudcroft Lodge, with a fireplace, queen-sized four-poster bed and private bathroom. CJ hadn't argued much before letting Brady treat her.

"I don't know," Brady said, pulling up her feet and turning to face her. "It was all so wonderful. This is my favorite day of the year so far, I think."

"Mine too," CJ agreed.

The afternoon had been perfect. They had followed the loop road through the heart of the dunes, some more than fifty feet high, where all they could see other than the occasional yucca and saltbush was white sand rising and falling beneath the bright blue sky. At the designated picnic area, theirs was the lone car. They took turns changing into their PT kits and tennis shoes in the back seat. Then, after a mid-day meal of sandwiches and apples, they set out on a trail Marge had recommended, keeping an eye out for lizards and other local inhabitants. The only things they encountered, though, were dozens of pairs of tiny footprints crisscrossing the waves of white sand.

As they walked, Brady had linked their arms and CJ had strolled beside her, surprisingly content despite the vast, silent isolation of the dune field. It was as if they were in a strange land all their own, they'd agreed, far from any madding crowds.

"This reminds me of Lake Michigan," CJ had told Brady as they climbed a steep dune along the marked trail. "At Ludington, there are dunes even higher than this. My brothers and I used to climb up and run straight down into the lake."

"That sounds like fun."

"It was." But would they ever again have a chance—she clamped down on the bittersweet thought.

"It reminds me of snow," Brady told her. "I used to go skiing with my brothers in Utah, and we would drive along the mountain roads with the snow piled up on either side. The banks were almost as high as some of these dunes."

That summed them up: Brady, the Southern Californian who skied down mountains, and her, the Michigan girl who ran barefoot down sand dunes. But under the surface they were the same, weren't they? She could almost swear they were.

"Come on," she'd said when they reached the top of the dune, holding out her hand.

Brady took it, and together they ran down the dune, feet sinking into the sand with every giant step downward. At the bottom, Brady had pulled her to the ground, and they lay on their backs together in the sand, laughing, cowboy hats shielding their faces from the omnipresent sun. CJ had had the sense again that they were far from everyone and everything they knew, a place where they could be entirely themselves.

Now Brady smoothed the sofa cushion between them, firelight glowing in her eyes. "Are you saying today was better than your college graduation?"

"Yes, but that isn't saying much. Our speaker gave a lecture instead of a commencement address, more grim than celebratory in tone. I still remember a few of the things he said: that we live in a world where good doesn't always succeed unless it's backed by force. That those who believe in freedom and justice have to be willing to support their ideals through the use of power."

"Geez," Brady said, wrinkling her nose. "Welcome to the world, graduates. Now go kill and maim for your country. Or even better, die for it."

"That was the gist of it. Wasted, too—the crowd was mostly female students, 4-Fs and parents."

"We females could die for our country, you know, especially if we end up overseas."

"Did you put in for overseas duty?"

Brady nodded. "Did you?"

"Absolutely. I believed being a mechanic would help my chances. That was before I realized it would mostly be secretaries and clerks who would get to go."

"Who knew having a good MOS would work against us?"

"At least you got to see Europe before it self-destructed."

Brady's mother had taken her to Europe on the *Queen Mary* the summer after her high school graduation. They had spent two months traveling "The Continent" by train, staying in luxury hotels and dining in high-end restaurants.

"I don't know if I'm lucky or not," Brady said, frowning. "It's strange to think that some of the people I met on that trip are dead now. Quite a few, possibly."

"So many dead." CJ stared into the fire. *And so many more to come.*

Silence descended on the room, punctuated by the crack and hiss of the wood fire.

"Enough war talk," Brady announced. She stood up. "I have an idea."

Fifteen minutes later they were perched on a velvet-tufted bench in front of the fireplace, giggling and sucking melted chocolate from their fingertips. Their marshmallow sticks were skewers hastily borrowed from the restaurant downstairs where they had dined on roast duck earlier in the evening.

"Here," Brady said, mashing chocolate and marshmallow between two graham crackers. "Try this."

Cupping her hands under Brady's, CJ took a bite, humming as the combination of flavors hit her taste buds. This was heaven. What had Brady said about not wanting to go back to Fort Bliss? Except that if they didn't go back, they could be hunted down and arrested by MPs and then court-martialed. More likely, they would be fined, restricted to quarters and sentenced to KP and latrine duty for the foreseeable future. She wasn't sure which punishment would be worse.

"What is it about an open fire that makes food taste so good?" Brady asked as she finished off the s'more.

"Wood smoke, maybe?"

"That was supposed to be a rhetorical question."

"Oh." Her cheeks warmed.

"You can take the girl out of Michigan...I'll bet your campfire experiences aren't limited to the Girl Scouts, are they?"

"No. We have a fire pit out back. When I was younger, we used to have friends over to roast marshmallows and tell stories. Or someone would bring a guitar for a sing-along."

Brady shook her head. "I can't imagine growing up like you did, with tractors and plows and hay fields. Your childhood sounds like something out of a Willa Cather novel."

"Ooh, I love her writing."

"So do I."

They shared a smile, perched close together on the love seat, firelight flickering romantically on the walls of the narrow, cozy room.

"Besides, we're even," CJ added, "because to me, your life sounds like something out of a movie."

Brady had confessed to growing up in Beverly Hills on an estate that included an English garden and an Olympic-sized swimming pool, with friends and neighbors who worked in the movie industry.

"You're the one who gets to fly around in experimental aircraft," Brady pointed out, reaching for another marshmallow.

"True. Say, would you ever want to go up on a hop?"

"Would I ever! Maybe I could swing a story for the *Monitor*."

"Good idea. Now, hand over the chocolate, Buchanan."

"You'll have to come and get it," Brady said, eyes shining as she held the Hershey's bar aloft, the marshmallow on its makeshift stick still clutched in her other hand.

"How mature of you," CJ said, pretending to be disdainful. Then she tickled Brady until she dropped the chocolate bar.

"You're lucky I didn't skewer you," Brady said. "Didn't your parents teach you never to tickle someone holding a sharp object?"

"Uh, no, that would be more of a big brother lesson."

"Tell me about it."

They ate s'mores until their stomachs hurt, and then they watched the fire die down, the smell of wood smoke competing with the scent of burnt sugar.

"Have you heard from your brother in Italy recently?" Brady asked after a while.

"A few days ago. He said he's waiting on orders, something about a new command."

"I bet it's the Fifteenth under Jimmy Doolittle. I heard they're splitting the NAAF between northern and southern Europe so they can cover more territory."

"Wait—*the* Jimmy Doolittle? As in, Doolittle's Raiders?"

"That's the one."

Doolittle was famous for his role as leader of an assault on Japan in April 1942, during which sixteen B-25 medium bombers took off from an aircraft carrier in the Pacific and bombed strategic targets on mainland Japan. While it hadn't caused significant damage to Japanese military or industrial sites, the boost to American morale more than made up for the loss of the bombers, the majority of which were destroyed when their crews, running low on fuel, bailed out off the coast of China.

"Can I write and tell my parents?" CJ asked.

"Better not. I wasn't even supposed to tell you."

"Oh. Well, thanks."

"I'm actually keeping an eye on that area of operation myself."

CJ hesitated. "Because of Nate?"

"Yes." Brady reached for the poker. "I think I'll build up the fire again. It's getting cold outside."

At almost nine thousand feet above sea level, Cloudcroft was significantly colder than El Paso. The desk clerk had said it might even snow overnight. Perhaps they would get stuck in the mountains, CJ thought, and be forced to spend another night at the lodge. Gee, what a disappointment to be marooned a hundred miles from base with Brady.

She watched as Brady added another piece of wood and a handful of kindling to the fire and then adjusted the logs until the flames began to lick at the new tinder.

"For a city girl, you sure know your way around a fire."

"I told you, my grandparents took us camping every summer. Those were some of my favorite times growing up."

"Without your parents?"

"That must sound strange to you, coming from such a happy family."

"We weren't always so happy. I'm not sure my parents can ever be truly, not after losing a child."

Brady touched her shoulder. "I'm sorry, I didn't know. What happened?"

It had been years since CJ had told someone the story of Henry, born after Pete and before Rebecca, the youngest. When Henry was almost two, all of the Jamieson kids came down with a cold. By the time their family doctor instructed them to take Henry to the hospital in Kalamazoo, the cold had progressed to pneumonia. A day later he was gone, and a week later they buried him. CJ hadn't known they made caskets that small.

"He was this sweet little kid," CJ told Brady, her throat tightening despite the fact Henry had been gone for a decade and a half. "He loved animals. He was always so happy. It was almost like he knew he had to pack a lifetime into a couple of years."

"How old were you when he died?"

"Seven. Things were never quite the same after that. I don't think my father will ever forgive himself for not taking Henry to the hospital sooner."

"Even if he had, Henry still might not have made it."

"I don't think my father sees it that way. The worst part is now he could lose two more sons. I don't know what he'd do..." She trailed off. It was unlucky to mention the possibility of death. Anyway, she didn't have to. Brady's brother's unit was stationed not far from the front lines. Chris had written Brady about coming under artillery fire more than once.

"I can't even imagine," Brady said. "You would think we would have learned from the last war, but apparently not. I hope this will be the last time. Maybe we won't have to watch our sons go off to war."

Our sons—she said it so easily, as if the notion of having children was a given. Maybe her dream of becoming a writer was the kind of dream you could put on hold while your children were young. An academic career, on the other hand, wasn't as flexible. Sean had been right on that count, at least.

"Do you want children?" CJ asked.

"Of course. Don't you?"

"I don't know. I think so."

Brady poked at the logs again, sending a cloud of sparks wafting into the chimney. "Nate wants us to start a family as soon as he gets back."

Was that what *she* wanted? CJ didn't ask. Instead, she chose a safer question: "What kind of work will he do after the war?"

"His father offered him a position in his company. They're wholesale grocers. They supply some of the largest chains on the West Coast."

Nate would be a good provider—people always needed groceries. CJ could already see Brady with a tow-headed baby in her arms, another on the way. She would be a good mother, one any child would be lucky to have. But would she be happy with a husband she had agreed to marry because she couldn't see any other choice?

Brady shifted away from her on the bench. "Janice thinks I'm crazy."

"Why?"

"Because…" She paused and bit her lip. Then, "I've been thinking of breaking it off with Nate."

"You have?"

"I have."

CJ sat up straighter, watching the fire intently. She was afraid if she looked at Brady, she wouldn't be able to stop herself from blurting out the words inexplicably reverberating in her mind: *Yes, please, yes!*

"Obviously," Brady said, "I don't want to 'Dear John' him. He's one of my best friends. The last thing I want is to hurt him. But I don't know what else to do."

CJ aimed for objectivity. "Wouldn't it be better to do in person?"

"It would, except that I don't have any idea when I'll see him next. Meanwhile, his mother and his sister keep writing me these letters about how lucky he is to have me supporting him while he's off serving his country. I feel like I'm lying to everyone. The thing is, I don't love him, not the way I'm supposed to. I shouldn't have to keep pretending, should I?"

Her eyes pleaded for support, understanding, empathy. But all CJ could think was, *She doesn't love him. Thank God, she doesn't love him.* Then she wondered at her own elated reaction. She should feel sorry for Brady, shouldn't she? It wasn't like Brady's confession of non-love for her fiancé had anything to do with her.

"I can't tell you what to do," she said. "It has to be your decision."

"I know, you're right. It's just, what if I meet someone else? I can't cheat on him. I could never do something like that."

For a moment, CJ didn't breathe. "Have you met someone?" *Please, don't let it be Charlie*, she thought. Then again, every other GI she pictured was nearly as awful.

Brady stared into the fire. "I didn't say that."

Did that mean she had or hadn't? CJ caught herself, wondering again at her own oddly self-interested response. A best friend *would* show support, understanding, empathy. If she didn't, what did that make her?

"I'm sorry," she said. "I wish I could help."

"You are helping," Brady said. Then her eyes narrowed. "Saving some chocolate for later?" And she leaned close to brush crumbs from the corner of CJ's mouth, her fingers lingering.

Oh, God. CJ felt herself flush as she recognized the urge filling her—she wanted to capture Brady's hand and hold it to her lips. She wanted to touch her pale throat, the curve of her chin, the freckles on her cheekbones.

She stood up and backed away, understanding all at once how a spooked horse must feel.

Brady's smile faded. "What is it?"

"Nothing. I have to pee."

Then she blushed harder because she hadn't meant to be crude in front of Brady. Brady, who she wanted to kiss; Brady, who…her breath catching, she clamped down on her racing thoughts. This couldn't happen. It was fine for the Kates and Tobys of the world, but it wasn't right for her. What would her parents think? What would her brothers say? If they found out, they would never let her near Rebecca or Pete again.

"The bathroom's right there," Brady prompted.

More to the point, what would Brady think? Here she was looking for support from a friend, and CJ was busy picturing—

"Mm-hmm," she said vaguely, and shut herself in the bathroom.

A gilded mirror hung on one wall. CJ leaned against the elegant ivory sink beneath it and stared at her reflection. Her cheeks were pink, from the fire as much as from the turmoil suddenly enveloping her. Something clicked in her mind, and she remembered the night after she'd met Brady, when she examined herself in the barracks mirror trying to figure out what had changed. This was it. This was why Charlie and Janice reacted to her the way they did. They cared about Brady, and they knew CJ's motives were far from pure. Even if she hadn't admitted it to herself until now.

Twenty-four hours, she reminded herself, dashing cold water against her face. Only one more day, and then they would be back on base.

"You can do this," she muttered to her expression. Then she shook her head. Here she was in a hotel room in New Mexico alone with the woman she had discovered she was, well, attracted to, and all she could think about was getting back to Fort Bliss where privacy was nonexistent and intimacy next to impossible. If she hadn't felt like throwing up, she might have laughed at her own absurdity.

By the time she'd peed and brushed her teeth, there was no more delaying. Steeling herself, she opened the door and headed back into the room, where the four-poster bed seemed to leap out at her. The bed she and Brady would be sharing. Alone. All night.

Brady, already clad in a green silk nightgown, brushed past her. "My turn," she said, not meeting CJ's eyes.

Of course she would wear silk.

CJ changed into her own cotton nightgown, then turned out the lights and crawled into bed. Her head hurt, which seemed a fitting conclusion to a day that had started so well and veered so dramatically off course at the end. The clock on the wall ticked off the minutes, hands barely visible in the light from the dying fire, and then Brady opened the bathroom door.

She paused, her eyes on CJ. "Are you tired?"

"Mmmm." She rolled over onto her side, facing the wall. "Goodnight."

The bed shifted as Brady slipped between the sheets, the warmth of her body seeming to hover tantalizingly close. Just as CJ made up her mind to turn and face her, Brady settled onto her own side of the bed.

"Goodnight," she said in a voice so quiet CJ couldn't tell what she was thinking—irritated or indifferent, wishful or disappointed.

But then, she was the wishful one, wasn't she? The one who wanted to slide over to Brady's side of the bed, to press her lips to Brady's as the firelight cast shadows on the wallpaper and the night grew colder outside. Instead, she hugged herself tightly. Brady didn't want her, not like that. She was normal. She wanted children and a writing career, comfort and safety, a life that couldn't possibly include CJ except as a friend.

Oh, God, she thought again, squeezing her eyes shut. *What am I going to do?*

CHAPTER EIGHT

She was awake before sunrise, unrefreshed after a restless few hours of sleep. Her head still ached and her mouth felt dry, as if she'd had too much wine at supper the previous evening. In the night she had awakened—which meant she must have slept, though it felt like she hadn't—to find Brady snuggled up to her, one arm across CJ's chest, head on her shoulder. CJ had lain motionless, inhaling the now-familiar scent of strawberries and lavender, trying to resist the urge to give herself over to cuddling with Brady. After all, it was cold in their room, and it was natural to seek warmth from the person sleeping beside you.

What wasn't natural was how much she wanted to kiss that person. In fact, there were all sorts of laws against it—civil, cultural, not to mention martial. Even so, she couldn't seem to stop herself from turning her head slightly so that her lips brushed against Brady's forehead. Immediately she pulled back and held her breath, but Brady slept on beside her. What was it about her that made CJ feel so good? And how could such a feeling be criminal, as the Army claimed? Irregular, yes; abnormal, perhaps. But a crime? That part didn't make any sense.

At some point in the early hours of the morning, she awakened again to find that Brady had moved away. A mix of disappointment and relief assailed her. She lay in the dark listening to the clock tick, the pipes in the walls gurgle, the building creak above and below. The closeness she'd felt to Brady in the middle of the night had faded, leaving the same fear that had nearly paralyzed her the night before. What was she going to do? And how would she ever face her parents? She had always tried to be a good daughter. How would she be able to look them in the eye now, knowing she wasn't the person they believed her to be?

Beside her, Brady rolled onto her side, silk nightgown bunching in a way that made CJ long to reach out and smooth it across the curve of her exposed side. God, what was wrong with her? It was like a switch had been thrown the night before, and now she didn't know how to turn off the desire to touch Brady. Castigating herself, she slipped out of bed and dressed quietly in her PT dress and GI pants. Then she left the room, feeling bereft as soon as she closed the door between them. For God's sake, she was acting like a lovesick girl mooning over the boy who didn't know she existed. Or, to be more precise, a lovesick girl mooning over a girl who would probably hate her if she knew.

Cut the sappiness, Jamieson, she told herself. By nightfall they would be back on base, back in their separate barracks surrounded by their squad mates. The thought produced a wave of contradictory emotions, but she ignored them. She needed space from Brady, that much was clear. Space and time to figure out how to get back to normal.

Downstairs, she greeted the front desk staff and headed into Rebecca's, the restaurant named for the lodge's resident ghost, according to the menu they'd read the night before. The dining room was almost empty, so she picked a table near the window with a view out over the resort's well-tended grounds. A waiter brought her coffee, and as she sipped the reviving liquid—her mother prized the curative powers of coffee, especially when it came to headaches—she studied the portrait of the restaurant's namesake on the far wall. Red-haired and blue-eyed, this Rebecca looked nothing like CJ's dark-haired, dark-eyed little sister.

CJ was on her second cup when Brady, dressed in her own PT kit and cowboy hat, slid into the seat across from her. CJ's heartbeat accelerated, and she cursed inwardly. She'd hoped that her attraction to Brady had been a product of their lovely day, of the cozy fire-lit room, of too many sweets before bedtime. But as Brady gazed at her across the table, she couldn't will away the leaping pleasure she felt at the sight of her. Brady entered a room, and suddenly the room seemed brighter, happier, more interesting. CJ had convinced herself that her feelings for Brady fell well within the bounds of female friendship. Now there could be no more pretense.

"Good morning," she said, congratulating herself on the neutrally welcoming tone she managed to dredge up.

"Is it? I thought maybe you'd left," Brady said, the seriousness of her gaze belying her light tone.

"Where could I have gone?" CJ pretended to joke back. In fact her flight instinct had clamored so loudly on the way downstairs that if there had still been passenger trains running between Cloudcroft and Alamogordo, she may have been tempted.

Brady shrugged. "I don't know. I woke up and you weren't there."

"I couldn't sleep."

"What, you missed Ethel's snoring?"

"So it would seem."

CJ and the other D-lites, as they flippantly referred to themselves, had complained enough in Brady's presence that she knew all about Ethel Treece's deviated septum. Similarly, CJ knew the intimate details of Clara Jefferson's penchant for crunching peanut brittle in the middle of the night even though she'd never actually met Clara, a founding member of Company A.

The waiter brought another cup of coffee, and CJ watched as Brady stirred in fresh cream. How did she make even the simplest of actions seem graceful?

"Did I do something wrong last night?" Brady asked, her gaze firmly fixed on the table top.

"What? No."

"Then are you upset with me because I said I was thinking of ending my engagement?"

"Not at all." She paused. What could she tell Brady? Not the truth: *I realized I want to be your boyfriend, except I'm a girl, so…* At this, she couldn't hold back a slightly hysterical snort of laughter.

Brady stared at her. "Is this funny to you?"

"No, it's not. I mean, you're not. I was laughing at me."

"Did you want to share the joke?"

"Not really."

Brady blinked, and then she shook her head. "What's going on, CJ? If I did something wrong, I'm sorry."

"I told you, you didn't do anything wrong." With two cups of coffee and minimal sleep to embolden her, she reached across the table and took Brady's hand. It felt soft and strong in her grasp, and all at once, she had a feeling that everything would work out. Everything would be fine. "I couldn't sleep, all right?"

Brady glanced down at their clasped hands. "All right." She squeezed CJ's fingers softly. "If you're sure."

"I'm sure." And then, because she knew she should, CJ let go of Brady's hand. Almost immediately the sense of loss she'd felt that morning leaving their room accosted her. Trying to shrug it off, she gestured outside where the rising sun angled through acres of evergreens. "It didn't snow after all. You still up for a hike this morning?"

"I am if you are," Brady said, sounding more like her usual self.

"First I need food. But after that, I'm up for anything."

"Anything?" Brady repeated, watching CJ over the rim of her mug.

"Well, not anything…" she started uncertainly. She was saved by the arrival of their waiter. Brady turned her flirtatious smile on the unsuspecting septuagenarian, allowing CJ time to compose herself.

Had Brady done that on purpose? If so, it meant she knew how CJ felt about her, which was surely a fate worse than a month of KP. *She couldn't know*, CJ assured herself, turning her attention to the breakfast menu. Brady could never find out.

* * *

By nine, they had paid the bill and loaded their gear back into the car. Sylvia, the older woman at the front desk, had recommended a trail half a mile from the lodge on the way back down to Alamogordo. She had even given them a rough trail map that the lodge kept on hand for "you young types," as she called them.

"Do you have water?" she'd asked, eyeing them suspiciously.

"Yes," Brady said, far more tolerantly than CJ would have expected. "And food."

"Hmph," Sylvia harrumphed, folding her arms over her sizable breasts. "Extra clothes? Because the weather here can turn before you know it."

"We have sweaters," CJ said.

Winter in the Southwest was tricky, they'd been told. High desert country could be hot and dry or cold and snowy. Or somewhere in between, as it had been since they'd left Texas the previous day.

Had it only been a day? CJ sighed. *Unbelievable.*

"And do you know the signs of mountain sickness?" Sylvia wanted to know.

Brady nodded, but CJ made the mistake of admitting she didn't. Helpfully, Sylvia ran down the list of afflictions lowlanders often experienced while vacationing in the thin air of the Sacramento Mountains: nausea and vomiting, dizziness, fatigue, loss of appetite, unsteadiness and shortness of breath.

"If you feel any of those things, you turn right around, get in your car and drive down to Alamogordo as fast as you can. Mountain sickness is nothing to sneeze at, you know," she scolded them.

"Sounds like a hangover," Brady commented as they left the lodge a few minutes later.

Or lovesickness. CJ sighed again.

They drove out of Cloudcroft slowly, watching for the turnout their erstwhile tour guide had mentioned. She couldn't get over the differences between Cloudcroft and Alamogordo. Even though she'd known to expect an evergreen forest twenty miles from White Sands, she'd been astounded by the changes along the narrow, twisty road that led from the floor of the Tularosa Basin to the resort town. The sun had been setting as they headed out of Alamogordo, the uneven road instantly starting to climb and remaining at a steady upward grade the entire way with a few pulse-stopping turns above nothingness. Despite the darkening sky, there had been plenty of light to see the transformation from desert to canyon, with rocky, sedimentary cliffs all around, and then again from canyon to forest.

Halfway up they'd pulled over on a narrow turnout to take a break from the occasionally nail-biting drive. The view of the canyon they were passing through—Fresnal, according to the area map—had been spectacular. They'd even caught a glimpse of dunes glittering off in the distance. Back on the road, the changes had accelerated, with scrub brush turning the landscape more green than red and Ponderosa pines beginning to dot the foothills on either of side of the road. Soon trees blanketed the land as far as they could see, except in asymmetrical jigsaw patches owned by logging companies. The transformation was complete—from desert to forest in twenty very long miles.

As Sylvia had promised, the turnout was half a mile down the main road from town. They parked the car, stowed their supplies in the rucksack CJ had borrowed from the hangar and set off along the trail. The beginning went almost straight up, the dirt track with log steps in the steepest spots winding between deciduous trees with branches mostly bare of leaves. They took it slowly, stopping to catch their breath regularly in the thin mountain air. Finally the trail widened and leveled out, and they kicked through the fallen leaves, smiling at each other as the trail meandered over a hilltop.

"This reminds me of Massachusetts," Brady said.

"Reminds me of home." CJ gulped in air, but somehow it didn't feel like enough.

Brady paused. "Are you okay?"

"Fine," she said, plastering a smile to her face. The trail wasn't that long. Damned if she'd quit before they even got going.

A little ways in, the trees parted, offering an unrestricted view of the wooden railroad trestle below that spanned the Mexican Canyon and, beyond it, all the way to the floor of the basin, where miles of white dunes shone beneath another sunny sky. Today there were enormous cumulus clouds moving slowly through the jet stream; from where they stood, they could see cloud-shaped shadows stealing across the earth's surface.

The railroad trestle, used to transport logs from the mountains down to Alamogordo, looked like a roller coaster, they agreed.

"Do you like roller coasters?" Brady asked.

"Sure. Do you?"

"I love them. There's one on the boardwalk at Santa Cruz. I'll have to take you there after the war."

She lifted the camera and took a few shots while CJ stared unseeing at the view. The thought of visiting Brady after the war struck her almost painfully. How could they possibly remain friends? For that to happen, she would somehow have to get over this awful crush. Which, she had to concede, was the perfect name for the feeling currently pressing in on her.

The trail wound on, some stretches featuring shaded forest hiking, others affording long views of the valleys and ridges nearby. CJ gulped water from her canteen and waited to feel better, but the headache, which had returned full force, and growing nausea refused to abate. Maybe she should tell Brady she wasn't feeling well.

A half hour of steady walking in, CJ shed her sweater and tied it around her waist.

"Are all those muscles from working on engines?" Brady asked.

"No." CJ cleared her throat. "They're from throwing hay and working with the horses."

Unlike some of their neighbors who had depended on a single crop, her family had diversified: maple syrup in late winter; asparagus in the spring; cherries, blueberries, sweet corn and wheat in the summer; and squash, potatoes and pumpkins throughout the fall. And, of course, celery throughout the summer and into the fall—Kalamazoo wasn't known as Celery City for nothing. As a result, even during the lean years of the Depression, the farm had produced plenty of food to support seven humans and an assortment of other creatures, including their horses.

"*You* threw hay?" Brady asked. "I didn't know women did that."

CJ kept her eyes on the trail where raised roots and loose rock kept trying to trip her. "My parents managed the farm like a cooperative. We all learned every aspect of the daily running of the property. We each had a specialty too, something we were better at or liked to do more than anyone else. For Joe, it was cultivating. Alec can plow and plant straighter than the rest of us. My mom's good at gardening, my little sister is an excellent cook and my dad and little brother are great carpenters."

"And you?"

"Engines." She ducked under bent branches that waved gently in the breeze. "Unfortunately, while helpful in securing my current MOS, being good with engines is hardly transferable to the real world."

"What is the real world, anyway?" Brady countered. "I grew up thinking life was one way, and then I went back east to Smith. Talk about a foreign culture. I'm not always sure which is real now."

"I think I know the feeling."

"Because of the Army?"

"Something like that."

As they continued on, CJ started to actively worry. Sylvia had said mountain sickness was nothing to sneeze at, and while she couldn't be sure it wasn't the previous night's realization making her want to empty her stomach at the edge of the trail, Cloudcroft's elevation seemed the more likely culprit. Maybe they should turn back. In fact, maybe they should head home early. She wasn't sure she could take a whole day alone with Brady without giving herself away. Besides, as soon as they were back at Bliss she was going to corner Toby. She had questions that needed answering.

Typical, she thought as the trail descended from a stand of pine and fir trees into a wide alpine meadow. She discovered something new about herself and what was her first instinct? To conduct research. *You can take the historian out of the library...*

Brady seized her arm, effectively squashing any thought of interrogations or libraries, and whispered, "Look."

A hundred feet away, an elk lifted its antlered head to stare back at them. At least CJ assumed it was an elk, given it was the size of a small moose but possessed deer-like antlers. The massive beast turned in an almost leisurely manner and walked away, two female elk following in his wake. Brady released her arm to snap photos, the camera's shutter clicking away as the elk vanished into the forest at the far end of the meadow. Then she turned back and grabbed CJ's hand.

"That was amazing," she said, eyes shining.

"Yeah." CJ smiled back lopsidedly, nausea interfering with her guilty enjoyment of Brady's nearness.

Brady looked at her more closely. "Are you sure you're okay? You don't look so good."

"Thanks a lot," she quipped, but then she ruined the moment by belching, the taste of coffee and fried egg bitter on her tongue.

Brady's grip tightened. "You feel sick, don't you? Could it be mountain sickness?"

"Um, it's possible."

"You shit!" Brady fumbled with the map. "I can't believe you didn't say anything sooner. What were you thinking?"

"I'm sorry," CJ offered, taken aback by her vehemence. She'd never heard Brady swear before. "I didn't realize."

"Of course you didn't. You're from Michigan." She chewed a fingertip, staring at the map. "It's too late to turn around. We're already halfway around the loop, and there's a more significant climb if we go back the way we came."

"It'll be okay. We'll go back to the car and head down to the valley, like Sylvia said."

Brady stared at her, brow furrowed. "This is serious, CJ. A friend of my father's died of a pulmonary embolism in Argentina, and he was only a little higher than we are here."

Higher, as in more drunk? As if from a distance, CJ heard herself giggle.

Brady's gaze narrowed. "Honestly? Do you always laugh at inappropriate moments?"

"I don't think so. Maybe it's the altitude."

"Uh huh. Let's go."

They started off down the trail again, taking it slower than before. Brady kept asking her could she breathe, was she dizzy, did she think she might vomit? If CJ hadn't been mortified by her body's weakness, she might have enjoyed having Brady fuss over her like a worried hen. As it was, she merely felt like a dolt. Again. Feelings of inadequacy seemed to come with the territory when Brady was around.

If it hadn't been for that last hill, the one they'd struggled up at the start of the hike, they probably would have made it back to the car unscathed. But as they started down, a wave of dizziness washed over CJ. This time when yet another root tried to trip her, she lost the contest. She felt herself falling, heard Brady's shout, tried in vain to catch herself as she bounced off more exposed rocks and roots. The fall seemed to last an inordinately long time. She had time to wonder if Brady would curse at her again, to notice that her hat was no longer on her head. Finally she managed to brace herself against one of the conveniently placed log steps. Although crashing into it with the full force of gravity behind her was less than optimal.

Almost immediately, Brady was leaning over her saying her name worriedly. Great. She must have looked like an idiot, pitching headlong down the hill.

"I'm okay," she said, sitting up and dusting herself off. Then she felt it—a sharper pain in her head and something warm sliding down the right side of her face. She reached up and pulled away fingers covered in blood.

"Your forehead," Brady said, eyes wide. "You must have hit it."

CJ didn't remember banging her head, but then again she hadn't been completely aware of what was happening to her body. The fall itself hadn't been all that frightening. It was the fact that she might have plunged all the way down the steep slope that made her want to throw up. Or maybe that was the mountain sickness again.

Brady held her shoulders. "Do you have a concussion? Did you break anything? Are you bleeding anywhere else?"

CJ checked herself over, flexing muscles and testing joints. "I don't think so." Even the cut on her head didn't hurt too badly. Later, she knew, once the adrenaline from the fall wore off, she would be in pain. But for now, everything seemed to be in working order.

"Thank God." Brady pulled her into a tight hug.

Despite their awkward position on the ground, their bodies fit perfectly together. *Of course they do,* CJ thought, briefly giving herself over to the press of Brady's softness against her. If she'd known all it would take to get Brady to hug her was to fall off a mountain…

Then she caught herself and pulled away. "I'm okay," she repeated, eyes fixed on the ground. "But we should probably get back to the car."

Brady leaned away from her. "You're right. Do you think you can walk down? Your head looks pretty bad."

CJ touched the cut. "I don't think it's very deep. But hey, at least you get a chance to use your first aid training from basic."

"Not funny." She stood up, holding out one hand, CJ's missing hat in the other. "Ready?"

"As I'll ever be."

But as soon as she was standing, Brady linked their arms.

"Let go." CJ tried to disengage. She was starting to feel like a letch, knowing that Brady's gestures were a product of mere friendliness. "I don't want to take you with me if I decide to go all paratrooper again."

Brady tightened her grip. "If you think I'm letting you fall, you're insane."

"But—"

"This is not open for discussion. Now march, soldier."

While they were both privates, Brady did technically have more stripes on her sleeve. Anyway, CJ felt too ill to argue. She picked her way down the steepest section of the trail, diligently trying to avoid treacherous roots hidden beneath dead leaves.

At last they reached the turnout. Her ribs ached, along with one wrist and the other ankle. She had probably earned herself a profanity-laced dressing-down from Griggs. The master sergeant did not appreciate it when his personnel took it upon themselves to get injured off-duty, thereby making him redo his duty roster.

"Friggin' unacceptable, Jamieson," she could already hear him thundering at her at roll call. Assuming she made it to roll call.

Brady pulled a first aid kit from the car's trunk.

"I didn't know you brought that," CJ said.

"I was a Girl Scout too, remember?"

CJ started to laugh but stopped as the motion vexed several of her aches.

"Sit on the passenger seat," Brady ordered grimly, pushing back her hat. "Let's get you cleaned up, and then we can figure out whether or not you need a hospital."

CJ did as Brady directed, trying not to gasp as the iodine stung her scalp. Brady was efficient but gentle, her brow lowered over her pale blue eyes in what seemed to be a semi-permanent expression.

"Think I'll get a Purple Heart?" CJ tried, but Brady's features didn't alter.

She was so close, the arc of her collar bone beneath the open PT dress directly in CJ's line of sight. It would be so easy to lean forward and press her lips against the smooth flesh at the hollow of Brady's throat. So easy, and so disastrous. Clenching her fists, she remembered Brady lying on her side in bed the night before and the nearly uncontrollable urge she'd experienced to touch her then too.

Crushes were abominable. Why hadn't anyone warned her?

"I'm sorry," she said as Brady replaced the cap on the small iodine bottle.

At last, Brady's gaze softened. "You don't have to apologize."

"No, I do. It wasn't fair of me to put you in this position." *In more ways than one.*

"I'm not worried about what's fair, CJ. I'm worried about you." She touched CJ's cheek, smoothing the skin she had rubbed clean.

Looking up at Brady, CJ had a renewed sense of dizziness. This time, though, it had little to do with elevation.

"I'm worried about me too," she joked, pulling away. If she hadn't, she would have arched into Brady's touch like an affection-starved barn cat. And that would be harder to explain away than a little dizziness.

While Brady busied herself putting the first aid kit away, CJ checked her reflection in the rearview mirror. Not as bad as she'd expected—no stitches necessary, if she was lucky—but not good either. In the mirror, she saw Brady close the trunk and then lean against the car for a moment, both hands over her face. Then she abruptly straightened and walked around to the driver's side.

"Are you sure you don't need a hospital?" she asked as she slid into the car. "There's probably one in Alamogordo."

"If we go to a hospital, we might get back late, and I for one would rather not be stuck with double latrine duty for the next month."

"Fine." Brady turned the key in the ignition. "But I'm taking you to Beaumont as soon as we get back."

"Yes, ma'am."

CJ leaned her head back and closed her eyes. A visit to the post hospital actually didn't sound so bad. She'd been thrown from more than one horse in her life; she knew that the pain was likely to worsen exponentially in the hours and days after a big fall.

Brady checked her mirrors and pulled onto the main road. Quickly she accelerated, taking the first curve faster than CJ liked. She reached out to touch Brady's arm, feeling the muscles tense beneath her fingers.

"Relax," she said. "It won't help if we end up at the bottom of a canyon."

Brady eased her foot off the accelerator. But she drove onward with her eyes fixed forward and her arms rigid, hands tight on the wheel at ten and two.

CJ rested her head on her balled-up sweater and tried to sleep, but halfway down the mountain road, Brady decided she might have a concussion. Convinced that the autumn air would keep her awake, she insisted they roll down their windows. CJ didn't argue. She figured she owed Brady that much.

The drive down to Alamogordo seemed to take half the time of the previous evening's drive up. Once they were down from the mountains and headed back to El Paso along Highway 54, a straight, flat shot between the two cities, Brady found a station playing big band music and turned up the volume, singing along off-key.

After ten minutes of this torture, CJ reached out and snapped off the radio. "Enough," she declared. "Your singing is giving me a worse headache than the fall did."

Brady glanced at her. "Do you still have a headache? What about your stomach?"

"My head hurts, but I don't have a headache. And my stomach feels fine. In fact, I'm hungry."

"What about your breathing?"

"Normal. See? I told you everything would be all right."

Beside her, Brady took a long, shuddering breath. And then, to CJ's consternation, she started to cry, tears sliding silently down her face.

"Wait." CJ scooted closer on the bench seat. "Hey, none of that. Everything's fine, I promise." Tentatively, she slipped her arm around Brady, telling herself it was okay this once.

Immediately Brady slowed the car and pulled over on the empty shoulder. As soon as they stopped, she turned and hid her face in CJ's neck. CJ held her close, aware of the muscles in Brady's back, the press of her breasts, the slight scent of wood smoke in her hair. They'd had that bathtub all to themselves and somehow they hadn't made use of it. Instantly the image of Brady naked, steam rising around her, assailed her, and she shut her eyes, trying to will it away.

"Shh," she said, rubbing Brady's back. "Shh, it's okay. I've got you."

Suddenly Brady pulled back and pummeled her shoulder. "You jerk. You scared me!"

"I know," CJ said, trying not to wince at this new pain. "I'm sorry, really."

"It's not your fault. I should have known something was wrong." Brady closed her eyes and wiped the tears away. Then she leaned her forehead against the same shoulder she'd struck and whispered, "I'm so glad you're okay."

CJ rested her cheek against Brady's hair. She remembered the moment in bed the night before when they had lain together, bodies touching from head to toe. She'd wanted to kiss Brady, yes. But even more she'd wanted to hold onto the sensation of having Brady so close. Now here was that feeling again—the sense that she could stay here like this forever, happily. This was the meaning of life, the reason human beings existed: to love and be loved.

Love? *Aw, crap. Crap and double crap.*

"I'm sorry," she repeated miserably. She was. Sorry for falling in love with her, sorry for lying to her, sorry for ruining the best friendship of her life. And yet, her feelings for Brady had walked the line between friendship and adoration right from the start. She just hadn't read the signs correctly.

"So am I," Brady murmured. And then she pushed CJ away, dried her eyes again and pointed the car toward El Paso.

CHAPTER NINE

"Are you sure you don't want to go to Tony's?" CJ asked as they neared the post.

Before the accident, they had planned to spend the afternoon near Alamogordo exploring an archeological site that was home to thousands of petroglyphs, and then drive back to El Paso in time for supper at Brady's favorite restaurant, Tony's Place, fifteen minutes south of Bliss. There they had intended to linger over margaritas and Southwest cuisine until their pass expired.

Instead, they'd eaten day-old sandwiches, apples swiped from the lodge and the last of their mess hall cookies as they followed the highway back to El Paso, stopping once to fill up the car's tank and their canteens.

Brady glanced away from the highway to consider her. "I think you should probably have that cut looked at. The last thing you need is an infection."

On one hand, CJ wasn't ready to relinquish the rare intimacy they'd enjoyed all weekend. But on the other, she couldn't wait to be away from Brady, whose gravitational pull she was finding almost impossible to resist.

They pulled into the post's main gate a few minutes before four. When the MP on duty caught a glimpse of CJ's bloody gash, he telephoned ahead to the post hospital and gave them directions to the correct building. The directions were necessary—William Beaumont General Hospital had recently expanded to more than a hundred buildings in order to provide specialized medical care to wounded soldiers returning from all theaters of the war.

Brady dropped her off at the designated building and went to park the car. Inside, a civilian employee took CJ's information and called in an Army nurse, who led CJ to an examining room. There she proceeded to ask a variety of questions, poke her sore spots and shine a light into her eyes. Eventually a harried doctor came in and concurred with the nurse's diagnosis—nothing broken, no stitches needed and no concussion. The nurse cleaned and secured the head wound with butterfly closures, dressed the worst of the scrapes on her arms and legs and sent her on her way with a packet of aspirin and a note excusing her from duty for the next twenty-four hours. Griggs would have to wait a day to chew her out.

She found Brady seated on a utilitarian sofa in the lobby, frowning down at an old issue of *Yank*. She'd never seen Brady as agitated as she'd been today. Had the day's events stirred up old feelings about the family friend who had died from elevation sickness? Or could she possibly...CJ stopped the thought. No use wishing Brady felt the same way. Number one, she didn't. And number two, even if by some miracle she did, it wasn't like anything could come of such feelings. The government owned them, and according to Uncle Sam, acting on romantic feelings for a member of your battalion was strictly *verboten*.

Brady jumped up when she saw CJ. "What'd they say? Is everything okay?"

"Other than a brain injury and some internal bleeding, I should be fine."

Brady started to smack her shoulder and then folded her arms across her chest instead. "Are you okay or not?"

"Sorry," CJ said for the tenth time that day, suddenly picturing Brady leaning against the car, hands over her face. Brady was right— she *was* a shit. "Nothing's broken, I don't have a concussion, and no stitches required. I just have to take aspirin for the next few days. Oh, and I get out of duty tomorrow." She reached for the door, then winced as her back constricted. Yep, there was the pain she'd been expecting.

"I'll get it," Brady said. "You're not very good at letting other people take care of you, are you?"

"Probably not," CJ admitted.

Except her mother. What she wouldn't give right now for a bowl of homemade turkey soup. But how could she ever face her mother again? She'd never been good at stretching the truth in her own favor. What would her mother and father think if she told them she'd fallen for a girl?

They stopped at Brady's barracks first. CJ waited in the car with the excuse that she could move the illegally parked vehicle if any officers or MPs were feeling officious. In reality, she wanted to avoid Janice, who, it seemed, had been right about her all along.

A short time later, Brady returned to the car looking cool and refreshed in a clean summer uniform, her hair pulled back in a colorful onyx barrette.

"Ready?" she asked, turning the key.

"You don't have to drive me, you know," CJ tried again. "I can walk."

"I'm driving you," Brady said, an edge to her voice that hadn't been there before. Then she smiled, an insincere offering CJ had seen her toss at countless GIs and other Wacs. "What kind of friend would I be if I abandoned you now?"

They drove the two hundred feet to CJ's barracks in silence. Brady insisted on carrying her bag inside for her, then waited in the car while CJ got cleaned up and changed. By the time they parked the LaSalle behind the officers' quarters and walked the short distance to the mess hall, the sun had set and evening mess was almost over.

CJ glanced around the interior of the converted barn, but her friends were nowhere to be seen. Either they had eaten already or they were eking out their weekend pass, as she and Brady had intended to do.

Supper was chipped beef with potatoes and green beans. Not quite the meal they had planned, but CJ hadn't eaten much that day. They ate quickly, chatting about the work week ahead. Brady was writing a story on the WASP company due to arrive at Biggs later in the week. Apparently, they were coming to Fort Bliss by way of Camp Davis in North Carolina to join the Sixth Tow Target squadron.

"That is one job I wouldn't want to have," CJ said. "You should see some of the cadets. They seem younger than my little brother even, and they're itching to shoot down anything that moves."

"You couldn't pay me enough," Brady agreed. "But it probably beats getting shot at by the actual enemy. I heard last week that bomber crews in the Eighth have a life expectancy of six to eight weeks."

CJ looked down at her plate. Her brother Alec might not be in the Eighth flying raids out of England, but he would soon be facing German fighters over Axis targets, assuming Brady's intelligence was accurate. What would his odds of survival be once the Fifteenth started their long-range bombing campaigns?

"I'm sorry," Brady said quickly. "I wasn't thinking."

"It's fine."

But it wasn't fine. Twenty-four hours earlier they had held hands and run down a gypsum dune, and now they were struggling to make small talk about the war. She longed to take Brady's hand again, to assure her that everything would be all right. But they were in the WAC mess hall, and besides, she wasn't certain everything between them would be okay.

Brady turned in their dishes and they headed back to the barracks, the now familiar line of the Franklin Mountains hulking black against the purplish horizon. They didn't talk as they walked, but occasionally in the twilight Brady's arm brushed against hers. CJ had to resist the urge to take her hand again. Was this what life was like for Toby and Kate? Were they constantly editing their behavior, second-guessing the way they interacted in public? Not that this was the same thing, of course.

They reached Brady's barracks first.

"Do you want me to walk you home?" she asked.

"That's okay. But thanks."

"If you're sure." Brady hesitated and glanced over her shoulder at the barracks door.

Not that again. "I'll see you tomorrow," CJ said, starting to turn away.

"Okay," Brady said, the single word somehow managing to sound forlorn.

CJ stopped. "Are you going to be all right? This weekend wasn't exactly easy on you."

Brady wrapped her arms around her middle, hugging herself in the descending chill of the desert night. "I'll be fine. I actually had a good time. Mostly."

"So did I."

"Right. You probably wish you'd gone to see the Andrews Sisters and saved yourself the headache of a weekend with me. Literally."

"But I don't." CJ stepped closer. How could she even think that?

"You don't?" Brady seemed oddly hopeful.

"Of course not. I'm glad we spent the weekend together. Honestly, I'm disappointed it had to end early."

"So am I." Brady looked over her shoulder once more and then, so quickly CJ didn't see it coming, leaned forward and brushed her lips against her cheek, perilously close to the corner of her mouth. "I'll miss you tonight."

As she turned and disappeared inside the barracks, CJ stared after her, dumbfounded. Had Brady kissed her? Heart thumping, she touched her mouth. If she had known the kiss was coming, would she have turned her head and kissed Brady back, right there in the WAC compound for anyone and everyone to see? Probably. And that was the part that frightened her most.

Mind churning, she limped back to her own barracks, no longer hiding the effects of the fall. She hadn't wanted Brady to know how much pain she was in—the very impulse that had gotten her into trouble earlier that day.

Jesus God, she thought, rubbing her temples. What now?

* * *

She was writing postcards in the day room when Toby and Reggie came in later that night, whistling at her bandages.

"We heard you were back here looking like you made a tour of the front lines," Toby said. "What does the other guy look like?"

"Was it a bear?" Reggie asked. "Or did Brady get mad and slug you?"

"Yeah, what did you do to set off the blonde bombshell?" Toby added, seemingly innocently. But then she and Reggie exchanged one of their looks, and all at once, CJ understood. They knew she had feelings for Brady. They'd known before she did.

She glanced around, but the other Wacs in the day room were busy talking and playing cards. "Actually," she said, lowering her voice, "I tried to kiss her and she walloped me."

They gaped at her, eyes wide.

Served them right, CJ thought uncharitably. Were they even her friends, or did they simply enjoy watching the unfolding train wreck of her crush on Brady?

"Now if you'll excuse me," she added pointedly, "I have some postcards to write."

Toby nudged Reggie. "It wasn't Brady. She's yanking our chains."

"Oh." Reggie laughed uncertainly.

"Come on, pal," Toby added to CJ. "Let's me and you take a walk."

"Why would I want to go for a walk with you?"

"Because you need someone to talk to, and I hope it can be me. Even if I have been something of an ass."

"*Something* of an ass?" she echoed.

"Easy, killer." Toby offered her a hand.

After a moment, CJ let herself be pulled up. "This doesn't mean I forgive you."

"I can live with that."

Outside, the compound was brightly lit, MPs on duty both outside and inside the gate. CJ had heard that they were so carefully guarded because sometime the previous spring a civilian had sneaked into one of the women's barracks late at night and attacked the sergeant in charge of quarters. Fortunately, her shouts had brought a dozen enlisted women to the orderly room, and they'd made short work of the would-be attacker.

"How long have you known about Kate and me?" Toby asked.

"A while. I went to university. It's not a new concept."

"So the idea isn't new, but the practice is?"

CJ shrugged.

"What did happen?"

"Do you swear to keep this to yourself? Well, you and Kate, since I assume you're going to tell her."

Toby nodded. "We do have some experience with secrets, you know."

So as they walked in a wide circle around the compound, going slowly in deference to CJ's sore ankle, she told Toby everything, ending with the kiss outside Brady's barracks.

"She said she would miss you?" Toby repeated.

CJ nodded, both miserable and semi-euphoric at the memory.

"Huh." Toby took a drag on her cigarette. "Interesting."

"What should I do?"

"I can't tell you what to do, CJ. Only you can decide what's right for you."

That sounded suspiciously like what she had told Brady the previous night.

"But," Toby added, "let me ask you this: If there were no rules against it, if your family and your church and your hometown didn't care one way or another, what would you do?"

That was easy. She didn't even have to think about it.

"It doesn't matter," she said. "They do care. Besides, I don't even know how Brady feels at this point."

"Don't you?" Toby gave her a dubious look. "She did kiss you."

"Not a real kiss. Anyway, she's engaged. And even if she wasn't, my family would never understand. I don't think I could hurt them like that."

"In my experience, ignoring how you feel doesn't make it go away. Besides, given the chance, your family might surprise you. Not everyone has a problem with gay people."

Gay people. That was certainly better than the denigrating "fruit" and "queer" she'd heard tossed around the hangar and the flight line. Much cheerier, as if falling for a member of your own sex were a happy accident rather than a potentially lonely, alienating experience that may or may not result in criminal charges.

"How long have you known you were, well, that way?" she asked, studying Toby.

While not traditionally beautiful, Toby was certainly attractive. She looked younger than she was, with smooth skin and rosy cheeks, deep blue eyes and dark brown hair cut shorter than the average WAC hairstyle. She didn't look like a girl trying to be a man, as the stereotype dictated. She looked more like a freshly scrubbed teenage boy the high school girls would all swoon over.

"I knew when I was a kid that I wasn't like other girls. So did my parents. We never talked about it, but my mother didn't pressure me to get married like she did my sisters. I used to take the train into New York all the time, and I managed to find places there for people like me. Eventually I moved to Manhattan. The Army has more than its share of gay people too, some who knew before they joined up and others who found out once they were in."

"Is that why you joined up?"

"Nah, I wanted to be part of something important. I was making better money working the assembly line in Newark, honestly, but I couldn't shake the feeling I should be doing more."

"So you're okay with it then? Being different?"

"It used to scare the crap out of me," Toby said. "But then I realized there were people like me everywhere, all in this sort of secret club, and it started to seem almost exciting."

"And now?"

"Sometimes I wish it was easier. I wish people didn't think of Kate and me as perverts or sick. It's this one small part of who we are, something we couldn't change even if we wanted to. Speaking of which, have you noticed the way Janice Evans looks at you? I'd watch out for her. Rumor has it someone in her platoon reported a couple of Wacs for being gay."

"What happened?"

"The higher-ups transferred them both to different posts."

"I thought it was an automatic blue ticket."

"With enlistment numbers lower than expected, it turns out they need us more than we need them. At least for now." Toby ground out her cigarette and pocketed the stub. "We better get back. You look beat."

"I feel beat. But thanks. For talking, I mean."

"Anytime." Toby clapped her on the shoulder. "Whatever you decide, I'll still be your pal."

CJ doubted the same could be said for Brady.

"Can I say one more thing?" Toby added.

"Of course."

"If you ever decide to explore the gay life, make sure you bring me along. I'll probably have to use a baseball bat to keep the girls off you."

"What?" CJ laughed out loud. Then she realized Toby was serious. "What are you talking about?"

"You're a cute girl. You just hadn't found your people yet."

She followed Toby back toward the barracks, their conversation coiling through her mind. Toby thought she was cute in the gay sense, which should probably horrify her but instead was actually quite flattering. Was this who she was supposed to be? Were Toby and Kate "her people," as Toby claimed? And if they were, could Brady be one of them too? Toby seemed to think it was possible. But what about Nate? Thinking about breaking off an engagement and doing it were two very different things, and everyone knew that getting involved as the other woman was a terrible idea. Cheating wasn't her style, and Brady had said herself that she couldn't do that to Nate.

Besides, now that she was away from Brady, she was starting to wonder if she might not have imagined everything. Maybe it had been the romantic inn and the adventure of being off-post together. Maybe if she waited it out, this miserable crush would pass, despite what Toby had said.

Worth a try, wasn't it?

* * *

In the morning, while her squad mates rushed about getting ready for drill and PT, CJ lay on her GI cot pondering her conversation with Toby. She had said there were gay people everywhere, including in the Army. Was Reggie? Probably. CJ had never seen her with a GI, and it wasn't like dating opportunities didn't abound on the post. Sarah clearly wasn't a member of the club, given her involvement with Jack. Who else? CJ watched the Wacs around her—Nancy, whose Marine husband was in the Pacific; Ruth, who was dating an Air Cadet even though the rules expressly forbade it; Rose, who was always asking Ruth about the Air Cadet's buddies; and Mary, who had short hair like Toby and had never mentioned a boyfriend, husband or fiancé. She had possibility.

Then again, possibility for what? Kate and Toby were proof that a banned relationship could be successfully hidden from military authorities, who were apparently less interested in policing such dalliances than they purported to be. For that matter, Ruth and her cadet boyfriend offered additional evidence that what the military didn't know couldn't hurt the individual soldier. But even if Brady did have feelings for her, there was still the slight matter of her fiancé to think of, not to mention how their families would react. It wasn't like they could ride off into the sunset.

No, she told herself again, better to avoid Brady and see if this thing between them, whatever it was, might dissipate on its own.

After the barracks emptied, she ate a banana Reggie had swiped for her, took more aspirin and went back to bed, rising eventually a little after eleven to officially start her day. At lunch she sat with the usual gang of D-lites, who demanded the story behind her cuts and bruises before they would tell her about the concert. CJ kept her tale short and light, ignoring Toby's occasional questioning look. Nothing had happened, she reminded herself, and she intended to keep it that way.

Brady came in late and sat with her usual group of friends. CJ felt her looking over a couple of times but pretended not to notice. She was determined to purge Brady from her system. She was absolutely not going to daydream about kissing Brady for real, or wonder what her lips would feel like, or remember the heat of Brady's body pressed against hers in the cold New Mexican night...

Reggie threw a french fry at her, and she returned to the lukewarm reality of tepid cheeseburgers, which they were lucky to have, given the national beef shortage.

A little while later she left the mess hall with her friends, turning resolutely toward the barracks as they started back to central base. She didn't wonder what Brady was thinking or feeling, really. She wished she were going back to work herself. Staying busy would have been better than having all this blasted time to think. Good thing there were always letters to catch up on. She hadn't written Joe in a week, which wasn't like her. He was less committed to their correspondence, but his mail was sometimes delayed for weeks, traveling through the censors and back to the States.

She hadn't gone far when her neck began to tingle. Then she heard her name. Slowing, she looked back, already knowing who it would be. As Brady approached, blue eyes glowing with the same pleasure CJ could feel sparking inside, the tingle spread. *Crap and double crap.*

"How's your head?" Brady asked, stopping before her.

"Fine. Better than it looks," she added, touching the bandage.

"I don't know. You look pretty good to me." And she smiled into CJ's eyes.

CJ felt her pulse jump, the tingle becoming more pronounced. *Stop it*, she told herself sternly. *Stick to the plan. You do not want to melt into her arms. You do not want to kiss Brady Buchanan in broad daylight in front of half her company.*

As the silence lengthened, Brady fidgeted, bouncing from one foot to the other. "Is there something we should, I don't know, talk about?"

"No," CJ said quickly. Too quickly—Brady seemed almost to flinch, the glow fading from her smile.

"Oh. Okay." She squinted toward central base before glancing back at CJ. "You planning to get some rest this afternoon?"

"Yep. Doctor's orders."

She longed to reach out somehow, to reassure Brady. *Remember Nate*, she told herself, focusing on Brady's engagement ring.

"And you wouldn't dream of not following orders." Brady took a step back. "I have to get back. See you later."

CJ forced a smile. "See you."

Brady rejoined her Admin friends and set out toward central base. CJ longed to stare after her until she was a speck retreating into the dusty distance, but instead she turned and marched back to the barracks. It was better this way. With a little distance, they would both realize that they could only ever be friends. It wasn't like there was any other choice.

Was there?

CHAPTER TEN

Over the next week, she worked diligently to avoid Brady, knowing that her willpower would crumble like the Maginot Line if they spent any time together. She tried to be subtle about her evasion, using her initial soreness as an excuse not to play basketball or softball, inventing duties to stick closer to the barracks than usual. In truth, the duty schedule had been revised, and she'd been assigned to KP for Thanksgiving—a serious piece of misfortune, the D-lites agreed.

The week dragged dully, the few points of color coming when she glimpsed Brady at PT, drill or mess. Fortunately, the nature of her work at Biggs kept her from dwelling too narrowly on her personal life. Flight lines and hangars were dangerous places; you could easily lose a finger if you weren't careful. Or worse.

On Wednesday a dust storm, not uncommon in West Texas, kept the hangar doors closed, engineering crews inside and airplanes on the flight line chained and covered for most of the morning and into the afternoon. CJ's crew played cards, messed about with heavy tools they weren't rated on and read tech orders for ships they would probably never get their grubby little hands on, as a particularly cantankerous Griggs reminded them. The storm finally cleared mid-afternoon, but there wasn't much they could do other than a basic check on aircraft with missing covers to make sure dust hadn't worked its way into sensitive engine parts. The evening crew, already the busiest of the three shifts, would have even more to do now, thanks to Mother Nature.

CJ and her squad mates were about to go off duty when the airfield's alert system screeched into action. In mid-November, the sun set by six each night, which meant it was already nearly dark outside when their shift ended. As multiple alarms began to howl across the airfield, CJ heard another sound: a massive explosion, like a thousand-pound bomb hitting the earth somewhere nearby. The ground shook, the brief metallic rattle of tools and hard stands joining in the broader alarm. Everyone in the hangar froze, exchanging worried glances. Then they rushed outside, looking for the source of the blast.

Residents of nearby hangars joined them as fire trucks and other emergency vehicles sped westward, and soon CJ saw it: midway up one of the mountains that bordered Fort Bliss raged a fire, its smoke plume barely visible against the twilit sky.

"B-17?" she heard Jill ask Griggs.

He nodded grimly. "Or a B-29."

Both heavy bombers were known for problematic takeoffs. If dust had worked its way into any one of the plane's engines, a successful takeoff over the Franklins would be next to impossible.

"What were they doing flying so soon after the storm?" Toby muttered to Reggie.

"And why would they head west?" Reggie shook her head, her face pale.

For a while, the crew still on duty watched the slow progression of emergency lights up the side of the mountain. Then Griggs ordered them all back to base. There was nothing they could do at the airfield. Nothing anyone could do.

They barely made supper. By the time they went through the mess line, most of the tables were empty. Brady and her Admin friends were nowhere to be seen, CJ noticed, simultaneously relieved and disappointed. It was better that way, she told herself as she sat down to eat with her friends.

No one was very hungry. They didn't talk about it, but clearly they were all thinking about the crew on board the fallen bomber. A B-17 crew was ten people, a B-29 eleven. A bomber being ferried cross-country might have a skeleton crew, but the plane that crashed wasn't one of theirs. That left Tow Target or one of the training outfits. Wasn't the new WASP squad due to arrive any day? Pushing dry meat she couldn't quite identify around her plate, CJ crossed her fingers that a woman pilot hadn't been at the controls. Like WAC mechanics, WASP pilots had to perform perfectly. Otherwise the reputation of all of womankind would suffer.

Later that night, she lay in bed unable to sleep. She kept seeing the fire at the crash site, a beacon through the dusty twilight, flames that had almost certainly consumed the flesh and bones of boys no older than her brothers. Exactly like her brothers, in fact, and Brady's brothers and Reggie's brothers and so many other mothers' and fathers' sons. It could have been Alec. Could at this moment be him somewhere in Europe burning to death in a plane crash after a flak strike or an attack by German fighters, enemy pilots desperate to protect their own families far below.

If they all wanted to protect the ones they loved, and no one really wanted to kill any other mother's son, how had they gotten to the place they were now, where an American B-17 crew in the Eighth had a life expectancy measured in weeks? Boys barely old enough to shave, some of them, and they were dying in droves over foreign soil, many of them crying out for their mothers as their lives ebbed away. She didn't think she would ever understand.

All at once, she wanted to go to Brady, to embrace her and feel the warmth of her skin, the steadiness of her pulse pounding at the base of her throat. She wanted to touch warm, living flesh, to love and be loved, to feel as she had that night in Cloudcroft when Brady had held her: safe and thoroughly at peace. It seemed the only thing to do in the face of such fear and grief—to reach out and grab hold of the one who felt like home, the one you knew must love you because every time you were together you could feel an invisible wire tightening between you, drawing you ever closer.

But even as she longed to go to Brady, there were so many reasons why she couldn't: Nate, their families, the Army, their government. So many reasons she had to stay in this lumpy bed, surrounded by the placid snores and faint breathing of her squad mates as tears slipped silently across her cheeks and dripped onto the soft cotton pillowcase her mother had sent from home.

* * *

In the wake of the B-29 crash, which they found out the following day had taken the lives of eleven men from the XX Bomber Command, the Transient Hangar was busy as ever with planes coming in from across the country. Some arrived dropping parts and coughing oil, and those were the ones that CJ treated with the utmost care. It was their crew's job to diagnose problems and fix them quickly so that the grounded bird could be back in the air as soon as possible. However, rushing and engine repair did not go together. The ground crew held the flight crew's lives literally in their hands, a fact of which Griggs was always quick to remind them.

Engineering crews, especially those working late at night, were not immune from casualties either. Sarah and Jill had told her about an incident on the flight line late one night the previous spring. An engineering crew in training had been performing a hundred-hour inspection on a P-39, including cleaning the cannon. The armorers had just reinstalled the gun with ammunition in the ammo can when they somehow accidentally fired off a round, narrowly missing a propeller technician. The practice round contained a tracer compound that made for a spectacular sight arcing over the flight line toward the distant mountains.

CJ lived with what she considered to be a healthy fear of making such a mistake. When Griggs called her and the other Wacs together at the end of the week, she assumed they were in for another lecture from the higher-ups on safety precautions, something the others had told her often followed an airfield crash. Instead, he removed his sergeant's cap and informed them in a serious tone that they were being transferred away from the Transient Hangar.

CJ sensed her own dismay reflected in her crew mates. Had this latest accident convinced the Biggs CO that the airfield was no place for women?

Griggs said gruffly, "Don't worry, you don't have to give up your wings. You've been requested is all. I would have blocked it if I didn't think you'd get all Amazon on me because it turns out y'all gripe the least out of any flock of penguins I've commanded."

"Where are we going?" Toby asked, eyes bright with anticipation.

"The Balloon Hangar."

"No kidding, Sarge?" Jill asked.

"Would I shit—I mean, would I kid you, Matthews?"

The Wacs began to talk among themselves. They'd heard the day before that the newly arrived WASPs had joined their sister pilots in the Balloon Hangar, home to the Sixth Tow Target Squadron. The Sixth's pilots flew Beechcraft trainers and obsolete Navy fighters on simulated bombing, gas and strafing missions. They also towed targets for the antiaircraft boys at Bliss to practice firing on.

Working the engineering crew in Tow Target was a peach of an assignment. They would no longer be relegated to the drafty Transient Hangar looking after ferry and transport planes merely stopping over on the way to someplace else. Instead they would be working on a real flight line, like the rest of the post's airfield mechanics. True, the Balloon Hangar didn't possess much of a flight line. Worse, it was the farthest out of all the Biggs hangars, situated right at the edge of the desert. But they could worry about transportation to and from the WAC compound later.

"Quit yer jabbering," Griggs finally said, but his tone was mild. "They're still bringing the girls in and getting the flights organized, which means I've got you through Thanksgiving. Now get back to work, and make it snappy."

For the rest of the day, CJ pondered the promise of the new assignment. Working with male crews was all right, but as female mechanics, she and her fellow Wacs were constantly asked to prove themselves. Did they know how to handle tools, were they capable of performing their duties during their time of the month, could they withstand the physical nature of airplane repair without complaint? Wacs were judged on separate standards from male crew members, even the civilian ones on loan from the airplane manufacturers. WASPs undoubtedly were familiar with the notion of double standards too. As pilots, even as auxiliaries, they were higher in the Army Air Corps pecking order than members of the ground crew. That meant the resistance they faced from male counterparts was probably that much more intense.

But even such a major airfield development couldn't entirely divert her from her turmoil over Brady, who had stopped trying to catch her eye by now. Fortunately, her other friends were skilled at distraction. On Saturday evening, Reggie invited her to play pool in the enlisted men's club. They had both grown up with the game, CJ on the table her father had built during one especially long winter, Reggie in the pool halls of her northern New Jersey home town. CJ had a decent time nursing a beer and making short work of the unsuspecting GIs who didn't think they could be beaten by a couple of Wacs. Still, it wasn't nearly as much fun as playing pool at the EW club with Brady or watching a movie with her, seated close together in the darkened post theater.

As they walked back from the club, pockets bulging with dollar bills they had scored off gullible GIs, the moon rose over the mountains in the distance. CJ looked for Orion, her favorite constellation, locating him above the horizon. Wasn't there a story about Orion the Hunter falling in love with one of the Pleiades, the Seven Sisters? Fantastic. Even the stars reminded her of Brady.

Who was she kidding? Their week apart hadn't helped her get over Brady at all. If anything, it had made her miss Brady more.

"What's going on with you and Brady, anyway?" Reggie asked. "It seemed like you were always together before last weekend."

"You know how it is when you make a new friend. At first you spend every waking moment together, but then time passes and you don't see each other as much."

"That sounds more like love than friendship."

CJ sighed. "It does, doesn't it?"

Reggie slung her arm around CJ's shoulders. "Don't look so worried. There are other fish in the sea."

"But I'm not interested in other fish."

She couldn't seem to stop herself from looking for Brady everywhere—at mess, on the training field, even tonight at the service club—hoping she might run into her even as she worried about what would happen if she did.

"Someday you will be," Reggie said. "Trust me."

"Sounds like experience talking."

"Indeed. 'Twas a fair lass back in Jersey that made me become a Wac. 'Let's join together, Reg,' she said. And so we did, and that was the last I saw of her. She went to Daytona, I went to Des Moines, and a month after basic I received a Dear Jane letter care of the United States Women's Army Auxiliary Corps."

"How long ago was that?"

"Four months."

"But you're single. What about all the other fish?"

"I was talking about her, not me. I'm still trying to mend my poor, broken heart."

And she wiggled her eyebrows at CJ, who laughed in spite of herself.

That night she lay in bed, sleep eluding her once again. The sounds of the barracks rose and fell around her, whispers between bunks, laughter, shushing, the inevitable snores. When she was home, she shared a bedroom with her little sister, but it was different to sleep among all these women. What would her squad mates think if they knew how she felt about Brady? Would they avoid her? Laugh at her? Turn her in? Then again, Toby and Kate weren't overly cautious, and the women in their company appeared to like Toby, whose mischievous smile could get her out of any scrape, it seemed.

It was funny. There were all sorts of laws against how she felt about Brady, laws CJ had always believed were as bigoted and unfair as the ones in the South that dictated where black people could sit on buses and in restaurants. Apparently it was easier to be objective about bigotry when it was directed against a group you didn't belong to.

But did she really belong to the same group as Kate and Toby? What about Sean? She had cared about him and mostly enjoyed what they did in bed, though they had never "consummated" their relationship, as he'd insisted on referring to sex. She'd known plenty of girls at Michigan who hadn't gone all the way yet. More who had, but without any reliable protection other than condoms, which were both user-dependent *and* difficult to find, abstinence had always seemed like the best option.

The fact that she hadn't ever been swept away by passion for Sean seemed to be a tipoff now. She'd never fallen madly in love with any of the boys in her classes at Kalamazoo Central, either. Looking back through this altered lens, she suddenly saw something she'd missed—her fixation on Laura Miller, a girl from nearby Plainwell who she'd played summer basketball with in ninth grade. Laura was a point guard, small and blonde and pretty, and CJ remembered now how she had agonized over whether to ask her out to the farm after summer league ended. Her mother had encouraged her to extend the invitation, but in the end she'd been too scared to branch out beyond the kids at school, most of whom she'd known since kindergarten.

At least, that was what she told herself. Now she realized she'd been frightened not of making a new friend but of her colossal crush on Laura, the cutest girl she was sure she'd ever seen. In fact, if she were honest with herself, Laura and Brady weren't the only girls she'd known who had made her feel all warm and fluttery inside. Brady was simply the first such girl she'd let herself get this close to.

In bed in the darkened barracks, window shades pulled against the outdoor lamps, CJ stopped herself. This line of thinking wasn't helping. If anything, it felt suspiciously like revising history, which in the academic world was rarely a good idea. But in this case, it might be more like discovering an important, previously hidden viewpoint than purposely altering known facts.

Briefly she allowed herself to dream of a not-so-distant point when she and Brady were an actual couple, living together and socializing with other women like them—Toby and Kate, perhaps, or one of the older couples she'd known at Michigan. But that version of the future was even more difficult to picture than the post-war world where she and Brady somehow managed to remain friends.

* * *

At mess the next morning, she was at the coffee urn when she sensed Brady's presence. She glanced over her shoulder, and sure enough, Brady was walking directly toward her. Their nearly telepathic connection was not helping matters in the least.

"Hey," Brady said.

"Um, hi."

Brady poured a cup of coffee, her gaze trained on the sideboard. "I feel like I never see you anymore."

CJ couldn't say the same. Brady had returned to her dreams the previous night in a repeat performance involving the four-poster bed from their room in Cloudcroft. She felt her cheeks color. "Sorry, work's been busy."

Brady turned to stare at her. "That's your excuse for avoiding me? Because *work* has been busy?"

"I'm not avoiding you."

"That's bullshit, and you know it."

Where CJ came from, women didn't curse. What was more, the Army frowned on swearing among Wacs. But Brady was right. It *was* bullshit. She missed her. Missed smoking on the steps, debating social theories over coffee, playing one-on-one basketball under the lights in the early evening hours after mess. These last days, she had been lonely even in the company of friends.

"It's not you," she said. "I, well, I felt like an idiot after the trip."

Brady frowned. "Why?"

"Because I didn't tell you I was sick," she lied, "and then I tried to catapult myself off the trail."

"That's why you've been avoiding me?"

CJ shrugged, not meeting her eyes. "Well, yeah."

"Oh. I thought it might be—I mean, I thought..." Brady ran her hand over her hair, touching the same onyx barrette she'd worn Sunday evening when she'd kissed CJ's cheek, her lips soft and lingering. "You know what? It doesn't matter. Forget it."

*Easier said...*CJ stared down at her coffee mug.

"For the record, I didn't think you were an idiot. I was just glad you were okay." Brady squinted out across the crowded mess. "But then, you already know that."

Another Wac approached the counter, and they waited in strained silence while she poured a cup of tea.

Then Brady looked CJ in the eye again. "Is there nothing you want to say to me?"

Was she joking? There were a thousand things CJ wanted to say. But she wasn't the one with a fiancé.

Brady bit her lip. "I guess that's it, then. See you around, CJ," she said, her voice husky, and turned to go.

CJ knew she should let her go. Brady wasn't likely to come after her again. In fact, she would probably never even look at her again, let alone talk to her. They would pass as strangers in the WAC compound, in the theaters and service clubs around the post, each possibly wishing the other didn't exist.

She gripped her Army-issue coffee cup tightly. And then, because she couldn't bear to let Brady walk away, she said it: "Wait."

Brady paused and glanced back. "Why?"

"Because I miss you." She sighed a little, knowing she shouldn't have admitted this fact.

"I miss *you*." Brady came closer again. "But you already know that too."

CJ closed her eyes briefly. "What do you want me to say? You're engaged to be married."

"I told you, it doesn't mean anything."

"You told him you would marry him. That does mean something, at least to me. And to him too, I would imagine."

Brady exhaled, her shoulders falling. "You're right. I'm still trying to figure it out." She hesitated. "What if I weren't engaged?"

CJ stared into Brady's eyes with their mismatched colors, at her hair pinned up beneath her garrison cap, at her flushed cheeks. God, she was beautiful. And yet…"I don't know. I haven't done any of this before."

"It's not like I have."

"You haven't?" she asked, trying not to sound thrilled by the news.

"No, CJ, I haven't."

Another Wac interrupted to pour a cup of coffee, smiling curiously at them. Brady offered what CJ thought of as her Public Relations Office smile and added powdered milk to her cup, stirring ever so slowly.

"What now?" Brady asked when the other woman was out of earshot.

"I don't know." The refrain was beginning to feel familiar. "I guess we keep avoiding each other, or we try to go back to being friends."

"Friends, then?" Brady asked, flashing one of her disarming smiles. But her eyes held a hint of vulnerability, as if she was afraid CJ might choose otherwise.

As she should. Brady had kissed her, and even though Brady probably didn't remember, CJ had kissed her too, in the middle of the night in Cloudcroft. They had both crossed that line willingly, and CJ wasn't sure she could go back.

But what other choice did they have? Avoiding each other made her want Brady more—"the Romeo and Juliet effect," as her English lit professor had called it.

"Friends," she said finally, holding out her hand.

Brady took it, and instantly CJ realized her mistake. As long as she didn't touch Brady, she might be able to pretend they were merely buddies, good old-fashioned Army pals. But with Brady's warm palm pressed to hers, her long, slim fingers holding CJ's, the charade fizzled.

"So, *friend*, do you feel like shooting some baskets this afternoon?" Brady asked, releasing her hand. "Assuming you're fully recovered."

"Can I invite Reggie and Sarah?" With friends as buffers, they were less likely to get into trouble.

"Of course. The more D-lites for me to beat, the better."

"Dream on, Buchanan."

Maybe this would work. But as she smiled into Brady's eyes, her stomach lurched.

"See you later?" Brady asked, looking away first.

"Absolutely."

She ignored the ever-present urge to watch Brady walk away. Everything would be fine, she told herself, heading back to her own table. They were grown women. They could do this.

"You two kiss and make up?" Reggie murmured as CJ slipped into her seat.

CJ shot her a baleful look as Reggie, who had spoken so softly that no one else heard, smiled and bit into a cinnamon roll.

Making up hadn't been difficult. But not kissing Brady when she knew her feelings were entirely mutual? That would be the hard part.

CHAPTER ELEVEN

As Thanksgiving neared, CJ settled back into the pattern she had fallen into before New Mexico. Weekdays were busy with drill, PT, work in the Transient Hangar and occasional dull orientation lectures or extra details, such as scrubbing the walkway outside the barracks. On weekends, she relaxed with her usual group of friends, but now Brady was back with them, sharing drinks at the USO club in El Paso, shooting pool at the EW club, swapping cigarettes on long walks around base and getting tipsy as enlisted women's bands played big band music late into the Texas night. She and Brady weren't quite as close as they had been before, but CJ made do with Brady's continued presence, reminding herself of the other option. Besides, it was self-indulgent to fixate on her romantic life, or lack thereof, with war raging across the globe.

Half a world away in Cairo, President Roosevelt was meeting with England's Winston Churchill and China's General Chiang Kai-shek to chart a course for the war in the Pacific. After that he was headed to the Middle East to meet with Churchill and Russia's Joseph Stalin to discuss strategy for the war in Europe. By the end of the month, it looked like the "Big Three" would have agreed on strategies for defeating the Axis powers on both fronts.

Meanwhile, American and Japanese troops were fighting gruesomely bloody battles in the Gilbert Islands. Every mention CJ caught of the fighting there chilled her because she knew Joe's division, which had successfully taken Guadalcanal in the Solomons earlier in the year, was either already in the area or on its way. Brady confirmed the week before Thanksgiving that Joe's division had moved into the Gilberts while Alec's unit had been mustered into the new Fifteenth Air Force, currently in the process of establishing its headquarters in Italy.

Sometimes when she was feeling sorry for herself, CJ would reread one of Joe's letters about the shelling his unit had withstood at Lunga Point on Guadalcanal or one of Alec's missives about the dangers of desert flying in Tunisia. She had joined the Army to help bring boys like them home faster. But while she worked hard six days a week, sometimes so hard that she could barely stay awake after evening mess long enough to complete a single letter, it still seemed as if the government had sent her to a summer camp of sorts where she got to monkey around with airplane engines and, in her spare time, play softball, sunbathe, go to movies and listen to music with friends.

Strange to think that the Army was giving her the space and time she needed to discover who she was—and to meet other people like her. Only childless women or those whose children were no longer dependent were eligible to join up, which made the WAC especially attractive to women whose lives were built around other women. It was ironic, really, that Uncle Sam was paving the way for homosexuals to find one another.

Now that she had named her difference, at least to herself, she went about her Army life with it near the forefront of her mind. At first she tried to tell herself that it was Brady she was attracted to, not women in general, despite her childhood crushes on other girls. She spent a couple of evenings paying extra attention to Jack's friends Mac and Sam, faithful dance partners to her and the others. But they didn't make her heart pound or her stomach lurch, and in truth, no man ever had, not even Sean. It would be so much easier if she could feel that way about a man. But while Mac and Sam and thousands of other boys at Bliss were nice, attractive even, they didn't move her the way Brady did.

Armed with her new insight, CJ watched women dancing at the EW club together, wondering if they were involved. She watched women in the mess hall, trying to figure out which ones were gay from the way they looked and how they interacted with other women. She didn't know many Wacs who matched the stereotype she'd heard bandied about in college: mannish women who formed unnatural relationships with other women because they longed to be men. But there were others who looked like Toby and Reggie: not particularly feminine and not overtly masculine. They were somewhere in between—just like she'd always been.

Her little sister, Rebecca, had been a typical girl right from the start—she liked to play with dolls, wore dresses and had little interest in learning about or operating assorted farm equipment. She would rather make a pie crust from scratch than help cultivate a wheat field. CJ, on the other hand, had always been a bit of a tomboy. Early on, her tomboy tendencies hadn't seemed unusual. But in high school, as girls in her class started to experiment with clothing, makeup and boys, she began to notice her own difference more and more.

One summer night while shelling peas on the back porch, she asked her mother, "Do you and Dad ever wish I was more of a, I don't know, regular girl? Like Rebecca, I mean."

Beside her, her mother stopped shelling. "Why would we want you to be someone you're not?"

Their belief in honoring the individual was what had led her parents to join the First Baptist Church of Kalamazoo, a progressive American Baptist congregation that preached that everyone has the right to have a relationship with God and that no one should tell someone else what to believe. FBCK supported each individual's right to believe as they saw fit, and refrained from baptizing members into the faith until they were of age to understand the commitment they were making.

Both of CJ's older brothers had chosen to be baptized, but she hadn't. By the time she came of age, she had already discovered a latent skepticism that wouldn't allow her to accept the church's contention that the Bible was the divinely inspired word of God or that it should serve as the final authority on Christian life.

The war had led her farther from the First Baptist path of peace and social justice. Pacifism was not always the righteous choice. The war had also made her question a notion she had once believed implicitly: that God is deeply and passionately involved in human history. What kind of devoted god could let Japanese soldiers bayonet Chinese infants? Or allow SS soldiers to wipe out entire European villages? Or look on silently as both sides bombed civilian center after civilian center? It seemed more likely that rather than determine the course of life on earth, God now wept for humankind.

Her church would have disagreed with this conclusion, but CJ had made her peace with that aspect of her difference years ago. Now she wondered what the faithful members of the congregation like Mrs. Anderson, her religious education teacher for most of her life, would say if she revealed the yearning in her heart. FBCK members believed everyone was a child of God; would her parents' closest friends, the Graafs, still treat her with tolerance, kindness, acceptance if she chose to follow the path of homosexuality? Though it wasn't as if she had a choice. Surely a compassionate God would not create people who loved members of their own sex and then banish them to hell for falling in love. But she knew what Pastor Ben would say to that: "Love the sinner, not the sin."

As much as she loved her parents and their church, she could not accept that what she felt for Brady was a sin, not when it felt like the only rational thing in this currently fouled-up world.

* * *

CJ's Thanksgiving KP assignment was fast approaching. The only good thing about having to spend the day in the mess kitchen was that she was going to appreciate Thanksgiving weekend that much more. Non-essential post personnel had both Saturday and Sunday off in recognition of the holiday, and Kate had secured two-day passes for the D-lites. Their destination: downtown El Paso, close and inexpensive, with ready access to Mexico via the international streetcar lines.

It was Toby's idea to go to the Juarez race track. Her father had loved horse racing, and she had spent her formative summers at Belmont with him, betting on the races and cheering on their picks. Her father always chose horses with unlikely names, she said, like Starstruck Omelet, Son of an Owl or Whistle Pixie.

"The trolley will pick us up in downtown El Paso, take us across the border to the race track and bring us back to the Hilton. What do you say?" she asked, looking around the mess hall table.

"I'm in," Sarah said.

"Me too," Reggie said.

"Me three," Brady added.

CJ glanced at her, startled. Brady was coming with them? Even with half a dozen buffers along, she wasn't sure it was a good idea to spend forty-eight hours together away from Fort Bliss.

A little while later, when Brady excused herself to take her coffee cup to the window, CJ followed.

"Hold on," she said, catching up.

"What?" Brady's smile was innocent.

"Shouldn't we talk about this weekend?"

"Oh, that." Brady continued on to the KP window and dropped off her cup, then tugged CJ toward the door. "I wanted to talk to you anyway."

"You did?"

The thought of a serious discussion with Brady made her sweat, despite the coolness of the late fall evening. Had Brady changed her mind? Did she think they were better off avoiding each other, after all? But if she did, she wouldn't be making plans to come to El Paso with them, so that couldn't be it.

Hope began to rise in CJ. For what, she knew exactly, but she didn't want to jinx it. She stopped the smile threatening to split her face and followed Brady out of the mess hall.

On the porch behind the officers' quarters, Brady sat down on the top step and offered her a cigarette.

She accepted it, took a puff, but didn't sit down. Instead she stood, facing her. "What? Tell me."

Brady looked out across the softball field. The post lights didn't reach very far inside the fence, which left much of the field dark.

"I wrote to Nate," Brady said. "I broke off the engagement."

CJ nearly choked on her cigarette. "You did? When?"

"Last night."

"And you mailed it?"

"I did."

Brady had done it. She had actually done it. "Oh my God."

"I'm not sure God has much to do with this."

"It wasn't because of me, was it?" CJ asked, suddenly feeling awful for the Army lieutenant about to receive a Dear John letter post-stamped—ironically—Fort Bliss.

"No," Brady said, gazing up at her. "Or, well, maybe. I mean, it was mostly because of me. But you figured significantly in the timing."

"Brady…" She turned away. "I don't know. This doesn't feel right."

Brady came down the stairs toward her. "I thought this was what you wanted."

"It was. It is."

"Is it?"

She looked at her feet. "It's all I've wanted, ever since I found out he existed."

"CJ." Brady reached out and took her chin. "Look at me."

She did and froze at the look in Brady's eyes. For a second she thought Brady was going to kiss her right there, but instead she took CJ's cigarette and stubbed it out.

Suddenly Brady smiled. "You're it!" And she sprinted out onto the softball field.

Laughing, CJ forgot about Nate. She forgot about heavy bombers and amphibious landings, prisoner of war camps and death marches as she followed Brady into the dark outfield.

"Where are you?"

"Here," Brady said, materializing in front of her.

They were in the shadows now, but moonlight shone off Brady's blonde hair and her collar insignia, a bust of Pallas Athene, the WAC's patron saint.

CJ stopped a few feet away. "You know what this means, don't you?"

"What?"

"You're free."

"I am." Brady paused. Then, in a lower voice, "Come here."

Hesitantly, CJ stepped forward. The Articles of War, her family, Nate even flashed through her mind. But then she realized that none of those things truly mattered, not at that instant. Life was too frighteningly brief to risk passing up the kind of happiness she felt when she was with Brady. Hadn't the war proven that you couldn't take your own continued survival for granted, not for an instant?

Brady met her halfway, and then they were in each other's arms, CJ's hands at Brady's waist, Brady's hands tangling in her hair. CJ wasn't sure who started the kiss, but that didn't matter either. They had both been waiting for this moment. Their lips were soft at first and then firmer as they tried to get closer still. CJ felt Brady's lips part hers, their tongues touch. She opened her eyes in shock at the sensation. She hadn't known kissing could feel like this, hadn't realized her body was capable of such feeling. Then she slid her leg between Brady's and tackled her to the ground, catching her as they both fell.

"Hey," Brady said, laughing up at her.

"Is for horses," CJ said, and then she leaned down and kissed her again.

Beneath her, Brady tugged her closer until CJ's body pressed against hers, breast to breast, hip to hip. CJ kissed Brady harder, her breathing increasingly ragged. She needed to feel Brady's skin. She reached for Brady's tie and tugged it off, dropping it in the short grass. Brady tugged hers off in return, clearly in favor of the plan. CJ had just undone Brady's top button when she froze. Were those voices?

She lifted her head. The basketball court, bathed in lights from the officers' quarters, was no longer empty. Reggie, Toby and a few other Maintenance Wacs were out there now, bouncing a basketball as they settled on a game.

"They can't see us, can they?" she asked, suddenly panicked.

Brady sighed. "No. I promise."

CJ rolled off and lay on her back, looking up at the wide night sky as her breathing evened out. She couldn't believe she'd flung caution so far to the wind like that, but it felt good. Better than good. She had kissed Brady, finally, after weeks of dreaming about it.

"Are you okay?" she asked, glancing over at Brady.

"I'm good." She watched CJ. "What about you?"

"Marvelous." She rolled over and rested her chin on Brady's shoulder. "We kissed."

Brady smiled. "I'd say so."

"Do you know how long I've wanted to do that?"

"Um, since the day you ran into me at the PX?"

"Um, you ran into me."

"And I've been thankful ever since that I did."

"Aww." She reached up and kissed Brady again, slowly this time, savoring the fact that she could.

After a while they straightened their uniforms and walked the long way around the officers' quarters. Then they returned to their spot on the steps, so stealthily that the basketball players didn't notice them at first. Brady sat on the top step, and CJ sat one step below her, leaning against her knees.

Life didn't get better than this, she thought, happiness uncoiling inside her until she felt she must be glowing from head to toe. She and Brady were finally together. Sure, there was KP hell to get through, but soon enough it would be the weekend. And then they would have forty-eight hours together away from the post, beyond the reach of military authorities.

"Would you like to share a room Saturday night?" Brady asked.

This telepathy thing was kind of great, after all.

"I would love to," she said, glancing back at Brady.

They smiled into each other's eyes, and this time CJ didn't feel the need to look away. No more avoiding each other, no more pretending they didn't feel what they were feeling.

"Jamieson!"

CJ rolled her eyes at Brady and looked out at the court. "What?"

"Get your butt out here and even up the teams," Toby said.

"She can't," Brady shot back. "She's busy."

Toby's eyebrows lifted while Reggie smiled broadly.

"In that case, never mind," Toby said, turning back to the game.

Play restarted, and CJ snuggled back against Brady's legs as Orion chased the Pleiades and the sliver moon rose higher overhead.

* * *

Her euphoric state carried her to Thanksgiving Day. For KP duty, she was paired with Mary, the radio technician who had never mentioned a boyfriend. Mary had a ready smile and capable hands and made an excellent KP partner, CJ discovered during the breakfast rush. She was willing to split the less pleasant jobs and approached whatever they did, from washing pots and pans to cleaning the mess hall tables and floors, with an easygoing shrug of the shoulders.

After breakfast, the dictatorial cooks ordered them to peel a veritable mountain of potatoes in preparation for Thanksgiving supper.

Mary handed CJ a knife and asked, "Fancy a bit of peeling music?"

The post radio station was playing Christmas tunes, as was every other station, even the Mexican ones. CJ had heard Bing Crosby's new release, "White Christmas," and its B side "I'll Be Home for Christmas" twice already, and it was only mid-morning.

At ten, she took a break to listen to Brady deliver the news, still amazed that someone like Brady would want to be with her. They had been inseparable since their kiss Monday night, or as inseparable as it was possible to be as active-duty Wacs. Tuesday night they'd had to attend an orientation film with the rest of their company, yet another installment in the series *Why We Fight*. They had arrived late and sat at the back of the room snickering at the film's morally superior tone and thinly veiled propaganda until at last a nearby sergeant had dismissed them. She'd winked at CJ as they slipped out the back, and CJ realized there might be some unexpected perks to belonging to the gay secret society after all.

At the end of the news broadcast, Brady said, "This next song goes out to a certain someone suffering through holiday KP duty. You know who you are."

The opening notes of "Begin the Beguine" floated into the kitchen, and CJ smiled to herself as she picked up yet another potato from the barely diminished pile.

"You're pals with Brady Buchanan, aren't you?" Mary commented.

CJ started guiltily, trying to compose her features into a less dreamy expression, and nodded.

"I heard she Dear Johned her fiancé."

She'd known news got around fast, but this seemed excessive even by Army standards. "That's right," she said cautiously.

Mary smiled sideways at her. "Must not have been true love."

"Couldn't have been," CJ agreed.

She hummed along with the song as she peeled onward. Another dozen hours or so of KP to get through, but there would probably be a sizable break after the noon mess when she and Mary would be able to go back to the barracks and rest. And later, Brady had offered to come by and massage French hand crème into her GI-soap-reddened skin, and, well, that was something to be thankful for, wasn't it?

For a moment she gave into temptation and imagined Thanksgiving on the farm. Her parents were at home this year, playing host to the DeWitts from down the road, whose sons were all off serving in some fashion or another. Her mother had written CJ's first week at Bliss to tell her that Jacob, the youngest of the four boys, had been killed during advanced training in Virginia when the Army truck he was traveling in had rolled into a ditch. CJ could picture Anna and Peter DeWitt, her dark braids graying now, his hair mostly gone. She could see Jacob too, a few years younger than she was, a pale kid with unruly hair and glasses trailing after his older brothers. He had been a late baby, unexpected, and had always struggled to keep up with the other three, who had doted on him.

His parents had been both proud and relieved when he was selected for military intelligence. "Shows how smart he is. And I don't mind saying it'll keep him away from the front lines," CJ had overheard Anna DeWitt tell her mother a few weeks before she left the farm. "Between you and me, I don't think our Jacob is cut out for fighting."

Now he was dead and buried with full military honors, her mother had written, and his parents were left grieving a senseless loss. As if some wartime losses made more sense than others. She knew what her mother meant, though. At least if you died fighting for your country, your death might be construed to mean something. An automobile accident while on maneuvers was simply bad luck.

In a way, CJ was relieved she wouldn't be at home to share Thanksgiving with her parents and the grieving DeWitts. But even as the thought entered her mind, she chastised herself. Where was her generosity? Her sense of charity? True, she was head over heels for the first time in her life and wanted to hold onto her joy as long as she could. But there was also the fairly large issue of what her parents would think if she told them the truth. She couldn't imagine lying to them, but she couldn't picture telling them about Brady, either. What did other gay people do? Did they tell their families, or did they distance themselves so that they wouldn't have to risk rejection?

"What's your favorite Thanksgiving pie?" Mary asked as they started on another pile of potatoes.

"Pumpkin," CJ replied straightaway, pushing away any lingering thoughts of home. She was in Texas with no extended furlough in sight, and her news about Brady was not something that could be shared with her family in a letter. Subject closed. "What's yours?"

"Apple. With vanilla ice cream, of course."

And they were off and running on a common GI theme—favorite foods from pre-war civilian life before sugar, butter and cooking oil were rationed, before SOS and griping became customary mealtime staples. Then again, they knew they had it better than the boys overseas, who were forced to survive on C-rations and whatever local delicacies their quartermasters could drum up. CJ told Mary about some of the concoctions her brothers had written about in their letters: Australian sheep tongues in Guadalcanal, along with bug-infested rice seized from the Japanese and whale fat rolled in seaweed, and in North Africa lamb cutlets, sheep intestines and shish kebabs.

She really was blessed, she knew. There would be plenty of turkey, mashed potatoes and cranberries to go around at supper mess, even if she would be working through most of the meal. In another few hours she would see Brady again, if only through the kitchen window. The next day would be her last in the Transient Hangar, and then there was the weekend away to look forward to. On Monday, she and the others would start their new assignment with Tow Target and the WASPs. Somehow she had a feeling that more and better hops awaited in her future.

It was hard to believe now that she had ever regarded her transfer to Bliss as a calamity. Monterey County might have ocean breezes and smooth sand, but it didn't have Brady or their friends. For all she knew, the post commander at Ford Ord was stricter or the WAC command might take themselves overly seriously or any number of other unwelcome realities. Aeschylus had written, "In war, truth is the first casualty." But for her, it was the opposite. Somehow she had landed in the place where the right combination of people had allowed her to figure out who she truly was. For that, if nothing else, she would always be grateful to the Army.

Then she remembered the feel of Brady's hand in hers in the darkened post theater the previous night, the way their shoulders brushed as they'd walked back to the WAC compound with their friends, how Brady had smiled at her when no one else was looking. She couldn't wait for the weekend when they would be alone, gloriously, amazingly alone, for an entire night.

She would enjoy this brief spate of happiness while she could, because one thing about the Army was certain—it didn't like its soldiers to get too comfortable.

CHAPTER TWELVE

Every weekend, soldiers from Fort Bliss caught the streetcar into El Paso, where they enjoyed USO shows and dances, free entrance to museums and galleries and discounts at restaurants and bars. Ten minutes away across the US-Mexico border, Juarez offered horse racing, a large city market and a wide range of less reputable entertainment options such as gambling establishments, all-night bars and, though the WAC command purposefully didn't mention it, brothels.

GIs received more forthright advice about the dangers of the Mexican city, Jack and his friends reported over beers at the service club the night before the D-lites' weekend away. To combat the spread of venereal disease, Fort Bliss soldiers were encouraged to pick up condoms at prophylactic stations, open around the clock, before going off-post. MPs also patrolled brothels and other off-limits establishments ("olés," as Bliss personnel called them) on both sides of the border, arresting any soldier caught on the premises. In spite of these prevention efforts, an entire building at Beaumont General Hospital had been set aside to treat soldiers with serious cases of VD—gonorrhea, syphilis and the like.

Mac held up his glass of beer and parroted the military doctor from a health education training film male GIs were forced to endure: "'Drunkenness is responsible for much venereal disease.'"

In the same Cary Grant tone, Sam added, "'Most men know less about their own bodies than they do about their automobiles.'"

Kate chimed in, "Funny—most men know less about the female body than their automobiles too," and there was general hooting around the table.

That night Jack accompanied them as far as the women's compound, where he and Sarah said a long, semi-private farewell. Kate's influence in obtaining overnight passes didn't extend to the rest of the Army, so Sarah would have to leave Jack behind this weekend. His eighteen weeks of AA training had already morphed into twenty-two weeks, which meant he could be transferred to another post or to overseas duty at any time, like everyone else at Bliss. Because of this, Sarah had considered staying on base with him. But in the end, she said, she couldn't pass up the chance to get away for a night.

After breakfast mess Saturday morning, the D-lites—of whom Kate and Brady were honorary members, everyone agreed—caught a streetcar from the post to downtown El Paso, where they transferred to the line that would take them to the race track in Juárez. The ride cost a dime, and soon they were on Stanton Street headed for one of the international bridges that connected El Paso to Mexico. CJ shared a seat with Brady and was aware of Brady's leg pressing against hers as they rode over the Rio Grande.

"Have you ever been to Mexico?" Brady asked, leaning into her, supposedly to get a better look out the window as they crossed the international border.

"No," she said, more interested in contemplating Brady's eyes and lips than what lay beyond her window.

Brady smiled and elbowed her. "The view's out there."

"I prefer the one inside," CJ said, and then blushed. Anyone could have heard her. She ought to be more careful.

"I can't argue with that," Brady said softly, gazing back at her with eyes that clearly communicated her desire to kiss CJ silly, as she had done every chance they'd gotten that week. Unfortunately, that wasn't all that often—living on base hemmed in by barbed wire and observed closely by MPs and their own officers didn't allow many opportunities to break the Uniform Code of Military Justice.

Reggie, seated directly in front of them, glanced back and wiggled her eyebrows suggestively. CJ turned to the window. This *was* her first foray into Mexico. Perhaps she should pay attention.

Not long after they crossed the Rio Grande and merged onto Avenue Lerdo, the Mexican counterpart to Stanton Street, CJ began to see a difference between the sister cities. The blocks in El Paso were orderly and neat, laid out according to plan. But south of the border, the buildings didn't match their neighbors as well, almost as if they were haphazard afterthoughts. The street's edge was sprinkled liberally with booths, handcarts and individual vendors selling their wares to passersby. She had never seen anything quite like it—rickety tables stacked with scores of Mexican blankets; narrow shelves overflowing with religious figurines carved from wood and stone; and woven mats displaying silver necklaces and turquoise earrings. On some street corners, wizened old women hunched on the ground, hawking a variety of wares from their blankets.

"This isn't the real Mexico," Brady told her, frowning out the window.

"What do you mean?"

"Border towns aren't good representations of Mexican life or culture. Sometime I'll take you to Mérida, this amazing colonial city near Cancún. The cathedrals are hundreds of years old, and there are Mayan ruins nearby along with the sweetest little fishing village you could imagine."

CJ wasn't sure she could imagine a Mexican fishing village at all, sweet or otherwise. She stared at Brady, aware as she rarely was of the gap between their backgrounds and experiences.

"Don't look at me like that. Everyone in Southern California vacations in Mexico."

"Everyone?"

"Well, maybe not everyone. But plenty of people. It's like Canada for you. You've been to Niagara Falls, haven't you?"

She had. Montreal and Toronto, too. Her parents had been big on family trips, even during the hard years of the Depression when not everyone had the opportunity or ability to travel. Seeing different countries and cities was crucial, her parents had maintained, to the development of a world view that allowed for difference. Although how different CJ would turn out to be, she doubted anyone could have predicted.

The streetcar route took them away from the commercial streets commonly traveled by visitors and into the heart of the small city, site of an important siege that had spilled temporarily into El Paso during the Mexican Revolution thirty years earlier. El Paso buildings reflected the city's American Southwest identity, with tiled roofs and Spanish colonial architecture interspersed among brick edifices with squared-off roofs and stone gargoyles. Similarly, Juarez buildings reflected the border city's multitude of identities and influences. While the architecture was more eclectic than El Paso's, with elaborately decorated pink adobe structures facing functional factory buildings, single-story slum dwellings and palatial haciendas, it was also, conversely, more uniform.

Signs in Spanish advertised Mexican businesses, from magazine stands to radio repair shops. Women wore colorful shawls and skirts, while children ran barefoot along the dusty roads, calling out to one another in Spanish. In the alleys, stray dogs dug through trash as groups of young boys chased after homemade soccer balls. She recalled her own childhood, playing baseball and basketball with her brothers and other farm kids. It was the same idea except that here, the options were limited by lack of space, equipment, organization. And she'd thought America had it bad in the years leading up to the war. Looked like every day was the Depression here.

The streetcar deposited them at the race track, where they bought discounted tickets and found seats together in the upper tier of the grandstand. Toby and Reggie went to place bets while the others stayed in their seats, watching the horses line up for the next race.

CJ, it turned out, was the lone member of the outing party who had never been to a horse race.

"But I've participated in a few," she insisted. "That counts."

"Are we talking an actual track with spectators or cross-country farm field racing?" Brady teased.

"Well, we called it a track, anyway," CJ said, pretending to be miffed.

"Did you at least win?" Sarah asked.

"No. My mare Molly and I were no match for the competition."

Her brother Alec had always had a way with horses. In more than one letter, he'd mentioned he couldn't wait to get back home to see Jay, his gray gelding. Horses didn't understand about military service, he'd written. There was no way to explain to Jay that his absence wasn't voluntary, that he hadn't left home because he wanted to. CJ knew what he meant, only unlike her brother, she had no intention of returning to farm life. In her case, she *had* chosen to abandon Molly. Although leaving her in the care of her parents was hardly abandonment. Rebecca and Pete doted on her too, so it wasn't like she wasn't well cared for.

Molly never seemed to hold her absences against her. Whenever CJ strolled into the barn, her childhood horse merely whinnied welcomingly and bumped her soft muzzle against her pockets, looking for the carrot or apple bits CJ wouldn't dream of setting foot in the barn without. Lately, each time she left the farm, CJ had wondered if she would see Molly again. When the mare's life ended—and it was a good life as horse lives went, CJ knew—would she regret not having spent more time with her? Would a deeper understanding of slave narrative conventions and fugitive slave experiences make up for the knowledge she had chosen to leave behind a beloved friend? For that matter, that she had left behind her entire family?

"I had a horse named Molly once," Sarah said, her tone wistful.

"So did I," Brady said.

"*You* had a horse?" CJ stared at her.

"A polo pony. She lived at the stables so I didn't see her much, especially after I left for school. But I rode her every week for years."

"You played polo?" Kate asked. "Honestly?"

Brady shrugged. "Everyone back home played."

CJ wanted to ask if Nate played too, but she didn't want to remind Brady of the letter she'd penned. She hadn't received a response from Nate yet and didn't expect to for another week, at the earliest. Even if her letter had gone by air, it still had to reach Nate's assigned post station, be censored, get transferred to microfilm, cross the ocean, arrive at the receiving station and be reproduced, sorted and (finally) delivered to Nate's unit. American troops in Italy weren't currently on the move, much to the disappointment of the Allied command in the ETO, which meant Nate's mail would find him more easily. But it was more likely that the letter would travel from its New York APO to the correct Italian receiving station by ship, and even the fastest ship took a week to cross the Atlantic. More than likely, Nate wouldn't receive word that Brady didn't want to marry him until sometime next week or after.

Not that CJ had spent much time thinking about the letter's overseas journey.

Seated beside her on the narrow wooden bench, Brady leaned into CJ, smiling. She promptly pushed V-mail shipments from her mind and returned instead to the warm Mexican sun and the company of some of her favorite women in the world. Her first trip to a country other than Canada and her first horse race warranted notice. The other possible first that awaited her, mere hours away now instead of the days she'd been counting down, made her mouth dry. Nervous or not, she would soon find herself alone again in a hotel room with Brady Buchanan. This time, she was pretty sure the first thing she would notice would be the bed.

Toby and Reggie slid in beside them just before the colorfully decorated horses and their riders entered the starting gate.

"Everyone has to cheer for Wacky Hooch!" Reggie announced, grinning.

"Wacky or WAC-y?" Sarah asked, and they all laughed.

Then the starter pistol rang out, the gates shot up and the horses were off.

"Go, Wacky Hooch!" CJ called.

Beside her, Brady shouted encouragement. They paused, smiling at each other, and then refocused on the track, where Wacky was running dead center of the pack. Middle was better than last, CJ thought, and then she forgot to think as Brady's hand found hers.

In what seemed like no time, the horses were rounding the turn and clattering into the home stretch. Wacky was gaining, and the six Wacs jumped to their feet almost as one to cheer their horse on, heedless of nearby track goers who were more interested in the novelty of a group of American women in uniform than in the race unfolding below.

* * *

As it turned out, the view was the first thing CJ noticed after they returned to El Paso and checked into their hotel room. Or rather, their rooms. Brady knew someone who knew someone, which meant that while the rest of their party occupied average-sized quarters on the hotel's second floor, Brady and CJ were shown to a suite on the fifteenth floor.

As Brady tipped the bellboy and closed the door behind him, CJ crossed to the wall of windows in the suite's living area, gazing out over the city's north side toward Fort Bliss and the Franklin Range, both tinged sunset pink. The Hilton was the tallest building in the city, but CJ was amazed to discover that she could see all the way to the white-peaked Sacramento Mountains. Somewhere up there was Cloudcroft, tucked in among the forests and canyons.

"What do you think?" Brady asked, coming to a stop out of reach. She clasped her hands before her. "Do our accommodations meet with your approval, miss?" Her tone was light, but CJ noticed that her knuckles were white.

Could Brady be as nervous as she was? The thought gave CJ the nerve that had failed her earlier when Brady had reached for her hand in the elevator. She had shaken her head at Brady, nodding at the bellboy's back. In return, Brady had leaned against the elevator's rear wall, arms folded across her chest.

Now CJ reached for Brady's hands and gently pulled them apart. She wove their fingers together, tugging her closer until their hips met. Then she pressed Brady's arms to her sides and leaned forward until their lips were mere centimeters apart.

"The accommodations are more than serviceable." She waited, eyes on Brady's lips, dimly aware of the lights of El Paso flicking on below them as winter twilight fell early across the city.

Finally Brady made a sound low in her throat and narrowed the remaining distance, capturing CJ's mouth with her own. Her lips were insistent, but CJ kissed her slowly, languidly, still holding Brady's arms at her sides. There was no hurry. Tonight they had all the time in the world. There would be no bed check, no snoring neighbors, no morning reveille or breakfast mess. Tonight they would be alone in this suite of rooms with doors that locked, a fire flickering in the fireplace and a bottle of champagne chilling on the glass-topped dining table.

At that moment, a banging sounded at the door, and CJ heard Reggie's unmistakable voice calling, "Fort Bliss Military Police! Open up in there!"

Really, that wasn't funny, CJ thought, pulling away from Brady to scowl at the door.

"Your friends have lousy timing," Brady said, touching her hair.

"So now they're my friends?"

"They always were," Brady said, moving to open the door, a smile pinned to her face. "Come right in, Mr. MP. We weren't doing anything wrong."

"I'm sure," Reggie said archly as she and the others filed into the room. And then her eyes widened. "Holy moly, CJ. What'd you do to deserve the special treatment?"

"Nothing," Brady said, her eyes on CJ. "Yet."

CJ felt her cheeks flame as her friends bit back smiles and looked any place but at her.

"Say," Sarah said, moving toward the window, "can you see the alligator pool from up here?"

The others crowded around the window, oohing and aahing at the expansive view. Sure enough, they decided, it was barely possible to make out the shadows of the handful of alligators that lived in a fenced-off pond in San Jacinto Plaza, nicknamed La Plaza de los Lagartos for the tourist attraction that had been around since the 1880s. By the time Sarah's timely inquiry had been answered, CJ had recovered from her brief bout of mortification. She wouldn't look at Brady, though, as they left the suite and piled into the elevator, headed out on the town for supper.

Fitting six adults into a cab was difficult, but they managed. Reggie and Sarah rode up front with the driver, while the two couples squeezed in together in back. Brady held CJ's hand, and by the time they reached Ashley's, a Mexican restaurant north of downtown, she'd given up all pretense of displeasure. How could she feel anything other than happiness when they were together?

Jack and Sam were waiting when they arrived. Sarah actually squealed, a sound CJ had never expected to hear from the usually reserved, level-headed mechanic.

"I thought you couldn't get away tonight?" she said, her arms around Jack's neck in a rare public display of affection.

"We have to be back for bed check, but Mac took my detail. He said he couldn't stand the moping," Jack said, leaning down to kiss her.

"Looks like it's me and you, Meatball," Sam said, corralling Reggie around the neck.

Reggie shrugged and slipped her arm around his waist. "When in Rome…"

Ashley's was popular with the Fort Bliss crowd for its tacos and enchiladas. They had to wait for seating together, sipping margaritas and sangria at the bar, but at last they were able to push two tables together. A harried waiter took their order and practically slung their food at them when it arrived, but CJ felt sorry for him. Then again, his tips on this one night would probably amount to more than her weekly pay. Privates didn't make much in Uncle Sam's employ.

At one point, CJ thought she saw Janice picking her way through the crowded tables. But then a lanky GI well on his way to inebriation stumbled into their table, and CJ lost the Janice-look-alike in the crowd. Not that it mattered if Janice knew Brady and CJ were out with the rest of the D-lites. They had been off-post together before. Nothing was particularly different about this weekend.

Except that everything *was* different, of course. Brady was laughing at something Kate had said, but as if she felt CJ's gaze on her, she glanced across the narrow wooden tabletop. Their eyes caught and held, and CJ felt warmth flowing through her body, flushing her skin. Everything had changed. All anyone would have to do was look at them to know.

"Do you want to get out of here?" Brady asked, her voice low.

CJ nodded quickly. Did she ever.

They rose, dropping money on the table to cover their mostly uneaten meals.

"Wait a minute," Reggie started, but Toby elbowed her.

"Hope your headache feels better," Kate said, smiling up at Brady.

"Thanks," Brady said after a pause, her own smile slow. "I'm sure it will."

As she and CJ wove through the crowd arm in arm, CJ heard Jack ask why she was leaving if Brady was the one with the headache.

"Not that kind of headache," Sarah said.

CJ glanced back and saw Jack's eyes widen in comprehension. Crap, there went her secret. Would he write Sean and tell him? Would Sean inform everyone they knew that the Army had turned her queer? If they did, she didn't care, she told herself as she and Brady hustled out of the restaurant and headed for a taxi stand a few blocks away. She was lucky to have Brady, and she knew it. She wouldn't mind if everyone knew. Well, everyone except her family, of course. And the Army. And maybe some of her friends back in Kalamazoo.

Before the old doubts could set in, she slipped her hand into Brady's and tugged. "Come on," she said, racing down the sidewalk. "I've heard exercise cures headaches."

Brady laughed and followed her.

They were back at the hotel in no time, riding up the elevator with the same bellboy who watched them out of the corner of his eye as the car slowly climbed to the top of El Paso's tallest building. Brady and CJ behaved, standing a full foot apart the whole time, but in the mirror of the polished metal doors, CJ could see the way their bodies angled toward each other as if connected by invisible ties.

As soon as the elevator doors dinged closed behind them, Brady caught her hand and backed down the wide hallway toward their corner suite, kissing CJ as they went. She didn't pull away this time, but leaned into the embrace and guided Brady ahead of her. No one was around, which was good because the margarita she'd had while waiting for the food she hadn't eaten had officially gone to her head. She wasn't sure she would have been able to stop kissing Brady even if MPs *had* materialized at the other end of the hall.

Brady fumbled with the lock on the door, and then they were falling into the suite and hastily slamming the door behind them. Kicking out of her brown pumps, Brady turned and pushed her against the door.

"God, CJ," she murmured, "I've been waiting to do this for so long."

"So have I."

And then they were kissing again, the door solid against her back supporting her as her hands slid to Brady's waist, investigating the curve of her body beneath her uniform jacket. She felt so good, CJ didn't want to stop what they were doing, not ever.

When Brady broke contact finally, CJ tried to hold on. But Brady backed away, smiling seductively. "Come with me."

Heart thundering, CJ followed her into the bedroom. The suite occupied the northwest corner of the fifteenth floor, with the living area looking out over north El Paso and the bedroom's wall of windows facing west. The sun had long since set, and the new moon was impossible to see in the dark mantle of stars that stretched to the horizon. Brady led her to the bed and then turned away, disappearing into the bathroom. CJ stepped out of her own low heels as she heard a match strike. When Brady returned, her face was lit by a flickering candle. She set the candle on the bedside table and turned back to CJ.

As she watched, Brady unbuttoned her uniform jacket and cast it to the floor. She reached for her WAC tie, but before she could loosen it, CJ stilled her hands. "Let me."

In the dim light, she could see Brady watching her as she tugged the tie free and started on her shirt; could see, too, Brady's bottom lip caught between even teeth as CJ's hands slipped beneath her open shirt and pressed the cloth away, sending it to the floor. Swallowing hard, she reached for the clasp on Brady's skirt, and soon Brady stood before her, a pale goddess glowing in candlelight.

Brady leaned forward and whispered, "My turn," her breath raising goose bumps on the sensitive curve of CJ's neck.

Slowly, Brady unfastened her jacket. When it too had fallen, she grasped CJ's tie and pulled her forward for a quick, hard kiss. CJ's legs almost buckled, but she held to Brady's waist, enjoying the feel of her warm, supple skin.

Brady started to melt into CJ's touch. But then she stopped, shaking her head a little. "Not yet," she said, and CJ could see her frown adorably in concentration as she set to work on first her shirt buttons and then her skirt zipper.

CJ felt the military-issue cloth slip down her thighs and calves and kicked it away. Like Brady, she stood nearly naked in purposely un-GI underclothing. Instead of the WAC-issued khaki rayon slip and fitted knickers, Brady wore a pale green silk bra trimmed with lace and a matching panty-slip, while CJ wore a short white rayon slip and matching briefs. Neither wore stockings, which meant that when CJ reached out and pulled Brady against her, she felt Brady's bare legs intertwine with hers, just like in Cloudcroft. But now they were both wide awake and gazing into each other's eyes.

Brady tugged the straps of CJ's slip over her shoulders. When CJ tensed, she paused. "Is this okay?"

"Of course," CJ said determinedly, glad her body was in shadows. She and Sean had only ever been intimate with the lights out. But she wanted to see Brady, so she would have to get used to the idea of Brady seeing her too.

Soon the rest of their clothes lay on the floor around them.

"Kiss me," Brady whispered, wrapping her arms around CJ's neck. "Please."

And then they were falling onto the queen-sized bed, arms around each other and mouths pressed feverishly together. CJ couldn't help noticing how soft Brady was, how smooth her skin felt, so different from Sean's coarser limbs. She hadn't known holding a woman would feel so perfectly right. She kissed Brady as if she were starved for her, and in a way she was. Ever since Cloudcroft she had wanted this—to run her hands along the contours of Brady's body, learning her dips and curves, her ticklish spots, the places that made her moan. To dip her tongue into the hollow of Brady's throat and taste her skin while Brady gasped beneath her. To kiss her way down Brady's arms to the tips of her fingers, and then again along the arc of her spine to the gentle rise of her hips. To touch Brady where no one else got to, to make Brady hers. Even though she knew she didn't have the right, she wanted Brady to be hers. No one else could have her—not Nate or Charlie or any of the other lovesick GIs who were always coming around. Brady belonged to her.

In return, she belonged to Brady. She was Brady's to kiss, to caress and explore with outstretched fingers, mouth and tongue. Sean had touched her in the same places, had even used his mouth in similar fashion to rouse her to a passion of sorts. But he had never made her feel like she did now—weightless yet anchored to the bed by a fierce ache that only Brady could generate and only Brady could assuage. Heat rose in her as Brady's mouth dipped lower, and CJ closed her eyes, gripping the expensive sheets. This was real love, she realized as a pink light took form against her eyelids and seemed to travel the length of her body, following the path of Brady's mouth and hands. This craving and this ache, this need and this desire so overwhelming that she could only clutch the sheets more tightly and give herself over completely to the feeling of Brady turning her inside out, to Brady loving her so fully that nothing else mattered, nothing else existed except the heat and the light and their two bodies joined as one.

Afterward, Brady stretched out beside her, one arm across her waist, cheek resting against her shoulder.

"Mmm," was all CJ could say. Her head was actually spinning a little and not because of the margarita.

"Mmm is right," Brady said, her voice low and sexy.

CJ felt a flicker of renewed heat. How could the sound of her voice have that effect? She stretched too, pointing her toes at the wall of windows as the candle cast shadows across the ceiling and walls.

"Holy moly," she said after a moment.

Brady laughed.

"I'm serious," CJ said, turning onto her side so that she could peer into Brady's eyes. "I had no idea it could be like that. Honestly, no concept."

Brady shook her head, smiling. "I didn't either."

"You're incredible," CJ said, catching one of her hands and kissing it slowly.

"You're the incredible one." Brady rolled on top of her, peppering her neck with kisses.

"No, you are."

As Brady's hips arched into hers, she felt the fire return in earnest. What was wrong with her? Was this normal? Did she care if it wasn't? *Nope*, she decided, flipping Brady over.

"Clearly we need another run," she said in a serious tone, leaning on her elbows above her. "You know, to ascertain which of us is in fact the incredible one."

Beneath her, Brady's eyes sparked. "Clearly." She slid her hands down to the back of CJ's thighs, and CJ forgot to think as desire surged through her and she willingly lost herself again in Brady's kiss.

* * *

Later, they ordered room service—chicken with mushrooms in red wine, sautéed spinach, white rice and roasted yams. When the food arrived, CJ went to the door dressed in her suit jacket and skirt while Brady hid out in the bedroom. Once the curious waiter had gone, CJ stripped again and they pulled on luxurious robes that bore the hotel's insignia. Seated cross-legged on the bed, they fed themselves and each other, washing down the meal with champagne.

"Why do I always feel a thousand times drunker on champagne?" CJ wondered aloud, spearing a forkful of chicken and spinach and offering it to Brady.

As Brady held the fork steady, her thumb stroked CJ's palm suggestively. "Because of the carbonation," she said and took the bite.

The whole thumb-stroking bit had made CJ's mind go temporarily blank. "Sorry, what?"

Smiling smugly, Brady offered her a spoonful of rice and yams. "The carbon dioxide in champagne accelerates the rate at which your body processes the alcohol. Champagne gets into your bloodstream faster than other drinks, so you feel its effects more quickly."

CJ lifted her eyebrows. "Sexy *and* intelligent. No wonder I love— um, being with you so much."

Whoa. Maybe she should slow down on the bubbly. Confessing her true love was not part of the plan.

Brady's head tilted. "I could say the same about you."

Snorting, CJ swallowed a bite of chicken. "Good with engines, yes. But no one has ever called me sexy, to my knowledge."

"You're adorable, and you don't even realize it." Brady leaned in to kiss the corner of her mouth. "I knew the first time I saw you that you would be like this."

"Like what?" CJ asked, her eyes on Brady's lips, so tantalizingly close again.

"Intense. Fiery. Passionate."

It was like she was describing someone else, and yet at the same time, CJ knew what she meant. Being with Brady like this, here, tonight, had unlocked a part of herself she hadn't even known she was holding in check. She loved Brady, but even more, she loved how she felt when she was with her—strong and smart and attractive. Sexy even.

"It's because of you."

"Good," Brady said, and offered her another bite of the delicious food.

A little while later, Brady cleared the empty plates and dishes while CJ ran a bath in the oversized clawfoot tub. Then they shed their robes and climbed into the hot water, facing each other from opposite ends.

"What do you think the others are doing right now?" Brady asked, a smile playing about her lips as she slid her hand along CJ's calves.

"The same thing we are. Except Reggie and Sam, of course."

"I don't know," Brady said. "I distinctly heard Reggie mention when in Rome…"

"Not a chance."

"Would you like to place a small wager?"

CJ angled her head to the side. "What are the terms?"

"If they hook up, then you have to spend Christmas with me."

"And if they don't?"

"That's up to you. I'm sure you'll think of something," Brady said, her voice lowering as her hand crept higher.

CJ felt the same heat rising inside her, swift and exquisite. Again? Then Brady's hand settled on its objective and she forgot to wonder as she tilted her head back against the tub's cool enamel edge, steam and desire dimming her vision.

The water had cooled by the time they stumbled to bed and collapsed beneath the sheets, arms and legs intertwined. CJ fell asleep quickly, and when she woke in the night to find Brady snuggled up against her, she smiled and drifted contentedly back to sleep.

CHAPTER THIRTEEN

Sunlight streamed in the suite's wide windows the next morning, waking CJ. Rolling over onto her side, she gazed at the sleeping woman beside her. Last night had really happened, hadn't it? Brady's eyes were closed, her eyelashes pale smudges against the darker marks beneath her eyes, testimony to their late night. Her blonde curls were tousled from their bathtub sortie, and reaching up, CJ felt her own normally tame hair standing up every which way. She must look a sight, but she didn't care. She felt better than she could ever remember feeling on any other morning, contentment coiling inside her like a physical manifestation. Or maybe that was exhaustion.

Moving closer, she kissed Brady's shoulder. Brady sighed a little in her sleep, her lovely lips curving upward. She clearly knew how to sleep in. CJ, on the other hand, was conditioned from farm and Army life to rise early. Pulling on a discarded robe, she slipped quietly from the bed. In the bathroom, she used the toilet, brushed her teeth and smoothed back her unruly hair as best she could. Then she returned to the bedroom and stood quietly, watching Brady sleep. God, she was a lucky, lucky woman. She leaned in and kissed Brady's forehead, remembering the morning in Cloudcroft when she'd wished for a train to spirit her away from Brady and her own newly realized, decidedly queer feelings. How much had changed in a month—it was almost shocking, in the best possible way.

In the living room, she called room service and ordered fresh fruit, waffles, juice and coffee. Then she sat on the loveseat, replaying the previous night in her mind as the sun rose over El Paso. With Sean, being intimate had almost always been his idea. She'd thought that was the way things worked, but after last night, she understood that her perception of herself as a supposed good girl was skewed, based on a thoroughly false set of pretenses. After last night, she knew she was no more a good girl than Brady was. Even now the memory of Brady's body beneath hers, their lips and fingers tracing fiery trails against each other's skin, made her heartbeat accelerate. She touched her tongue to suddenly dry lips. Hiding her feelings for Brady the person was one thing. But trying to hide her newly awakened passion for Brady's body? Honestly, she wasn't sure she was going to be able to accomplish such a feat.

The food arrived and the bellboy had barely left when CJ heard water running in the bathroom. Soon Brady emerged, robe-clad and sleepy, an almost tentative smile on her lips.

"I thought maybe you'd left," she said.

Apparently their weekend in Cloudcroft was on her mind too.

"Not a chance." Rising, she took Brady in her arms, thrilled by the fact that she could. "I didn't want to wake you."

"That was sweet." Brady hugged her tightly. "Good morning."

"Good morning." CJ rested her cheek against Brady's still-messy hair. "How did you sleep?"

"Amazingly. You?"

"The same."

Brady shifted, focusing on the dining table. "Ooh, coffee. And pineapple! I knew I brought you along for a reason."

"And here I thought it was for my conversational skills," CJ quipped.

Brady looked up at her through her lashes. "After last night, I'm pretty sure you know which skills of yours I particularly prize."

CJ felt her cheeks flame. Maybe her good-girl notion of self wasn't so far off, after all.

Over breakfast, they shared the complimentary newspaper the waiter had brought. Brady hadn't been reading the front page for long when she blanched.

"What is it?" CJ asked quickly, her mind going first to Nate. Then she caught herself. Brady and Nate were over, finished, kaput. He was no longer first in her mind. Or he shouldn't be.

"We bombed Berlin again. This article claims a third of Berlin is in ruins, with thirteen thousand dead and half a million homeless."

"That many?" She should be used to the numbers by now, but destruction on such a scale eluded comprehension.

At least the news that had upset Brady had nothing to do with their brothers. Or with Nate, for that matter. While CJ envied the ease with which he had assumed an accepted position in Brady's life and family, she didn't wish him harm. She pictured the children who must number among the German dead and homeless, of the widows and widowers, the families left childless or parentless. It didn't seem fair that she should be so happy this morning when hundreds of thousands of people on the far side of either ocean were mourning their dead, searching for food for their hungry children or otherwise trying to resist the machinery of a war that had swallowed them up in a maelstrom of destruction never previously conceived, let alone achieved.

Brady caught her hand. "It's a nasty war, isn't it?"

CJ held her gaze across the glass-topped table. "It is."

"That's why I feel so lucky to have found you." Brady squeezed her hand, paused, smiled again. "I love you, you know."

CJ stared at her. There she went, surprising her once again. "I love you too," she said, smiling back.

"You'd better." Brady leaned forward to kiss her.

She loves me! CJ closed her eyes against the morning sunlight. Lucky, indeed.

As the kiss began to deepen, a familiar pounding sounded at the door.

Brady drew back, her brow lowered. "Your friends are in serious trouble." Before CJ could respond, Brady stalked to the door and threw it open. "This had better be good."

Reggie recoiled a step. "Uh, sorry to interrupt," she said, looking away from Brady's barely cinched robe. "The others wanted me to, you know, um, find out what you two are, well, up to?"

CJ bit her lip, trying not to laugh at the sight of the normally verbose Reggie struggling to find words. Clearly, she had drawn the short stick on this one.

"What's wrong with the telephone?" Brady demanded, tugging the flaps of her robe together.

"I see now that the telephone would have been a much better idea," Reggie agreed, glancing over her shoulder back down the hall. "Anyway, we're going for a walk around town if you want to join us."

"We have plans," CJ called from the table, waving briefly at her squad mate.

"Great. Fantastic. If you change your mind, we're having lunch at Paso del Norte. See ya."

And with that, she retreated down the hall as if she were under enemy fire. CJ couldn't blame her. Brady had been angry with her a couple of times, and it had scared the bejesus out of her too.

"Now, where were we?" Brady said, smoothing her hair back and offering CJ a patrician smile.

As she neared the table, CJ caught Brady's hand and tugged her onto her lap. "I believe we were here," she said, and began to kiss her again.

* * *

They stayed in that morning and made full use of the suite, reading the newspaper cover to cover, completing the crossword puzzle while lounging on the loveseat and, later, enjoying another long hot soapy bath that necessitated a sojourn to the bedroom and additional, separate baths afterward. But the hotel's official checkout time was noon, and eventually they decided that their weekend of decadence should probably come to a graceful end, one that didn't involve the staff forcibly removing them from the suite.

A little past noon, they reluctantly buttoned each other back into their "A" uniforms and bade farewell to the suite.

"We'll be back, won't we?" Brady asked, pulling the door shut behind them.

"Of course we will," CJ said as they walked arm in arm to the elevator.

In fact, she wasn't certain they would be back. They had both put in for overseas duty before they met. What if the Army in its bureaucratic ineptitude sent one of them to the Pacific and the other to the ETO? What if Brady got promoted to write for *Yank* magazine? What if CJ's squadron got transferred to another post on the home front? They could both be sent anywhere the Army wished, anytime it chose. They were no longer free citizens of the United States. For now, they belonged to Uncle Sam, a short-sighted sort of relation who was far more concerned about himself than about their health or happiness.

Fifteen minutes later they walked into the stunning lobby of the Paso del Norte Hotel, crowned by a massive stained-glass dome custom-designed by Tiffany's when the hotel was built thirty years earlier. Across the way, Toby and Reggie waved at them. Smiling back, CJ approached the long table where their friends sat. She and Brady were an official couple finally, and here were practically the only people in the world who would be truly happy for them.

"I guess we don't have to ask how your night went," Toby said, smiling up at them.

Brady and CJ exchanged a glance as they sat down. For once, CJ didn't bother to hide her feelings. "Let's just say the suite more than lived up to expectation."

"I'll say," Brady said, gazing back almost as adoringly.

"This calls for a toast," Toby declared.

"Hear, hear," Reggie added, grinning.

A waiter was summoned, and soon everyone at the table was lifting crystal glasses of champagne.

"To our friends CJ and Brady," Kate said, gazing at them. "May you be good to each other always."

"To CJ and Brady," the chorus rang out.

CJ focused on Jack, who was smiling almost as broadly as the rest of the group. He nodded at her, and she nodded back. Then she glanced at Brady, smiled into her eyes and drank her champagne. Life was good, right here, right now. That was all anyone could ask.

"So what did you all get up to last night?" Brady enquired, shifting the focus.

Sarah told them that Toby and Kate had invited everyone back to their room after dinner for an evening of tequila and dancing. An El Paso radio station had broadcast a live show from the Palomar Hotel in Los Angeles with featured entertainers the Harry James Band and vocalist Frank Sinatra.

Brady leaned in and murmured, "Maybe we should have joined them after all."

"Are you kidding?"

"Yes. I am definitely kidding."

After lunch, the group headed out to walk around El Paso again. One of Toby and Reggie's favorite pastimes was to salute male officers who were walking with their girlfriends. Inevitably the officer would scowl at them as he was forced to remove his arm from around his companion to return the gesture, and the Wacs would walk on, snickering. Usually CJ considered this game juvenile, but today she understood the motivation behind it. Even if they hadn't been Wacs, there was no sidewalk in America where she and Brady could stroll with their arms around each other, pausing to kiss whenever they felt like it. Inconveniencing those who didn't even know how good they had it might be juvenile, but it was also immensely satisfying.

As they walked around El Paso checking out department store Christmas displays, CJ found herself looking at more than only male officers differently. Before the war, most American women didn't wear pants outside the comfort of their own home. But women now filled all sorts of positions traditionally denied them, which meant more were wearing pants in public. She gazed with new appreciation at female store clerks, taxi drivers, train operators, even construction workers. Before Brady, she hadn't spent much time thinking about women she didn't already know. Now she noticed which ones wore their pants suits well, which ones were particularly attractive, which ones returned her appraisal boldly. *This* is *fun*, she thought, grinning over at Toby as they passed a woman hotel valet who winked at them.

Then Brady elbowed her, and she started guiltily.

"Don't tell me you're a wolf in sheep's clothing," Brady said into her ear.

The feel of Brady's breath on her skin gave her shivers. "I'm no wolf."

The hours slipped away as the group split up to pursue competing interests. CJ and Brady bought postcards and Christmas gifts to send home, and then stopped at a bookstore and lost themselves in the stacks. Every once in a while one would find the other to compare notes, but otherwise they wandered the aisles separately.

Normally CJ preferred nonfiction. Today, however, she found herself browsing the fiction section. She stopped at a placard marked "W," scanning the shelves more carefully. There it was: Virginia Woolf's *Orlando*. The novel was an avowed favorite of Marjorie Quinlan, a history professor at Michigan who specialized in nineteenth century abolitionist and women's rights literature. Everyone at Michigan knew that Marjorie lived with Helen Brooks, an instructor in the chemistry department. They didn't broadcast their relationship, but they didn't hide it either.

"Whatcha reading?" Brady asked, looking over her shoulder.

CJ held up the book.

"Interesting. I haven't read much Woolf."

"She's not exactly a Romantic," CJ pointed out.

"No, but she does have certain other redeeming qualities."

"Did you find anything good?"

Almost sheepishly, Brady showed her Gertrude Stein's *The Autobiography of Alice B. Toklas*.

CJ laughed. "Looks like we had the same idea."

"When in doubt, read a book."

Her smile slipped a little. "Do you have doubts?"

"No, it's just an expression." Brady rested her chin on CJ's shoulder momentarily. "Why, do you?"

"Of course not."

Still, she glanced around to see if anyone else had noticed Brady practically embracing her in public. Nearby, at the end of the aisle, a store employee was building a "New Releases" display. She caught CJ's eye and smiled a little, the telltale look in her eyes. Lucky again.

A little while later, the same employee rang up their purchases. She looked at their selections, commented on their uniforms—"Fort Bliss, then?"—and, right before they left, reached under the counter for a book.

"You might be interested in this title," she said. "This is the British edition, but it's about to be released in the States under the title *The Middle Mist*."

CJ held the book while Brady read over her shoulder: *The Friendly Young Ladies* by Mary Renault. They read the inside jacket copy and exchanged a look. Then CJ handed the book back.

"When does it come out?"

"In the spring. If you call the store in March, we can set aside a copy for you."

"Thanks." Brady smiled at the woman. "We'll be in touch."

Then she caught CJ's hand in hers and tugged her toward the door. Outside in the Texas sun they released each other and started along the sidewalk, shoulders brushing with each step.

"Do you think she was…?" Brady asked.

"Um, yes! She couldn't take her eyes off you."

"Nuh uh. She was watching you."

"Nuh uh," CJ echoed, laughing as she bumped Brady's hip with her own.

Suddenly Brady sighed.

"What?"

"I wish I could kiss you, right here in front of the whole world."

"I know. Me too." But her stomach roiled at the thought.

Up ahead, a pair of MPs stalked toward them along the El Paso sidewalk, sunlight shining off their distinctive white helmets, their black arm bands unmistakable. If they were to catch her and Brady making out, would they arrest them and haul them back to base? It probably wouldn't help their case to be caught carrying literature written by known homosexuals.

"Anyway, nobody said life was fair," she said, quoting her father.

"I can't believe *you* would say such a thing. Doesn't that violate your vow of eternal optimism?"

"Optimism and realism are not inherently contradictory."

"Says who?"

"Says me."

They continued along the sidewalk, sparring lightly, bodies nearly touching. It wouldn't take a genius to work out what was between them. The girl in the bookstore had figured it out immediately. What hope did they have of hiding it from the people they worked and shared quarters with?

As the MPs neared, Brady put more distance between them. CJ knew why, but the knowledge didn't stop the disappointment that washed over her.

"Good afternoon, boys," Brady said, flashing them a flirtatious smile.

They touched their helmets and returned the smile. "Ladies."

Then they were past, and CJ found herself maintaining the distance purposely, even when Brady tried to drift closer again.

"What?" Brady asked.

"Nothing."

"It doesn't seem like nothing."

CJ hesitated. "You flirted with them."

Brady sighed. "CJ, you and I are in a banned relationship, are we not?"

"Yes."

"And the Articles of War are pretty clear about such relationships, right?"

CJ made a sound in her throat. "I understand *why* you smiled at them, but I don't have to like it, do I?"

Brady looped their arms together, tugging her closer again. "Of course not. In fact, I'm glad you don't."

CJ felt herself sliding into Brady's eyes, and she remembered the previous night when Brady had arced above her, face and skin lit by the flickering candle, the lights of El Paso far below them.

"Don't look at me like that," Brady murmured, her gaze dropping to CJ's lips. "Otherwise we'll be out of the Army long before the duration."

Would that be so bad? CJ looked away and continued along the El Paso sidewalk, her arms and legs swinging in step with Brady's. They still had a few hours before they had to be back on post, before they would have to say a chaste goodnight without any outward display of affection. That would be their life moving forward: sneaking around looking for places to be together, hoping they wouldn't be found out even as they almost wished they would. While life outside the military might not be easy for gay people, at least they could enjoy as much privacy as they wanted in their own homes. Besides, Toby had said there were places for people like them.

Brady stopped to look into a shop window, and CJ paused beside her, studying their reflection in the glass. What was she worrying about? Brady loved her. The rest of the world—their families, their school friends, the war even—were too far away to matter. What mattered was the woman at her side, smart and funny and sassy, and the amazing future that lay before them.

Turning, Brady held out her arm. "Shall we?"

CJ took it, and together they strolled along the El Paso sidewalk, blending their voices to the tune of "Begin the Beguine."

CHAPTER FOURTEEN

On Monday morning, CJ's crew reported en masse to the Balloon Hangar at the southwest edge of the airfield. Not too long ago she had been new to the Transient Hangar, but this transition would be different. Instead of a lonely replacement soldier, this time she was part of a crew that had long since proven itself to its previous squadron but was now starting over with a group of mostly male, somewhat skeptical officers, ground crews and flight crews.

The Sixth Squadron's commanding officer, Major Zachary Pederson, welcomed them with a neutral nod and passed them off to their new crew chief, Master Sergeant Harold Whimple, a dough-faced boy with a pleasant smile and receding hairline. Whimple gave them their assignment—Flight C—and introduced them to the other members of the squadron, the aforementioned dubious males. Once they had checked out tools from the tool shop, Whimple showed them their equipment lockers and gave them an extended tour of the area, including the two low wooden buildings that bordered the hangar.

"This," he said, pausing before a door marked PILOTS ONLY, "is Flight C's ready room. Your pilots report every morning at eight o'clock, Monday through Saturday, which means you do too."

CJ and Toby exchanged a look. With drill, PT, mess and the long hike to the airfield to contend with, they were going to be sorely challenged to reach the Balloon Hangar on time each morning.

"I know what you're thinking, and I've already requested a couple of drivers from Transport for you," Whimple added.

"Thank you, sir," Jill said, speaking for them all. "That's really generous."

"Don't thank me yet. You'll be working longer hours once the existing crews rotate out for overseas duty. Sometimes you'll even be expected to go out on antiaircraft maneuvers and RON in the desert. Any problem for any of you on that front?"

They shook their heads quickly, exchanging grins. Antiaircraft artillery maneuvers that required them to remain overnight—RON— in the desert would make them the envy of the rest of Maintenance. Except Transport, maybe. Drivers and mechanics already had a pretty nice deal going, particularly when it came to off-post duty.

"Good," Whimple said. "Then let's meet your pilots."

His crisp knock was answered by a tall, willowy redhead in shirt and tie but no cap. Or, currently, shoes. In fact, there were cotton balls stuffed between her brightly painted toenails.

"Come right in, Whimpy," she drawled. "And who do we have here?"

Though they dressed in Air Corps officer uniforms, complete with insignia and wings, the WASPs weren't regular military. Technically they were civilian personnel attached to the Army; salutes weren't required. Still, there was something about the redhead that commanded attention, other than the faint blush her words had evoked in the crew chief.

"These are the new members of your engineering crew," Whimple said as he brushed past her uninvited, waving the Wacs into the room.

Reggie went first, smiling assuredly at the handful of female pilots arrayed about the ready room. CJ followed, noting the women as well as their surroundings. The room had a curved ceiling and was decorated with desks, tables and chairs along with a couch. Two armchairs in a corner were currently occupied by a pair of WASPs with rapidly clacking knitting needles. A bookshelf lined with books whose covers depicted a wide range of aircraft sat near one armchair, as if encouraging casual reading, while the arced walls sported maps of the Southwest, pictures of military planes and instructive posters on formation flying: the Sneak Attack, the Scissors Movement and the Sisters Act, among others.

At one of the tables, three WASPs were busy with a card game. Two of the three folded their cards and rose with friendly smiles to greet them. The third, a blonde with a swept-back do and a diamond ring on one of her pinkies, eyed them over the fan of her cards before reluctantly laying her hand face-down. Then a yapping sounded, and the blonde reached under the table.

"Shush, Spicket," she said, pulling a fluffy-haired Pomeranian onto her lap. "They're friends."

"Spicket is our mascot," the redhead told the staring GIs. "Being civilian has its perks."

Soon the room was filled with the murmur of women getting to know one another. CJ found herself talking to a petite brunette pilot with a freckled nose and an affable smile.

"Nell Charles," the pilot said, holding out a hand.

CJ shook it. "Caroline Jamieson."

"Everyone calls her CJ," Sarah put in, also shaking the WASP's hand.

"Well, everyone calls me Chippy," Nell confided, shrugging her shoulders as if to say, *What can you do?*

Nell, they learned, hailed from Lincoln, Nebraska, where she had gone to college and worked for a few years as a high school music teacher before the war. She listened to Sarah and CJ's back stories, smiling easily, before turning to meet the others on the crew. Sarah and CJ moved on to Pinkie, the redhead, a former corporate pilot for the Coca-Cola Company. With more than a thousand flight hours to her name along with both civilian pilot and instructor ratings, Pinkie had been selected as commander of Flight C. As such, she said, she was particularly curious to know their backgrounds. The other pilots were slightly less forthcoming but similarly inquisitive, their questions centering mainly on the mechanics' training and preparation. CJ couldn't help wondering if the WASPs had subjected the male engineering crews in the Sixth to such a vigorous interrogation.

After a while, Whimple raised his voice above the din. "Hate to say it, ladies, but the tour must go on."

Pinkie, Nell and Holly, another brunette card player, and Jo and Shirley, the knitting duo, bade them friendly farewells, but Em, the blonde with the dog, merely nodded as the engineering crew filed out of the ready room.

The Wacs talked among themselves as they followed Whimpy—*Master Sergeant Whimple*, CJ corrected herself mentally—out to the flight line for a tour of the squadron aircraft. Consensus was that Nell and Holly were the standouts when it came to friendliness, while Miss Emily Gardner Thompson, a Grosse Pointe debutante and recent Vassar graduate, stood out for her unsociable attitude.

"She's a Seven Sisters girl, don'tcha know," Jill said, rolling her eyes. Then she glanced quickly at CJ. "Sorry. I mean, they're not all bad, are they?"

CJ frowned. Did the entire battalion know about her and Brady? Then she pictured Brady in the hotel room—*their* hotel room—and her frown faded. She couldn't quite believe that the weekend had happened. All through PT this morning she had stared at Brady's lithe form engaged in physical activity and remembered their own rather strenuous activities Saturday night. Not to mention Sunday morning…

Toby elbowed her, and she returned suddenly to the Balloon Hangar flight line, to the mid-morning sun angling across the desert like a beacon. God, it was barren here. Sometimes the lack of anything growing still startled her.

"Did you hear them say they're in bachelor officer quarters?" Reggie said. "Must be nice to have your own room."

"Makes sense, though. If Congress ever gets around to making them Regular Army, they'll be second looeys, minimum," Toby pointed out.

"I'd bet next month's pay Pinkie rates a gold leaf," Reggie said, referring to a major's insignia.

Even Whimple agreed with this assertion. "Every time I look at her my hand itches."

The Wacs could sympathize. The importance of saluting a superior had been drilled into their heads during basic training. CJ had actually saluted a Pepsi-Cola truck driver at Fort Des Moines, much to the driver's amusement and her own mortification.

"There are more WASPs in the squadron, aren't there?" Sarah asked as they headed back outside.

"Six more," Whimple told them. "Three are out on missions right now, one is checking out on a new ship and the other two are right over there." He pointed to where a pair of women in AAF shirtsleeves sat on lawn chairs near the external entrance to Flight C's ready room, faces lifted to the sun. "You'll meet them in good time. Now, who wants to see some birds?"

As they approached the Sixth's flight line, CJ couldn't help but smile. Whimple was a good man, and so far he seemed to be treating them like male soldiers—except for an utter avoidance of profanity. *Give him a few days*, she thought, stopping in front of the first plane they came to, an A-24 Navy Dauntless diver. It was a beauty, though its tri-color paint had seen better days. Beside it, an A-25 Helldiver (christened "the Beast" by Navy pilots for its poor handling qualities) rested, nearly as beat up and even more impressive. Both were single engine, which CJ found to be a slight disappointment after all her training on twin and quad engine aircraft. But they were lovely ships, so she pushed her disappointment away and listened as Whimple described the types of missions the squadron's planes were used for.

Divers like these were employed to simulate strafing, diving to buzz gun positions and troops on maneuvers in the nearby desert; on tracking missions, allowing antiaircraft gunnery crews to train with moving targets; on low-altitude night missions, dropping flares on troops and gun emplacements; and to lay smoke screens. Medium bombers towed targets, while Beechcraft trainers were primarily used to train ground-based radar operators and to provide practice for antiaircraft searchlight crews.

The next aircraft on the line was a B-26 Marauder, a twin-engine bomber known in the flying community as "the Widowmaker" for its tendency to crash during takeoff and landings. The boys in the Sixth didn't like to fly this ship much, Whimple admitted, but several of the new WASPs had expressed a desire to check out on her as soon as possible.

"Any Thunderbolts?" Toby asked.

"A speed jockey, hmm? No, the Navy divers are it for fighters. For now, anyway. If Pinkie has her way, we'll soon have Thunderbolts, Cobras and a heavy bomber or two at our disposal."

The WASPs had a reputation as overachievers among the Air Corps, always eager to get their hands on new aircraft. Part of it, CJ suspected, was that this was the first time American women had been allowed to fly military aircraft, and they knew this opportunity wouldn't be extended forever. Just as women factory workers were likely to be sent back to hearth and home as soon as their wartime services were no longer required, female pilots could expect to be cut from the military as soon as the war ended, possibly sooner. Even the WAC wasn't authorized to exist for more than six months after the war's official end, whenever that came.

They didn't get their hands dirty that morning. Instead, they read tech orders and manuals on the ships they hadn't encountered previously—the Beechcraft trainers, especially the AT-7 and -11, and the C-45. Many ferry pilots who stopped at the Transient Hangar for fuel and RONs were piloting combat-ready bombers and fighters.

When Toby asked if the hangar was always this quiet, Whimple explained that there was a surplus of personnel in the Sixth currently, both flight and engineering crews, but that male pilots and mechanics alike would soon be rotating out of Biggs.

The Wacs were quiet for a moment. Then Toby voiced the concern they all shared: "To combat duty?"

"Some of them, yes."

"Because of our arrival?" Jill asked.

"Yours and the WASPs," Whimple said. "That's the intent of the women's services, isn't it? To release a male counterpart for combat? It's what you all signed up for."

True. But CJ had never had to directly face a man whose home-front position she was taking.

That wasn't the only difference between their previous assignment and this one. At the Transient Hangar they had rarely seen the same airplane twice. Now they would be working on planes used day after day to dive-bomb Fort Bliss troops, American boys like Jack and Sam whose most fervent wish was to survive training and get through whatever lay beyond it. This responsibility seemed more awesome— and more immediate. If their crew failed to successfully repair a ferry plane, chances were slim they'd ever know. But if they made a mistake on one of these beauties, the pilots on their flight crew might be injured. Or worse. She hadn't realized until advanced training how common casualties were in the Army in general and in the Army Air Forces in particular. The WASPs were putting their lives in the Wacs' hands, for better or worse. No wonder they wanted to be sure of their training.

"It's not at all what I thought it would be like," CJ told Brady that evening as they lay out on the softball field, hidden in the shadows. Her head was pillowed on Brady's stomach, and she could feel Brady toying gently with her hair as they watched the constellations slowly shift overhead.

"What do you mean?"

"I don't know. I thought I would be more useful."

"At least your contribution is tangible. When you work on an engine, there's a visible outcome, something that can be quantified."

"Your articles seem quantifiable to me."

Brady made a sound of frustration. "But we're so limited in what we're allowed to write. It's not real, what we do. It's not much better than propaganda."

"Do you honestly think so?" CJ asked, rolling onto her side. She could barely make out Brady's features in the darkness of the outfield.

"I don't know. Maybe. We're supposed to protect morale, to report on positive outcomes, but it's a war. Do you know how many troops we lost at Tarawa? Do you know how many casualties a day there are right now in Campania?"

CJ shivered at the mention of Tarawa. Joe's division had been involved in the attack, and she hadn't received a letter from him in weeks. Not that there was any connection. She often went weeks without hearing anything from her brothers. But still.

"I don't want to know," she said. "Neither do you, and neither do the boys here. It's better if they don't know the reality they're about to face, isn't it?"

"Probably." Brady sighed. "No, you're right. I wouldn't want them to worry more than they already do. I'm just tired."

"The *Monitor* comes out tomorrow, doesn't it?"

"You know me well."

She knew her schedule anyway—she'd had to wait extra interminable hours to see her after Brady stayed late at work and grabbed dinner on base with her coworkers, as she often did on Monday nights.

They were both quiet, and then CJ leaned forward and kissed Brady's cheek. "I guess ignorance really is bliss."

"Very funny," Brady said, and turned her head so that CJ's next kiss landed squarely on her lips.

But the darkened field wasn't entirely private, and bed check was fast approaching. After a little while, they separated reluctantly, straightened their uniforms and walked home through the brightly lit compound.

"This is not how I want to say goodnight," CJ said as they reached Brady's barracks.

"I don't want to say goodnight at all," Brady replied, looking at her with such naked longing that CJ could barely resist touching her.

"Don't look at me like that."

"Like what?"

"Like you wish we were back at the Hilton."

"I *do* wish we were back at the Hilton."

Gazing into Brady's eyes, CJ felt a physical sensation of falling. Then a door slammed nearby, snapping her out of it. They were no longer avoiding each other, but the Romeo and Juliet effect still applied, clearly.

"When can you get another weekend pass?" Brady asked.

"I don't know. I can ask Kate to work her magic. You?"

"I'll call in a favor if I have to."

They lingered a little longer, torturing themselves and each other, until a group of Company A Wacs approached, laughing and talking.

CJ backed away. "See you tomorrow?"

"You better."

As she retreated, CJ passed the Admin Wacs. Janice was there at the center of the group, and automatically CJ started to look away. But then Janice did something unexpected: She nodded at CJ, not overtly friendly but also not the least bit hostile. CJ nearly tripped. Then she nodded back and continued on her way.

She remembered Brady's assertion that Janice wasn't bad, once you got to know her. Was it possible Brady had been right?

* * *

That week, when she should have been paying attention to her new assignment and her new crew chief and her new responsibilities, CJ was distracted. She kept thinking about Brady—her slightly crooked smile, the soft hair at her nape, the way she chewed on her pinkie finger when she was worried about something. She kept remembering the feel of Brady's skin against hers, like silk; the soft sounds she made when their naked skin touched; the sight of her in the tub in their hotel room, freckled cheeks flushed, eyes closed, mouth turned up in pleasure.

It was downright disconcerting to be in the middle of wrenching out a bolt when all of a sudden her mind was hijacked by a remembered sight or scent. And then she would feel her own cheeks flame and hope against hope that no one else in the vicinity had mind-reading capabilities.

On Thursday at supper, Kate slid in next to her. "You owe me, my friend."

CJ set her fork down. "No. Truly?"

Kate nodded, and CJ threw her arms around the smaller woman, nearly crushing her.

"Thank you, thank you, thank you!"

"Is there a reason you're manhandling PFC Delaney?" Toby asked, bumping CJ's mess tray with her own as she slid onto the wooden bench.

CJ released Kate and beamed at Toby. "She's a genius."

"I know." Toby sipped her coffee. "How did she demonstrate her intellectual prowess this time?"

Kate shook her head at Toby, eyes crinkling at the corners.

"She arranged passes for Brady and me."

Reggie leaned into the conversation. "You know, there are so many comments I could make, CJ, I'm not even sure where to begin."

Sarah elbowed her. "Then don't."

For the hundredth time that week, CJ felt the blood rush to her face. Now all her friends were thinking about her and Brady, perhaps picturing them back in the suite on the fifteenth floor—naked.

Well, it wasn't like they wouldn't be soon.

CJ lifted her chin. "You're jealous," she said to Reggie, smiling to take the sting out.

It was Reggie's turn to redden, and immediately the attention shifted from CJ to her buddy, who had been spending a noticeably significant chunk of time at the Balloon Hangar in the general vicinity of one of the new WASP pilots, a Miss Josephine "Holly" Hollingsworth.

"There is nothing lovers love more than love," her Shakespeare professor had liked to say. Finally, CJ understood what she'd meant.

* * *

"Is Holly even gay?" Brady asked.

It was Sunday morning and they were lying at opposite ends of the couch in "their" suite. They had checked into the room in the middle of the previous afternoon and spent the rest of the day ravishing each other, eating supper naked in bed, having their way with one another again, taking not one but two baths (one last night, one this morning after sleeping late) and dining in for breakfast. Now, mid-morning, they were engaged in divvying up the newspaper as well as the last of the breakfast fruit.

"Holly? Absolutely." CJ popped an apple slice in her mouth.

"How do you know?"

"Because she went to a women's college."

"Hey, now," Brady said, tickling the bottom of her feet.

"Kidding. She mentioned a 'friend' she lived with in New York after college, who she fell out with right before she joined the WASPs. It was pretty obvious."

"It sounds pretty unobvious to me."

"If you saw her, you'd probably change your tune."

Holly was one of those rare women who didn't care what anyone else thought. She wore her blonde hair clipped short and said she wouldn't be caught dead in a skirt. Still, her face was angelic, her smile sweet. Reggie had been smitten instantly.

"I don't think she's the 'Josephine' I interviewed for the *Monitor*," Brady said. "Did you know there are two in their company?"

"Two Kayes too."

"Which one is the Vassar girl?"

"Em, from Grosse Pointe. Nell says when they were in training at Sweetwater, Miss Gardner Thompson didn't care to march in step. Their squadron commander was always in trouble because of it."

"I know the type."

"I'll bet you do."

"What's that supposed to mean?"

"Nothing," CJ said, smirking.

"Admin Wacs drill better than the rest of you lot. There's a reason Company A wins the blue ribbon every month."

"There is. I believe it's called brown-nosing."

"Hey! Take that back," Brady said, tickling her again.

CJ giggled and squirmed away.

Gossip and company insults momentarily exhausted, they returned to the newspaper. Brady, in possession of the front page, read aloud from a report on the recently completed meeting in Tehran between Roosevelt, Churchill and Stalin. The main goal of the conference, according to the article, was to agree on the best way to hasten Germany's defeat and reduce her military might for the future safety of Europe. However, the leaders were delaying official word on the conference's outcome due to a massive surge of German counter-propaganda.

"Do you think they agreed on a second front?" CJ asked.

"That would be my bet."

"France?"

Brady nodded, and they looked at each other across the length of the loveseat. A landing in France would require an almost unimaginable quantity of troops—American troops, specifically. The British had taken the brunt of the North African campaign. How many lives would it cost to crack the Nazi stranglehold on Northern Europe?

"When?"

Shrugging, Brady looked away, gazing out over the browns and reds of El Paso and the surrounding area. "Six months? No more than a year, I'd say."

A year—and where would they be then, either of them? The war might be over in a year. Or the Germans might rebuff the Allied attack, and yet another new, bitter phase of this global conflict would begin. There were rumors that the Germans were working on a "super" weapon that could wipe out an entire city. CJ had heard another rumor that a company of Wacs was helping on a super-secret American version of the same project.

In reality, what was the difference between killing forty thousand civilians over several months, as the Germans had done during the Blitz; in a week, as the Allies had done in Hamburg back in July; or in a single night with a super-bomb? What about the hundreds of thousands of Soviet men, women and children who had died in the Nazi siege of Leningrad, still going on at this very moment after more than two years of bombardment? Civilian casualties were civilian casualties; the numbers were dizzying, unimaginable, unreal when contemplated from the untouched interior of North America.

More subdued now, they turned back to the newspaper: 1,500 tons of bombs had been dropped on Berlin; the Eighth Army had driven six miles up the Italian coast toward San Vito; and November's war plane production had set a record with an average of one airplane completed every five minutes.

"Every five minutes?" CJ did the math in her head. "That means twelve an hour, which is, what, two hundred forty plus forty-eight, so two hundred eighty-eight airplanes every single day last month."

Brady whistled.

"I know," CJ agreed. "That's a lot of planes."

"I was whistling at you. For a history major, you're surprisingly good at math."

CJ attacked the nearest foot, tickling Brady until she begged for mercy. Then she kissed Brady until she begged for other things, and that was an even better use of their limited time alone together.

The weekend went too quickly, as it was always going to do, and soon it was time to pack up and leave the suite. Downstairs, CJ waited near the hotel bar while Brady settled the bill. The amount was equivalent to a week and a half's pay at their grade, but Brady handed over a check as if the amount were of little interest.

"How are you paying for this?" CJ asked as they walked across the lobby, headed for the outside world. "We've spent nearly a month's pay in a week, and that doesn't include Cloudcroft."

"I've been at Bliss longer than you," Brady said, dodging her eyes.

They emerged into daylight, and CJ stopped on the sidewalk. "But you're not using Army money, are you? That check was from your bank in L.A., and you're not the type to wire your pay home."

Brady pulled out a cigarette, still avoiding her eyes. "Want one?"

"No thanks."

She waited while Brady inhaled the smoke and released it in a handful of orderly rings. *Don't get distracted*, she told herself sternly, looking away from Brady's lips. Only a few hours before that mouth had been on her neck, her belly, her—well, it didn't bear remembering right now. Or at least she couldn't bear to remember it without wanting more, and more naked time with Brady was out of the question. In fact, she couldn't be sure when they would enjoy such time again. Damn it.

"I have a trust," Brady finally said.

"A trust?"

"From my grandparents. My brothers and cousins and I all have them. They were meant to pay for school, and whatever's left is ours to do with as we please."

"So what you please is decadent weekends in a Texas hotel with your illicit female lover? How nonconformist of you."

Brady put her head back and laughed in the way CJ loved—spontaneous and free, as if she didn't care who heard her. People on the street glanced their way, smiling indulgently, and CJ felt a surge of pride as they walked on, headed for their favorite bookshop. *She* had made Brady laugh like that. What was more, Brady loved *her* more than anyone else in the world, the same way she loved Brady—madly, desperately. Blissfully.

Thank God for the Army, and thank God for Texas.

Amazing how many things she'd never thought she'd say or do that she now found herself routinely doing and saying. This couldn't last; she knew even as she marched along the sunny El Paso street with Brady, their arms and legs swinging in unison almost by habit, that at some point the war would end and so would the Women's Army Corps, and they would be mustered out and sent home. This adventure, this temporary leave from reality could not continue indefinitely. She didn't even want it to, knowing the cost in lives and suffering the continuation of the war meant.

Still, they were here, now, together. And when Brady caught her arm and pulled her into a shop to look at jewelry—lockets to hold each other's photos, but not matching, of course, so as not to attract attention from their fellow soldiers or CO—she told herself to focus on the here and now. Because as any soldier knew, tomorrow couldn't be guaranteed, not when you were in the service of the good ole US of A.

CHAPTER FIFTEEN

A few days later, CJ was checking a faulty fuel line on the Helldiver when she heard a whistle. Pausing mid-twist of a wrench, she ducked out from under the airplane's nose to see Nell, the WASP from Nebraska, smiling at her.

"Hiya, mechanic." She was dressed in a khaki flight suit and leather bomber jacket with the WASP mascot—Fifinella, Disney's "good" little gremlin—on the front, AAF wings on one sleeve and the Sixth's insignia on the other. A parachute bag dangled from one hand.

"Hiya, flygirl," CJ said, returning the smile. "What can I do for you?"

"I'm scheduled to take up a couple of ack-ack boys to check the 197th's concealment this afternoon, but the throttle on the AT-11 has been sticking a little."

CJ wiped her greasy hands on the handkerchief she kept in one pocket of her coveralls. "Do you want me to take a quick look?"

"Actually, I was hoping you'd come along as my nonrated mechanic."

CJ stared at the petite pilot, who was now grinning even wider. "Is the throttle really sticking?"

"Officially, yes. Unofficially, I'd rather not be up there on my own with these fellows. Besides, I heard you were asking about hops."

CJ winced. "Whimpy wasn't supposed to rat me out."

"How else would we know you weren't just another groundhog?"

Penguins, dodos, groundhogs—why were the nicknames pilots had for their ground crew so unflattering? Why couldn't they be gazelles or cheetahs or some other perfectly respectable animal that happened to lack functional wings?

"I would love to go," she said. "Let me square it with the boss."

"Already done. All you need is a parachute."

"Swell," CJ said. "Thanks, Chippy."

"You're more than welcome. See you out there in five," she said, nodding toward the runway where the Beechcraft trainer was already waiting.

Ten minutes later, CJ was buckled into the copilot seat in the Beechcraft's cockpit beside Nell, who was running through the tech orders over the radio with Major Pederson in the flight control tower. Two officers from the 197th Antiaircraft Artillery Battalion were also aboard, squeezed together into the bombardier's compartment in the aircraft's nose. The nose boasted walls of reinforced glass that afforded its occupants unrestricted views of the landscape over which the plane cruised. From where she sat in the copilot's seat, two steps above the bombardier's compartment, CJ had almost the same unrestricted view.

She gazed at the cockpit controls, easily identifying most of the instruments. While she spent most of her time mucking around the guts of assorted aircraft, she had read her fair share of tech orders. She had also taken a turn during advanced training in the much-maligned Link Trainer, an indoor flight simulator the Army Air Corps used to train pilots to fly and navigate by instrument. The Chanute Field CO had believed that every mechanic should have a feel for the machines they were working on, and that meant two hours in the Blue Box. Out of her training company, CJ had earned the highest marks in the Link, a fact she had made sure to share with Alec, her Air Corps brother.

"Have you ever flown before?" Nell asked.

It took CJ a moment to realize that she was being addressed. "Once."

"Which ship?"

"AT-21 Gunner."

Nell whistled. "Beauty. What I wouldn't give to get my hands on her." And she winked at CJ.

CJ looked away. Nell, she suspected, was another member of the club. She had spoken of working as a teacher in Lincoln, where she shared a house with two female colleagues who had offered to take care of Louis, her German shepherd. Not once in the week CJ had known her had she mentioned a man other than her father or older brother, a crew chief on a B-25 in the Fifth Air Force. Besides, her best buddy was Holly, and CJ had learned that queer birds tended to flock together. Safety in numbers, Toby and Reggie claimed, but CJ had a feeling it had more to do with seeing yourself reflected favorably in others.

Preflight checks complete, Nell fired up the Beechcraft's twin engines and guided her down the runway away from the Balloon Hangar. When the control tower gave them the green light, she increased throttle, preparing for takeoff. CJ watched out the windshield as they taxied down the runway. She could feel wind buffeting the small plane. Picturing the burning bomber up on Mount Franklin, she wondered suddenly if she should be worried. Her squad mates had slapped her back when she came in for a parachute, but Brady didn't have any idea she was going up. If something happened, she wouldn't even know CJ had been on board. Who would tell her? Sarah? Kate? Their CO? She wouldn't be able to grieve, either, not the way a boyfriend or fiancé could.

Then they were lifting off, and CJ forgot to worry as the miracle of flight seized her—the pull of gravity as they rose into the sky, the shrinking of her everyday life below, the expanding of her horizons in every direction. To her left, past Nell's shoulder, Mt. Franklin loomed large and imposing. CJ glimpsed the blackened earth where the B-17's crew had met their deaths, but then Nell turned the wheel and guided the Beech toward the desert, where the 197th's Engineering Camouflage Unit had been out on extended field exercises for the past week. Jack had heard that these boys would be shipping overseas in the near future to help pave the way for a second European front, a rumor Brady would neither confirm nor deny. If the 197th did see combat, and it seemed likely they would, their lives would literally depend on their ability to conceal their guns and equipment from enemy aircraft intent on finding them.

Nell set a heading northeast of the airfield and leveled out at a thousand feet above the desert floor.

"We'll fly in a grid pattern," she said into her headset. "If anyone sees anything, call it out in hour hands."

The officers up front nodded and gave a thumbs-up. CJ added her eyes to theirs, but every so often her gaze strayed to the mountains east and west, the darker blue sky overhead, the distant sprawling dunes of White Sands and the snow-capped peaks of the Sacramento Mountains. When they turned and took a different tack, she pushed thoughts of sand dunes and cowboy hats from her mind. Forty-millimeter automatic cannons, fifty-caliber antiaircraft machine guns and ninety-millimeter tank guns—that was what the sandy-haired officer with the Errol Flynn moustache had said they were looking for.

Shortly after they passed Condron Field, a Biggs outpost ten miles east of the Organ Mountains, Nell spotted the first telltale sign.

"Reflection at four o'clock," she said calmly, dipping the nose in that direction.

CJ looked hard, and there it was again: a single flash of light as the sun shone off something metallic in the seemingly empty desert below. Now it was like a puzzle coming clear—once she knew where to look, her brain assembled the rest of the pieces. She blinked, and her eye discerned netting, guns, even the short shadows of soldiers.

One of the officers cursed matter-of-factly, and the other asked Nell for their heading and altitude. She recited it and smiled over at CJ as the two officers discussed the engineering unit's defenses in more detail.

"The good thing is," Nell told her, "they could have taken us out by now. If we were an actual threat, that is."

CJ pictured the enormous guns on the ground with their gaping mouths trained on their small aircraft. Once again, she could secretly appreciate the values that kept her from having to choose between a graduate deferment and combat. If she were a man, would she be able to do the job required of her? Or would fear win out?

Lucky for her, she would probably never have to find out. Meanwhile the men in the AT-11's nose and the woman seated beside her too, for that matter, faced their fears routinely. For the officers, the worry probably had to do with losing trainees. That worry was even greater for the Air Corps. Rumor had it that more American flight crews had been killed so far in training than in combat. Far safer to be part of the regular armed forces—except that there was Tarawa and more battles like it in the near future, no doubt. She pictured Joe in his sports magazine pose with a bat over his shoulder, all-American smile gleaming, brown hair caught by the breeze. She couldn't imagine him crawling across a booby-trapped beach on an isolated atoll in the Pacific, covered in sweat, grime and the blood of his brothers in arms. She simply couldn't picture him there, not her sweet-tempered big brother who had taught her to ride, to throw a football, to repair a flat. He had never told her she couldn't do something because she was a girl. Alec, on the other hand, had routinely refused to have her on his team, be it basketball, baseball, football. As a result, CJ had usually beaten him. Alec may have been a decent athlete, but he was no match for Joe. Then again, who in their narrow childhood circle was?

The officers asked Nell to circle the area a couple of more times, and then they turned for home, the sun high in the navy blue sky.

"Jamieson, do you have a driver's license?" Nell asked after she had pointed the aircraft in a straight line toward home.

"Yes."

"And are you a good driver?"

Suddenly it dawned on her where this line of questioning might be headed. "Yes," she repeated.

"Then why don't we see how you do with a different kind of wheel. Go ahead and grip it, lightly. The trick is to keep the altimeter at twelve hundred."

The AA officers had gone quiet and were gazing back at them now. CJ could almost hear their thoughts: *Not one woman driver, but two!*

Then the control column was in her hands, and she was moving it slightly, automatically adjusting to the air currents. It really was like driving, she realized, except that the road was made of air, not asphalt. Her Link training came back to her, and she relaxed into piloting the AT-11, her mind focused intently on the information her hands and arms were transmitting to her brain.

"Look at you," Nell said after a few minutes. "You're a natural, Jamieson."

CJ risked a glance away from the altimeter. "I am?"

"Seems I might not be able to get away with calling you a groundhog anymore."

"What a disappointment…" CJ bit back a gasp as a gust of wind threatened to wrest the steering column from her hands.

"It's okay. You don't fight it as much as you ride it out, like a bicycle going down a hill. Watch."

She took her own controls again, and once they were through the rough patch, they flew the plane together back to Biggs, each holding onto one of the steering yolks. Nell even let her turn the plane and line it up with the runway before assuming control for the landing.

CJ tried to play it cool as they taxied back to the Balloon Hangar, but she couldn't stop the grin from splitting her face. She, an Air Corps penguin, had flown an airplane! Wait until Brady found out.

"Nice job, Private," the sandy-haired AA officer said, while his swarthier companion nodded.

"Thank you, sirs," she replied cheerfully, following them from the cockpit.

Jill and Sarah were waiting on the tarmac as they disembarked.

"How was it?" Sarah asked.

"I flew!" CJ practically shrieked.

"She did," Nell confirmed, laughing.

"We knew that, dummy," Jill said, heading toward the Beechcraft. "Anything mechanical to report, Nell?"

"Nope. She did beautifully," the WASP said, gazing at CJ.

"I flew the plane," CJ clarified. "Nell let me take the controls on the way back."

At this, Sarah and Jill turned and gave the WASP an incredulous look.

"It's okay," she said, still looking amused. "I'm rated as an instructor. Most of us are. Besides, the Kansan is designed for training."

"Bombardiers, maybe," Jill said. "But pilots?"

CJ smacked her squad mate's shoulder none too gently. "You're just jealous."

"Damn right she is," Sarah agreed. "As will be the rest of the crew."

"Don't worry," Nell said. "I don't think we're in danger of winning the war anytime soon. There are plenty more hops where that one came from if you play your cards right."

And with that, she winked at CJ once more, slung both of their parachutes over her shoulder and strolled toward the Balloon Hangar, humming a tune CJ recognized as the Army Air Corps song:

Off we go into the wild blue yonder
Climbing high into the sun;
Here they come zooming to meet our thunder,
At 'em boys, give 'er the gun! Give 'er the gun!

* * *

CJ looked for Brady at dinner that night, but she didn't see her. She lingered at the mess hall even after her own friends had gone, half-concentrating on an old copy of *Yank* someone had left behind, but Brady and her Admin buddies never showed. Finally CJ headed back to her barracks to write letters and wait. Bed check arrived before Brady did, and CJ lay in her cot with doubt nibbling at her mind. Was Brady angry with her? Was she okay? Could the honeymoon be over that quickly?

To distract herself, she replayed the afternoon flight in her mind, feeling the steering column jumping beneath her touch, the responsiveness of the AT-11 when she turned the yolk, simultaneously pulling the elevator up to maintain altitude throughout the turn. Nell had said she was a natural, and CJ believed her, even if the pilot was a bit flirty. But CJ had felt comfortable at the plane's controls. Perhaps she should think about going for her pilot's license. Flight technology was sprinting ahead, spurred by ever-increasing demands of the air war. No doubt the industry would continue to surge even after the war ended.

She stared up at the barracks ceiling, chewing the inside of her cheek. Would she be a historian or pilot after the war? A wife or an illicit lover? The choices facing her were interesting, anyway.

At PT the next morning, she caught Brady watching her. Relief flooded her as Brady waved, smiling, and she waved back. Brady wasn't angry with her, apparently. *Whew.*

"Where were you last night?" she asked at breakfast. She and Brady were seated alone at a table far from the mess line that wound outside and down the rickety wooden steps.

"El Paso. Geraldine Hunt is engaged, and she wanted us all to meet her fiancé, who's in town on furlough before he ships out."

CJ's stomach dropped a little. Brady hadn't thought to bring her along to socialize with her work friends. But of course she hadn't. How could she? Still, it didn't seem fair. Brady went out with her and the D-lites regularly, but ever since they'd started seeing each other, she'd stopped inviting CJ along on Company A adventures. What did it mean that they could be themselves with CJ's friends but not with Brady's? Then again, it had been that way right from the start. No reason to think that being in love would change anything.

Squaring her shoulders, she looked Brady in the eye. "Are you ashamed of me?"

"What? No, of course not." Brady stared at her. "I thought we were past all of that."

"I did too."

"Is this because I didn't invite you along last night?"

CJ nodded.

Brady's expression softened. "I'm sorry. I would have, except we went straight from work. Besides, you would have been bored silly. Trust me."

Trust me.

That was the problem, CJ thought later as she rode to work with the rest of her squad in the back of a transport truck, the winter sun creeping above the eastern horizon. After their shaky start, she wasn't sure she trusted Brady entirely. Having to hide their relationship didn't help in the faith department either. But CJ wasn't hiding their relationship, not from her friends. Brady was the one pretending to the people who had known her best and longest in the Army that she was the same person they had always assumed her to be.

And what if she was? What if what they had together was merely a matter of comfort, of convenience? Except that being with another woman while serving in the US Army was neither comfortable nor convenient. No, Brady must love her. Otherwise, why would she risk so much?

Geraldine was lucky. CJ pictured the pretty redhead who worked in the PRO with Brady. She could show off her engagement ring secure in the knowledge that their friends, families, the world even supported their relationship. Maybe her parents wouldn't like her husband-to-be; maybe a sister or a friend would like him too much. But people of all nationalities were rooting for her, even if she didn't realize it.

* * *

The rest of the work week went quickly as CJ read tech orders (TOs), took apart unfamiliar engines and passed the time getting to know the members of Flight C. The pilots were averaging a run every second day, which meant they spent a lot of time reading TOs and waiting around for a chance to check out on a new airplane. CJ and her squad mates weren't nearly as busy here as they had been in the Transient Hangar. Whimpy kept saying that would change after the start of the new year, but for now, pilots and mechanics alike had more down time than they knew what to do with. Carol had found a stray kitten on base and started bringing the tiny creature daily to the hangar where anyone not on the assignment board would dutifully spend her time carrying the kitten around and making cat toys out of bits of string and cloth. Spicket was perhaps the only Balloon Hangar resident displeased with the new addition.

On Thursday, Reggie got her first chance at a hop with Holly during a tow target run. On this type of assignment, the squadron's specially equipped B-25 would tow a large, flat-panel cloth target behind it on a 2,500-foot steel cable, while the AA boys on the ground tried to hit the target with forty-millimeter shells. Holly invited Reggie along to serve as tow operator, the soldier who ran the crank that released the target cable.

"Heck yes!" Reggie squeaked. She cleared her throat. "I mean, sure, I'd be happy to."

She and Holly were in the air for much of the afternoon, flying straight lines back and forth above the artillery fields. When Reggie finally returned to the Balloon Hangar with her parachute bag in hand and a dreamy look fixed to her face, Toby elbowed CJ.

"Do you think the smile is for the B-25 or its pilot?"

"I was wondering the same thing."

With Geraldine's boyfriend in town for such a short time, Brady was AWOL from CJ's life that week. The PRO Wacs and their GI colleagues were in El Paso or at the men's enlisted club every night, and though Brady had invited CJ along, she hadn't taken her up on the invitation. Spending time with people who looked down their noses at her didn't appeal, not when she could go to the movies or out for drinks and pool with her own buddies. She tried to tell herself that the situation didn't mean anything, but she missed Brady. How was it that they saw each other less now that they were a couple?

Meanwhile, Nell had pulled night duty, so CJ also hadn't seen her much. Antiaircraft ground troops at Bliss were being trained to use massive searchlights to locate airplanes at night. Pilots who were instrument-rated, like Nell, would fly back and forth in the dark while the troops scanned the skies. AA officers also liked to use searchlights for tow target practice at night. It was dull to fly these missions, Holly reported, but at least the lights kept them wide awake. Once the searchlight caught her, a pilot was unable to see the horizon or anything else outside the aircraft, which was why she had to be instrument rated.

On Friday, when another dust storm grounded pilots and engineering crews alike, Holly invited Reggie and her "pals" into the WASP ready room to drink Cokes and play poker. At first, Em, the Vassar girl, looked askance at their presence. But after she learned that she and Toby had once lived on the same block in New York's Greenwich Village, she thawed a bit.

After three awful hands, CJ tossed down her cards. "I'm out." They were playing for pennies, and if she lost much more, she wouldn't be able to buy Brady's Christmas present—a waterproof, shockproof sports watch Brady had lingered over during their stroll through El Paso the previous weekend.

CJ pushed away from the table and paced the length of the room to where Jill and Carol, a pretty young Texas pilot, were playing with the kitten. Dropping to the floor beside them, she sat cross-legged and played with the cat while Jill and Carol chatted. Carol had recently arrived at Biggs from Avenger Field in Sweetwater, while Jill had gone through Chanute six months before CJ had. They were talking about men when CJ joined them.

"I ran into a couple of boys I knew from home," Carol was saying, "who are now P-63 pilots. I don't know what it is, but peashooter pilots are so much more fun than bomber pilots."

"Aren't they?" Jill agreed. "We're not allowed to date officers, you know, but there were a couple of ferry boys who came through Transient regularly with their Cobras, and, boy, was I tempted to break regulation for them!"

The two women giggled, and then Jill glanced at CJ and covered her mouth with her hand. CJ smiled at her and remained where she was through a discussion of a lieutenant in Flight B who had invited Carol out for a drink, but whose wife and children had shown up at the officers' club the very next day.

"I thought for sure he was a wolf," Jill said, shaking her head.

Spicket chose that moment to charge their little group, eager to inform Kitten that she had overstayed her welcome. CJ jumped up, the Pomeranian firmly in her grasp.

"Come on, buddy," she said to the dog. "Let's leave this corner to the feline members of the company."

Jill smiled almost apologetically at her, but CJ touched her shoulder as she turned away. She was glad that Jill, the youngest member of their crew, had found a friend among the newly arrived group of WASPs. Jill hadn't batted an eye when everyone teased Reggie about her sudden interest in flying. In fact, she and Sarah had joined in the razzing with gusto. Still, it couldn't be easy being outnumbered. Immediately her mind went to Brady. How could Brady prefer to spend time with her Company A friends? Unless she didn't feel outnumbered among the Admin Wacs. Maybe her infatuation with CJ was running its course, and she was even now setting her sights on a male GI.

Thoughts like that would drive her crazy. As her father always said, it was better to focus on what you could control than what you couldn't. Spicket securely tucked under her arm, CJ wandered over to one of the arced walls to study the formation posters, stroking the dog's soft fur absently. Formation flying spooked her. To move through the air at one hundred fifty miles per hour with another plane's wings mere feet from your own—she couldn't quite grasp what would be fun about it. Necessary, yes. In combat, formation flying helped pilots maintain visual contact with each other and offered bombers protection against smaller, quicker fighters. It also allowed heavier craft to conserve fuel on long missions. But enjoyable?

"Let me guess," a voice drawled at her elbow. "The boy-crazy talk was a bit much for you."

CJ glanced at Nell's face in profile. "A bit."

"They're young. They don't know any better."

Not like we do, her expression seemed to add. CJ knew from that look that her suspicions about Nell were correct: The WASP was indeed a member of the secret club. Although how secret their club was seemed to be arguable these days.

"I guess they don't." CJ patted Spicket as the dog butted her head expectantly against her forearm.

"She's taken quite the shine to you," Nell observed.

"Animals are easy. They don't ask much."

"No, they don't." Nell reached out to stroke the dog's silky ears. "Unlike people."

The pilot's eyes were narrowed, and CJ wondered if she detected a touch of wistfulness in her voice. Had she, like Reggie, sacrificed a relationship to contribute to the war effort?

The door to the ready room blew open suddenly, and Master Sergeant Whimple strode inside, slapping his hat against his leg.

"Goddamned dust," he exclaimed.

The gathered Wacs and WASPs paused, all eyes on the crew chief. CJ knew the female pilots had noticed it too: The sarge had cursed in front of them. Finally, he saw them as his crew instead of as a bunch of females.

"What?" he asked.

"Goddamned dust," Reggie echoed, and the rest of Flight C joined in with their own curses and laughter.

Beside her, Nell grinned, and CJ smiled back. It was good to belong. Rare, perhaps, but that only made it more extraordinary when it happened. In her arms, Spicket yipped, setting off a fresh round of laughter. Even the dog could recognize a breakthrough when she saw one.

* * *

That night, CJ was trouncing Toby at a game of pool when the EW club door opened and in walked Brady, brushing dust from her wool jacket. She looked around deliberately, her gaze stopping when it fell on CJ. She smiled slowly, and CJ felt her stomach tingle in the old way.

"What's that you say?" Toby asked. "You forfeit? Why, certainly, I accept."

"Funny." CJ handed her stick to Mary, who had called next game. "All yours, buddy."

They met in the doorway between the bar and billiards room. Brady paused before her, still smiling, and CJ barely stopped herself from pulling Brady into a tight hug.

"Hi," she said softly.

"Hi," Brady said, her tone matching.

"I thought you were going to El Paso again tonight?"

"I did. But I caught a cab back to the post."

"Why?"

"Because I missed you, and I realized we don't know how much time we have here, any of us."

CJ's eyebrows lifted slightly. Usually Brady, her sunny Californian, left the worrying to others.

"Not because the end of the world is upon us or anything," Brady added. "I mean we could be transferred at any time. Besides, while I'm happy for Gerri and Bob, I'm getting a little tired of hearing about their plans, to be honest."

"It's not fair, is it?"

"Not fair at all," Brady agreed. Her gaze dropped to CJ's lips. "I'd really like to kiss you right now."

"While I have no objection to that, unfortunately, Uncle Sam does."

"Let me worry about him," Brady said.

"Gladly."

They waved at their friends, and then they practically skipped out of the EW club. Brady led CJ through the dark winter night, between buildings, along narrow sidewalks, past bored MPs who somehow didn't seem to notice a couple of giggling Wacs slipping by in the night. This time, CJ knew exactly where they were headed. She had seen the Jeep parking lot during takeoff and landing from the AT-11 earlier in the week, and wouldn't be needing the stars to find her way back to the WAC compound. In the months since that first night in the Jeep lot beneath the unfamiliar West Texas sky, Bliss had begun to feel like home. What was more, so had Brady.

They climbed into the back seat of one of the Jeeps and snuggled up together, as close as their winter uniforms would allow. Brady leaned her head on CJ's shoulder, and CJ rested her cheek against Brady's hair.

"Much better," Brady said, sighing.

CJ tightened her grip in agreement. They didn't talk. They didn't need to. They simply sat close together while the searchlights split the sky overhead and the ack-ack guns sounded in the distance. CJ wondered briefly if Nell or Carol or one of the Kayes was up there flying grids in among the searchlights and exploding shells, and then Brady was turning her face toward hers, and for a while, CJ willingly gave herself over to the woman in her arms. Brady was right. None of them knew how much time they had here. For now, Brady's kiss, her touch, was enough. For now, being with Brady was all she could imagine she would ever need.

CHAPTER SIXTEEN

"I can't decide if seeing her from a distance makes it easier or harder," CJ said, pausing in sweeping up metal shavings from the hangar floor.

They did a cursory cleaning at the end of every shift, but Saturday mornings were reserved for once-weekly tasks like scrubbing the cement floor and polishing the Balloon Hangar's steel trusses.

Toby elbowed Reggie. "Young love. Aren't they sweet?"

Reggie snorted. "A regular Bonnie and Clyde."

"Thanks a lot." CJ flicked the pile of shavings at Reggie's shoes.

At the same time, Toby swatted the back of Reggie's head, knocking her fatigue hat to the floor. "Have some respect. You might someday be in love again yourself, if you're lucky."

Reggie bent to retrieve her cap. When she straightened, she was blushing to the tips of her ears.

"Hold on," Toby said. "*Are* you in love?"

"No. Yes." Reggie shook her head. "I don't know!"

"You don't say," CJ said, exchanging a smile with Toby.

Together they sat Reggie down on the nearest bench and extracted information from her while other members of their crew flitted around them. Holly, the WASP, had taken Reggie to dinner the night before in El Paso, and they had even shared a kiss before Reggie had to report for GI night duties.

Toby pushed her hat off her forehead. "You told us you went to the club with Jill."

"I didn't want everyone to know. She's civilian, so fraternization doesn't apply, but you know how people talk. The last thing I need is for the major to get wind of it and have one of us transferred."

"How did you leave it?" Toby asked.

"I'm supposed to see her tonight at her quarters. You'll come with me, won't you? Both of you? I don't want to go alone."

She sounded panicked. Reggie was a prankster, but even though she had made light of being Dear Janed, CJ knew that her ex-girlfriend's betrayal had hit her hard.

"Of course we will," Toby said, her arm around Reggie's neck. "It'll be great, you'll see. You're a good egg and so is Holly."

"She is, isn't she?" Reggie asked.

"Absolutely." CJ squeezed her shoulder.

As they set up ladders to reach the upper trusses, CJ wondered if other bases had as much opportunity for gay women to meet and mingle as Bliss offered. She had heard that other posts varied widely in their acceptance of Wacs, depending on the attitude of the Army command. The same was true for Negro units. Bliss had a Negro antiaircraft regiment, and like Wacs, black GIs were segregated from the rest of the base in their own area, with separate officers, living quarters, mess halls and clubs. CJ had glimpsed a handful of the men around base and had noticed that they almost always traveled in groups—like Wacs. Safety was a major concern for black soldiers at the post, according to Brady. Earlier in the year, Fort Bliss had played host to two separate racial disturbances in which black troops were beaten and pelted with rocks by white troops. Ill treatment of black soldiers in the US Army didn't stop at physical assault. Brady had read a report that soldiers from Negro units received blue ticket discharges at a significantly higher rate than did white soldiers. Hardly surprising in a country operating under Jim Crow.

CJ still remembered the letter to the editor she had read in *Yank* that described the treatment a group of black soldiers had experienced while traveling through Texas. When they tried to buy a cup of coffee at a railway station lunchroom, they were refused service and ordered to go around back to the kitchen. While they stood outside, they observed a group of German POWs be led into the lunchroom, seated at booths among other white customers, fed whatever they wanted from the menu and even given cigarettes. Black soldiers were good enough to die in combat defending American democracy, but that didn't prevent them from being regarded as racially inferior, even when compared to the European fascists they were tasked with fighting.

Gay soldiers may have to hide their relationships from military authority, but they were lucky that hiding was even an option. Lying was not ideal, CJ thought as she applied a wire brush to the nearest truss, but she didn't think she had to fear being assaulted for being gay. Then again, there was a reason WAC trainees were taught to remain clear-headed and to avoid being alone with male soldiers. What would happen if Charlie or some other spurned GI figured out they were together? Would Brady's physical safety be compromised? Would her own? Or would the GI in question merely turn them in?

Any resulting investigation into misconduct could extend to Toby, Kate, Reggie, even to others she didn't know. Maybe she and Brady should be more careful. The current look-the-other-way approach favored by the Fort Bliss command could change any day, especially if the war continued its steady progress toward Allied victory. She remembered Toby's words: "They need us more than we need them. At least, for now."

Cleaning day always dragged, but at last the clock struck noon and the Wacs caught a ride back to the women's compound. At lunch mess, Brady joined their table a little earlier than usual, clutching her usual cup of coffee.

"Hi," CJ said, gazing at her unrestrainedly.

"Hi." Brady smiled into her eyes. "How was cleanup day?"

"A tad more painful than usual." CJ pulled up her sleeve to display the purpling bruise on her forearm. "Turns out spilling soapy water on a ladder and then climbing said ladder is not advisable."

"CJ," Brady exclaimed, tugging her arm closer. "Did you go to Beaumont?"

"Nah. It'll be better in a couple of days."

"I made sure she put ice on it." Sarah was a staunch champion of the curative powers of ice.

"Thanks, Sarah." Brady gave CJ's arm a last squeeze and let go. "What are you doing tonight?"

"Well," CJ said, glancing at Reggie, who gave her a look half begging and half threatening, "I think we're going to meet up with a few of the WASPs at their quarters. I know you have that engagement dinner in town, but you're welcome to join us."

"I was going to say the same thing to you, but it sounds like you already have plans."

What would Brady do if CJ announced she wanted to be her date to dinner, after all? But even as she considered changing plans, she realized she didn't want to. An evening with her buddies at the WASP BOQ sounded far more enjoyable than a fancy meal with people who resented her presence.

"Too bad," she said, shrugging. "Your dinner sounds like fun."

"Liar. It sounds like drudgery. I'd rather come see how the other half lives. Didn't you say they're in bachelor officer quarters?"

"Yep. They took over an entire building. One night, this ferry pilot came stumbling into Pinkie's room. He claimed to have no idea that WASPs were billeted anywhere on post, let alone in that building."

"Likely story," Brady said, which was what CJ had thought. "What did Pinkie do?"

"She offered to get hold of the MPs and have him escorted to his billet. Naturally, he declined."

Brady laughed out loud. That was definitely one of CJ's favorite sounds in the world. She couldn't imagine ever tiring of it—or of Brady, for that matter.

As they walked back to the barracks after lunch, Brady looped her arm through CJ's. "I'll miss you tonight," she said, her voice low so the others wouldn't hear.

CJ's stomach fluttered. "I remember the first time you ever said that to me."

"You do?"

"Of course. I was sure I must have misunderstood. How could you possibly be feeling what I was?"

"But I was. I thought you'd figured it out the night before and that you couldn't wait to get away from me. When I woke up in that inn all alone…" She shuddered a little.

CJ pressed Brady's arm closer to her side. "I know. I'm sorry about that. I was so scared you were going to figure out I had this massive crush on you and never speak to me again. Or worse, turn me in."

"You're kidding." Brady stared at her. "Why would I do that?"

"Obviously I know now that you wouldn't, but you were still a mystery to me then. Toby says someone from your company did actually turn in a couple of girls."

"She probably means Lois and Jane. One day they were here, the next they'd been shipped off as replacement soldiers to God knows where."

"So they weren't discharged for being in a banned relationship?"

"I'm not even sure they were in a relationship. If they were, it didn't end up on their record."

"How can you be sure?"

"I'm an Admin Wac, remember?"

"If only I could forget."

They walked on side by side through the winter sunshine, arms and legs automatically moving in unison. Shortly before they reached CJ's barracks, Brady paused and glanced over her shoulder before asking, "Do you worry about being discharged because of us?"

"A little," she admitted. "Don't you?"

"Not especially. What worries you about it?"

CJ tilted her head. "My family finding out, I guess. I know it's not the same for us as it is for the boys. I mean, who's going to ask us for our military papers after the war? But even so, I don't think I could lie to my parents."

"I could."

"Really?"

She made a sound in her throat. "My parents aren't like yours, CJ. They're not interested in helping us find out what we're good at or what we love, not unless it involves marrying the right person for our social class and settling down to the type of life they expect of us. I can't be myself with them. They wouldn't allow it, and frankly, it's always been easier to go along with what they wanted."

CJ remembered the wistfulness in Brady's tone when she'd talked about becoming a science writer, how she had fussed with her engagement ring. "Nate was the right person for your social class, wasn't he?"

"My parents certainly thought so, even after he…" She trailed off, shook her head. "Anyway, I don't want you to worry. We'll be okay. I promise."

"Do you know something I don't?"

"Not some*thing* as much as some*one*. Now come on, didn't you say Company D has a new puzzle with our name on it?"

CJ followed her, troubled by what Brady hadn't said. Even after Nate what? And who at Bliss was supposed to be looking out for them? But Brady was clearly determined to enjoy the rare afternoon together, and they couldn't talk openly in front of the other Wacs in her barracks. As they lazed away the afternoon in the women warrior-bedecked day room listening to records, their heads bent over a thousand-piece puzzle of Yellowstone National Park, CJ was conscious of time slipping away too quickly. All too soon Brady was rising and stretching and making a regretful farewell, and CJ was left in the cheerful day room feeling like some of the color had drained from the world again.

The feeling didn't last long. Soon Reggie was rushing around fretting over her hair and makeup. CJ had never seen anyone debate so thoroughly the color of her lipstick.

"That one," she said when asked, pointing to one of several look-alike reds. She glanced at Toby, who pursed her lips, hiding a smile.

"I can see you, you know," Reggie said as she backed away to find the iron for one more pass at her "A" uniform.

She worried all through dinner about spilling food on her jacket. At one point, as Reggie went to refill her water glass—coffee would leave her with coffee breath, of *course*—CJ shook her head at Toby and Kate.

"Boy, am I glad I'm not in her shoes anymore."

"So are we," Toby said, and Kate nodded emphatically.

"What do you mean?"

Kate's eyebrows rose. "Do you know how torturous it was to watch you moon over Brady and not be able to say or do anything?"

"You probably wanted to tell me to get on with it already."

"No," Toby said, "it wasn't like that. We knew where you were at, and we knew what it would take to get where you are now. That's all."

"Aww," CJ said, smiling at Toby and Kate. They were so danged sweet, both separately and together.

"Aw, what?" Reggie asked as she returned to the table.

"Aw, don't you look cute." Kate laughed as Reggie turned bright pink again.

The WASP BOQ building was in the center of the post, about half a block from the officers' mess where the pilots dined and a block from the officers' club, where the pilots had privileges despite their in-between status. They were also right next door to the barber shop—"in case we need a shave and haircut," Holly joked as she gave them a tour that evening. Each woman had her own room with a cot, a chair, a closet, a shelf and a tin wastepaper basket, and because they didn't have to obey military regulations, the WASPs had decorated their personal spaces with non-GI quilts and curtains. The building had its own telephone and a large community bath that the dozen women shared, along with a day room decked out with tables, chairs, rugs, curtains, pillows, ashtrays, a wireless set and even a battered old piano someone's boyfriend had had delivered. This was where Holly ended the tour, inviting the visiting Wacs to make themselves comfortable.

Many of the WASPs were out on a Saturday night, but a handful occupied the day room, engaged in assorted forms of entertainment. The Wacs hadn't been there long before Holly and one of the Kayes pestered Nell to play the piano. She gave in with a good-natured shrug and took a seat on the rickety bench, cracking her fingers dramatically before starting in on a tune CJ thought sounded familiar, possibly from her Girl Scout days. The WASPs in the room broke into what was clearly a favorite song:

> *He was a big bold man, he was a desperado*
> *From Cripple Creek way out in Colorado*
> *And he horsed around just like a big tornado*
> *And everywhere he went he gave his WAR HOOT!*

After that, they cycled through old favorites and more recent hits. CJ watched Nell, impressed. She didn't seem to need sheet music at all. In fact, a couple of times at a request she stuck out her tongue a little and muddled her way through a first verse, picking up speed as she found her groove in the second.

Then Reggie called out, "'I Got a Gal from Kalamazoo!' Or should I say Brady does."

Toby elbowed her.

"What?" Reggie rubbed her ribs. "It's hardly a secret."

It was CJ's turn to redden as all eyes went to her. Then the opening notes of the requested tune sounded, bright and lively, and she smiled gratefully at Nell for the diversion.

Soon their drafted pianist insisted on taking a break, and they passed bottles of beer and cigarettes around, settling back on the low orange couches arranged near the wireless. The WASPs had an ongoing competition, CJ knew from down time in the ready room, that centered on one-liners featuring the hapless French military. Once the alcohol started flowing, it didn't take long for the jokes to roll.

"How many Frenchmen does it take to guard Paris?" an older WASP named Betty asked.

"Nobody knows," Kaye said. "It's never been tried."

"Why did the French plant trees along the Champs-Élysées?" Nell chimed in.

"So the Germans could march in shade," Holly replied.

"What does 'Maginot Line' mean in German?" Kaye asked.

CJ knew this one. "Speed bump ahead."

Reggie had been practicing too: "What's the first thing the French Army teaches in basic?"

"How to surrender in ten languages," Toby said, and the two Wacs grinned at each other.

"Going to war without the French on your side is like going hunting without your accordion," Kate put in, smiling as everyone else laughed.

The humor was a tad harsh, but American soldiers had a bone to pick with the French, whom they viewed as all but derelict in duty. The ease with which the French had surrendered to their German neighbors not once but twice irked the average GI because now, as in the last war, American soldiers were being asked to lay down their lives while the French waited to be rescued. Certainly the French Resistance was doing its part, but the French military? Not hardly, from the American standpoint.

The beer kept flowing and the cigarettes burned brightly as the wireless set played big band tunes. After a brief foray into camp rumors and current events, the WASPs settled into what CJ recognized as another favorite pastime: telling and retelling flying stories.

Josephine "Josie" Parker, a thin blonde with strong tanned forearms and a Georgian accent, started them off: "Kaye and I were flying a strafing mission in formation one day in Helldivers, and we had already finished our strafing and were on the way back to base when we saw a guy in a Jeep. We dove toward him, but instead of getting out and taking cover like the rules of engagement said, he had the gall to wave at us. So Kaye says over the radio we should go back for another pass. This time we come really, really close, and he jumps out of the Jeep and into a ditch. Meanwhile the Jeep keeps going right on out into the desert boondocks. We flew over one more time to find him—he'd taken off his white T-shirt and was waving at us in surrender."

"Nell has a similar story," Holly said. Nell shook her head warningly, but Holly ignored her. "With strafing, you come down out of the sun and buzz the troops. They're supposed to pretend it's real and take cover. But with gas missions, it *is* real—when we're over the boys, we hit a button on the Helldiver stick and let loose the gas from under the wings. This way the troops can practice getting their gas masks on under pressure.

"This one morning back in September, Nellie here goes out on her mission, pushes the button to release the gas and heads back toward base, mission accomplished. On the way back, she caught some of the troops skinny-dipping in a stock tank. Like any good pilot, she decided to buzz them. But the men at the airfield that morning had loaded the gas incorrectly. When she pulled out of the dive, the gas released. Fortunately, the boys had enough sense to duck under the water and hold their breaths. But Nellie didn't know that. She called up base and told them she had killed the whole group. There was an investigation and everything, but they didn't find her at fault. The CO told us it happened once before, except the gas released over a parking lot and stripped all the paint off the officers' cars."

"I remember that," Toby said. "It was right after our company arrived last spring. We told each other that at least we couldn't get blamed for that screw-up."

"You girls take a lot of heat from the boys too?"

"Of course. We're women who have dared to invade their male domain, aren't we?"

"That we are," Holly agreed.

To get back at her friend, Nell shared a story about how Holly had crashed a radio-controlled aircraft. "There she was, hanging upside down in the safety pilot seat, unable to move. There's a reason they call it the safety pilot, you know. You're not supposed to let the plane crash."

"It wasn't my fault the plane hit a mound of dirt on landing. As I recall, you and Betty were in the control ship."

"Wait, were you okay?" Reggie put in, frowning.

"I was fine," Holly reassured her. They shared a look, and everyone else in the room suddenly found somewhere else to focus their own gazes. Except Kaye.

Almost gleefully she said, "You think that's scary, wait until you hear about the time Pinkie came down from towing a target with a split cable."

"Kaye," Nell said warningly.

But Reggie had already bit. "What do you mean, a split cable?"

"You know how the tow operator cranks out the target at the beginning of target practice and cranks it back in at the end of the run?"

Reggie nodded. She knew very well, having served in this role a couple of days earlier.

"Well," Kaye said, pausing to take a gulp of beer, "lots of times the boys shoot the cable, which is understandable. They're trying to hit the target and the cable is attached to it. But on this particular mission, the tow crank guy went back at the end of the run, and it only took two cranks for the end of the cable to come whipping in—the gunner had missed the target by a couple thousand feet."

CJ glanced at Reggie's face. She was trying to look tough in a way CJ recognized, but her cheeks were pale. CJ didn't blame her. If it were Brady up there getting shot at by prepubescent boys who thought women shouldn't be allowed to fly… Except it wasn't the gunner's fault he'd almost shot down the plane instead of the target; it was squarely his instructor's responsibility.

"Hey, don't worry." Holly moved closer to Reggie on the couch. "It's not that dangerous, what we do. Most of the accidents happen in training, and our squadron is pretty well-trained at this point."

Reggie nodded, but CJ could tell she was still troubled.

"Tell you what," Holly said, and leaned forward to whisper in her ear. Immediately Reggie perked up, and both women rose to their feet.

"Um…" Reggie grinned at CJ and the others. "I'll see you back at the barracks later, okay?"

Without the guests of honor to keep it going, the party broke up shortly thereafter. Toby and Kate offered to walk CJ home, but she told them to go on ahead. It wasn't quite nine thirty yet, and she felt like stretching her legs. Mostly, she wanted to give them time to themselves. Such opportunities were rare, as she well knew. For a moment she wondered where Brady was, but she knew—inside the marble and gypsum confines of Paso del Norte, where their friends had toasted them their first weekend together. The temptation to hop on a streetcar and crash the dinner party was almost overwhelming.

"Feel like company?" Nell asked.

"Sure," CJ said, grateful for the suggestion. The last thing she needed was to show up at the restaurant like a love junkie.

As they headed for the exit, she glanced over at Nell. The smaller woman was dressed in a cotton sweater and her "general's pants," as the WASPs referred to their khaki uniform pants. Like many things WASP-related, CJ hadn't gotten the story behind the nickname. The pilots seemed to have a penchant for shortcuts and inside jokes. In some ways, she envied them their civilian status. Frankly, she was tired of wearing skirts. For the past few years, she'd taken advantage of changing cultural mores to wear pants nearly all the time, but the WAC had strict rules about maintaining a feminine appearance—as if the appearance of women in Army uniforms could somehow be softened by a straight-line skirt.

The temperature had dropped, and Nell grabbed a pair of bomber jackets from the downstairs closet on the way out. CJ's lapel read, "Booker."

"Is this Pinkie's?" she asked, faintly alarmed by the prospect of wearing the squadron commander's jacket.

"Don't worry. She and Em are on a date with a couple of captains from the other end of the field. I'll have the jacket back long before they are."

Once outside, CJ was grateful for the coat's warmth. Her wool uniform jacket was warm enough, but it actually felt like winter tonight. Or winter in Texas, anyway. Back home the farm was covered in snow, according to her mother's latest letter, and her father was now dressing in his warmest clothes each morning to go out to the barn.

"Hard to believe Christmas is two weeks away, isn't it?" Nell asked, taking a drag on a cigarette as they walked together beneath a nearly full moon. "No snow, and most men acting like holidays are just another excuse to get drunk."

"They do seem to like their booze here."

"It's because it's so cheap in Juarez. Some of the girls call any excursion south of the border a 'rum run' now."

"You're kidding."

Army regulations being what they were, it wasn't like Wacs could bring back so much as a bottle of beer to the barracks. In addition to pants, Wacs were expected to avoid drunkenness and other forms of lewd behavior. After an evening in the WASP BOQ, she was starting to think she had joined the wrong branch of the armed forces. Snug and warm in her bomber jacket, she tried to imagine what it would be like to be a WASP, flying missions out over White Sands, dining in the officers' mess and socializing in the OC. Everyone loved a pilot, it seemed, or wanted to be one, even though the casualty rate was so high.

"Did you have a good time tonight?" Nell asked, breaking the somehow comfortable silence.

"Very. BOQ is a pretty nice setup."

"Don't we know it. When we first arrived on base last summer, they didn't seem to know what to do with us, so we were billeted in WAC officers' quarters. But the WAC officers had long since taken over the smaller rooms, leaving one large room for the six of us to share."

"Was this in the WAC compound?"

"No, it was before the cavalry brigade left for staging, when the Wacs were billeted on main post near the nurses. Those first ten days were awful. Two girls couldn't have a conversation without the others jumping in with their opinions."

"Gee, I feel so sorry for you."

Nell scrunched up her nose, seeming to remember that CJ, an enlisted woman, slept every night in a room full of potentially opinionated women. "I'm sorry, I didn't mean that how it sounded."

"Sure you did. How did you end up in BOQ?"

"Jackie Cochrane herself, head of the WASP, flew in to Biggs to set straight the powers that be. We moved the very next day."

"Bet you were glad to have a room of your own."

"Still am. But for a while, I sort of missed those Wacs. It was nice to be around women like us, even if they were Regular Army. That's why when we heard about you girls, we pestered the major until he got you transferred to Tow Target. I hope that was okay," she added. "We didn't stop to think that maybe you would prefer to stay where you were."

"I can't speak for everyone, but I like Tow Target. Our last sergeant was tough. Whimpy seems more even-keeled."

"And the work?"

"Better too. It's nice to get to know the ships we work on—and their quirks. In Transient, it was nearly all routine checks and quick fixes."

"It's the opposite for us. The ferry line is what most WASPs aspire to."

"Why is that?"

"Well, it's the reason we were hired, in theory, to deliver aircraft from factories to airfields. In fact, it's what the majority of active WASPs do. Besides, you get to fly the newest of the new. I don't know if you've picked up on it yet, but some of the girls are all about pursuit."

"Is that what you would rather be doing? Ferrying fighters around the country?"

Nell smiled, her teeth flashing white in the base lights. "I thought it would be, but after a few months here, I realize I'm more of a homebody. We get letters from the ferry girls, and one night they're in New York City, the next Chicago and a few days later, L.A. To be honest, it sounds like too much moving around for me. They also don't get any variety in their missions like we do. One day I could be flying strafe, the next gas, the next searchlights."

"How did you become a pilot anyway?"

"When I was a kid, the barnstormers came through our town. My father paid five dollars to take me and my brother, the two eldest, up for rides. That was it. I was hooked. After college, my brother and I bought a single-engine Taylorcraft with another friend. I managed to log five hundred hours before the ferry service was formed."

CJ remembered the barnstormers who had passed through West Michigan, former military pilots from the First World War who flew around the country selling rides in surplus Curtiss Jennys purchased from the government after the war. Almost every summer when she was little, CJ had longed to go up for a ride, but even a few dollars had seemed like too much, even during good times. Now she wondered if her parents might have willingly donated the funds to the cause if she had asked. And if they had, would the bomber jacket she currently wore bear her name instead of another woman's?

They walked on, chatting about the shared experience of having older brothers overseas on bomber crews. Nell was easy to talk to, CJ realized, which shouldn't be a surprise. They had so much in common—they had both been raised in Midwestern farm communities; their parents were Roosevelt liberals who believed strongly in a compassionate God and in education as the path to betterment; and they had both attended state universities where students like them were given a window onto lives that didn't involve marrying a boy from back home and settling on a hundred acres not far from the family farm. They had each left those lives to seek a different path and ended up here at an Army Air Corps base in West Texas, serving their country to the limits that country would allow.

In the midst of another comfortable silence, Nell asked, "Who's Brady?"

The sudden change of subject jolted CJ, and she nearly stopped walking. "Oh. Um, she's my friend from Admin."

"Your *friend*," Nell repeated, stressing the term. "And where is she tonight?"

"At an engagement party for one of the girls in her squad."

"I see."

Did she? While CJ was fairly certain Nell preferred the company of women too, the pilot had yet to confirm this supposition. Without verification, there was no way CJ could risk revealing herself, not even to someone who was becoming a friend.

At the gate to the WAC compound, CJ took off Pinkie's jacket and handed it to Nell, who accepted it with a slightly chivalrous bow.

"Thanks for the company," CJ said, folding her arms across her midsection. Geez, it was cold for Texas. "You sure you'll be okay walking back alone?"

"I guarantee it. By the way, I have to say, your friend Brady is a lucky woman. I hope she knows it." And she waved jauntily as she turned and strode away.

CJ nodded at the MPs and hurried toward home, rubbing her jacket sleeves as she went. Usually she considered herself the lucky one, but it was nice to know someone else thought Brady was. Even if Nell was a flirt, she was a cute flirt who might someday be persuaded to teach her how to fly.

As she neared the barracks, she pictured the barnstormers in their Jennys performing spins, dives, loop-the-loops and barrel rolls while aerialists walked on the wings, hopped from one plane to another and even, once, played tennis in midair above her parents' fields. Where were those pilots and wing walkers now?

And then she wondered if the same performers had ever made stops near Kalamazoo and Lincoln, if the same Jenny that had carried Nell up on that first important airplane ride might not have made loop-the-loops over CJ's farm too, way back in the day when flying seemed like nothing more than an exhilarating game and global war belonged, they were certain, firmly in the past.

CHAPTER SEVENTEEN

At breakfast the next morning, Reggie was floating so high that she seemed to soar above the teasing jabs her friends leveled at her. CJ participated with half her brain, the other half intent on watching for Brady. But Brady didn't show.

Sparse attendance wasn't unusual for Sunday morning mess. Sunday was the one day of the week they were allowed to sleep in, and plenty of women stayed out late on Saturday night, since bed check was an hour later than the rest of the week. But CJ had fully expected to see Brady after spending their second Saturday evening apart since they'd met. The last one had been during the Week of Denial, as CJ mentally termed the unhappy period she'd spent avoiding Brady.

"Did you see her this morning?" she finally asked Kate. They were in different squad rooms, but it was possible.

"No. Sorry," Kate said, squeezing her shoulder.

CJ waited until the Wacs on KP began cleaning up before she finally gave in and walked over to Brady's barracks. At the door, the Wac on day duty was none other than Marjory from Albany, the post librarian.

"Hi CJ. Looking for Brady?"

"I am. Is she here?"

"She's asleep. But I can let her know you stopped by."

Apparently, Marjory was not going to allow her inside Company A's barracks. Would she even tell Brady about this conversation? She seemed almost friendly, which was a switch. In fact, the hostility that Janice and her cronies had habitually leveled at her appeared to have faded in recent weeks. Was that a good sign or bad?

"All right," she said finally. "Thanks."

It wasn't like she didn't have plenty to keep her busy, CJ told herself as she headed back to her own barracks. Letters, laundry, gossip and a recently published slave narrative her mother had sent a few days earlier were all clamoring for her attention. She would gladly focus on something other than her absentee girlfriend.

Shortly before noon, she stepped into a shower stall in the barracks bathroom. The day was half over, and she had already finished her weekly laundry and area detail, written three letters to friends and family and smoked a cigarette with Reggie and Sarah on the back stoop. Still there had been no sign of Brady. Maybe she would be at noon mess. Just in case, CJ took extra time with her shower routine. Toby had convinced her to cut her hair shorter and style it a little differently. The upsweep was more difficult to maintain than her old-fashioned bob, but she had to admit, it made her look more sophisticated. As a plus, Brady said she loved it.

At the mess hall, she scanned the room without luck—Brady wasn't there. Had something happened at the engagement dinner? Stomach rumbling uneasily, she joined the line to wait for a plate of chicken mushroom casserole. She doubted she'd be able to finish the overly generous portion. Serving sizes were based on the average height and weight of male soldiers. As a result, most of the Wacs she knew had gained ten pounds since joining. Fortunately, PT, drill and the strenuous nature of airplane maintenance kept CJ lean and strong. In fact, she had noticed her body slimming down, as if any baby fat that had managed to survive the farm had finally given up the ghost. She'd even paid Brady's tailor in El Paso to take in her uniform slightly, so that now everything fit nearly perfectly.

She had almost reached her table when she felt a tap on her shoulder. *Brady*.

"There you are." CJ paused, taking in the sight before her. Brady's hair was in disarray, her skin pale, eyes bloodshot and red-rimmed. "Wow. Are you okay?"

"How can you look so sparkly?" Brady asked, squinting. "And no, for the record, I am not okay. In fact, I don't care if I ever see a bottle of tequila again."

"You got drunk last night?"

"Gee, your powers of deduction are amazing."

CJ felt herself bristle. "You don't have to be nasty."

"No, I know. I'm sorry." Brady bit her lip. "My head is splitting and I haven't been able to find any place quiet enough to sleep."

Military housing wasn't exactly easy even when you felt healthy. But add in nausea and a headache—not to mention other alcohol-related ailments—and CJ could imagine a squad room in a crowded barracks might be nightmarish.

"Look," Brady added, "I only stopped by to find you. You look great, by the way. Fresh out of the shower?"

She nodded, feeling a little less silly for taking such pains with her appearance.

"I wish I had the energy to say something about joining you, but I really need to go back and lie down. I'm sorry again."

"It's fine. Is there anything I can do?"

"No, but it's sweet of you to ask. Marjory said you stopped by this morning."

"She told you?"

"She did."

They shared a look, and CJ thought she read in Brady's eyes a similar sense of cautious optimism toward the shifting attitudes of the Admin Wacs.

"Do you think they know?" CJ asked, her voice low.

Brady nodded, and the look on her face became grim again. "I have no doubt some of them know. I'll have to tell you about it. Are you up for dinner at the club?"

"Um, sure." CJ quelled the urge to shake the mystery out of her. Engaging Brady in vigorous motion of any kind probably wasn't the best idea right now.

"Swell." She started to turn away. Then she paused and asked, "How was your night, by the way?"

"Great."

"Good, I'm glad. How's five for dinner?"

"Perfect."

"Okay, see you then." Brady started to lean toward her but caught herself. "Sorry," she said, flustered, and backed away.

"It's okay," CJ assured her, even though her pulse said otherwise. Brady had been about to kiss her, there in the middle of the crowded mess. Such a brazen violation of military law would have to be punished by more than a transfer, wouldn't it?

Looking even paler than before, Brady gave her a half-wave and headed for the exit. CJ resumed her trek to the corner the D-lites favored. She'd been so looking forward to seeing Brady, but now she almost wished she hadn't. The fact that Brady had somehow felt the need to drink herself into near oblivion the night before with her supposed friends, combined with the cryptic comment about those friends, raised so many red flags CJ wasn't sure which worry to chew on first.

Remember, she told herself, hearing her father's calm, familiar tone, *better to focus on what you can control than what you can't*. At that moment, she was having trouble determining what might be under her control as opposed to the long list of things that categorically weren't.

"Everything okay?" Toby asked as she slid onto the bench beside her.

"Honestly? I'm not sure."

"I hear you. Women." Toby gave her a knowing look.

"I hear you too," Kate commented. "Because I'm sitting right next to you."

"I didn't mean you, sweetie," Toby said, offering her girlfriend a gallant smile. "You know that."

Kate rolled her eyes, but she smiled back at Toby. "Whatever you say, hon."

Later, as they walked back to the barracks, Toby slowed to wait for CJ. "Do you want to talk about it?"

"I don't know if there's anything to talk about."

"Okay. Well, you know my door is always open."

"That's because squad rooms don't have doors."

"Don't be so literal, Jamieson." Toby shoved her mid-stride.

"Hey," CJ said, laughing, and shoved her back.

They jostled a bit, then straightened their garrison caps. As CJ walked on with her friends, some of the day's luster returned. Whatever had happened, Brady still loved her, judging from the almost-kiss; and even looking like something the cat dragged in, Brady was still as appealing as ever. In fact, possibly more so, for here was evidence that Brady was no more perfect than she was. Here also was proof that their relationship was strong enough to withstand instances when one or the other of them wasn't at her finest. With Sean, she'd always felt like she had to be on her best behavior. He never wanted to see her when she was sick or stressed over exams. Talk about a red flag—she'd missed so much in their relationship.

Thank God they hadn't married, she thought now, shivering in the cool December sunshine. What a disaster that would have been, especially if she'd gotten pregnant. Raising children took a sense of humor and a certain amount of irreverence, or at least that was what she'd gleaned from watching her parents with her younger siblings. In hindsight she could see that with Sean, she had experienced neither. Meanwhile, with Brady there had been both from the start. Too bad having children together was not an option.

Brady wanted kids, that much CJ knew. She had always assumed that she would have a family too. But in her case, even if Brady were to vanish from her life tomorrow, she wouldn't go back to dating men. Was the same true for Brady?

Probably, CJ realized as she followed her squad mates into their home away from home, she should find out.

* * *

The walk to the EW club, located not far from the gate to the main post, took longer than usual. Brady was a tad less pale than she'd been at lunch, but the smudges beneath her eyes were nearly as dark. She had cleaned up nicely, though, and now looked as if she were about to go on a date. Which, CJ supposed, they were.

"In my mind I'm holding your hand," Brady said, smiling sideways at her.

"Same here." CJ returned the smile. "You look like you're feeling better."

"Toast and a Bloody Mary work wonders."

"You had a Bloody Mary?"

"Minus the booze. I don't think hair of the dog works, do you?"

"I don't know. I've never been drunk enough to need it."

"Why doesn't that surprise me?" Brady's voice held a note of fondness. "You're so good, CJ."

"Am not."

"Yes, you are. It's good to be good. I know I can trust you no matter what."

Chewing her lip, CJ remembered her own doubts. Were they about Brady, or were they more about herself? Being in love was supposed to be all flowers and romantic music, not constant worry. Oh, well. She'd get the hang of it. She just needed practice.

Brady slowed even more. "I *can* trust you, right?"

"Of course. Now move it. We want to get there before they run out of food, don't we?"

At the club, they picked a table in the corner of the sparsely occupied dining room. Sunday was hardly a popular night to go out at Bliss. Most soldiers, male and female alike, were busy recovering from Saturday night and getting ready for the six-day work week. The jukebox in the opposite corner played a rotation of recent hits. After they ordered—chicken noodle soup for Brady and turkey and mashed potatoes for CJ—the opening chords of "I'll Be Home for Christmas" sounded from the speakers.

Brady expelled a breath. "And here I was starting to feel better."

"I don't know, I kind of like it."

"So did I, the first hundred and forty-two times I heard it."

CJ waited a minute and then said, as she'd wanted to do ever since lunch mess, "Do you want to tell me what happened last night?"

"Not particularly, but I think I have to." Still she sat there playing with the napkin on her lap.

"It's okay. Whatever it is, you can tell me."

"I know." Brady sighed. "Your friends are so great about everything. I wish mine could be. I've been spending all this time with them this week, trying to convince myself that nothing has changed, but it's not true. I'm different, whether they know it or not."

"Did somebody say something?"

Brady nodded.

Their food arrived then, and CJ waited impatiently for the server to move away again. Then, "Janice?" she asked, a heat borne of anger rising in her chest.

Brady leaned back. "No, of course not. It was Charlie. I overheard him make a comment about my missing engagement ring and how he'd heard…" She stopped, shook her head, took a sip of ice water. "God, I don't even want to repeat it."

On one level, CJ didn't want her to repeat it, either. But at least with Charlie, whatever nonsense he spouted came from jealousy.

"Maybe it's not that bad," Brady tried. "I'll just say it, okay? Okay, here it is: He told Mick that I should transfer to Company D since everyone knows D stands for dyke and I obviously like"—she paused to grimace, lowering her voice almost to a whisper—"*pussy* so much."

CJ felt her mouth form an actual O. "He said what?" But as Brady stared at her, eyes wide, she shook her head quickly. "I meant that rhetorically. Please don't say it again. Not ever."

Brady bit her lip and then suddenly she giggled.

"Is this you laughing inappropriately now?" CJ asked, but she felt her own lips begin to curve.

Brady nodded, trying to hold the laughter in, but it was no use. After several seconds, it burst out of her, overwhelming Bing Crosby's smooth tones.

"I mean," she said, trying to catch her breath, "he's right, isn't he?"

"That's not the point." CJ was smiling now. "Although it is great. I mean, I'm a big fan myself."

Brady gazed at her across the table. "I'm so glad you're here."

"Even if it means you feel like you don't belong with your friends anymore?"

Her smile slipped. "Especially because of that. It's too late—the genie's not going back in the bottle now. Besides, it isn't all of my friends or even most of them. You should have seen Janice. When I hinted around at the kind of comment Charlie made, she grabbed him and hustled him out of the restaurant. One of the other girls said she saw her slap him. Can you believe it?"

In fact, she couldn't. Clearly, Brady had been right about Janice all along.

"Well, I'm glad to know there are some women in your squad on our side." She raised her beer glass. "A toast: To the Wacs of Company A. May they continue to broaden their horizons. And also, may they not get us kicked out."

"I'll drink water to that."

As they ate, CJ's gaze kept finding its way back to Brady's face, lit by the candle at the center of the table. The flickering light reminded her of their first weekend together at the Hilton. As more Christmas music serenaded them, she thought of the bet they'd made that first night. Now seemed like as good a time as any to call it in.

"You know," she commented, "Reggie most definitely did not sleep with Sam over Thanksgiving weekend."

Brady's brow rose. "And you mention this because…?"

"Because we had a wager."

"Oh, that," Brady said airily.

"Don't pretend you don't remember."

"You didn't set any terms, as I recall."

"I thought I'd borrow yours." CJ paused. She didn't know why she was so nervous. This was Brady, after all. "I put in for a three-day pass for Christmas, and I'm hoping you'll do the same."

"What did you have in mind?"

"A trip to the Grand Canyon, actually. There's a hotel on the South Rim, the El Tovar, that sets aside a certain number of rooms for active duty servicemen. One of the rooms is ours if we want it."

"The Grand Canyon?" Brady asked, a slow smile breaking across her face. "But we only have a few days. How would we get there?"

"There's an airfield near the South Rim, and I happen to know a pilot or two who might be willing to give us a lift. Even if they're not, as an Air Wac I can tag along on any military flight that has the space."

"Really?" Brady's eyes got a little brighter. "Are you sure you wouldn't rather be here with your friends?"

"Of course not." CJ longed to reach across the table and take Brady's hand. She lowered her voice. "I love you, and I would love to spend Christmas with you holed up in a hotel room at the Grand Canyon."

"I love you too." Brady brushed away an errant tear. "I'm sorry, I don't know why I'm being so emotional."

"Probably because you haven't slept much, and you didn't know I had a romantic bone in my body."

"I think you're very romantic. And it's not your bones I'm interested in, anyway."

CJ paused. "I don't suppose you feel up to a trip to the Jeep lot?"

"No." Brady sighed. "I wish I did. Rain check?"

"Anytime."

As the music played on, they discussed holiday traditions. Each year, CJ's family went for a walk the week after Thanksgiving to pick out a tree, usually a small evergreen from a crowded grove in need of thinning. They would cut it down, bring it back to the house and spend a day or two adorning it with family heirlooms and homemade decorations. Brady's mother, on the other hand, hired someone to pick out their tree and, what was more, to decorate it with rented ornaments.

"You rent ornaments?" CJ repeated. "I didn't know you could do that."

"I always wanted a Christmas like yours, with carols and pie and hot apple cider. I always said that when I had my own family, we would make new traditions."

"You can be part of mine. Next year, or the year after, whenever the war ends, we'll have Christmas in Kalamazoo. It'll be great."

"You think so?"

"I do," she said with considerably more certainty than she felt.

She wanted the future she'd offered up. More than anything, she wanted her parents and siblings to open their hearts to Brady. Would it happen? She wasn't sure. But as Toby had pointed out, not everyone was prejudiced against gay people. Until proven wrong, she would hold out hope that her parents were as open-minded as they had always professed.

"In the meantime," Brady said, "we'll have the Grand Canyon. It can be our tradition."

"For now," CJ conceded. She raised her nearly empty glass to Brady. "To Fort Bliss. May we be so lucky to call it home for the duration."

"Plus six." Brady clinked her glass.

As she drank, CJ felt her heart swell and settle, a little fuller now. She and Brady were in this for the long haul, both of them. If only the Charlies of the world would let them alone, not to mention the Army and their COs and anyone else who had a problem with two women in love…

"Tell me about last night," Brady said. "Is BOQ as swell as everyone says?"

"Better," CJ said, and filled in the details of her evening out. For some reason, she started to leave off the bit about Nell walking her home, but then she backtracked. It wasn't like she had anything to hide.

Brady's head tilted. "She walked you all the way back?"

"It isn't that far. BOQ is right near the men's OC."

"I know where it is. Isn't she the one who took you up on that hop?"

"Yes."

"Huh."

"What's that supposed to mean?"

"Nothing."

She wasn't jealous, was she? Admittedly CJ had been spending time with Nell, who could be something of a flirt. But Brady had nothing to worry about. Who in their right mind would think of ditching her for someone else?

After a moment, Brady smiled across the table at her. "Thanks for tonight. And thanks for being patient this week. I've been missing you, more than you know."

"I've been missing you too."

Maybe she'd imagined Brady's brief flash of insecurity. Lord knew she had misinterpreted plenty since joining the WAC. Nothing like casting yourself into a river whose current you had no idea how to navigate.

"Tomorrow is *Monitor* night," Brady added, making a face, "but after that I'm yours. What do you say?"

"I say it's a date."

"Good."

Smiling into Brady's eyes, she couldn't help but think of the hotel room awaiting them on the South Rim of the Grand Canyon. Christmas couldn't come soon enough.

CHAPTER EIGHTEEN

The flight board at the Balloon Hangar usually filled up Monday morning with the week's anticipated duties, but there were always last-minute missions requested by the AA officers or bigwigs who needed a ride here or there. When CJ heard on Tuesday afternoon that an extra searchlight mission had been added for that evening, she wasn't surprised. The unexpected part was seeing her name on the board next to Nell's.

"Hold on," she said, catching Whimpy's arm. "Why is my name up there?"

"Your pilot requested to have you aboard as the tow operator." His eyebrows rose. "Do you have a problem with the assignment, Private?"

"No, sir. Absolutely not."

Flying at night would be a whole new experience. Her brother Alec's crew was part of a night bomber squadron, and while he had never been much of a poet, his letters during advanced training had been filled with the unimaginable beauty and strangeness of the world at night from twenty thousand feet.

She checked the board again. They would be towing targets for the boys on the ground to locate first with radar, then with searchlights and finally with fifty-caliber antiaircraft machine guns. At two thousand feet, they wouldn't need oxygen like on some missions. That was probably why Nell had added her—for a night flight, this one required minimal extra preparation or precautions. The image of a split tow cable popped into her mind, but she pushed it away. She had been at Biggs for two months now, and she hadn't heard of a single incident of friendly fire.

Although that was exactly what she might face at the mess hall, she reflected as she caught a ride back to the WAC compound with the rest of her squad. Brady was waiting outside her barracks when she arrived, as they'd previously arranged. The plan was that CJ would get cleaned up and they would grab a bite to eat at the club before heading out to a movie on main post.

"Howdy, soldier," Brady said, coming to meet her as she jumped out of the truck.

"Hey."

Sarah, Toby and Reggie patted CJ on the back and then smiled nervously at Brady before ducking around her to scurry into the barracks. Brady glanced from their retreating backs to CJ, her eyes narrowing.

"What's going on? Don't tell me you're breaking our date."

"Not intentionally."

"Let me guess—you have the chance to go up on a hop and you don't want to miss it."

"How did you know?"

"Because you have that look you get when flying is involved." She paused. "Is it dangerous?"

"No more than any other mission," CJ said, deciding on the spot that Brady probably didn't *need* to know that gunners would be firing forty-millimeter shells and fifty-caliber rounds in their general vicinity.

"Fine. But you better not make me a war widow, got it?"

"I won't." CJ pulled Brady into a rare public hug. "Thanks for understanding. I knew I loved you for a reason."

"Uh-huh. If you hadn't sprung the whole Grand Canyon bit on me, I'm not sure I would be quite so forgiving."

She read magazines in the day room while CJ scrubbed grease from under her fingernails. Then they walked to the mess hall together, chatting about their holiday plans. Brady's pass had been approved, which meant the Grand Canyon trip was a definite go. Now they had to figure out how to get there without wasting most of their time traveling.

"I'll ask Nell tonight," CJ said. "I bet she'll know how to fly standby on a holiday weekend."

Beside her, Brady slowed. "You're going up with Nell tonight?" Before CJ could respond, she added, "No, of course you are. Who else would it be?"

So she *hadn't* imagined it the other night. CJ paused outside the mess hall and waited until a trio of Wacs had passed them. "Wait, you're not jealous, are you?"

"Should I be?"

"Of course not."

"Do you even realize how much you've talked about her lately?"

"I've talked about going up in an airplane with her. And yes, I have been getting to know her. We have a lot in common. That doesn't mean anything."

"Is she gay?"

"I don't know." CJ looked away, remembering the flirty smiles Nell had leveled at her, the comment about Brady being a lucky woman. "Maybe."

"Does she know you have a girlfriend?"

"Not in so many words, but I have mentioned you."

Brady folded her arms across her chest. "I know you have this Pollyanna approach to everything, but how can you not see what's right in front of you?"

"You've never even met her. Why do you have to think the worst of people?"

"Because I'm usually right. Can you honestly say she hasn't given you any signals?"

CJ hesitated. "She flirts a little, but it's harmless. Anyway, you do it all the time."

"The difference is," Brady said, lowering her voice as a contingent of Admin Wacs approached, "I don't flirt with anyone I'm interested in."

"I'm with *you*, Brady. You know how I feel about you."

At that, she sighed. "I know. You're right. Go. Have fun. I'll see you tomorrow, okay? Just be careful."

She touched CJ's arm briefly, and then she spun and waved at the women from her company, smiling the smile that CJ suspected most people didn't know was fake. Janice, however, wasn't most people.

"I thought you were going to the club?" she heard Janice say.

Brady's response was muffled as she looped her arm through Janice's and turned into the mess hall.

After a minute, CJ followed. She couldn't very well stand in line behind them, though, so instead she went to grab a cup of coffee. The caffeine would come in handy later, no doubt. By the time she got in line, there were at least a dozen women between her and Brady's crowd. The distance didn't stop Janice from turning around and sending her a look. So much for the ceasefire.

When she slid in at her usual table with a tray of spam and eggs and hot cakes, the kitchen staff's idea of a nutritious weeknight meal, Sarah whistled.

"Went that well, huh?"

CJ shook her head.

Beside her, Toby and Kate were being their usual adorable selves, kidding each other about a letter Kate had received from her mother inviting Toby home on Kate's next leave. How did they do it? How did they make navigating the potential quagmire of a secret gay relationship in the US Army look so effortless? Apparently they trusted each other.

Must be nice, CJ thought, glancing across the mess to where Brady sat with her friends, her PRO smile firmly in place.

* * *

She should have listened to her gut, she realized a couple of hours later as live shells burst in different-colored puffs directly ahead of the B-26, making a soft, cushiony-looking pattern that belied its deadly purpose. The AA troops weren't shooting at the target—they were shooting at the plane. She'd had a feeling that going up tonight would be a mistake, but she'd managed to convince herself she was uneasy about her conversation with Brady. Now, as Nell shoved the stick forward, increasing the Marauder's air speed in an attempt to evade the exploding shells raining deadly shrapnel all around them, CJ held tight to her copilot's seat and tried to keep supper where it belonged—inside her belly, not sprayed all over the instrument panel.

A dozen different ways of dying flashed into her mind: flak that pierced the plane's armor and struck a major blood vessel; a cockpit fire; an electrical failure that left the airplane flying blind; a direct hit to the gas tank. Or what if flak killed Nell or left her unconscious and CJ somehow had to try to fly the plane? A twin-engine Beech trainer was a far cry from a medium bomber that routinely stalled and crashed on landing if it dropped below one hundred fifty miles per hour during approach.

Don't make me a war widow. Brady's comment now seemed eerily prescient.

As they climbed higher, Nell radioed back to base with their position. With a live-fire exercise there shouldn't be a lot of other aircraft out in the area, but that wasn't the issue.

"We're heading home," she told the tower. "Find us a runway, will you?"

"Negative. Your orders have you flying in pattern until twenty two hundred hours," the disembodied voice came back.

"I'm aware of that," Nell said, her hands clenched on the controls as the Marauder out-paced the antiaircraft artillery. "The thing is, the boys down there apparently can't tell the difference between a target and a plane, so I'm revising the orders."

There was silence at the other end. Then CJ heard muffled orders being shouted in the background. Soon the same voice came back, almost apologetic now, and asked, "Are you hit?"

"Not for lack of trying. I'll have my on-board engineer give her a look." She signed off and glanced at CJ, her voice losing its hard edge. "You okay over there?"

CJ nodded, hoping she didn't look as green as she felt. "Other than tasting my supper twice."

"Don't worry, we're out of range by now. Do you feel up to making a visual check while I take us home?"

"I'm on it."

CJ unbuckled her safety restraint and began to walk the bird from nose to tail, checking for any sign of damage. It was a relief to have something to do. Nell must have understood that she needed motion to distract her from reliving that first awful flash of recognition that at any second a live shell could tear through the plane—and both of them. At the rear, she cranked the target back in, unsurprised to find the cloth sleeve untouched.

The firing range was twenty-five air miles from Biggs. In no time, Nell was lowering the landing gear and asking her to buckle back in for the final approach. CJ held her breath as the massive plane roared down and kissed the runway, bounced once and settled groaning onto the landing gear. Then she breathed out her terror, willing away the tears that for some reason saw fit to sting her eyes now that they were safe.

"It's okay," Nell said, taxiing the B-26 toward the Balloon Hangar at the far end of the field. "It's completely normal to cry after a close call."

CJ tried to clear her tight throat. "Has anything like this ever happened to you before?"

"Not friendly fire. But once, before the war, I got caught in a whiteout. It was all I could do to find my way to a nearby field and wait out the storm. For a while, I thought I might never go up again."

"I know the feeling."

And to think she had passed on a date with Brady for the chance to get shot at by their own troops. What she wouldn't have given to be in a dark theater with her now, watching Fred Astaire and Eleanor Powell dance across the screen.

"Give it some time," Nell said. "The beginning was pretty amazing, wasn't it?"

CJ couldn't argue. Night flying under the stars and the still mostly full moon, which had seemed enormous rising over the Sacramento Mountains, had more than lived up to her expectations. Everything had been so clear: the moonlight sparkling off White Sands and the snowy peaks of the Organ Mountains, the lights of El Paso twinkling far in the distance. If the moon hadn't been so bright, Nell had told her, they would have been able to see the Milky Way. But as it was, she would have to settle for the sense that the moon was nearly close enough to fly to, if only they had enough gas.

A Jeep zipped up beside them as they were unloading their gear from the belly, and two men raced toward them.

"Are you all right, ma'am?" the first one asked, trying to take Nell's parachute bag from her.

"Not so fast," she said. "I can schlep my own gear."

"What about you, miss—uh, Private?" the other boy asked.

They got shot at and suddenly became damsels in distress? CJ stiffened her spine, hoping the remnants of her tears didn't show in the shadows. "I'm fine, thank you."

Five men emerged from the hangar and hurried in their direction— the Sixth's night engineering crew. Fortunately, they only had eyes for the squadron's lone Marauder.

"Don't worry," Nell said, "she's in fine shape. Lucky for us the boys in the 197th need a little polishing."

Major Pederson was waiting in the ready room for them, along with a WAC private secretary who looked distinctly unimpressed with their brush with AA fire.

"How are you, Charles?" the major asked. Then he seemed to notice CJ and coughed a little. "And you, Private...?"

"Jamieson, sir." She saluted.

"At ease. Now tell me, what happened up there?"

As the major and Nell discussed heading, position, tow cable length and radio communications, CJ watched the Wac record notes in neat shorthand in a wire-rimmed notebook. Maybe she should have picked an Admin MOS too. With a college degree, she could have had her pick. It would certainly be easier than her current work. But while being a secretary or other type of clerk would probably have kept her from getting shot at, it wouldn't have given her the chance to watch the moon from mid-air rising over distant mountains.

After fifteen minutes, the major let them go with a final caution not to discuss the evening's incident with anyone. Military accidents were considered top secret.

"But it wasn't a real accident," CJ commented to Nell after the major and his assistant left. "Surely we can tell our friends."

"Technically, we can't. I'm a civilian, though, so I can probably have a little latitude. You, however, are Regular Army, and that was a direct order from a superior."

So was not kissing girls, and clearly she had found a way to justify her transgressions on that front. Still, this situation was different. Morale was tricky, and she didn't want to be the cause of a loss of it among any of the AA units about to ship out.

The first two boys, control tower technicians, were waiting outside the hangar when they finally emerged.

"Can we give you girls a ride back to your quarters?" one asked.

"Sure. How about a lift to WASP BOQ?" Nell answered. As CJ started to protest, she added, "We have a tradition—anytime one of us survives a near-miss, we get together and share a bottle of single-malt Scotch. You may not be a WASP, but I think tonight qualifies you for honorary membership."

This sounded so much like a line that CJ could almost hear Brady's disgusted snort. But she had to admit, a glass of Scotch sounded good. Maybe the booze would help her work out how to get around the orders that officially barred her from telling Brady about the mission.

The two boys chatted them up as they drove the three miles back to WASP BOQ. Surprisingly, CJ found herself following Nell's lead and flirting a little along the way. They were clearly enamored with the idea of female pilots, and Nell encouraged the adulation by sharing brief stories about her prewar flying life. The driver asked her out on a date as the Jeep rolled to a stop at her quarters. Nell thanked him and told him it was against regulation, but wasn't he sweet.

As the Jeep pulled away with a friendly horn beep, CJ said, "It's not against regulation, is it?"

"No, but they don't know that."

Inside, several members of their squadron stared at them in surprise.

"What are you doing here?" Pinkie asked, checking her wristwatch. "Mechanical problems?"

"Nope." Nell paused dramatically. "It's Glenfiddich time, ladies."

There was a mix of gasps and cheers around them, and then Pinkie disappeared into the downstairs kitchen and returned with the Scotch. Nell handed CJ a glass and turned to the gathered pilots.

"To faulty radar and inexperienced AA troops," she said, lifting her own glass. Then she knocked back her drink.

Quickly CJ did the same, barely keeping herself from coughing as the liquor hit her throat hot and hard. Almost immediately she felt some of the shakiness she'd been carrying since the flight fade. She pictured Brady sitting cross-legged on their bed at the Hilton shortly after they'd made love for the first time, feeding her supper in bed and explaining how champagne gets into the bloodstream faster than other drinks.

A pang of loneliness hit her harder than the Scotch had, and she closed her eyes, trying to tune out the murmur of voices around her. Brady had barely nodded at her when she left the mess after supper. What would she think if she found out that CJ had survived a friendly fire incident and, instead of looking for her, gone back to WASP BOQ to have a drink with Nell?

She opened her eyes and set her glass down. This wasn't right. She shouldn't be here. Catching Nell's eye, she gave a little wave and headed for the door.

"Where are you going?" Nell asked. "The party's just beginning."

"Not for me." She touched Nell's arm. "I don't think I said this earlier, but thank you for getting us down in one piece."

Nell hesitated, and her eyes seemed to darken as she stared at CJ. "I didn't say it either, but I'm sorry for putting you in that position. Sometimes I forget that not everyone signed up for the life and death part of the job."

CJ smiled, trying to lighten the moment. "It wasn't like anyone forced me to take a night flight. Honestly, I was more afraid of you getting hurt and me being stuck trying to land the notorious Widowmaker."

"You probably would have set her down perfectly on the first try. I mean it, not everyone is as naturally talented in the air as you are."

Rolling her eyes, CJ laughed. "I bet you tell all the girls that."

"Not *all* of them," Nell said, smiling. "Do you want company?"

"I don't think so. But thanks."

Nell walked her out to the street. Then, as they paused on the sidewalk outside the BOQ, she pulled CJ into a tight hug.

At first CJ stood unmoving in the circle of the smaller woman's arms. Nell's warmth seeped into her, comforting after the earlier scare, and she noticed the scent of cinnamon and cloves, the curve of breasts against her own, the strength of the arms that held her. All at once, Brady's words sounded in her head—*how can you not see what's right in front of you?*—and she pushed away.

"I, um…" She trailed off uncertainly. Was Nell making a pass, or was she simply reacting to the emotional evening?

Nell tucked a strand of CJ's hair back behind her ear and tugged on the brim of her Hobby hat. "Get outta here, soldier. I'll see you tomorrow, okay?"

CJ nodded and turned away. At the corner near the officers' club, she glanced back and saw Nell standing under the street lamp outside her quarters, smoking a cigarette. CJ's stomach rumbled uneasily at the thought of tobacco, and she walked on, the taste of Scotch and spam making her long for a glass of warm milk and a hot water bottle for her bed.

She looked up at the sky as she walked, trying to find comfort in the familiarity of constellations. Back home the stars and moon would be tracing a similar arc across the sky, Orion and the Big Dipper and Cassiopeia wending across the northern night sky. Inside the family would be gathered about the fireplace, Rebecca and Pete listening to serials on the wireless set and reading magazines, her mother darning socks, her father whittling delicate animal faces out of pieces of pine and cedar. What if their plane had been shot down tonight? Would her family have received a telegram or a visit from a WAC officer? Would her remains have been found, or would her parents have received an empty casket, like the families of the B-29 crew killed in the crash on Mt. Franklin?

She tried to clear her mind, but the images kept coming—her mother sewing a gold star onto the window banner where once there had been blue; her casket being carried by her father, brother and family friends out to a plot in Riverside Cemetery near her little brother, her father's father, who died before she was born, and his mother, who passed a year after baby Henry; family and friends gathering at their house afterward for food and fellowship, precisely as they had done after Henry's funeral.

This, of course, was the same sequence of events she had previously imagined. Except that every other time she'd been there in her service uniform—at the church, in the cemetery, at home afterward—because always in the past it had been one of her brothers killed in the war, Alec or Joe whose star had turned from blue to gold. Not her. Not a woman soldier stationed on the home front. She was even less likely to die than

Jacob DeWitt, the neighbor boy with the glasses and the non-combat rating.

When she reached the WAC compound, she went straight to Brady's barracks, but the Wac on duty reported that Brady wasn't home. She backtracked to the enlisted club, but Brady wasn't there. Where the hell was she? CJ caught herself. Just because she'd broken their date didn't mean Brady had to stay home sulking. Charging out around base or town wouldn't do much good. She could be anywhere.

Disheartened, CJ found a seat at the club's bar and ordered a beer to chase down the Scotch. It tasted good and seemed to keep the uneasiness shadowing her at bay, so she ordered another and then another. By the time Sarah and Jack found her, she was having a hard time keeping her eyes open.

"CJ," Sarah said, pausing beside her. "Aren't you supposed to be flying tonight?"

"I was. We flew into—" She covered her mouth, giggling. "Oops. Can't tell you. Top secret!"

She licked her lips, wondering why her tongue felt double its usual size. Too bad Brady wasn't there. She would probably know why alcohol made your body feel all swollen and fuzzy. Not to mention dizzy. As she stood up, the floor seemed to tilt beneath her, and all at once she was back in the cockpit of the B-26, flak bursting in beautiful, deadly puffs around them.

Sarah reached out and caught her as she lurched. "Hey now, I've got you. You're okay."

She leaned her head against Sarah's shoulder and felt a sob tear from her throat. Strange, she hadn't even realized she was crying.

Jack came around her other side and they helped her out of the club. Afterward, CJ vaguely remembered sitting in the day room drinking coffee with Sarah and Mary, her KP buddy, who spoke in low voices that were hard to track. But mostly, the rest of the evening seemed to seep past in a blur. By the time bed check rolled around she had sobered up somewhat, enough to get herself ready and into bed without incurring the wrath of the sergeant in charge of quarters. Then she lay on her cot, hands clenching the thin sheets as the ceiling spun overhead. *I'll never drink again*, she vowed over and over, willing the dizziness to pass.

Only later did she notice that not once had she vowed to give up flying.

CHAPTER NINETEEN

The cold air helped at PT the next morning. CJ went through the exercises at a far lower rate of effort than usual, trying to pick Brady out of the crowd of Admin Wacs. But every time she thought she saw her, someone shifted and the Wac who might be Brady disappeared. After a while, CJ stopped trying to find her and focused on making it through PT and drill without throwing up. No wonder she had never gotten that drunk before. There was nothing redeeming about the experience, as far as she could tell. The alcohol had helped her forget the terror of the previous night's mission temporarily, but it had left her a weeping mess in the end. Some GIs insisted on getting drunk several times a week. Were they crazy?

A warm shower helped even more, enough that she decided she might as well try breakfast. Sarah and Reggie walked with her to the enlisted mess, their arms over her shoulders.

"Toast," Sarah said.

"And coffee," Reggie added. "Possibly a banana, if your stomach feels up to it."

"I am capable of feeding myself, you know."

Her friends laughed in a way that clearly communicated their opinion on the matter.

At that moment, Brady approached the mess with her own gang. CJ started to smile, but the automatic pleasure she felt at the sight of Brady dimmed as she took in the grim set of her girlfriend's mouth, her lips a tight slash of red. Had Brady somehow heard what had happened? But no, she looked angry, and it wasn't like she would blame her for the AA unit's mistake. Or CJ didn't think she would anyway.

The two groups met near the entrance, and for a split second no one moved. Then Sarah and Reggie nodded hello and headed into the building, leaving CJ alone to face the trio of Admin Wacs. Brady murmured something to Janice and Marjory, and with last hard looks at CJ, they headed inside too.

"Hi," she said tentatively.

"Hi." Brady stared at her, brow furrowed.

"What's wrong?"

"Not here," Brady said cryptically, glancing around as more women passed them on the way into the mess.

In silence, CJ followed her toward the nearby parade ground, trying to figure out what could have happened since supper the night before. Other than her own brush with death, of course.

Brady stopped suddenly and pinned her with a look.

"I know what happened with you and Nell last night."

"You do?" The friendly fire incident had taken place two thousand feet above the desert many miles from the airfield. The official report probably hadn't even been issued yet. "How?"

Brady seemed almost to deflate, the dark smudges beneath her eyes standing out against her pale skin. "You're not going to deny it?"

"Why would I? I wanted to tell you last night but I couldn't find you."

"That's because I went to the movie we were supposed to see together while you were off with your little WASP friend." She shook her head. "You're worse than a man. At least they try to cover their tracks."

"Hang on. I wasn't *off* with anyone," CJ started.

But Brady was already turning away. "I'm not interested in your excuses."

"They're not excuses. Come on, Brady, don't do this."

At that she hesitated, glancing from CJ to the mess hall and back again.

"Look, the reason I stopped by WASP BOQ was to have a drink because that's what they do when they nearly get shot down. I had one drink and then I went to look for you."

Brady blinked rapidly. "What do you mean, you were nearly shot down?" Her arms lifted, but CJ took a step back. She didn't want Brady to touch her. Last night it was all she'd wanted, but not now.

"I'm sure the incident report will come across your desk." She swallowed hard against the nausea threatening to rise again. "Did you really think I would lie to you? That I would cheat on you?"

"No, but Gerri said she saw you with Nell on the street, and you weren't exactly talking." She crossed her arms, hugging herself. "You told me you had to work last night, CJ. What was I supposed to think?"

"You were supposed to think something must have happened. Because to be honest, I needed a lot more than a hug from a friend last night. I needed you."

Brady held out her hands, supplicating now. "I didn't know. How could I have known?"

"You couldn't. But you could have believed in me. You should have trusted me. God, Brady!" CJ rubbed her temples. The morning sun was giving her a headache.

"I'm so sorry." Brady came closer. "I'd decided the thing with Nell was all in my head, and then Gerri told me…I felt like a fool."

"Well, now I feel like one." CJ closed her eyes briefly. Somehow she was wearier than she'd been since the start of basic training. "I can't do this right now. I have to go."

Sarah had suggested she get to the hangar early to talk to Whimple. They needed their crew chief on their side in case the Biggs CO decided to use the previous night's incident as an excuse to get rid of women pilots and mechanics entirely.

"Okay." Brady's voice was soft, her expression earnest. "I am sorry, CJ. If I'd known what happened…"

"I know. It's fine." She started to turn away but stopped when Brady caught her elbow. The touch was gentle, sweet, and it was all CJ could do not to lean into it. She was so tired.

"It's not fine. You're right. I should have trusted you. Let me make it up to you, please?"

CJ felt the sting of tears and shook her head. "I have to go. I'm sorry."

And with that, she turned and walked away, leaving Brady standing alone on the parade grounds. It wasn't even that hard to do—she just left her there on the dusty field, and she didn't look back, not once.

* * *

At mid-morning break, Toby practically strong-armed her out to one of the Beech trainers for "a little chat."

"Sarah told me about the state she found you in last night," she announced as they each claimed a seat in the cockpit. "Care to share the particulars?"

"That would require breaking a direct order."

"Wouldn't be the first time. Or the last."

CJ filled her in, ending with the scene she'd had with Brady that morning. "I don't get it, Toby. One minute she's telling me how she knows she can trust me, and the next she's sure I'm lying to her. It doesn't make any sense."

"I don't think her doubts are personal. She was willing to cheat on her fiancé to be with you, wasn't she? Think of it this way—if she was capable of it, why wouldn't you be?"

"Right, and it's more about her than it is about me, and so on and so forth." She waved a hand and smacked her elbow on the steel-armored wall beside the copilot's seat. "Ouch! Damn it."

"It *is* more about her. When you get involved with someone, you don't get to pick and choose the parts you like. Besides, you know she's partly right."

"What? I would never cheat on her."

"I don't mean about you." Toby gazed at her meaningfully and grabbed the trainer's controls, pretending to fly it.

"What's that supposed to mean?"

"Come on, you must have seen the way Nell looks at you. And let's not forget—she did let you fly a plane. Clearly she can't resist you."

"You're hilarious. Oh, wait, no you aren't."

"I'm serious! Remember how I said I was going to need a bat to keep the girls off you?"

"You're full of crap." She tilted her head. "So are you saying I shouldn't worry about Brady being jealous?"

"That's up to you. But be careful with Nell. I doubt she has Brady's best interests at heart. Or yours, for that matter."

Break ended and they filed back to their respective assignments. Whimple had calmed her fears that morning and set her to work on sluggish ailerons on one of the Helldivers. Replacing the worn spars in both wings and recalibrating the chord balance tabs was more than a single day's work, but she was grateful for a task that required so much of her attention. Busy work or even no work, which happened more often in Tow Target than it had in Ferry Command, would have left her too much time to dwell on friendly fire—both of the AA and girlfriend variety.

As it was, the night flight kept returning to her at odd moments. The reflection of sunlight off a window reminded her of the searchlights that had pierced the sky before the flak began exploding around them, while the clatter of the hammer drill sounded like gunfire. How did her brother do this day in and day out? How could he walk and talk after an actual combat mission? And how did he write letters at all, let alone ones that maintained the illusion that he didn't face the possibility of a terrifying death each and every time his crew went into action?

She managed to fixate on her girlfriend only at lunch, despite the fact that Brady remained a no-show. CJ kept an eye out throughout the meal, wondering what she would say if she saw her. What did the morning's argument, if it could be called that, mean? Were they speaking, or were they taking a break? By the time she got back to work, she had already decided to skip supper. Instead of riding back with the rest of the WAC crew, she stayed late at the hangar to work on the Helldiver and grabbed a quick supper at the club on her way back to the barracks. She didn't see Brady, which was a relief, she told herself sternly as she lay in her cot that night trying not to notice the sizable hole in her heart.

It had been easier the first time she'd resorted to avoiding Brady because they hadn't admitted to being in love yet. But if they loved each other, why couldn't they figure out how to be together?

The next day, when Brady waved at her hopefully across the mess hall at supper, CJ waved back but didn't make any move toward her. Brady had actually believed she was capable of cheating. Then again, she couldn't pretend she didn't find Nell attractive. Occasionally she remembered their hug—the scent of Nell's hair, the feel of their bodies pressed together, however briefly—and she had to admit that Toby was right. Brady's jealousy wasn't entirely unfounded. At some point, CJ would have to stop being a coward and tell her as much.

On Friday morning as she poured herself a cup of coffee, CJ felt someone pause beside the battered sideboard.

"Hi," Brady said softly.

As she glanced up into familiar blue eyes, CJ resisted the temptation to hurl herself into Brady's arms. "Hi."

"Do you think we could talk?"

"I was about to ask you the same thing." Silence wasn't getting them anywhere. Besides, she missed Brady. "Do you want to have supper in town tonight?"

Brady's eyebrows lifted slightly. "That would be nice."

They settled on Tony's Place. Brady would already be downtown covering a story for the *Monitor*, so they agreed to meet at the restaurant. Then they lingered at the sideboard, watching each other with sideways glances as they stirred powdered milk and granulated sugar into their mugs.

Finally Brady said, "I'm glad we're going to talk."

"Me too." And she was, even though the conversation wouldn't be easy.

Brady squeezed her shoulder and headed back to her side of the mess while CJ returned to her own table. Now she just had to make it through the work day.

The Flight C board was nearly empty, with only a handful of missions that would require preflight and postflight checks. Looked like another day of poker and tech orders, storytelling and kitten time. Great. Now she would have more time on her hands to worry about her date with Brady.

"How about a game of basketball?" Reggie suggested.

Someone had rigged up a half-court between the buildings with a hoop protruding from the outer wall of the hangar so low that CJ barely had to jump to tip the ball in.

They divided up into teams—WASPs versus Wacs, naturally—and everything was going splendidly until Holly decided to outright tackle Reggie. The rest of the players summarily kicked the pair of troublemakers out of the game, after which they sat on an old saw horse poking and tickling each other while the match went on without them.

CJ knew that she and Brady had been like them in the beginning. It had felt like having blinders on—whenever Brady was around, her vision had seemed to home in on her to the exclusion of all else. It wasn't like that as much anymore. Brady was always with her now, in the back of her mind. Except when she flew—flying drove everything out of her mind, even Brady. This wasn't a problem in and of itself. The problem was that she had been sharing the miracle of flight with a woman whom she found more than passably interesting.

Maybe it was her imagination, but her current life almost seemed to resemble some darker version of *The Philadelphia Story*. Unlike the characters in the film, she was discovering that right and wrong, jealousy and fidelity weren't quite as black and white as the screenwriter had made them out to be.

* * *

After lunch, she surveyed the quiet hangar. The basketball game had kept her busy in the morning, but now the rest of the day yawned ahead. Maybe this would be a good time to get a head start on clean-up day activities. Nothing like honest work to keep you honest, her mother always said.

She was mopping the hangar floor when Nell walked in. The pilot had flown another night mission the previous night, CJ knew, searchlights only this time. As was the WASP custom, she'd taken the morning to sleep in. No one wanted a sleepy pilot at the controls of a bomber. Now she approached CJ, her smile as tentative as Brady's had been earlier. For the first time, CJ recognized the power of having two women vie for her attention—it was immensely flattering, especially for someone boys had rarely seemed to notice.

"Haven't seen you much the last couple of days," Nell said, hands in the pockets of her khaki pants.

"I've been around." CJ leaned on the mop handle.

"Did you hear they busted the captain whose trainees shot at us back to first looey?"

"They didn't!"

"Even a broken-down Widowmaker costs a million dollars to replace, don'tcha know."

Despite herself, CJ smiled. Nell was so easy to be around. Then she caught herself. That was the sentiment that had gotten her into trouble to begin with. What if their positions were reversed and Brady had come to her gushing about a new coworker from the PRO? The thought made her slightly ill.

"Anyway," Nell said, taking a coin out of her pocket and rubbing it between her thumb and forefinger, "I was wondering if you'd like to take a hop some weekend. The major lets anyone who completes three missions in a week take a plane out."

Weekend flying for fun rather than military purposes? It sounded amazing, which of course Nell knew. CJ released a breath.

"I would love to, but I can't."

"Why not?"

"I think you know. Don't you?"

Nell gazed at her for a long moment. Then she slipped the coin back in her pocket. "Your girl."

CJ nodded, hoping she didn't look as nervous as she felt. She had never actually told anyone about Brady before. At least, not in so many words.

"All right." Nell smiled crookedly at her. "But the offer stands, no strings attached. You could even bring your lady friend if you wanted."

CJ pictured Brady's face if she relayed the invitation. Honestly, pigs were more likely to sprout wings than Brady was to accept.

"I'll keep that in mind."

"I hope so. Have fun mopping, Private." Nell tipped her head gallantly before strolling out of the hangar, whistling "I Got a Gal."

CJ went back to cleaning, trying not to wonder if she would ever get to go up on a hop again. There would be more flying in her future, there had to be. After all, she was an Air Corps Wac.

* * *

The restaurant was crowded when CJ got there a little before six. She added her name to the list and took a seat at the bar.

"What can I get you?" the bartender, a boy a little older than her, asked with a slick smile.

"Tonic on ice."

"Sure you don't want a little gin with that?"

"Positive."

Her stomach barely stopped short of turning over at the mention of alcohol. As she took her first sip of tonic, she wondered when she would be able to drink again. Sean had liked gin and tonics, and she had liked the taste on his lips. Often on weekends they would go out to a jazz club or to one of their friends' apartments, where they would smoke and drink and listen to music while they debated constitutional principles of presidential power, the role of the market economy in early modern Europe or whether England actually could have won the Revolutionary War. Sometimes Sean, Jack or one of their other buddies would drink too much and spend part of the next day in bed, but they seemed to rebound faster than she was now.

It was Friday night in Ann Arbor too. Was Sean there, wrapping up final papers and grades for the courses he TAed? Or was he home already in Grosse Pointe Farms, back in his childhood bedroom in his family's roomy colonial two blocks from Lake St. Clair? His parents had kept his room exactly as it had been when he graduated from high school, a shrine to his athletic and academic achievements with baseball trophies, model train sets and a still-overflowing bookcase. No wonder he had assumed she would go along with his plans for the future. Everyone else always did.

Engrossed in memory, she didn't notice Brady until she slid onto the stool beside her.

"I hope that look isn't for me," Brady said lightly, smoothing her hair back.

"No." She smiled ruefully. "I was thinking of my ex."

"What brought that on?"

"Gin and tonic." She lifted her glass. "Minus the gin."

"Poor baby," Brady said, smiling at her. Then her smile faltered, and she looked away. "A Lone Star, please," she added, nodding at the bartender.

He popped the top off the bottle of beer and leaned in, sliding it across the bar to her. "There you go, sweetheart."

She stared him down. "Last time I checked, I wasn't any man's sweetheart."

Beside her, CJ smiled into her glass. God, she'd missed her. Infuriating, fascinating woman. How could Brady have seriously believed anyone else would come close to measuring up?

The bartender held up his hands and backed away. "Whoa, lady soldier. No offense intended."

With a last withering look, Brady took a sip of her beer. Then she glanced at CJ and held up her bottle. "To Friday night in the city."

"I'll drink to that."

Being away from the base was a relief. It wasn't like they didn't have to be careful here, but the atmosphere was different, a relaxed air of friends focused on good food, drink and conversation.

"Thanks for suggesting this," Brady said, picking at the paper label on her bottle.

"Thanks for meeting me." She hesitated. "I've missed you."

"I've missed you. But how is it that we seem to say those three words to each other more than any others in the English language?"

"I don't know about that." CJ lowered her voice. "I can think of three other words I've said to you more often than those."

Brady watched her. "Does that mean you still do?"

"Of course." She placed her hand on the bar as close to Brady's as she dared. "My feelings haven't changed."

"Even though I'm a lousy girlfriend with next to no faith in you?"

"I prefer to think that you struggle occasionally with jealous tendencies, but that deep down you know you can trust me."

"Oh, CJ," Brady said, resting her chin on her hand, "how can you be so forgiving? I'm glad you are, of course, but I'm a bit in awe."

"I don't have a choice, do I?"

"I don't know about that. I would think you could probably have your pick at this point."

"Funny, I would say the same about you."

They looked at each other, and CJ noticed the care Brady had taken with her hair, her makeup, her dress uniform. She was so beautiful, but she was also so much more than a beautiful woman. CJ loved the way she laughed, the adorable inverted "V" that formed between her eyes when she tackled a crossword, how she knew more simultaneously about Hollywood starlets and nineteenth-century British poets than anyone CJ had ever met. But most of all, she loved the way Brady looked at her with eyes the color of a summer sky and usually as open.

Now, however, her eyes flickered, and Brady looked down at the bar, rubbing its polished surface. "I have to tell you something."

That couldn't be good. Before CJ could respond, the restaurant host called her name and led them to their table in a corner near a wall adorned with framed photographs of famous restaurant patrons. Clark Gable stared down at them as they took their seats and accepted menus from the host.

As soon as the host had scurried away, CJ said, "So…?"

Brady set her menu on the table. "Do you remember how I told you I thought you were good and that I could trust you?"

"Of course."

"Well, that's kind of a big deal for me because—" She stopped, picking at her beer bottle again. "I don't know why this is so hard. People are dying on the other side of the world, and I can't even talk about something that happened years ago."

"It's okay. Take your time," CJ said, despite the fact that she really, really wanted to know what Brady was about to share. Or maybe she really, really didn't want to know. Kind of a fifty-fifty chance either way.

Brady swallowed another sip of beer and met CJ's gaze. "Nate cheated on me in college. I had no idea he was seeing a shopgirl in New Haven for most of our junior year. We split up for a while, but he begged me to come back. Eventually I did, but it was never the same."

CJ reached across the table and took her hand, holding it lightly. "I'm sorry. That must have been awful."

"It was." She shook her head. "I might not have found out if one of his friends hadn't developed a crush on me. He told me about Cathy in an attempt to break us up. Nate denied it at first, but one night he got drunk and confessed everything: how he'd been sleeping with her for months, how he loved her but knew his parents would never accept their relationship."

Jackass, CJ thought darkly. Worse, a cowardly jackass. "And that's why you've been having a hard time trusting me?"

Brady nodded. "The thing is, I love you a thousand times more than I ever loved him. If you did cheat on me…"

"I wouldn't. That's not who I am. And by the way, Nate must have been certifiable to fall in love with anyone other than you."

"You're sweet to say that. But no matter what happened in the past, there's no excuse for me to not trust you. You deserve better."

CJ was trying to figure out how to broach the idea that perhaps she could have handled the Nell situation better herself when Brady focused behind her, frowning. Glancing over her shoulder, CJ discovered Janice headed straight for their table, her face composed in serious lines.

"What is it?" Brady asked, half-rising.

"Sorry to interrupt," Janice said, nodding at CJ, "but there was an emergency phone call for you from California. Your parents need to talk to you as soon as possible."

"Oh, God." Brady's voice broke a little. "No, no, no, not Chris. It can't be."

"Maybe he was injured," Janice said, sliding her arm around Brady's shoulders. "Maybe he's on his way home on a troop ship this minute."

"Do you think?"

"It's possible. You won't know until you call home."

CJ dropped a few dollars on the table to cover their drinks and hurried after Brady and Janice. Outside a cab waited at the curb, meter running. As soon as they'd slid in, the car took off.

In the back seat, CJ sat on one side of Brady, Janice on the other, each holding one of her hands. Brady had composed herself and now sat grimly silent, her knuckles white. CJ pictured Chris, blond and almost as attractive as his younger sister in his official Army portrait, which Brady kept in her locker. Then she pictured her own brothers, one fighting his way through the Gilbert Islands, the other freezing in a wooden shack in the mountains of Italy as his unit tried to ready an abandoned airfield for long-range bomber attacks. What if the phone call had been for her? Stomach churning, she redoubled her grip on Brady's hand.

"It'll be okay," she said. "Everything will be okay."

Brady squeezed her hand back but didn't answer as the cab drove onto base.

At the gate to the WAC compound, CJ and Brady piled out and hurried back to Company A's barracks, leaving Janice to pay the driver. Brady didn't bother signing CJ in. She simply took her by the hand and brought her down the hallway to the orderly room.

"Buchanan," the sergeant in charge of quarters said, nodding at Brady and then frowning slightly at CJ. "I have a message for you from the Red Cross, but you might want to take it in private."

Brady shook her head. "She stays."

"Okay," the sergeant said dubiously, her eyes resting on their linked hands.

CJ started to extricate her fingers, but Brady held on tighter.

"The message, please, Sergeant Matthews?"

The sergeant adjusted her glasses, glanced down at the piece of paper on her desk and read aloud, "Please have Private Buchanan call home as soon as possible for information about a family emergency. It is not, repeat, *not* about her brother Christopher."

Brady's grip loosened, and then she turned and wrapped her arms around CJ's neck, hiding her face as a sob overtook her.

Janice came in then and looked at CJ, eyebrows raised.

"It isn't Chris." CJ smoothed her hand across Brady's back. It wasn't her brother. So what, then, was the emergency?

After a minute or two, Brady gathered herself and made the phone call. CJ could hear a woman's voice at the other end as soon as the operator put the call through, but she couldn't make out distinct words.

"Hello, Mother," Brady said, her back stiffening. "Yes, I received the message. Yes, that was the right procedure. I agree, the Red Cross is doing a wonderful job." She paused, tapping her foot against the linoleum floor. "That's all right. Perhaps you could tell me why you called?"

The woman's voice sounded again, and as CJ watched, Brady's face slackened. Her eyes grew blank, and she shook her head. "That's not possible. He wasn't on the front lines."

As Brady stopped and listened again, CJ wondered who they were discussing. Was it a cousin? A friend? But as the voice at the other end kept going and Brady's eyes filled with tears, CJ knew: It was Nate. Nate, who had written entertaining missives about officers' dinners and boorish Brits and swimming parties in the warm, salty waters of the Mediterranean. Nate, who Brady had Dear Johned a few days before Thanksgiving in a letter she still didn't know whether or not he'd received.

"When?" Brady finally asked, her voice dull now. "All right. Thank you, Mother. Yes, I'll let you know. Yes, tell them I'll be there. Goodbye."

She handed the phone back to the sergeant, who made a notation on a form. "Everything all right at home, Buchanan?"

"No, it isn't." Brady reached for CJ's hand again. "My fiancé was killed in action. I have to go home."

CHAPTER TWENTY

"What do you mean, your fiancé?" CJ asked. "You don't have a fiancé anymore. Do you?"

They were alone on the back porch of the barracks, and Brady was crying quietly, tears sliding unchecked down her cheeks as she gazed back at CJ.

"Of course not," she said, sounding weary. "You know I don't. But as far as the rest of the world is concerned, Nate and I are still engaged."

"You haven't even told your parents?"

"No, only my brother knows. I was waiting until I heard from Nate. I assumed I would have heard something by now."

Brady had reported receiving a handful of letters from Nate since she'd sent hers ending the engagement, but his correspondence had remained upbeat. Clearly he hadn't received her last letter yet. Or maybe he had. Perhaps even now his final, posthumous letter to Brady was winging its way across the world.

"So the whole time you were giving me a hard time about Nell, you were pretending to be engaged to him?"

"That's different," Brady said. "Surely you see."

"I thought I did."

Suddenly she felt the need to put space between her and Brady. She backed down the stairs to the ground, her feet slipping a little in the Texas dust.

"CJ, you know I love you. Nate knows too…" She stopped. "I mean, he knew. At least, I think he did."

CJ had never pressed Brady for details about that last letter; she'd figured it wasn't any of her business. Now she asked, "You told him about me?"

"Not by name," Brady admitted, gazing down at her from the top step. "But I did tell him I'd fallen in love with someone else and that I was breaking off the engagement so we could be together."

"Oh." CJ chewed her lip. That was fairly significant.

"I didn't tell anyone here," Brady added, "because I thought it might offer us some protection. In case people started to talk."

"Wacs gossip? You think?"

Brady tried to smile. Then she turned away, her head bowed. Quickly CJ climbed the stairs and tugged her into her arms.

"It'll be okay," she said, her cheek tousling Brady's hair. "I'm not going anywhere, I promise."

Later, as they sat on the top step sharing a cigarette, Brady related her mother's end of the conversation. Nate had been killed two weeks earlier, but his parents had just received notification that morning. The officer who came to their house told them a German bomber attacked the forward communications unit he was inspecting. Apparently he had been assigned to an Allied team touring frontline switchboards.

"You didn't know?" CJ asked.

Brady shook her head. "He probably wasn't allowed to tell anyone."

She hesitated, but she couldn't keep the question from escaping: "Does this make you wish you hadn't broken up with him?"

"No. It may sound awful, but I wish I'd done it sooner. I should never have agreed to marry him in the first place."

CJ didn't think it sounded awful. Before tonight, she'd conceived of Nate as a fellow like Jack or Mac or Sam, affable and generally good-intentioned. She'd felt sorry for him, possibly even a bit guilty for stealing his girl. Brady's confession had changed all of that. He may have died fighting for his country, but the damage he'd inflicted on her back in college was still very much alive.

"What now?" CJ asked as their shared cigarette burned down to nothing.

Brady leaned against her. "Now I go home and pretend to be the loving fiancé one last time."

She winced. "You do?"

"I'm not doing it for Nate, or for me. Well, maybe a little for me, but mostly it's for his parents. He's their only son, and they're more fragile than my parents. Besides, they've always been good to me. I think I might have wanted them as in-laws more than I wanted him as a husband."

CJ nodded reluctantly. "I get it. You're going home to do the right thing. That's one of the reasons I love you, because even though you pretend otherwise, you're a good egg."

"So are you. I'll miss you," Brady added, her chin resting on CJ's shoulder. "More than you know."

"I think I know." CJ kissed her slowly, trying to help in the one way she knew how.

At the sound of footsteps, they flinched apart.

"Relax," Janice said, "it's me. But you two have got to be more careful. I could have been anyone."

* * *

"You look like someone kicked your puppy."

"She does, doesn't she?"

CJ glanced over her shoulder to see Reggie and Toby walking along the dirt road behind her. She'd left Brady a little while before, but instead of going straight back to her barracks, she'd decided to take a walk around the compound before bed check.

"What are you two up to?" she asked, deflecting the comment.

Reggie's smile was smug. "We just said goodnight to our ladies. What about you? How was your date?"

"Not so good," CJ admitted, and quickly filled them in on the evening's events.

"Oh, no." Toby slid an arm around her shoulders. "I'm sorry, pal."

"What about Christmas at the Grand Canyon?" Reggie asked. "You were both so excited."

With the holiday a week off, CJ had asked Brady the same question.

"It's not like you'll have a hard time finding someone else to take," Brady had replied. As CJ stared at her, she'd added quickly, "Like Sarah or Reggie, I mean. But do me a favor? Don't take Nell."

CJ had snorted. "I don't think there's any danger of that. I let her know there would be nothing extracurricular between us, not even flying."

"You did?" Brady's eyes brightened momentarily.

"I probably should have done it sooner—you were right about her, I think. But I really like flying."

At that, Brady had rolled her eyes. "Gee, I hadn't noticed."

Now CJ glanced at her friends. "I don't want to go without her. Do either of you want the reservation?"

Toby shook her head. "Kate and I got tickets to Albuquerque. She has an aunt who lives there—an unmarried aunt who seems awfully interested in meeting me."

"I'll take it," Reggie volunteered. "Holly's been dropping comments about going away together ever since I told her about your plans."

"In that case, it's all yours."

As Reggie whooped and leapt into the air, CJ exchanged an amused look with Toby. At least someone would be able to use the room.

Back at the barracks, CJ got ready for bed, surrounded by her laughing, chatting, griping squad mates. A few others were as quiet as she was, and she wondered what pain their silences hid: trouble with a superior officer, a relative missing in action, a gold star banner in a window back home? There was no way of knowing what the person beside you was going through unless she opened up and let you in. And even then, there was no real way of sharing how that person felt, even if they told you in no uncertain terms. CJ knew Brady was grieving Nate, but she had no idea what it would feel like to lose a boy she'd known since kindergarten, the one she had once thought she might settle down and raise a family with. She hadn't known Sean all that long, and besides, he was safely back in Ann Arbor with his deferment.

The wireless in the day room was playing holiday tunes, but CJ couldn't get into the spirit. This time last week she'd been planning the Grand Canyon surprise, and now she was facing a lonely Christmas in Texas without her closest friends, let alone her girlfriend. She had no doubt Brady would be home well before the holiday. In cases of compassionate leave on the home front, the military machine rolled quickly. As soon as the request came in from the Red Cross verifying Brady's family emergency, the paperwork chain would start. Within forty-eight hours, she would be granted leave to attend Nate's memorial service. By mid-week, she would probably be back in L.A., back in the house she had grown up in with the family and friends who knew her as a version of herself that CJ had never met. Would Brady revert to who she had once been? Or would she remain the woman she had become?

CJ wished she could be sure of the answer.

* * *

The military machine moved even faster than expected. After noon mess the next day, CJ found herself driving Brady to the train station in the same car that had taken them to Cloudcroft what now seemed like eons ago.

"I wish you didn't have to go," she said as she drove. "Are you honestly not coming back until after New Year's?"

"I'll be back on the third, maybe sooner."

"It sounds like forever. Promise you'll call on Christmas?"

Brady nodded. "I would call you every day if I could."

They had agreed that talking frequently would not only cost a fortune but also raise suspicion. They couldn't risk written correspondence for the same reason—their mail was guaranteed to be read by their company censors. For the next two weeks, they would be operating on near radio silence.

Their hands lay clasped together on the seat, and CJ could feel Brady watching her.

"I wish you were coming with me."

"Really?" CJ glanced at her, then back at the road.

"Really."

"And what would you tell your parents?"

"That you're my illicit female lover, of course, and they'd better get used to seeing us together."

"You wouldn't!"

Brady smiled a little. "You never know. Depends on how much they infuriate me."

"In that case, I think I'm glad I'm not going with you."

The Union Depot lay on the opposite side of town from the post. With its six-story bell tower and Victorian spire, it was hard to miss once you got past the crowded brick and sandstone blocks of downtown El Paso. CJ parked the car and helped Brady with her small hard-backed suitcase.

"You aren't really, are you?" Brady asked as they walked toward the station entrance.

"Aren't what?"

"Glad you're not going with me."

"Of course not."

"Good. Just checking."

Inside the cavernous central waiting room, sunlight shone down on the patterned marble floor from large windows that ringed the third floor. While Brady went to buy a ticket, CJ slouched down on one of the wide oak benches in the middle of the room, leaned her head back and closed her eyes. She hadn't slept much the night before. Whenever she did doze, she would wake up thinking about Nate and the direct hit the mobile switchboard unit had taken from a Luftwaffe bomber. A plane like her brother's, like the bombers Nell and Holly flew—one not very different from the Beechcraft she herself had flown—had released the payload that destroyed the communications installation where Nate and a half dozen other soldiers were working to support the Fifth Army's Italian campaign.

She couldn't stop picturing him as he looked in the photo Brady kept in her locker along with her brother's—young and faintly Robert Taylor-esque in his tennis sweater, with wavy dark hair and a crooked smile. He and Brady would have been a knockout couple, his darkness next to her light. Their children would have been gorgeous too, no doubt. Had he heard the airplane overhead? Had the soldiers inside the mobile unit known they were about to die, or had the bomb struck suddenly, without warning? What was it like to die in a bomb attack? Did you feel your body ripped asunder, or was your soul released before your physical self could die, as some African tribes she'd read about believed?

"There's a train in half an hour," Brady said, sitting down next to her so close that their hips touched.

"So soon?" CJ glanced around automatically to see if anyone was watching them. As women in uniform, they still attracted a decent amount of attention. But surprisingly, they were the lone soldiers in the sparsely crowded station.

"I know." Brady hesitated, and when she spoke again it was in a low tone. "I wish I could hold your hand."

"I wish I could do more than hold your hand." Being close enough to touch but unable to do so was torture. At least she wouldn't have to suffer that particular torment for the next couple of weeks.

Brady grabbed her hand and tugged her toward another section of the train station, suitcase in tow. CJ followed, not realizing her intent until Brady led her into the women's restroom, glanced under the doors to check for patrons—there weren't any—and then pulled her into one of the stalls, leaving her suitcase under the row of sinks.

"What are you…?"

Brady pushed her back against the stall door and kissed her. CJ shut her eyes and leaned into the kiss, even as she was amazed by her ability to do so. They were in a public restroom in a train station that MPs regularly patrolled. And yet, Brady's grief and longing were so raw that she felt herself melting into her arms, losing track of when and where they were. Brady kissed her desperately, and CJ kissed her back just as urgently, her hands slipping inside Brady's uniform. Two days apart had seemed like a lifetime. How would they make it through two weeks?

When the door creaked open and an older woman's voice sounded, followed by a response from a younger woman, CJ and Brady froze, eyes open again. They waited while one of the women used the facilities and washed her hands, chattering to her companion the entire time about miserable stock prices and the dearth of farm equipment, thanks to the war industry. When the door opened again and the women's footsteps receded, CJ leaned her forehead against Brady's.

"What are we doing?"

Brady pulled away. "Janice is right. We do need to be more careful. But sometimes when I get close to you I can't think, not even a little."

They straightened their uniforms and repaired their lipstick, and then they returned to the wooden bench in the waiting room.

"Will your parents be waiting at the other end?"

"No, they'll probably send Isabel." As CJ stared, she added, "Our housekeeper, remember?"

"I remember." She shook her head.

"What? It's what everyone does at home."

"I'm sure it is."

They sat in silence for a little while, CJ trying not to notice Brady's proximity. Too bad she couldn't sneak onto the train with her. If they had a sleeper car, they would find plenty of ways to amuse themselves on the long trip across New Mexico, Arizona and California.

"How far is it, anyway?"

"Eight hundred miles. I'll be home by tomorrow night."

All that valuable time they could be spending together, wasted. The ridiculous Army with its arcane rules—why shouldn't she go with Brady? After all, how exactly was her work with Tow Target supposed to make a difference in the war? It wasn't like she was a pilot or training to be a navigator or bombardier. She understood why soldiers facing combat needed to be controlled, regimented, reduced to tiny cogs in the military wheel. But she and Brady were lowly privates who would never see combat, like thousands of others who'd volunteered to serve and found themselves stationed on the home front. What would it hurt to allow them a bit more freedom?

Still, she had signed away her personal liberty willingly. Someday the war would be over and she and Brady would be free to go anywhere they desired, anytime they chose. But for now, when Brady's train was called, all she could do was walk with her to the track, hug her tightly for as long as was wise—perhaps a little longer—and then let go with both hands as Brady boarded the train and found a window seat from which to wave as the train whistled and slowly, slowly chugged out of the station, taking what felt like most of her heart with it.

She watched from the platform until the train was out of sight, and then she got back in Brady's friend's car and drove up the Franklin Mountain access road. Midway up was a vantage point, and she pulled the car over and climbed up on its hood, leaning back against the windshield to watch clouds and airplanes move overhead at vastly different speeds. The day was warmer than usual for the season, and soon she was shrugging out of her newly tailored winter overcoat. When the quartermaster had issued it to her two months ago, the coat had hung off her almost comically. Now it fit perfectly, just as Brady's did.

Nell was right—it didn't feel like Christmas without snow, evergreens, nativity scenes. People here seemed to favor Mexican holiday displays over traditional American decorations. It was easy to stare up at the bright Texas sky and forget that in a matter of days her family would get together with relatives far and near to celebrate winter solstice, the shortest day of the year, followed closely by the birth of Jesus. There would be caroling parties, wreaths on doors, stars and popcorn strings on trees, the annual collective reading of "A Visit from St. Nicholas" on Christmas Eve before a dying fire, with stockings hung and spiced apple cider mulling on the stove. She could smell the cedar boughs and the pumpkin pie, hear her mother's and father's voices raised in harmony as they sang "Silent Night" and "The First Noël" while Rebecca played along on the piano.

The sounds and sights of home were so vivid against her closed eyelids that she was almost surprised when a gust of warm air swirled dust against the hood. Rubbing the grit from her eyes, she gazed out over the sprawl of El Paso and Fort Bliss.

Damn you, Nate. Why did you have to go and get yourself killed?

* * *

Back at the barracks, she signed up in the orderly room for a phone spot. Saturdays and Sundays were popular calling times, but she managed to squeeze her name into a fifteen-minute slot before supper.

It took the operator forever to connect to her family's line, and then she came back and reported it was in use. Probably one of the neighbors—they shared a line with the DeWitts, Smalls and

Andersons, which made getting through difficult sometimes. The line stayed busy, so finally CJ asked the operator to interrupt whoever was on the line and let them know that she was trying to reach her parents from Texas. A moment later, CJ heard her mother's voice: "Caroline? Is that you?"

"Hi, Mom." Suddenly her throat was tight and she could barely see through blurred eyes.

"What's wrong, honey? Are you all right? It isn't one of the boys, is it?"

CJ tried to swallow back her tears. "No, everything's fine. Well, not fine. My friend Brady, you know, the one I was supposed to go to the Grand Canyon with? We found out her fiancé was killed in Italy. She's on her way home for the memorial service right now."

"Sweetheart, I'm so sorry." She paused. "I didn't realize Brady had a fiancé."

"They grew up together in L.A. That's where she's going now."

"Poor girl. You tell her we're thinking of her, won't you?"

"Of course. How are things at home?"

She sat in the hard-backed chair at the orderly's desk, aware of the sergeant flipping through a magazine a few feet away, and listened as her mother described the weather, the fields, the animals and the rest of the family—everyone except her sister. As the call went on, CJ realized her mother hadn't mentioned Rebecca, not once.

"Why aren't you talking about Rebecca? Is she all right?" There was silence at the other end, and CJ gripped the handset more tightly. "Mother? What's wrong with Rebecca?"

"I wasn't going to tell you, honey. I didn't want to ruin your Christmas. It's not like there's anything you can do."

"Oh my God, what's wrong?"

"She has scarlet fever," her mother admitted. "She's been in bed the last week or so, and as you can imagine, she is not very happy with the world right now. I'm sure you remember the feeling."

CJ was thirteen when she came down with scarlet fever, and she didn't think she would ever forget having to be quarantined in her bedroom for three weeks while the bacterial infection worked its way through her system. No one else in the family had had it before, so her brothers and sister had all gone to stay with their grandparents while she'd remained home with her parents throughout the entire quarantine period. After she got better, they'd cut her hair short, burned her bedding and clothes, and disinfected everything else. That had been worse than the illness itself, she remembered.

"How is she? Is it bad?"

"No, we've been lucky. It seems to be about as mild for her as it was for you. Dr. Forrest thinks she should be fine in a couple of weeks."

"Is she on quarantine?"

The sergeant's head lifted at this.

"Yes, poor thing. I think she's read every magazine and most of the books in the house."

"Are you home from school too?"

"The administration thought it would be best not to have me in the classroom, and I wanted to be home anyway, so I started my Christmas break early."

"What about Pete?"

"He's fine. He's staying with the Youngs for now, so of course he and David are on Cloud Nine."

David, her brother's best friend from the Boy Scouts, lived on a nearby farm. Something clicked in CJ's head. Scarlet fever was a serious illness with few treatment options, and since CJ had already had it, she was the lone member of her family who couldn't catch it again. By rights, the military should let her go home to help nurse her sister back to health.

"Mother, can you do me a favor? Write down what I tell you. If everything works out, I might be able to come home for Christmas."

"Not really?"

"Really. Now here's what I want you to do."

* * *

On Monday morning, Lieutenant Kelly held her after drill.

"At ease, Private," she said when CJ saluted. "I understand you have a family emergency."

"Yes, ma'am. My little sister has scarlet fever, and because I'm the only one in the family who's already had it, my parents are hoping I can come home to help out."

"I see." The lieutenant gazed out across the company parade grounds. "It seems to me that I heard something about one of your friends in Company A being out on emergency leave. This doesn't have anything to do with her, does it?"

CJ's lips were suddenly dry. "Well, no. Wait, what do you mean, ma'am?"

"I mean, if you were to tell me that you were going home to Michigan, and then it was discovered that you, shall we say, *detoured* someplace else, that would be a violation of the Uniform Code of Military Justice."

Stunned, CJ made the mistake of looking the lieutenant directly in the eye. What she saw was not judgment or condemnation so much as it was concern.

Quickly she averted her eyes. "Yes, ma'am. But to be honest, it wouldn't have occurred to me to take any detours. I'm a bit homesick, and my family could use the help."

"Good," Lieutenant Kelly said. "I suspected as much, but I felt it was important to let you know where the Army stands on such matters."

"Yes, ma'am."

"Your paperwork will be processed this morning. Stop by my office after noon mess, and we'll get you home to your family, Private. Are you planning to avail yourself of Air Corps travel resources?"

"Yes, ma'am."

"Let me know if you need anything else. Dismissed."

CJ saluted and jogged off to breakfast. Toby and Reggie had always claimed the lieutenant was one of their kind. This conversation proved that if she wasn't, then she was at least on their side, which might be even better. On the other hand, it also indicated that she and Brady were on the higher-ups' radar. Maybe no one else had noticed the intimate underpinnings of their friendship. After all, Lieutenant Kelly was the only WAC officer who routinely took part in proceedings of the Fort Bliss Sporting Club.

Later, at the Balloon Hangar, CJ was completing an inventory of one of the rolling toolboxes when Nell leaned against the nearest steel truss, dressed in her bomber jacket with a parachute strap slung over one shoulder. "Howdy."

"Hello," CJ said, looking up at her.

"I heard you had a family emergency, and I wanted to see if I could help." As CJ frowned, she held up her hands. "I told you before, no strings attached. I thought I could fly you a leg closer, maybe. It's what we do when we go on leave."

"As tempting as your offer is, I'm planning to go standby this afternoon. But thanks. I do appreciate it."

Still Nell lingered. "Is it serious, the emergency?"

"I don't think so. My little sister has scarlet fever, but so far it doesn't seem too bad."

"I had that as a kid." Nell shook her head. "I read every single book in my room four or five times before they finally let me out."

"Me too. That's why my parents were hoping I could get home—no one else has had it."

"That and it's Christmas." Nell gave her a half-smile. "Good luck, CJ. Happy Christmas."

"Happy Christmas."

It was nice of her to offer, but CJ had told Brady she wouldn't be spending time with Nell outside of work, and she didn't plan to break her word the first chance that came up. *Maybe the second*, she told herself, remembering with a sigh how it had felt to fly the AT-11 back from the firing ranges.

A half hour later, an Air Corps captain with a Ferry Squadron patch on his uniform stopped by the hangar. CJ saw him chatting with Whimpy and was somehow unsurprised when her crew chief nodded in her direction.

"Private Jamieson?" The slim good-looking captain paused before her. His jacket bore the name "Vandenburg," which reminded her of home. Southwest Michigan was saturated with Dutch names due to the presence of Holland, an old Dutch settlement there.

She dropped a propeller wrench and saluted quickly. "Yes, sir."

"At ease. A little bird told me you're on your way home to Michigan on emergency leave. Is that true?"

"Yes sir."

"It's your lucky day then. I'm on my way to Romulus with a Gooney Bird. You're welcome to hitch a ride if you think you can find your way home from there."

Romulus, the main AAF ferry center, was a couple of hours from home by train.

"I think I can manage," CJ said, smiling at him. "Thank you, sir. But how did you...?"

"The Air Corps takes care of its own," he said, and winked. "Now, how soon can you be ready?"

She glanced at the clock on the wall. It was nine thirty. "An hour?" she hazarded, hoping that when Lieutenant Kelly said her paperwork would be ready "by noon mess," she actually meant by, say, ten thirty.

"That'll give me time to grab a bite to eat. Which reminds me—you might want to bring some extra vittles along for the ride. It's a ten-hour flight, and I don't plan to stop along the way."

With that, he spun on his heel and walked back to a waiting Jeep.

"Blimey." Reggie had been standing nearby eavesdropping, as had half their squad. "You better hurry. Those ferry boys don't wait around!"

"Get a move on," Whimpy added. "And Jamieson."

"Yes sir?"

"Have a very merry Christmas. Antonelli, drive her back to pick her up her gear, will you?"

"Yes sir," Reggie said.

The next hour was a whirlwind. There were farewells to proffer, food to order from the club—Reggie volunteered to wait for it while she grabbed her already-packed suitcase from the barracks—and paperwork to be completed rather hastily. Then Reggie was driving her back to their old digs, the Transient Hangar, where there was a reunion of sorts as her old mates hugged her, loaned her a bomber jacket that had been left behind by some unfortunate pilot— "Lieutenant Hendricksen," according to the name on the lapel—and fitted her with a parachute.

Soon Reggie was driving her down the flight line to the waiting C-47 Skytrain.

"Thanks again for the hotel room," she said, guiding the Jeep past the seemingly never-ending rows of bombers and trainers. "Holly is super excited and so am I. I've never been to the Grand Canyon before."

"Neither have I."

"We'll get you there one day. In the meantime, have a good time with your family. I hope your sister gets better soon."

"Thanks, Reggie." She hugged her tightly before hopping out of the Jeep. "Have fun. See you in ten days!"

Reggie beeped the Jeep's horn and drove away.

CJ approached the twin-engine monoplane, the military's standard transport craft. Every branch of the US military and all of the major Allied nations flew some version of this plane, known for its dependability. Certainly it wasn't as sexy as the other aircraft she'd taken rides on, but it made an ideal choice for the fifteen hundred air miles that lay between Texas and Michigan.

The navigator helped her aboard while the pilot and copilot ran through the tech orders and conversed with the control tower.

"Glad you could make it, Private," Vandenburg said, nodding at her over his shoulder. "You might as well buckle up and settle in. It's going to be a long ride."

"Yes, sir," she said, buckling into one of the inward-facing metal bench seats in the cargo area. She checked her watch. Ten thirty-five. If all went well, meaning no weather or mechanical delays, they would be in Romulus by eight thirty that night. After that, Lord knew what the next leg of her journey held in store. At least she would be in Michigan.

As the plane's engines sputtered and coughed, CJ closed her eyes and prayed: *Please, God, hold us in your hands.* Then she watched out the nearest square passenger window as the airplane taxied onto the main Biggs runway and prepared to take off. The world outside was a now-familiar brown expanse edged with blue sky. She wondered what she would find at home. Gray skies? Icy roads? Her father had written that what snow they'd gotten had mostly melted by now, but that didn't mean a storm couldn't dump three feet on them overnight. Maybe she would have a white Christmas, after all.

If she couldn't have Christmas with Brady at the Grand Canyon, a hometown holiday was the next best thing. *Better, even?* But her mind rejected the thought. Two nights in a hotel with Brady, gloriously, luxuriously alone would have been well worth missing Christmas in Kalamazoo.

Someday, she thought, gazing out the window as the runway fell away and the plane turned toward home.

CHAPTER TWENTY-ONE

As she crossed the runway, wind blasted beneath her skirt. Not for the first time during the long day, CJ wished she had worn tights. She had only been in Texas for a few months, but somehow she had managed in that short time to forget her many years of winter training. How ridiculous that she should be so unprepared.

Captain Vandenburg led her into the ready room, empty at that time of night. "My desk's right here. Help yourself to the phone."

"Thank you, sir," CJ said. "You're being very kind."

"Kindness has nothing to do with it." His brown eyes sparkled despite the long, exhausting flight. "Pinkie promised me a date if I delivered you here safely, so I'm looking after my investment."

"Pinkie..." CJ trailed off. She should have known Nell would find a way to help her.

"Do you need a phone book?" he prompted, checking his wristwatch.

"No." She picked up the receiver and dialed a number by heart. "Sadie? It's CJ. What are you doing right now?"

Half an hour later she was seated in her former apartment with a cup of hot cocoa in her hands, undergoing an interrogation by two friends who had been a year behind her at Michigan. Sadie

Beckdorf was the daughter of a progressive, slightly flaky mother who had bounced around the country for years before finally settling in Cleveland. Perhaps in response to her mother's eternal flightiness, Sadie was one of the steadiest, most responsible people CJ knew at school. Her roommate, Tricia Flowers, was the opposite—intelligent but scattered, sweet but entirely too trusting. They had jumped at the opportunity to take over the lease of her brownstone apartment when she graduated.

"Your last letter said you wouldn't be home for months, possibly longer. How are you here now?" Sadie asked.

CJ explained about her sister's illness and the emergency leave. Then she asked her former schoolmates how classes were going and sat back to listen as they filled her in on history department gossip. It was amazing how far removed she felt from the world that she had happily inhabited since leaving home after high school.

At one point, Sadie and Tricia exchanged a look she couldn't quite read. She sat up a little straighter. "What?"

"It's Sean," Sadie said. "Have you heard?"

"Heard what?"

"He joined the Navy. He's leaving for basic training in a couple of weeks."

"He what?" She shook her head in disbelief. "But he had his deferment. I don't understand."

"Some people are saying he did it because of you," Tricia said, pushing back her long hair.

"Trish!" Sadie's tone was reproachful.

"It's okay," CJ said. "Ultimately it's his decision. I just have a hard time picturing him in the military. He's always been so against the war."

"I thought you would want to know. Are you planning to see him while you're on leave? Tristan said he's on campus for another couple of days."

Tristan was another of their friends, a pacifist whose heart murmur had given him a graceful out from military service.

"I wasn't planning on it," she admitted.

"Are you not even friends anymore?" Tricia asked.

"It didn't end well."

"Because you met someone in Texas?"

CJ blinked. Here was the first test, the first person from her old life to ask about her new life. Except that wasn't entirely accurate. "Does anyone here keep in touch with Jack Sawyer?"

"Tristan and he write."

"And he sometimes shares news about me?"

They nodded.

Perhaps it was easier, having the decision made for her. Now she wouldn't have to choose whether or not to lie to her friends from college. Soon enough she would have to make that choice with her family. Sometime in the next few days, in fact.

"Does Sean know?"

"That you're involved with someone in Texas? I don't think so," Sadie said.

"What's he like?" Tricia added, leaning forward in her arm chair near the fireplace. "Is he handsome? Where is he from? Jack told Tristan he's never seen you happier."

Crap. Jack had chosen to protect her, after all. But of course—he couldn't have put the true nature of her relationship in a letter. The officer in his unit in charge of reading the enlisted men's mail was required to report any violation of Army rules, especially a violation of the Articles of War like mutiny, aiding the enemy, murder, arson and, oh yes, sodomy.

That meant the need to decide still existed.

"Jack is right," she said. "Do you have any bread, by the way? I could die for a piece of toast."

"Of course." Tricia jumped up.

As soon as her roommate was gone, Sadie asked, "Did things not work out with your new beau?"

"It's not that." CJ sipped her cocoa. Sadie had always seemed to harbor a bit of hero worship for her and Sean, the older, more accomplished students in the department who took home scholarships and awards at every turn. How would she take the news that CJ was gay?

"Was he sent overseas? Is that why you wanted to come home?"

"No, it's not anything like that. It's, well, it's…" She hesitated. It wasn't too late to lie. She took a breath. "You know Marjorie Quinlan, right? And her friend, Miss Brooks in the chemistry department?"

Sadie nodded, head tilted slightly to one side. Her eyes narrowed, and then she gasped and covered her mouth. "You? No. You're saying you're—like *them*?"

CJ bit her lip and nodded, keeping her eyes on Sadie's even though she wanted to look away, wanted to jump up and make her way outside into the cold, gray streets. Fight, flight or freeze, as her basic training instructors had termed the automatic response to perceived danger.

"But what about Sean? You were happy together. I saw you. You were planning to get married!" Sadie's voice was almost accusing.

Tricia poked her head out from the nearby kitchen. "Everything okay?"

Sadie blinked rapidly, still staring at CJ. "Fine. How's the toast coming?"

"Ready in a jiffy," Tricia said brightly, and vanished again.

"I'm sorry to spring it on you like this." CJ set her mug on the low coffee table where she used to pile her textbooks haphazardly. "I can leave if you'd prefer."

"Don't be dramatic. You caught me off guard, is all. Can I at least have a minute to get used to the idea?"

"Of course. Sorry."

"Stop apologizing." Sadie's voice softened a little. "This must be hard for you too."

"A bit."

There was silence, and then Sadie asked, "Does anyone else know, other than your girlfriend?"

This last bit was said ironically, and CJ squinted at her, trying to determine whether the irony came from disappointment, amusement or some other cryptic emotion altogether. "Some friends in Texas, yes, but not anyone from here. Except Jack."

"Jack knows?" She shook her head. "I guess what they say about Wacs is true then."

"I've heard a lot of things said about Wacs, and very few of them are true."

Tricia came back then with her toast and her bubbly questions about CJ's love life, but Sadie guided the conversation in another direction before announcing they should probably let CJ rest.

"You've had a long day. I hope the couch will be okay?"

"I've always loved this couch. Besides, it's better than the cot I'm used to," CJ assured her. "Thank you."

Sadie nodded, and then, while Tricia went to get bedding from the hall closet, added quietly, "I always thought you and Sean would end up together, with this perfect academic couple's life. I suppose I took it a little personally when I heard you were with someone else, and now to find out it's a girl...But it's none of my business. I say if you're happy, good for you."

Still, as they took turns getting ready for bed in the little bathroom that had been CJ's ever since she moved out of the dormitory after freshman year, Sadie wouldn't quite meet her eyes. After the two girls retired to their twin beds in the room where CJ had spent more than a few nights with Sean, she could hear whispers on the other side of the wall, and she wondered if, after all, she should have lied.

Sleep eluded her, for reasons that defied understanding. She'd spent ten hours on a cold, juddering airplane that had taken her halfway across the country, and she was finally being given the opportunity to sleep in a room where she would be the lone occupant. This morning, she had awakened in the dimly lit squad room in West Texas, and now she was preparing to sleep in her former apartment in Ann Arbor, listening to the wind rattle the window panes just as she had the previous winter and the winter before that and the winter before that. How could she be transported so suddenly from her new life into her old? How did she make the pages of her life story fit together? Or maybe they couldn't—maybe each page was an entirely new addition, placed into the book after the ones that had come before.

As she watched the flames in the brick-faced fireplace give way to ash, she wondered where Brady was. It would be earlier in L.A. Perhaps she was at dinner at a restaurant in Hollywood, where Los Angelenos with trust funds typically ventured. Was she with old friends too, trying to decide what to share? Had she confessed the truth to anyone, or was she biding her time in L.A., waiting to escape back to Fort Bliss? Which was a slightly ridiculous thought. No one in their right mind would give up silk and celebrity parties for khaki and communal living, but that was exactly what Brady had done when she joined the Army. Which life would she choose if she had it to do over?

For that matter, which life would CJ choose? But she already knew the answer to that. She liked her work with Tow Target, looked forward to each new day in the Balloon Hangar. Besides, she wouldn't trade falling in love with Brady for anything. The entire plane ride to Michigan, when she wasn't looking out the window marveling at the clouds and the dark sky overhead and the changing land masses below, or chatting with the crew—Vandenburg was from a Dutch enclave in Washington state, not Michigan—she had daydreamed about Brady. Reminiscing about their weekend in New Mexico had occupied her for some time, especially after she realized that recalling their two weekends at the Hilton led to certain desires probably better not dwelled upon when she was stuck on a plane for ten hours with three men she didn't know.

Actually, probably better not to dwell on those memories here in her former sitting room either, she thought, her eyes tracing the familiar pink wallpaper with its pale yellow stripes and blue roses. The two girls in the other room no doubt already considered her sexually depraved. She didn't need to add fuel to the fire, so to speak.

"Brady," she whispered. She closed her eyes, picturing blonde curls, clear blue eyes, red lips that tasted of clove cigarettes and Lone Star beer.

Lieutenant Kelly's warning came back to her, and she realized now the wisdom in her commanding officer's counsel. Because if she didn't know it could cost her so much, she might be tempted to find her way back across the country in time to spend Christmas Eve in L.A.

* * *

The train ride home took two and a half hours. At the station in Kalamazoo, she passed the public telephone booth and continued out to the taxi stand. She had surprised her parents a few times when she was in college, and their joyful response had always made her feel particularly loved. Right now she could use the extra sentiment, especially as she still wasn't sure if she should tell her parents about Brady. Sadie's response had done little to bolster her confidence on that front.

Their property was fifteen minutes from the train station: a few blocks west and a dozen or so more north, and there it was. Kalamazoo went from red brick storefronts and factories to red painted barns and alfalfa fields fairly quickly.

CJ had the cab drop her off at the foot of the long circular driveway. Suitcase in hand, she walked briskly up the gravel drive to the two-story farmhouse, winter sun cutting weakly through the gray haze overhead. With Rebecca quarantined, her parents would be home, most likely in the kitchen at the back of the house getting ready for the mid-day meal. They would be spending the holidays at home too, foregoing the usual day-trips to Detroit to see her mother's family and to Muskegon to see her father's brother and his family. His other siblings lived farther away, and CJ's mother didn't like to travel in winter.

As she neared the house, the first thing she noticed was the foot-long, bright red sign attached to the front door: "SCARLET FEVER. Keep out of this house by order of the Board of Health." It was official then. Somehow seeing the sign brought home the seriousness of the situation. Most people came through scarlet fever fine, but in a few it could cause rheumatic fever or other complications. Accustomed to worrying about her brothers in their separate combat zones, she hadn't considered worrying about her little sister.

A curtain flickered in the upstairs bedroom she and Rebecca shared whenever she was home, and then a shape appeared at the window: Rebecca, waving furiously at her. CJ smiled and waved back. Even from here, she could see the telltale rash scalding her sister's face, chest and arms—it looked like a terrible sunburn with tiny red bumps, as she recalled from examining her own diseased body in the mirror on the back of the closet door. Little wonder Rebecca was excited to have a visitor. Any change in routine would make the quarantine period go by faster.

Ignoring the Board of Health's warning, CJ opened the front door and stepped into the vestibule, where she dropped her suitcase and stepped out of her shoes. Then she opened a second set of doors and walked into the front hallway.

"Hello!" she called. "Where is everyone?"

Rebecca's head poked out from the second floor, peering down at her from the top of the stairs that lay directly ahead of the front door. "CJ!" she said in a stage whisper. "You're home!"

"Hiya, kid." She smiled up at her younger sister. Other than the rash, Rebecca didn't look sick. CJ's worry faded as she unzipped her borrowed bomber jacket.

In a moment the door to the kitchen swung open, and her mother strode forward, wiping her hands on a dish towel. Quickly Rebecca made a shushing motion and vanished back toward the bedroom. She probably wasn't "allowed" to leave the bedroom. CJ recalled sneaking out a few times herself.

"Caroline," her mother said, smiling broadly. "You're certainly a sight for sore eyes."

"So are you," CJ said, tears pricking her eyes as her mother tossed the towel on a sideboard and pulled her into a warm hug. She had never gone this long without seeing her mother. It had been even longer for the boys. Did they miss home as much as she did?

Her father emerged from the kitchen looking hearty and hale and unaccountably older in his usual work uniform: plaid flannel shirt and blue jeans with creases. "CJ?" he said, making it sound like a question, and then he enveloped her and her mother in his broad, strong arms.

Family hug, she thought, remembering years of such embraces. Usually they involved additional participants.

"Nice jacket," her father commented, smoothing down the leather collar.

Her mother held her away at arm's length. "And who is Lieutenant Hendricksen?"

CJ wondered if she'd imagined the note of hope in her mother's voice. "We've never met. His lost jacket has become my gain."

"Doesn't wearing it constitute impersonating an officer?" Her father was a volunteer member of the Michigan State Troops, a reserve corps formed after the Michigan National Guard had been called into federal service.

She half-smiled. "It's a minor impersonation."

"Look at you," her mother put in. "How is it you've only been away half a year and yet you seem all grown up?"

"I don't look any different," CJ protested. "Except maybe for the permanent grease stains under my fingernails."

"That's not true. You're—I don't know, exactly. You seem surer of yourself than the last time I saw you. Do we have the Army to thank for that, or is there something else going on?"

CJ's cheeks warmed, and she turned away to hang her coat and hat on the curved wooden coat tree in the vestibule.

"The Army does have a tendency to reveal your true nature," she said. "Now what do I smell cooking? I'm starving!"

"Your mother is making your favorite, of course." He cast his wife an affectionate look. "Turkey soup and garlic toast."

She filled them in on her trip as they headed into the kitchen, where a large pot bubbled on the white enameled electric range. Funny, she still thought of this stove as "new" even though her father had bought it for her mother half a dozen Christmases ago to replace the old green Windsor stove that had come with the property.

"The soup is for supper," her mother said, "but there's plenty of turkey for sandwiches. Why don't you wash up and go say hello to your sister? I'm sure she'll appreciate physical contact with someone other than Dr. Forrest and Nurse Green."

"Poor kid. When did the quarantine start?"

"It's been a week and a day already. You should have seen how excited she was when we told her you were coming home."

Upstairs, CJ had barely knocked when the bedroom door flew open and Rebecca launched herself into her arms.

"Geez, big sis, what took you so long?"

Laughing, CJ picked her up and whirled her around like she always did when she came home from college. Then she pretended to stagger. "Boy, oh boy, little sis, you're getting too big for me," she recited from the script she'd memorized long ago.

"Are you taller?" Rebecca asked, peering up at her.

"No, you're shorter."

"I'm serious, you look taller. Maybe it's the hair." She stared at CJ. "I like it. Most girls couldn't pull it off, but short hair suits you."

"I'm not most girls and neither are you." She flopped onto her old bed against the far wall and surveyed the room. Her star charts and world maps had long since been replaced with posters of Errol Flynn, Tyrone Power and an anonymous bare-chested sailor, but an object on the desk was new. "Mom and Dad bought you a radio?"

Rebecca sat down at the desk between the twin beds. "They only got it because they felt guilty for locking me in for a month."

"I had scarlet fever, and I don't remember them springing for a radio."

"That's because they probably didn't make wireless sets this small back in the olden days."

CJ wrinkled her nose. "Gosh, and from my own sister." She rose and made a move toward the door. "I guess if you're going to feel the need to be obnoxious…"

Rebecca flew to the door, blocking it with her body. "I'm sorry," she said, wheedling like she used to when she was little. "I promise, I'll be nice. Please don't leave me alone!"

"I won't, kid." She ruffled her sister's hair. "I like your 'do, too. Rollers?"

"It's called natural," she started in her haughty teenager's voice. Then she caught herself. "I mean, thanks."

"Uh-huh."

While Rebecca talked a mile a minute about her unbearable eight days of solitude, CJ rifled through the closet. Some of her old clothes were still here, shoved into a back corner. She pulled out a pair of pants, one of Alec's hand-me-down chambray work shirts and a red wool cardigan. There were skirts and blouses from her university days too, but these suited her better.

"Don't you have to stay in uniform?" Rebecca interrupted herself to demand.

"Not when I'm at home with two guests or fewer," CJ said over her shoulder. "Given the lovely quarantine notice on our front door, I doubt we'll be having visitors."

Rebecca giggled.

CJ backed out of the closet, wool socks and leather boots in hand. "Will we?"

It turned out that Fred Dodge, Rebecca's latest in a long string of boyfriends, had sneaked a ladder up to the bedroom window several nights previously and talked to her through the glass. The conversation barely lasted a minute before their father discovered the boy perched against the side of the house at what he claimed was a dangerous angle. He insisted on escorting Fred home immediately and informing his parents of the whereabouts of their son—and their ladder. Then he set up a rope with a bell attached to it below the window sill to prevent anyone else from trying such a "stunt."

"I don't think he has to worry," Rebecca said glumly. "It's been far too cold for anyone else to come see me."

Ah, the ingenuity of teenagers in love. Or, really, anyone in love, she corrected herself, remembering her urge of the night before to hop the first AAF flight to Southern California.

While CJ changed into the outfit she'd picked out—"boys' clothes," Rebecca deemed them snootily—her sister turned on the wireless.

"What's on?"

"*The Romance of Helen Trent*," Rebecca said, turning up the volume.

"On that note, I'll be back in a little while."

"Uh-huh."

Rebecca was staring at the radio as if the soap opera actors might somehow materialize from inside it. CJ left the bedroom, stopping to wash her hands with hot water and soap before heading downstairs. Her mother had reminded her of the quarantine routine—wash your hands every time you even thought of the patient, basically—but she would have recalled the protocol on her own. It didn't seem that long ago since she'd been the one stuck in that bedroom, her life on hold while everyone else's continued on without her.

"She's into the soaps, isn't she?" CJ commented as she and her parents carried turkey sandwiches to the oak oval dining table in the alcove off the kitchen.

"She says she even dreams about the characters sometimes," her mother said.

"Better than nightmares, I guess."

She took a bite and sighed in appreciation. Everything tasted wonderful—the bakery bread, the turkey her mother had baked and seasoned, the cold potato salad served on the side. How she'd missed her mother's cooking.

"I don't know." Her father lifted an eyebrow. "Dreaming about soaps sounds like a nightmare to me."

"So how are you?" her mother asked. "Your letters are always so cheerful, but I know life in the military can't be all hops and three-day passes."

"Look at you with the lingo. And you're right, Army life isn't without its difficulties." *Friendly fire incidents and rules against dating fellow Wacs, for example.* "But in general, I'm happy."

Her parents exchanged a look.

"What?" she asked, looking from one to the other.

"Nothing. It's just, well, you always did like rules," her father said.

Her mother nodded. "You seemed happiest when there was an established structure of some sort—school, team practices, field rotation schedules."

"Swell. I sound like an automaton."

"Not at all," her mother insisted. "You like order, that's all. Your ability to create order from chaos has allowed you to excel in whatever you put your mind to."

"It's probably coming in pretty handy in the service too," her father added. "Have we mentioned lately how proud of you we are?"

"A dozen times, at least." Even her mother was nodding and smiling, eyes warm as of old. Had she finally forgiven her for breaking up with Sean? Brady's image flickered through CJ's mind, but she pushed it away. She wasn't ready to risk losing her mother's good will again. "Anyway, tell me everything. How is Pete's team doing?"

She ate heartily as her parents filled her in on her brother's basketball exploits, enjoying the talk of familiar people and places. She hadn't realized how homesick she was until now. She wondered briefly if Brady's homecoming was similarly edifying, but how could it be? Brady wasn't close to her family, not like CJ was. For a moment she wished she could be in California with Brady, holding her hand through what had to be a difficult, lonely time. Then again, it wasn't like they could actually hold hands in front of anyone. She remembered how her parents had welcomed Sean into their home, how her mother had smiled fondly whenever they sneaked off together for a turn on the porch swing or a tour of the farm. Somehow she doubted she and Brady would experience the same reception here or in California.

After lunch, she delivered a sandwich to her sister and let herself be sucked into an episode of *Jack Armstrong, All-American Boy*. It felt slightly decadent to lie on her childhood bed listening to the radio. Even though keeping her sister company was precisely what she was here for, she couldn't shake the feeling that there must be work she should be doing.

When *The Lone Ranger* came on, she pulled herself away and headed out to the barn. It was a low-sky kind of day, and she surveyed the winter landscape. She had missed the place of home almost as much as the people. Despite the fact it was currently barren and gray, the land here pulsed with the promise of returning life. When she looked out across the rolling hills, she saw summer ponds and autumn trees, winter clouds and spring fields all at once. Unlike Texas, Michigan was always on the cusp of change.

The first stop she made was the corral near the alfalfa field. Bessie and May, the milk cows, were huddled near the barn, but Molly and Jay, the horses, were eating from a pile of hay near the windbreak on the other side of the corral. When Molly saw CJ climbing up on the split-rail fence to whistle, she whinnied in reply and trotted over. CJ had come armed with carrots and apple slices, of course, but she waited until Molly drew close and nuzzled her coat pockets before pulling them out.

"How are you, girl?" She gazed into the mare's liquid gold eyes and rubbed her muzzle as she munched the treats. "It's been a while, hasn't it? You probably thought I wasn't coming back, but I promise I always will. As long as I can, anyway."

She was thinking of the night flight with Nell, of course, but also of the look in her mother's eyes after she refused Sean's proposal. Would she still be welcome here if she told her parents conclusively there would never be a wedding in her future?

Alec's horse, Jay, must have smelled food, for he came trotting over and butted his head against her bomber jacket. "Okay, okay," she said, laughing, and held her palm open. He sucked the apples and carrots up quickly before Molly could shoulder him out of the way.

Both horses' winter coats had grown in, and CJ removed her wool gloves briefly to feel inside their ears—cool but not cold, as they ought to be. They looked good, healthy and strong despite the old snow piled in the corners of the corral and the near-freezing temperatures currently hovering over the region. She was always amazed by the insulating ability of a horse's winter coat. Standing beside a thousand pounds of shaggy horse made her feel like a puny, naked human under all her layers.

When he realized she had run out of apples, Jay wandered off in search of other food sources. Molly lingered, though, watching her with one eye and then the other. She even butted her head against her chest, and this time, CJ knew the mare wasn't looking for food. She hugged her, pressing her cheek against Molly's cold, furry neck. How many times had they stood like this over the years? Any time she got to feeling lonely, thanks to the seemingly inexplicable differences between her and her schoolmates, Molly had always been there to pet, to hug, to commune with. The horse accepted her for who she was, loved her, even, the way kids her age couldn't seem to.

"She's missed you."

CJ turned to see her father watching them. "I think Jay misses Alec more."

Molly whinnied, and her father came over to stroke her nose and cough up a few apple slices from the pockets of his winter coat. Then the mare drifted away, following Jay on the search for more food.

They stayed where they were at the fence, watching the horses root around their winter grounds.

"For a minute there," her father said, "in that jacket and your brother's old hunting cap, I thought you were Alec."

"Sorry." She touched his hand with hers.

"Don't be." He smiled at her, green-gray eyes crinkling at the corners as he squeezed her fingers. "It's good to have you home. I'd prefer to have all three of you here, but I'm incredibly grateful you could fly in to surprise your mother. It does her heart good. Mine too."

"How's she doing?"

"All right, I think. It's hard not knowing where either of them is or even if they're all right. Brings back certain memories we'd rather not revisit. At least with you we know you're generally safe. Obviously not as safe as if you were in graduate school, but accidents can happen anywhere. Jacob's death proves that."

Clearly she wouldn't be sharing last week's antiaircraft incident anytime soon. "How are the DeWitts?"

"Grieving. There's nothing worse than losing a child, and they have three more in harm's way with no end in sight. I truly believed we had learned something in the last war. Apparently not."

His comment reminded her of something Brady had once said, and she thought not for the first time that her father would like her girlfriend. He had an affinity for strong women, and Brady was not only strong but bright. She wondered if they would ever meet. Then she caught herself. Of course they would. They had to, because she and Brady were going to be together forever. And if not forever, then surely for a long, long time.

"Enough war talk," her father said suddenly, pushing away from the fence. "Would you like to see the John Deere?"

"Of course."

She followed him into the barn workshop where a portable electric heater kept the temperature tolerable, aided by straw insulation and the hay loft. He had written to her in October about the ten-year-old John Deere he'd picked up at an estate sale. It needed a little work, but

Michigan winters were long. His plan was to have it up and running in time for spring planting.

They spent the rest of the afternoon tinkering with the tractor and discussing local news, national politics and the impact of the war on the current football season, both professional—Nagurski, a Bears fullback, had returned from retirement to help fill the manpower shortage, while the Steelers and Eagles had merged for the current season to become the "Steagles"—and college, which included "service teams" drawn for the first time ever from flight schools and other military training centers.

To CJ, standing at her father's side in the barn talking current events over an engine in need of work, it almost seemed as if the war had never happened. Except that they weren't discussing Joe's latest season with the Cubbies or Alec's most recent hunting escapade. The boys were oceans away, and there was no guarantee they were alive. Nate's parents hadn't been informed of his death right away, and she had heard stories of other families having to wait weeks or even months to learn a son's fate. Even in the familiar barn that smelled of alfalfa and motor oil, cow manure and lavender bouquets, even there she couldn't entirely escape the outside world.

"Speaking of flight schools," her father said, "how is it working with the Air Corps? They have a certain reputation as, how shall we say, lady killers?"

Despite his light tone, she could tell that he was genuinely worried about her safety. So she told him about the Wac from the motor pool who picked them up every morning and dropped them off each evening. She told him about the barbed wire fence around the compound and the MPs who patrolled the gate and surrounding areas. And as she described the varied measures in place to protect the women at Fort Bliss, outnumbered by men by more than twenty to one, her father visibly relaxed.

"Really," she summed up, "we feel very safe."

"That's good," her father said, nodding. "You know, your brothers and their friends are good men, but not all of us are."

She gazed at him across the tractor's frame. "You are."

"I was lucky, I had a good father. Plenty of boys don't have any father at all. I worry that will be the case even more after this war."

He pushed back his woolen cap, and she recognized the look that flashed briefly across his face. He still missed his father, who had died suddenly of heart failure a quarter of a century before; probably, he always would.

But at least her safety was one fewer thing for him to worry about. Then she remembered Brady, and it was all she could do to keep smiling and chatting. She couldn't tell him, could she? She had never lied to her parents before, but they already had enough to worry about without adding the fate of her immortal soul—not to mention her post-war prospects, should she be discovered—to the list. She would tell them someday, but it would be far kinder to do it after the war when their list of fears had been whittled back down to a more manageable number.

That was it, she decided as she handed her father a wrench. She would wait until after the war to tell them. For now she would put the future out of her mind and try to focus on enjoying her time in Michigan. Not every Wac got to go home for Christmas while the corps skittered along without her.

"This is probably easy compared to what you're used to," her father commented, giving the wrench a turn.

"I used to think all engines were pretty much the same."

"But not now?"

"Definitely not now."

"Tell me," her father said, his eyes glinting, "what was it like to fly a bomber?"

As CJ tried to describe to her father the unforgettable sensation of being in control of a twin-engine Beechcraft, she found herself transported back to West Texas with its blue sky and white-peaked mountains and sparkling gypsum dunes, its skeleton stripped bare for all the world to see. Could it be? Did she actually miss that godforsaken, dusty corner of the country?

She remembered what Brady had said about being torn between two places that both felt like home, and she realized—Brady, not Fort Bliss, was her home away from home. For now, she would have to remain CJ's secret, but it wouldn't be that way forever. One day when the world had settled back into uneasy peace, her parents would meet Brady and fall in love with her too. How could they not?

CHAPTER TWENTY-TWO

That night, Pete came home after supper to help with chores. He had grown three full inches since summer and was now almost as tall as his older sister. He was also trying to grow a moustache, which CJ found ridiculous. When she offered to help milk the cows, he insisted she stay with Rebecca. This was surprising mainly because the last time she was home, he had tried to dump his chores on her. Apparently a lot could change in half a year.

The evening passed in the upstairs bedroom with soap operas, puzzles and card games, amusements that became routine over the next few days. Pete came to the house before school and after supper each day while CJ slept in his room each night—*oh, blessed solitude!*—and spent the daylight hours moving between upstairs, downstairs and the barn. Occasionally her mother would sit in a chair on the second floor landing and chat with them from a safe distance, but Rebecca seemed to prefer having CJ's attention all to herself. She'd been like that as a small child too, always begging her big sister to play dolls or cart her around on her back.

It must have been hard for Rebecca to be the lone real girl in the family, CJ thought one afternoon as she groomed Molly in the relative warmth of the barn. Wait—she had just deemed herself as less than a real girl. Had the idea arisen by virtue of her tomboy tendencies, her sexual aberration or both? Possibly it was a chauvinistic view she'd absorbed without realizing it. Throughout the war, newspapers had printed opinion pieces declaring that the WAC and other military branches would masculinize women and disrupt their traditional roles as mothers and homemakers. Military and congressional leaders had initially laughed at the notion of women in the Army, until Pearl Harbor forced their hand.

Even then, Representative Edith Rogers's legislation to authorize formation of the Women's Army Auxiliary Corps took a year to be approved. The debate in Congress was acrimonious at times, with those opposed variously referring to the bill as "revolting," "a grave mistake," a direct challenge to "the courageous manhood of the country" and "the silliest piece of legislation…ever." A House representative from Michigan was quoted far and wide for his memorable comments about how women should stay home to "maintain the home fires" and do the cooking, the washing, the mending and all the other "humble, homey tasks" to which American women had devoted themselves— conveniently forgetting the suffragist movement and the gains early women's rights activists had made in the last century, advances that a decade of economic turbulence had almost completely undone.

The bigoted moron did have a point, CJ thought that night, lying in her brother's bed listening to the familiar creaks and sighs of the old farm house. She wished she had a cigarette, but her parents didn't allow smoking indoors, and it was one of those cold clear nights when your nostrils froze the second you stepped outdoors. The barn would be ten degrees warmer, but only an idiot would light up in a wooden structure filled with hay, straw and sleeping animals.

The thing was, the WAC did provide women an alternative to being a wife and mother. Wacs were serving all over the world—in Algiers and England, Hawaii and Iceland. They were cooks, telephone operators, mail clerks, drivers, mechanics, flight trainers. They were working on secret projects in the East and in the West (if Army gossip could be believed), maintaining confidential files, developing top-secret film and keeping up the morale of male troops. American women in droves were exercising their right to have a life outside of hearth and home.

All of that independence threatened some American men. Since she'd entered the WAC, CJ had heard countless stories involving the reactions of brothers, boyfriends, fiancés, even husbands serving overseas upon learning their loved one had joined the Army. Sisters were threatened with disownment, fiancées were ordered to return rings, wives were divorced all because the men in their lives believed the rumors that American servicewomen were little more than glorified camp followers.

She still remembered one woman in basic who'd received a letter from her brother that said girls who joined the WAVES or WAC or any other service branch were automatically prostitutes, in his opinion. He wanted to know why his sister and all the other female enlistees couldn't just stay home, be their "own sweet little selves" and leave patriotism where it belonged—with the men.

Another girl had cried quietly as the girls in her squad read a letter from her soon-to-be ex-husband. He'd written to tell her that he'd meant it when he told her she didn't have his permission to join the WAC. He wanted to come home to the girl he remembered, not some cartoon version of her. But she'd gone ahead and joined up anyway, and now he wanted a divorce because in his words: "I don't want no damn Wacko for a wife."

These men were controlling and insecure, but they also recognized an uncomfortable truth: The war was changing the men who left home to heed the call of duty, but also the women they believed had stayed behind. Apparently she had been smart to cut herself loose from Sean. Brady, on the other hand, was experiencing what happened when you allowed what someone else wanted to trump what you wanted for yourself.

At the thought of Brady, CJ felt tears gathering. She missed her, but even more she missed being on their own in Texas, well insulated from family expectations. At Bliss it was only the two of them, and they weren't beholden to parents or brothers or friends. They could do whatever made them happy without worrying about how anyone else would react.

Nothing would ever be the same again, she was starting to realize. Like Brady had said, the genie couldn't be put back into the bottle. Now that she was back under her parents' roof, she was beginning to wonder if the gap between home and Army, good daughter and secret homosexual, could ever be bridged.

* * *

The next day, after one too many rounds of Euchre and Crazy Eights, CJ taught Rebecca to play poker after swearing her to secrecy.

Somehow, she doubted their parents would appreciate her teaching the youngest member of their brood Texas Hold 'Em. Rebecca learned quickly and could soon, indeed, hold her own. The day before Christmas Eve, they were engaged in a match to determine who would control the radio dial when CJ heard a car in the driveway.

"Are you expecting anyone?" she asked her sister.

"Not likely," Rebecca said as she folded her cards face down and went to the window. Suddenly she perked up. "But it looks like you are."

CJ peered through the window, squinting in the rare winter sunlight gracing their property. Subject to lake-effect snow, Michigan was reliably dismal in the winter months. But today the sunshine glinted off the windshield of the familiar sedan pulling up the drive. Sean.

"How does he know you're here?" Rebecca asked. "Did you call him?"

"No, but I think I know who did. I'll be back soon, okay?"

"Don't hurry on my account," her little sister said, smiling conspiratorially at her.

CJ left the room without responding. How could the people who should have known her best not see how little she was suited to a relationship with Sean or any other man, for that matter? Toby and Reggie had figured her out right off the bat. Why couldn't her family see her clearly?

Quickly she washed her hands and pulled an Army-issue sweater over the white shirt waist she currently wore. The wool coat-style sweater was unmistakably military and therefore perfect—for some reason, she didn't want to face Sean in civilian attire. She was a soldier; dressing the part reminded her of that fact even here, where she'd lived the twenty-plus years of her life before the Army. She considered exchanging her twill pants for her uniform skirt, but pants were better for battle.

When she reached the downstairs, she glanced through one of the windows in the vestibule and saw Sean still seated in his car, staring at the front of the house. Apparently the Board of Health directive was doing its job. She didn't have to go out and talk to him. If she left him there, he would have to give up and go home, wouldn't he?

"Were you expecting him?" her mother asked quietly.

Startled, CJ glanced over her shoulder. "No."

"Right. Well, do you know if he's had scarlet fever before?"

"I'm not sure."

"Then you'll have to invite him to the back porch."

Clearly her mother was not about to allow her to leave her ex-boyfriend to languish ignored in his car. But why the porch and not the barn? Was she worried that CJ's father might send Sean back the way he'd come? Maybe that wouldn't be such a bad thing. Sean had obviously heard from Sadie and Tricia that she was in town. Had they also shared other, more delicate news?

"Fine. But he's not staying long."

She pulled on the bomber jacket, Alec's favorite sheepskin-lined hunting cap and a pair of her own gloves. Here went nothing.

The cold air hit as soon as she stepped out onto the front stoop. Behind the wheel, Sean was staring at the door as if willing her to appear, but when she did, he seemed taken aback. After a brief hesitation, he stepped out of his car and crunched across the gravel.

"Hello," he said, voice and eyes serious as he looked up at her. His hair was shorter, almost as if in preparation for basic training, and he had dark smudges beneath both eyes.

"Hello." She gazed steadily down at him from the top step, noting how little she felt. She had cared about him back at school, she knew she had, but those feelings were paltry compared to what she had now with Brady. Had he loved her the way she loved Brady? It didn't seem possible that love could be so out of balance.

"How's Rebecca?" he asked, glancing at the upstairs window.

She followed his gaze, unsurprised to see the curtain move. Who needed radio when there was a soap opera unfolding outside your front door?

"She's getting better." She paused. "What are you doing here, Sean?"

He shrugged. "I wanted to see you one last time before... Did Sadie tell you?"

"That you joined up? What were you thinking? You don't believe in killing or dying for the government. At least, that's what you always said."

"I don't believe in the right of any government to wage war. But it doesn't matter what I believe, not when so many people are dying. It's like you said—I'd rather be on the right side of history than be safe."

Had she said that? It did sound like something she would have professed at a party after a couple of glasses of wine or beer, a noble-sounding sentiment that didn't actually mean anything. In reality, their generation had been swallowed up by something over which they had no control or even any chance at impacting as individuals. The one way they could change the future was to sacrifice their bodies and souls en masse to try to stop Hitler and the Germans, Hirohito and the Japanese from killing and enslaving even more of the world's population. Appeasement hadn't worked. Only force worked, just as her graduation speaker had warned.

"Look, can we go somewhere to talk?" he asked. "That little coffee shop near the train station, maybe?"

"I can't."

He frowned. "Why? Is it against regulation?"

"Sort of, but in this case, my parents are the MPs." She nodded toward the side of the house. "Back porch?"

"All right." As they walked around the side of the house, dodging barren bushes and flower beds, he added, "Your father never did like me."

"That's not true." As he looked at her sideways, his eyebrows raised, she amended, "Well, maybe a little true."

"Is it because I don't know my way around a tractor?"

"I don't know. You'd have to ask him."

"No thanks." He pretended to shudder. "He scares me more than the Navy does. Your mom too."

"My mother? She's what, all of five and a half feet tall?"

"It's not her height, it's her presence. You have both, which makes you even more intimidating."

CJ shook her head. "You're full of crap."

"Not about this."

The screen door to the back porch was unlatched. CJ led the way inside, purposely choosing a wicker chair set away from the rattan couch. Sean skipped the couch as well and sat down on the porch swing. A host of memories came back to CJ—an autumn evening spent on that swing not long after they started dating and he came home with her to meet her parents; a winter afternoon when they'd escaped the holiday hassle to sneak a cigarette; that last night when he asked her to marry him and she told him she was joining the Army. But then it was her mother who sat beside her on the porch swing, looking crestfallen at the news that she'd sent him away.

"What did you want to talk about?" she asked, her heart hardening against him as she recalled their most recent encounter.

He stopped the swing. "I owe you an apology. I've known it for a long time, and when Sadie said you were back, I realized this was my chance."

"Okay," she said slowly. An apology was not what she'd expected.

"I should never have asked you to stay in Michigan. I should have been willing to compromise, instead of asking you to be the one to give up what you wanted."

"Is that why you joined the Navy? Because that's not compromise. That's abandoning your ideals."

"I'm not abandoning my ideals." He rubbed his palms against his corduroys the way he always did right before he taught class. "Whether I believe in this war or not, it's happening. You joined up to try to bring your brothers home sooner. What kind of man would I be if I didn't try to do my part?"

"A smart man. It was easy for me to volunteer because there's no chance I could end up on the front lines. But you could be made to fire antiaircraft cannons or engage in small-arms combat or any other number of terrifying things that involve killing or being killed."

He stared at her. "I've read the same newspaper articles you have, seen the same photos in *Life*. I've listened to my parents talk about how one of the Davison boys lost both legs when he stepped on a mine and they feel lucky he came home at all. Or how Chuck Padley's youngest burned alive in a plane crash when the cockpit latch got stuck. I know it'll be a matter of luck if I come back from this in one piece, but it's not like I have a choice, is it? I can't hide out in school while everyone else goes off to fight."

"But you don't believe in fighting!" She didn't know why she was arguing with him. Was she afraid it would feel like her fault if something happened to him in the war?

"Isn't not believing in fighting a bit of a luxury, though?"

He was throwing her words back at her—she'd used the same phrase the previous spring to call him out on his privileged status when he suggested they rent out an entire restaurant because he was tired of finding "their" booth occupied.

"So you did join up because of me."

He shrugged. "I probably would have done it anyway."

Probably? "This has got to be one of the worst apologies I've ever received."

"What, am I supposed to lie? Last time I checked, you weren't a fan of dishonesty. Or that's what you always said."

The bitterness in his voice alerted her, and she eyed him warily.

"Do you ever think about me?" he asked suddenly.

"Of course."

"But not very often."

She hesitated. "No."

He rose from the swing. "Did you even love me at all?"

"Yes. I mean, I thought I did."

He paced the length of the porch and stopped before her chair. "Which means what, exactly?"

"Sean…" She stood up and started to extend a hand to him.

"Don't," he spit out, shaking his head. "I can't believe I wasted so much time on you. Why did you let me think we had a future? We talked about getting married, and you never once thought to mention that oh, by the way, you were queer?"

She flinched and took a step away from him. But he followed, his face flushed.

"I defended you. I said I would know if you were a dyke, wouldn't I? But I guess there are some things the boyfriend finds out last. God, you must have been laughing at me the whole time!"

He was looming over her now, and CJ felt his hurt and rage like a palpable entity between them. But despite the fact that the hair on the back of her neck had risen, even though her palms were damp inside her gloves, she couldn't accept that he would hurt her. He was Sean, the first boy to make her feel beautiful, the first person she had spent the night with, the only man she had ever allowed to see her naked and vulnerable. He had never touched her in anger before; it was inconceivable that he would do so now.

And then a voice behind CJ said, "That is more than enough from you, young man."

She glanced back to see her mother standing in the doorway. Relief flooded her—*thank God*—followed quickly by fear. How much had she heard? Her mother wouldn't meet her gaze, and CJ knew immediately: *Everything.*

"I'm sorry," Sean said, his face white as he backed away a pace. "I wasn't—I wouldn't…"

"I know," her mother said, coming closer. "You've had a disappointment, but anger rarely solves anything."

CJ tried to swallow back her tears. She had made such a mess of things, and now Sean was going off to war and her mother had found out she was gay in the worst manner possible. There was silence on the porch, and she could hear wind whistling through the barren oak and maple trees at the edge of the backyard.

He found her eyes. "I should go."

She wanted to say something to ease the distance between them, something to heal the pain that seemed so raw in him even after all these months. But all she could manage was, "Okay."

Mind still churning, she led him back around the house, her mother close behind. Sean went to his car without another word and started the engine, lifting his hand as it caught. CJ waved back, and then he turned the wheel and drove down the long driveway, his eyes on hers in the rearview mirror until his car disappeared behind a stand of evergreens.

"Let's go in, shall we?" her mother said, voice falsely bright.

For the first time, CJ realized she was clad in a house coat and moccasins. "Of course. You must be freezing."

"Oh, I think I've been colder," she replied in the same sing-song tone.

Inside, CJ shed her outerwear, trying to think of something to say. "Thanks for coming to my rescue."

"It's what mothers do. Someday you..." She trailed off, her eyes widening, and quickly started away.

"Mom, wait."

For a moment, CJ thought she might not stop. At the kitchen doorway, she paused. "Yes?"

"I know you heard."

Her mother smoothed the front of her housecoat. "I don't know what you're talking about."

"I think you do."

"Caroline." Her voice was low.

"Look at me. Will you at least look at me?"

Slowly her mother lifted her gaze, revealing eyes that reminded CJ of a frightened doe. She was scared. Scared of her own daughter.

"We need to talk about this," CJ said. "Don't we?"

"Not here." She glanced toward the stairs, but for once, Rebecca wasn't spying from the landing. "Come."

CJ followed her to the kitchen and leaned against the counter, watching as the woman she'd always loved most in the world—until recently—poured coffee from a kettle into a chipped mug. She didn't offer CJ any as she turned to face her, one arm curved protectively against her abdomen.

"So, do you have any questions for me?" CJ asked, unable to stand the silence.

Her mother shook her head.

"There's nothing at all you want to ask me?"

She blew on the surface of her coffee. "I suppose there is something. Was what Sean said true? Are you..."

"Yes," CJ said, trying to ignore her fluttering stomach.

Her mother closed her eyes, and then she opened them again. "How can you be certain? It might be the Army and the people you've met there making you think this way."

"It's who I've always been, Mom. I just didn't realize it until now."

Her knuckles were white against the mug. "Well, I don't accept it."

CJ stared at her. "Excuse me?"

"I don't accept it. This is not how your father and I raised you."

"Are you joking?"

"I wouldn't joke about this."

"Whatever happened to wanting me to be the person I am? What happened to honoring the individual?"

"You can't expect me to sit by and watch you ruin your life. I wouldn't wish this fate on anyone, let alone my own daughter."

Her mother believed Brady would "ruin" her life? Lovely, smart, funny Brady who looked at her like she was the most amazing person in the world? CJ's anger rose, swift and bitter. "Well, fortunately not everyone is as narrow-minded as you are."

"Caroline!" She set her mug down on the counter top, hard. "Don't you speak to me like that, young lady."

"That's the thing, isn't it? I'm not that young anymore, and the last thing I want is to be a lady. I would have thought that would be abundantly clear."

She had never spoken to her mother in such a manner, and her heart raced like it did at the end of a round of calisthenics. All at once, she needed to escape. Pushing away from the counter, she headed for the hallway.

"Where do you think you're going?" her mother demanded.

"Out."

In the front vestibule, she grabbed her jacket and handbag before slamming outside. What a hypocrite! The award-winning school teacher, a scion of her church and community—no wonder she'd pressed CJ to accept Sean's proposal. She would rather her daughter be miserable than gay.

Adrenaline carried her to the barn, where she barely nodded at her father before swiping the keys to his sedan. Disbelief carried her down the driveway in Sean's wake, out onto the main road and into town. Anger took her to the train station where she sat, engine idling. She could catch the next train to Chicago and find her way back to Texas on her own. Her parents could send her suitcase on, if they could even be bothered. She could do it. She could leave the car keys at the information desk and send her parents a postcard from Chicago. What would her mother's response be—*I don't accept it*? She wouldn't have a choice, just like she didn't have a choice in who CJ chose to love. Not that loving Brady was a choice. Her feelings for Brady didn't involve reason or logic. If they did, she wouldn't be sitting here outside the train station in Kalamazoo considering running away from home.

Home. She pictured the Christmas tree in the front sitting room, a scraggly specimen culled not from their property during a family walk the first week of December but from the Meijer's store parking lot the day before she arrived. It had been hastily decorated with the usual ribbons and strings of popcorn, but her parents hadn't brought out the box filled with ornaments handmade over the years by CJ and her siblings. When she'd asked her father why they had foregone the usual family holiday traditions, he admitted that he and her mother didn't have the heart.

Their hearts were in constant danger, CJ remembered now as she sat outside the train station, of being broken in a way they remembered too well. Her mother's inadvertent discovery today must have been a reminder of that earlier loss, of the fear they lived with daily. CJ wasn't the person her mother had believed her to be, nor would she have the future everyone expected. There would be no wedding to help plan, no son-in-law to welcome into the family, no grandchildren to brag about, only a terrible secret to guard. It wasn't the same as losing a child to illness or war, of course, but it was a loss. She didn't have to agree with her mother or forgive her, but she did have to go back. If she didn't, the future happy Christmases she'd promised Brady wouldn't stand a chance. There may not even be a home to return to if she ran away now.

Still, she wasn't ready to face her mother again yet, so she parked the car and headed into the familiar station, leaving her jacket and GI sweater in the car. No one who saw her would guess she was a soldier out of uniform. After all, it wasn't like she was a man in civvies with an Army haircut to give her away. In the waiting room, she made a beeline for an empty public telephone booth near the newsstand. Pulling a change purse from her WAC-issued handbag, she added up the contents. Two dollars and thirty-four cents should buy her fifteen minutes or so. Assuming her call was answered.

She dropped a nickel in the pay box, dialed "0" for the operator, and asked to make a long-distance call. The long-distance operator took her information cheerfully and put her on hold. CJ held the receiver tightly, waiting as the line clicked. How many relays would it take? She had no way of knowing, but she kept track on her watch. Two minutes and ten cents later, a slightly accented female voice finally said, "The Buchanan residence. May I help you?"

"Hello." She cleared her throat. Isabel—it had to be her, didn't it?—sounded so far away. "Is Brady in?"

"She is. Who should I say is calling?"

"Caroline Jamieson." She resisted the urge to add "ma'am."

"One moment please."

The seconds ticked past, and CJ imagined a meter ticking along with them: one cent, two cents, three cents, four… The phone beeped, and she dropped more change in. *Come on, Brady*, she thought, suddenly desperate to hear her voice.

Then: "CJ? Is it really you?"

At Brady's familiar tones, her shoulders relaxed, the day's tension slowly easing out of her. "Of course," she said, forcing herself to sound cheerful.

"Dang it, you beat me to it. I was going to surprise you tomorrow. I couldn't wait until the weekend."

"You wouldn't have found me. I'm not in El Paso."

"You're not? Where are you?"

CJ quickly related the story of how she had come to be in Michigan. "But I'm in a booth at the train station, and I don't have much change, so…"

"Let me call you back. What's the number there?"

"That's okay, you don't have to—"

"I want to." Her voice dropped. "Please? I miss you."

CJ gave her the number quickly as Ma Bell demanded more tribute. Then the line went dead. She remained on the hard wooden bench, waiting for the phone to ring and connect her to Brady again. Hearing her voice had been wonderful but terrible, for the crackle of the long-distance line reminded her of how far apart they were, how long it would be before they saw each other again. Still, Brady had seemed happy to hear from her. Apparently she hadn't returned to L.A. and resumed the life of a society girl focused on wealth and prestige. Not yet, anyway.

The telephone pealed and she snatched up the receiver. "Hello?"

"Hiya, kid." Brady's voice was soft.

She sighed. "Hi."

"Have I mentioned how much I miss you?"

CJ allowed herself a smile. "Not nearly as much as I miss you. Tell me, how are Nate's parents?"

"Shell-shocked."

"When's the service?"

"Sunday. The casket will be empty—he's interred in Italy, and the family isn't sure if he'll be brought back after the war."

CJ had heard this type of news many times since Pearl Harbor, but it didn't get any easier. Sometimes the war seemed so far removed that it was hard to accept that those who had fallen were never coming home. She wondered if Nate's death felt unreal to the people who cared about him. Did they hold out hope that the Army had made a terrible mistake that would be revealed when he appeared upon their doorstep at the end of the war?

"How are you coping?" she asked.

"Fine. Amy, Nate's sister who was at Smith with me, flew in from New York." She hesitated. "She shared some interesting news that I'll have to tell you about when I see you. Otherwise everything here is the same. I'm the one who's different."

"I know. I stayed overnight with a school friend on the way home, and I felt so distant from that part of my life."

"Because of the Army or something else?" Brady asked innocently.

"More like someone else." She paused, trying to think how to word it. "Speaking of which, my mother knows about the Hilton."

"You told her about the *Hilton*?"

"Not literally, but I wasn't sure if there was anyone listening in at your end."

"Well, they're not. How did all of this come about?"

"Let's see. Sean dropped by today to ask if I ever thought about him…"

"He what?"

The account of Sean's visit took up another few precious minutes. Except that instead of the word "queer," she told Brady that he had accused her of being *happy*, which her mother had promptly overheard.

"Oh my God," Brady said. "Are you okay?"

"I'm fine. My mother, on the other hand, I'm not so sure of. Although unlike Sean, she did stop short of using Charlie's wonderful nickname for company D."

Brady paused. "I'm so sorry. That sounds awful."

CJ swallowed, her flippant tone fading. "It was. That's why I called. I needed to hear your voice. I couldn't wait until the weekend either."

"Poor baby." Brady's voice was soft again. "I hate that I'm the one driving you away from your family. I know how much they mean to you."

"It's my mother's intolerance driving me away, not you. I'd hoped for so much better from her. I didn't expect it, but I did hope."

"Maybe she'll come around. Give her some time."

"She'll have plenty of that soon enough. But I'm sorry as well. I promised you holidays in Kalamazoo, and now it looks like we might end up spending our Christmases exploring the Seven Wonders of the New World." She stopped, realizing how that sounded—as if she thought they would be together forever.

"I think that's a fabulous idea," Brady announced. "In fact, I'm going to pick up a travel guide before I leave the city. Planning our next five Christmases will give me something to do on the blasted train other than daydream about a weekend at the Hilton."

Their next *five* Christmases? CJ smiled again. "Don't I get a say in our future holiday plans?"

"We'll see."

"Yes, we will."

They were both quiet. Then Brady said, "I hate having to censor everything."

"It's becoming one of my least favorite activities too."

"I wish we were in the same room right now, preferably nowhere near our parents."

"They didn't find out about your happy state, did they?"

"No, though I have been tempted to let it slip."

"Hang in there. We'll be back at Bliss in, what, ten days?"

Brady groaned. "Now you're being cruel."

CJ pictured the bedroom Brady had once described as a cross between Scarlett's bedroom at Tara and the dream sequence in *The Little Princess*. She could almost see Brady sitting cross-legged on her carriage bed with the white lace bedspread, purple canopy and purple-and white-striped wallpaper she'd picked out in second grade—a dangerous age for anyone to be given the power to decorate her own bedroom. All at once, she missed her so much that her chest actually ached.

"I should go," she said. "This is costing your parents a fortune."

"They can afford it. But what's your exchange? Can I call you on Christmas like we planned?"

CJ hesitated. "Why not? It's not like my mother knows how integral you are to my *happiness*." She gave her the number, and then they wasted more time listening to each other breathe over the scratchy long-distance line.

Finally CJ said, "I really have to go. I'll see you soon, all right?"

"No, you won't. But I'll be thinking of you in Kalamazoo. Too bad I have no idea what Michigan looks like."

"Probably a lot like Massachusetts minus the mountains. What's L.A. like?"

"Picture El Paso minus Texans plus the ocean, movie studios and a million more people."

CJ laughed. "Got it. I think. Merry Christmas, crumpet girl."

"Merry Christmas, farm girl. Give my love to, you know, everyone there."

"Right back at ya."

They drew out their goodbyes another minute, until finally CJ forced herself to hang up. For a moment she stayed where she was, hugging her arms to her sides. If she closed her eyes, she could almost pretend that Brady was there holding her. The loudspeaker sputtered outside her booth, and she opened her eyes again, looking out on a familiar world that most definitely did not include Brady.

Bracing herself for the cold, she left the station and ran to her father's car. As she drove home along the sunny, wintry streets, she pictured the Hollywood sign, one of the few images of Los Angeles that came readily to mind. Someday she would ask Brady to take her to see it, and they would drive together along the streets of L.A., convertible roof open to sunshine and ocean breezes and the warm, warm air of Southern California.

When she got home, she parked the Ford in the barn and returned the keys to their hook. Then she went inside through the back door, stomping her feet against the cold. Her mother and father looked up from the kitchen table where they were sharing a mid-day dinner of roast beef sandwiches and cold cucumber soup.

"Hi, honey. Did you manage to clear your head?" her father asked.

She glanced at her mother, who gazed back, her own eyes neutral. "I told your dad about your visitor."

Clearly she hadn't shared Sean's revelation, though. This made CJ pause. She viewed her parents as a matching pair, perhaps because they had always tended toward a unified front.

"I don't mind telling you now I never did like that boy," he said. "I hope he didn't give you too hard a time?"

"No. Not at all."

"Rebecca's dinner is on the counter," her mother said. "Would you mind taking it up?"

CJ glanced at the kitchen counter, the scene of their earlier confrontation. Sure enough, there was a tray arranged with two plates, two glasses of apple cider, and a vase with a bundle of dried lavender. Apparently it hadn't occurred to her mother that she might not come home.

"In case we haven't said it enough," her father added, "thank you for helping with your sister. I know it means the world to her to have you here, and to your mother and me as well."

"You don't have to thank me," she said, retrieving the tray. "Rallying around each other is what families do, isn't it?"

She thought she saw her mother flinch and couldn't help a brief flash of satisfaction. But as she climbed the stairs, her smugness faded. What did it say about her that she wanted to hurt her mother the way she had been hurt herself? Brady was right. Family had always been important to her. But now that she was on a collision course with her parents' moral convictions, she couldn't afford to place as much value anymore on their feelings. If they could be close-minded about gay people, what else had they gotten wrong?

Upstairs, she sat at the desk in her old bedroom and allowed her little sister to grill her, careful to whitewash Sean's visit. The day dragged, and though her mother put on a good face at supper, CJ could sense her pulling away more every minute. She conjured Brady's face, trying to inoculate herself against the pain of her mother's withdrawal, but with Brady so far away, relief was temporary.

The desk was stocked with writing supplies, and she longed to compose a letter to Brady pouring out her thoughts, her worries, her love. Such a letter would not only be cathartic, it would also make her feel like they were closer. But she didn't get to write that letter, and neither did Brady. They couldn't even say they loved each other on the telephone in case someone somewhere was listening in. God, it was infuriating.

She thought of all the women she'd met in Iowa, Illinois and Texas who had written letter after letter to their boyfriends, fiancés and husbands declaring their love and pent-up passion, and then sent those letters up the chain to be censored by their officers. Or all the women who had sat at the barracks telephone singing out their love for their men. They had no idea how fortunate they were.

As she lay in her brother's bed that night, model airplanes and train tracks casting eerie shadows across the room, she realized that Sean had gotten his revenge, after all. The gulf opening between her and her mother was his doing. Toby had said not everyone had a problem with homosexuality, but so far CJ was oh for three—Sadie, Sean, her mother. Her mother, who was supposed to love her no matter what. Her mother, who believed in peace, tolerance and a loving God, but not, apparently, in her daughter's right to be happy.

CHAPTER TWENTY-THREE

"The President is giving a radio address this afternoon on the Cairo and Teheran conferences," her father said the next morning. "Your mother and I were thinking it might be nice to listen together. Can you tell your sister?"

"Sure. Upstairs or downstairs?"

"Upstairs. You know the rules, Caroline."

"But it's Christmas Eve. Can't we bend them a little?" When he lowered his newspaper to stare at her, she added, "Why are you looking at me like that?"

"If I heard correctly, you suggested we break a rule."

"I said 'bend.' And it's not like I've never broken a rule before."

"Oh, really," he said. "When?"

"At nearly every football game at Central sophomore year, for one. Carol Getz brought a flask to keep us warm, and you can bet it didn't contain hot chocolate."

Her mother, busy putting the finishing touches on Rebecca's breakfast, appeared unaffected by this most recent revelation—underage drinking probably paled in comparison to sexual perversion in her book—but her father frowned. "Caroline, I'm surprised at you."

"Relax." She took the tray from her mother. "I graduated at the top of my class, didn't I?"

She escaped from the kitchen before her parents could respond and high-tailed it upstairs. As she balanced the tray and entered the bedroom, Rebecca quickly tucked the letter she was writing—to Fred Dodge, no doubt—under her pillow.

"Don't worry, I'm alone," CJ said, setting the tray down on the desk. "But Mom and Dad will be up later. The President is giving one of his Fireside Chats on the conferences in the East this afternoon, and they want us all to listen together."

"What time?"

"I'm not sure."

"They better not preempt *Mary Martin* or *Ma Perkins* for a speech about some boring conference."

CJ drew in a calming breath, but the surge of oxygen did little to help. "Those 'boring' conferences were held to determine the outcome of the war. Do you honestly care more about people who don't exist than your own brothers?"

Rebecca had the grace to look chagrined. "Sorry. I didn't realize."

"Uh-huh. Now eat your eggs."

The day passed in the usual way until midway through the afternoon, when her parents arranged a couple of chairs a few feet from the girls' room as dictated by the Board of Health. CJ turned up the wireless set, and as the abridged family that they had become, they listened to their president's twenty-seventh Fireside Chat, broadcast from his home in Hyde Park on the Hudson.

"My friends," he began, as he always did, "I have recently returned from extensive journeying in the region of the Mediterranean and as far as the borders of Russia. I have conferred with the leaders of Britain and Russia and China on military matters of the present—especially on plans for stepping up our successful attack on our enemies as quickly as possible and from many different points of the compass."

Briefly he detailed the number of Americans serving overseas, from the Caribbean to the Middle East, before warming up to his main topic: the Allied leader conferences in Cairo and Teheran. In Iran, he had met Joseph Stalin in person for the first time. There, along with Churchill, they had "agreed on every point concerned with the launching of a gigantic attack upon Germany."

CJ heard her parents gasp, but she wasn't surprised to hear the president reveal that five million American service men and women would be overseas by the following summer. Nor was it surprising that General Eisenhower would lead the attacks on Germany. Ike had proven himself as commander of the North African Allied Expeditionary Force against Rommel's Afrika Korps and again in the invasion of Sicily and Italy.

President Roosevelt went on, praising American troops spending their second and third Christmases overseas for their hard work and sacrifice, acknowledging the families back home for their dedication and commitment. He warned that Americans needed to prepare for large casualty lists in the near future. "There is no easy road to victory," he cautioned. "The massive offensives which are in the making both in Europe and the Far East will require every ounce of energy and fortitude that we and our allies can summon on the fighting fronts and in all the workshops at home."

CJ glanced at her parents. She could see the fear in their faces, the same terror she felt in her gut. But she pushed the fear back, as she knew they and countless other Americans were doing at that very moment across the nation, tamped it down into a small, manageable thing. Her country needed her, and she was prepared to give whatever was required to do her part to rid the world of evil. They were the good guys working to free the rest of the world from tyranny. God must be on their side—assuming He took sides.

As the President wrapped up his address with a Christmas prayer, CJ found herself wondering if Brady was listening. And Joe and Alec, were they somewhere celebrating the holidays with their comrades, picturing the tree at home decorated as it had been every other year since they could remember, the serene prospect from the back porch so different from the views their current positions afforded? She wished they could all be here for Christmas, Brady and Alec and Joe.

Wishful thinking wouldn't help anyone, she reminded herself as the president's address ended. Her parents returned the chairs to their rightful places and then lingered outside the bedroom doorway, gazing at their daughters silently, eyes brimming with emotions that CJ couldn't quite identify. When they finally turned away, heads bowed and shoulders hunched, they looked aged, defeated.

Sons, CJ knew, were usually considered a blessing. But glad must be the parents now who had only daughters.

* * *

A short time later, the telephone rang. CJ's heart lurched—could it be Brady? Then she remembered they weren't scheduled to talk until the following day. Sighing, she turned back to the puzzle she and Rebecca were putting together for the fourth time in nearly as many days.

"Caroline," her mother called. "It's for you."

She was tempted to leap from her chair and bound down the stairs, but she forced herself to move at a more dignified pace. Downstairs she took a seat at the table in the front hall and lifted the receiver, aware of her mother in the kitchen ten feet away preparing Christmas Eve supper.

"Hello?"

"Hiya," Brady said cheerfully.

"Why, what a surprise to hear from you."

"Your mother is standing behind you, isn't she?"

"Close. We're having supper in a little while. What about you?"

"Me? Oh, I was lying here thinking about kissing my way down your luscious neck to your even more luscious…"

CJ coughed, her cheeks suddenly hot. "Brady," she whispered. "Party line, remember?"

Her laughter carried clearly across the thousands of miles that separated them. "I'm sorry. I couldn't resist. So did you listen to the speech?"

For the next few minutes they chatted about the radio broadcast, comparing notes on the conference takeaways. Brady had listened to the address alone, since Isabel was off for the weekend, her little brother was visiting his girlfriend and her parents were out with another couple.

"They left you alone on Christmas Eve?"

"Sure."

"And that doesn't bother you?"

"No. Should it?"

CJ lowered her voice. "I think I'm envious."

"Of what?"

"All of this would be easier if I didn't like my parents."

"In that case, don't be. I'm not sure who dislikes whom more at my house."

"I'm sorry," CJ said, wincing at her own obtuseness. "I shouldn't have said that."

"It's fine. It's not like I haven't said worse things myself."

"I know, but you get to. They're your family."

Brady paused. "Can I tell you something?"

"Of course."

"You feel more like my family these days than anyone else."

CJ rested her chin on her free hand. "I know just what you mean."

Later, after Brady made her laugh yet again and her mother had paused near the kitchen doorway one too many times, CJ reluctantly said she had to get going.

"All right." Brady sighed dramatically. "I suppose I'll have to find some way to amuse myself here alone on my bed in my skivvies…"

CJ groaned under her breath. "Thanks for that image. Now I won't be able to think of anything else."

"That was the plan. I love you, you know."

"I—" She caught herself in time. "Me too. Happy Christmas Eve."

"You too. Talk to you soon?"

"I hope so."

"Sweet dreams." The line clicked and Brady was gone.

As she replaced the receiver, she heard a noise at the top of the stairs. Rebecca, the little eavesdropper.

"Who was that?" her sister whispered.

"Brady, my friend from California."

"Is she your best buddy? Isn't that what they call Army friends?"

"Sure. She's my best buddy."

Among other things. But Rebecca didn't need to know that.

Her mother stuck her head out of the kitchen. "Could I have a little help in here, please?" she asked testily.

"Of course," CJ said, biting back her own irritation. The last thing she needed was to be barred from the telephone. She didn't think she was strong enough to resist the lure of the train station again.

* * *

On Christmas morning, instead of celebrating with friends and family like they usually did, CJ's family exchanged gifts on the second floor landing. Even then, Rebecca wasn't allowed to open hers for fear she might contaminate them with scarlet fever germs. CJ tried to talk her parents into celebrating Christmas later, after Rebecca was well again, but they wouldn't hear of it. She was home from the Army only for a week, they pointed out, and besides, the boys overseas didn't get to have Christmas at all, did they?

CJ's gifts from Mexico were a hit. Pete loved his riding bridle, her father was pleased with the leather belt and billfold, and her mother even smiled briefly at the sight of her shawl. Rebecca begged to be allowed to try on the blouse that Brady had picked out for her, to no avail.

"No wonder I like rules," CJ commented. "The apple doesn't fall far from the tree."

Her father snickered but ceased all movement as his wife cast him the withering glare she typically reserved for unruly classrooms.

Opening presents didn't take long, not like when they were kids. Afterward, they had breakfast—waffles and canned fruit from their garden, a Jamieson Christmas morning tradition—and then Pete and their parents got ready for the special Christmas Day service at First Baptist. They weren't planning to go, her mother had told her a few days earlier, but CJ had insisted. She was fully capable of looking after Rebecca. Wasn't that why she had come home?

"You came home because you should be home at the holidays," her mother had replied, touching her cheek. "But thank you. It would mean so much to us to be there."

How much had changed in a few days. Now her mother could barely hold her gaze without looking like the world was about to end. *Damn Sean, anyway.*

The Ford had barely vanished behind the trees at the end of the driveway when Rebecca said, "CJ, you know I think you're the best big sister anyone could have, don't you?"

She narrowed her eyes. "What do you want, brat? Spill it."

The younger girl hemmed and hawed, but finally she blurted, "Will you call Fred and tell him Mom and Dad will be gone for a couple of hours?"

"Rebecca!"

"Pleeeease? I'll keep the window closed, I promise. I think I'll die if I don't see him soon."

CJ knew the feeling, but in her case there was no possibility of assuaging it. "Fine. Far be it for me to stand in the way of young love."

"Really?" her little sister squealed.

"Really. But you can never tell Mom and Dad."

"I won't," she said, leaping off the bed. "I promise. You're the best sister ever, CJ, I mean it. I always tell everyone that."

"Easy, little miss bootlicker. I already said I would help."

Five minutes later, Fred's truck appeared on the driveway. Good thing there wasn't any snow or he might have crashed, the way he was driving. CJ bundled up and went outside to help him position the ladder, and then held it in place while he and Rebecca shouted their adoration through the closed second-story window. They were pretty sweet, she had to admit. Fred's ears were a tad too large, but he was a cute boy and he genuinely loved her sister, as evidenced by his willingness to risk life, limb and frostbite.

After Fred and his ladder had trucked home, CJ lay on her old bed throwing a tennis ball against the wall while Rebecca stared up at the constellation mobile CJ had built back in seventh grade and hung with their father's help from the ceiling.

"Isn't he dreamy?" she asked for easily the fortieth time.

"Hmm," CJ said noncommittally.

"Okay, once and for all, do you have a boyfriend or not?" her sister asked, also for the fortieth time.

"Once and for all, *again*, no. Why do you keep asking? The answer isn't going to change."

"Because I know you're lying," Rebecca stated. "You've got a new hair style, your clothes are tailored and you're wearing makeup."

"It's only a little lipstick and mascara," CJ protested.

"Like I said, you're wearing makeup. The fact that you're denying it makes me think you're involved with someone you shouldn't be. Oooh, are you having an affair with a married man?"

"For the last time, Rebecca, I'm not having an affair with any man. Now, knock it off. I don't want to hear about this again."

"Fine," her little sister said, reaching for the radio dial.

As the strains of holiday music filled the room, CJ rose. "I'm going for a walk."

"Rub it in, why don't you," Rebecca said crossly, picking up a magazine she'd already read cover to cover.

So much for being the best sister ever.

Downstairs, she pulled on outdoor clothing and went outside to visit with the horses. It wasn't as cold today as some Christmas Days she could remember, but it wasn't warm, either. She fed carrots and apples to the horses and went into the barn to visit with Bessie and May, the aging milk cows. The geese kicked up a fuss in their pen, so she ended up feeding them too. She liked geese. They made good guard dogs and their eggs were larger and tastier than chicken eggs.

After communing with the farm animals in the relatively fresh air, she felt better. At least she could come and go whenever she pleased. Rebecca had it far worse.

She was removing her scarf and gloves when she heard it—the telephone. Kicking off her boots, she ran for the hall table, socks slipping on the polished wood floor. "Hello?"

"Please hold for a long distance call from Beverly Hills, California," the operator said.

"I'm here!"

The line clicked and whirred, and then it went absolutely silent for a moment during which CJ considered how she could track down and strangle the operator who had lost the call. At last she heard Brady's voice: "Hello?"

"Oh my God," she said, laughing. "What are you doing? We just talked yesterday."

"I know, but it's Christmas, and we were supposed to be at the Grand Canyon," Brady said. "What did you end up doing with the room, anyway?"

"Reggie and Holly jumped at the chance."

"Huh. So I guess you were right about Holly—she really is happy."

"I would imagine she's ecstatic right about now."

"Can I get a rain check?"

"Of course," CJ said and settled down at the hall table to talk until the line gave out or her parents came home, whichever happened first.

"Merry Christmas, CJ."

"Merry Christmas, Brady."

* * *

The thing about flying standby was that it depended on flights that weren't necessarily scheduled and might not have any room on board even if they were. This meant CJ couldn't rely on another lucky ferry flight to get her back to base in a single day.

"How many days do you have to allow?" her father asked.

It was the day after Christmas, and they were out in the workshop again tinkering.

"Three," she admitted. "I should catch a train back to Romulus on Tuesday, to be safe."

"I wish I could drive you, but with gas and tire rations being what they are..."

"It's fine, Dad. I wasn't expecting a ride."

"I know, but it would be so good to take a little trip. I like seeing you in your element. Your mother and I still talk about the time we visited you in Illinois."

"You do? Why?"

"You're not a parent, so you won't understand," he said, measuring a length of wood for one of the planters her mother had requested for her spring flower bed. "But there's something to be said for watching your child grow up and achieve something you might not have expected they would, especially if it's not anything you would have wanted for yourself."

You're not a parent. He had said it so easily, whereas a similar thought had nearly paralyzed her mother in the wake of Sean's visit.

"Would you like to try the new handsaw?" he asked, clamping the two by four to the workbench and holding his Christmas present out to her. "Remember, it works on the upstroke."

CJ gripped the saw. She was pretty sure her mother had picked it out as an incentive to her father to build the planters she'd wanted for years now. Smart woman—and excellent saw, too. It cut through hardwood like butter.

"I think my mom worries I won't have children," CJ said into the telephone receiver later that afternoon. Brady had called her again, claiming that her parents wouldn't even notice the expense. "You know, now that she knows I'm happy."

"Pish," Brady said. "You don't need to be *un*happy to have children."

"Actually, I think it helps."

"That's because you don't live in L.A. Money can buy anything, especially in the land of make believe."

"Even children?"

"Think of how many illegitimate 'orphans' there will be by war's end. Not to mention all the European destitute arriving on our shores."

"So wait. You don't regard being happy as a deterrent to having a family?"

"Certainly it complicates matters, but no, I suppose I don't. Do you?"

She thought about it. "I guess not."

"Hmm," Brady said.

"Hmm, indeed."

As they dined alone in their bedroom that night, Rebecca asked, "Why would being happy stop you from having children?"

CJ threw part of a pickle at her sister. "Who taught you that snooping was okay?"

"No one," Rebecca said smartly, lobbing the pickle back. "I decided all on my own. Now answer the question."

"I can't." She rose and gathered their plates and silverware. "That topic is above your pay grade."

"I know you think you're funny, but you're not."

"I'd rather be not funny than funny-looking."

Reluctantly Rebecca smiled. Then she moved to the mirror and stared at the lines of peeling skin on her cheeks. "You promise this won't scar?"

"I can't promise, but mine didn't." CJ paused in the doorway. "Either way, peeling is a good thing. It means you're healing."

"So you say. CJ?" she added.

"Yes, bug?"

"I'm glad you came home. I know you didn't have to."

"That's not exactly true. I had to make sure you were okay, didn't I? Sisters stick together. Don't forget."

"I won't."

In the hallway, CJ set the tray on the floor so that she could wash her hands for what felt like the three hundredth time that week. Sisters were supposed to stick together, it was true, but that didn't mean they always did. Look at their Detroit aunts, Betsy and Rochelle, who had gone to Wellesley, married well and produced miniature versions of themselves and their husbands. They barely spoke to her mother, their younger sister, and her only crime had been to marry below their presumed station. That, and actually work for a living. What would they say when they learned of their niece's transgression? Her mother probably worried about their reaction too. Just what she needed—more fuel for her sisters' flaming disapproval.

CJ dried her hands and returned to the hall, wondering if Rebecca would still look up to her when she found out about Brady or if she would follow their mother's lead. For that matter, would their mom prove to be the same variety of apple as *her* mother and siblings, or would she reveal herself to be another type entirely?

There was no way of knowing for certain, she realized as she carried the dishes downstairs. She would have to wait and hope that her mother would decide to accept her for who she was—despite the fact her own mother had never seemed to accept her.

CHAPTER TWENTY-FOUR

On Tuesday morning, CJ's father let the sedan warm up in the driveway while she said goodbye to the rest of the family. Up in their room, Rebecca gave her a big hug and promised to write often, while Pete came outside to wave her away, a Jamieson tradition. Her mother, however, held her at arm's length, her eyes brimming with unshed tears.

"Think about what you're doing, Caroline. We only get one chance at life. Please don't waste yours."

Behind her, Pete gave CJ a quizzical look.

She took a breath, trying to push down her anger. An image of flak bursting at two thousand feet flashed through her mind, and she thought of Carole Lombard, who had died in a plane crash almost two years earlier on her way home from a war bond-selling tour. She and husband Clark Gable had fought before the trip, and much was made in the press about the lack of resolution in their relationship when she died. Shortly afterward, Gable joined the Army Air Corps and became a top gunner on a B-17 crew. In fact, his bombardment group had formed at Biggs before deploying to England.

"I know, Mom," she said, and pulled her into a close embrace. *Hugs fix everything*, her parents used to say when she was little and skinned her knee or lost a favorite toy. "I love you."

After a moment, she felt her mother's arms tighten about her. It only lasted a second, but brief was better than nonexistent.

Blinking back her own tears, CJ jogged down the front steps. At the bottom, she stopped to wave up at Rebecca, who gazed down forlornly from the bedroom window. CJ gave her little sister a V for victory sign, and then she was sliding into the car. She waved at her mother and Pete, still out on the stoop, and they waved back until the car rounded the same bend where she'd lost sight of Sean. She tried not to think of the events that might bring her home next: a memorial service, a tour-ending injury, some other personal family disaster. Maybe she wouldn't be home until the end of the war—although that wasn't such a bright thought either.

Unlike Brady, CJ's father followed the federal speed limit recommendations closely, so it took fifteen minutes to get to the train station where she planned to catch the eight thirty to Detroit. As they drove along the snow-free streets, they chatted about her mother's planters and the John Deere tractor, the animals and her younger siblings, but not Alec or Joe. CJ stuck to light subjects like work with Tow Target and her New Year's Eve plans—unformed as of yet, but with several possibilities.

He parked the car and went in with her, waiting while she arranged her ticket. Then they found a seat together in the waiting room. He took her hand in his, tracing the seemingly permanent grease stains on her knuckles.

"You know," he said, "you'll probably have to give your mother some time."

CJ looked at him quickly. Did he know? And if so, how?

"With the boys away fighting, she somehow got her heart set on your wedding. Now, as you know, Sean was not someone I would have chosen for you, but your mother got it into her head that your marriage would be a good thing for everyone involved."

"And then I broke up with him and ran off and joined the Army."

"You didn't run off." He squeezed her hand and smiled sideways at her.

She wanted so badly to tell him about Brady, to share her genuine happiness with him, but she couldn't risk losing him too. Not now. Instead she said, "What if there never is a wedding for me, Dad? What if I don't settle down and have the life Mom wants for me?"

"Because of your academic plans?"

She shrugged and glanced away, her gaze resting on the telephone booth where she had talked to Brady the day Sean blew up her relationship with her mother. "Maybe."

"Well, it *is* your life, and foregoing a family is certainly a safer option. But do you really want to stay safe, Caroline? Are you sure you want to miss out on everything a family of your own has to offer?"

"No," she said, looking back at his face etched with smile lines and sunlight, wind and laughter. He was such a good man. Would he think that her love for Brady was somehow a rejection of him? She forced a smile. "But I'm an Air Wac, remember? Safety is my middle name."

"I remember." He squeezed her hand again and looked searchingly at her, as if there was something more he wanted to say.

The loudspeaker crackled into life as the sound of an approaching train drew closer. Time to go. They rose and walked out to the platform together, his arm around her shoulders, her suitcase in his free hand.

"I read that women soldiers rarely have anyone to send them off," he commented. "Why is that, do you think?"

"Because we're headed to Texas or Iowa or Florida, not into a combat zone."

He stopped on the platform, set her case down and placed his hands on her shoulders. "I know you know this, but I'll say it anyway: I am *proud* of you, and I *believe* in you, Caroline. You are a fine young woman, and don't ever let anyone tell you otherwise."

"Thanks, Dad. That means a lot to me."

"Well, you mean a lot to me." He leaned forward to kiss her cheek. "Now get back to duty, Private. I will expect a letter after the first of the year."

"Yes, sir," she said, smiling, and saluted him.

She was turning away when he added, "One more thing. When the time is right, I would very much like to meet your friend. Brady, is it?"

CJ gazed at him, trying to figure out what he did and didn't know. "You would?"

He nodded. "She must be pretty special if she's as important to you as I think she is."

At first she didn't move. Then she dropped her suitcase and walked into her father's arms. "Thank you, Daddy," she whispered, pressing her cheek against the wool of his overcoat and breathing in the familiar scent of him—Old Spice, wood smoke, engine oil.

"I'm your father. You don't have to thank me." He kissed the top of her head. "Now you better go before they leave without you."

As she climbed aboard the train, she thought of what Toby had said—how you can't help who you love, how sometimes people can surprise you. It was uncanny how often she was right—except when it came to picking a winning horse.

The train was crowded with soldiers and civilians alike, and it took her a while to find an empty window seat. Her father was still there on the platform, his gaze fixed on the car she'd entered. As the train whistled and pulled out of the station, she waved briskly, trying to catch his attention. But he never did find her in the long line of railcars leaving Kalamazoo for points east.

* * *

Her trip back to Fort Bliss may not have taken three days, but it felt like longer. Fifty-two hours after she left Kalamazoo, the train she'd boarded in Dallas chugged to a halt at El Paso's Union Depot. An AA company fresh out of basic tried to convince her to join their convoy, but she politely declined. Instead she walked a few blocks to a nearby streetcar line and caught a ride downtown. There she found her way to a diner she and Brady had discovered during their second Hilton weekend and ordered a spinach omelet with Spanish rice and beans on the side. *Home again, home again*, she thought, sipping from her cup of Mexican spiced coffee. And yet if home was where the heart was, she should by all rights be in L.A.

After her mid-day meal, she walked around El Paso, still hung with Christmas lights. The weather was cool but nowhere near as cold as Michigan. It was a relief to be on her own after so much time cooped up with her sister. Though at least in Michigan she hadn't been reminded of Brady everywhere she turned—here there was the bookstore where the clerk had recommended the book about women like them; a block away was the shop where they'd bought their mismatched lockets; and on another nearby street was the tailor's shop where they'd had their uniforms fitted. In Texas, Brady was a distracting apparition hovering in the background wherever she went.

The feeling only intensified once she caught a streetcar to base. After she checked in with Lieutenant Kelly—"Glad to see you returned in good order, Private Jamieson"—she left the WAC officers' quarters and walked to her barracks, where she had soon unpacked. Her clothes were freshly laundered, other than the uniform she had been wearing for the last two days straight. Was it a good sign her mother had done her laundry for her before she left?

Feeling grimy, she slipped into a robe and grabbed her towel. She could smell diesel fuel in her hair from the harrowing B-24 flight out of Romulus. First the pilot had almost stalled on takeoff, and then when it came time to land near Kansas City, the landing gear had gotten stuck. Next she'd taken a seat on a Gooney Bird, this time with a cadre of Army nurses who lived up to their reputation as an entertaining bunch. When they landed in Dallas, they discovered that air traffic was officially grounded due to weather. She'd been lucky to find a seat on a train crammed with a variety of troops headed west.

But she was here now, she thought, turning the shower on as hot as she could tolerate. She emptied her mind and concentrated on relaxing her stiff neck, her hunched shoulders, her sore lower back. The healing powers of hot water had always amazed her.

"Private Jamieson!"

The cry startled her, and she glanced around the edge of the curtain to see Reggie, Toby and Sarah standing at the sinks, scrubbing grease from their hands in their usual end-of-work-day ritual. They grinned at her in the mirrors and waved, and she smiled back. It was wonderful to see them, even better than she would have guessed.

At supper mess, her friends crowded around the table asking questions about her holidays and talking over each other about their own. Sarah and Jack had rented a hotel room in Las Cruces for three days and rarely stepped outside, she admitted, her cheeks pink. Toby and Kate had had a lovely time with Kate's aunt, now confirmed as a member of the club, and had noticed the New Mexican scenery from their sleeper car window on occasion. Reggie meanwhile reported having a "glorious, life-changing experience" with Holly at the Grand Canyon.

"She thought the scenery was okay too," Toby quipped.

CJ wanted to be happy for her friends. After all, it was the season of giving, and they couldn't help that she had spent most of the past ten days looking after her sick kid sister while they had all spent the holidays in the arms of their respective others. Brady would be back early the following week, and they could try for another three-day pass then. Granted, passes typically weren't allotted to soldiers who had recently gone on extended leave, so they might have to wait a few weeks to be alone together. But their time would come. Eventually.

Her attempts at cheeriness must have been abysmal, because soon the table grew quiet.

Toby glanced at Reggie. "Go on, put her out of her misery."

"Tell her already," Sarah and Kate chimed in unison.

"Tell me what?" CJ asked.

"Wee-llll." Reggie grunted as Toby elbowed her. "Holly and I wanted to thank you for the hotel and all, so she talked the major into sending her and Nell to Burbank this weekend to pick up a P-38."

"We're getting a Lightning?" CJ asked, thinking they were trying to cheer her up with the news. "Swell. I can't wait to see her up close."

"You won't have to wait," Reggie said.

CJ frowned, not following.

"Holly requested you as their non-rated mechanic." As CJ stared at her blankly, Reggie crowed, "You'll be in L.A. for New Year's Eve!"

"Holy crap," CJ said. "I will?"

"You will," Toby confirmed.

"Holy crap!" she repeated, smiling so wide her face hurt. "I'm going to California!" Then she stopped. "Wait. Who's flying the P-38 back?"

"Nell won the coin toss, so you and your Admin friend will be hitching back to Bliss with Holly," Reggie said.

Whew. One bullet dodged. Brady wouldn't begrudge her a hop with Nell if it meant they would get to ring in the New Year together, would she? The fact that they would be flying back to Bliss together would soften the news, wouldn't it?

Looked like she would find out soon.

* * *

In the morning, CJ hurried back after drill to get cleaned up and retrieve her overnight case. After breakfast, she rode with the rest of her squad to the Balloon Hangar, where Nell and Holly were waiting with a spare parachute bag.

"Apparently our plan meets with your approval?" Nell asked, grinning.

"I'd say so," CJ said. "Thanks, by the way. This is great of you two."

"We aim to please," Holly said. "Besides, I owe you. That Grand Canyon experience was life-changing."

"So I've heard," CJ said, exchanging an amused look with Nell.

The plane they were taking to California was none other than the squadron's lone B-26, the craft that had seen her and Nell through their friendly-fire incident. They let her choose her seat, and she picked the bombardier's forward position in the aircraft's Plexiglas nose. To get to it, she had to crawl through a tunnel in front of the copilot's seat, similar to the setup in the AT-11. The fit was a bit tight with the parachute, but even though they'd checked and double-checked the bombsight doors, she still had to wear the chute. Just in case.

"How long will we be in the air?" CJ asked Nell through the headset.

"About three hours," Nell told her. "That'll get us to Burbank around noon."

"And when do we have to come back?"

Nell muted her headset microphone and leaned forward conspiratorially. "I'm turning around with the Lightning this afternoon, but I have a feeling you might have to ground this old bird for a couple of nights. Everyone knows how unreliable these flying bricks can be."

"What about Holly?"

"She'll be spending the weekend in West Hollywood with a friend from her aerial acrobatics days."

"Got it," CJ said, grinning back at her. Two whole nights with Brady—this time yesterday, she wouldn't have believed it would be possible.

Takeoffs and landings were the most dangerous parts of any flight. As the plane sped along the runway, CJ held her breath, keeping an eye on the nearby Franklins. Once they were past the mountains, she settled in to enjoy flying close to three hundred miles per hour through the air in a plastic bubble that afforded her nearly unrestricted views of the sky above and the land below. The Marauder might be crash-prone, but it could fly, as she well remembered from the evasive maneuvers Nell had run her through a few weeks earlier. They cruised at five thousand feet most of the way, except where there were mountain ranges to cross. Nell and Holly helpfully kept up a running commentary throughout on assorted deserts, national monuments and other points of interest they passed over.

The color of the earth intrigued her—brown, red and orange like the colors of an autumn landscape, along with the occasional snowy peak. But mostly the earth was brown, the jagged spines of hills and mountains visible beneath the surface much like the Franklin and Organ Ranges. Only when they were a hundred or so miles out of Los Angeles did the Palm Desert give way to the evergreen forests of the San Bernardino Mountains. Sunlight glinted off the ocean in the distance—her first sight of the Pacific—and she gazed in wonder at the foreign world below. The landscape was so different from the Midwest that it was hard to believe she was in the same country.

They made good time. By noon, as predicted, Nell was in the Lockheed Vega office signing for the new P-38 while Holly was negotiating with a bored sergeant to find out where to park the Marauder overnight, given its "heavy" handling on the way out.

"Go," Holly said to CJ when the sergeant wandered off to find someone else to pass them off on. "But be back here by noon on Sunday, and bring your girl."

CJ didn't need to be told twice. She skedaddled out of the hangar to a nearby ready room, looking for a telephone. An Air Corps lieutenant pointed her to a desk set, and soon she was asking the operator to put her through to Brady's exchange.

The woman CJ assumed was Isabel answered and asked her to wait, like last time. She assented, tapping her foot against the concrete floor of the ready room as the seconds dragged past.

"CJ?"

"Hiya." She couldn't help smiling at the sound of Brady's voice. "What are you doing?"

"I was about to go for a drive. Are you in Texas?"

"I got back yesterday," she said, which was perfectly true. "What are you doing tonight for New Year's?"

"Meeting some friends in the city. Why? What are you doing?"

"I thought I might go out on a date."

Brady was quiet. Then: "Wait. Why is the line so clear? Where are you?"

"At the Lockheed plant. You know, in Burbank?"

She winced as Brady let out a little scream.

"You're *here*? How are you here?"

"It's a good story, but I'd rather tell you in person. Can you come pick me up?"

"Heck yes! Where do I find you?"

CJ waved the friendly lieutenant over and quickly relayed the directions he gave her.

"I'll be there in half an hour. Don't go anywhere," Brady ordered.

"Yes, ma'am," she said, but the line had already gone dead.

The lieutenant offered to take her to the main gate. CJ accepted the ride in the Jeep but politely resisted his other, more personal overtures, including suggestions on where she and her friend should spend the evening. He gave up gracefully enough, and soon she was seated alone on a bus stop bench in the sun, waiting for Brady. In her head, she started a letter home: "Dear Family, I've been back for a day, and already I'm somewhere entirely new. Southern California for New Year's Eve—how crazy is that? I have the best friends in the world, that's for sure."

She'd gotten as far as the view from the Marauder's nose when a cute, red two-seater screeched around a corner and made a beeline for her. Brady, still refusing to even acknowledge the speed limit. She was out of uniform, dressed in a blue and yellow dress that revealed a fair expanse of tanned leg, CJ realized as Brady parked the car at the curb and leapt out, laughing.

"I can't believe you're here!" she said, hugging CJ.

"I can't believe how much I missed you."

"I can." Brady pulled away and gave her a radiant smile. "How long are you staying?"

"*We* have to report back on Sunday at noon to catch *our* flight."

Brady clapped her hands. "I get to fly back with you?"

"Holly even offered to detour over the Grand Canyon on the way. Unless you'd rather catch a train back?"

"Heck no." Brady looped her arm through CJ's and pulled her toward the car. "Two whole days together—how glorious. Any requests?"

"I don't care what we do as long as it involves food. And a room with a door that locks, preferably."

Brady's smoldering look made her breath catch. "I'm sure that can be arranged."

As they drove along roads edged alternately with farm fields and brand-new subdivisions, CJ watched Brady's face in profile. She looked relaxed and happy, her forehead unlined, smile lines crinkling at the corners of her kissable mouth.

"Are you staring at me?" Brady asked, glancing away from the sparse weekday traffic as the road took them between brown, tree-dotted hills.

"I am. I like your dress."

"I didn't want to take the time to change back into uniform."

The radio played Glen Miller—another celebrity turned Air Corps officer—as Brady drove quickly along streets she obviously knew well. CJ let her arm hang out the window, soaking in the sunshine and the sights and sounds of the city. There were palm trees everywhere, along with Spanish colonial and art deco buildings. She was really here. She was actually in L.A. with Brady.

Twenty minutes later, they turned onto a smaller road lined with palm trees (again) and large, handsome homes set back from the curb. As they slowed and turned into a gated driveway edged with thick bushes, CJ looked at Brady quickly.

"Are we where I think we are?"

"Don't worry. My father is at work and my mother is playing tennis at the club," she said, pressing a button on the dash.

The gate swung open, and as they headed up the driveway, CJ drew in a breath. From the outside, Brady's house resembled a Spanish villa, with a brick courtyard, tiled pool and separate guesthouse.

"*This* is where you grew up?"

"It's not that impressive. You should see the mansions a few streets over."

CJ gazed up at the two-story structure with its red tile roof, hacienda-style layout and rustic balustrades. "Are you trying to say this *isn't* a mansion?"

Brady's laugh echoed across the courtyard. "Come on. I'll ask Isabel if we can raid the refrigerator."

Inside, CJ's sense of wonder deepened. She'd known Brady was wealthy, but she'd never said anything about living in a museum. The large house boasted high ceilings with intricately carved wooden-beam construction, a Spanish red-brick fireplace, wood floors, a Spanish tile staircase and a sunny kitchen with a flagstone floor and gorgeous wooden cupboards. A dark-haired woman in a red dress and white apron stood at the stone-tiled counter, rolling out homemade flour tortillas.

"Isabel." Brady slid her arm around CJ's waist. "*Me gustaría que conocieras a mi querida amiga*, Caroline."

"Welcome, Caroline," Isabel said, in a warm voice CJ recognized from the telephone. "It's very nice to meet you. I have heard much about you lately from this one."

"Nice to meet you too."

"CJ just flew in from Texas. Any chance we could raid the icebox for a picnic?"

"I think we can do better than that for your guest," Isabel said. "Give me a few minutes."

"Which is her way of saying she doesn't allow anyone else in her kitchen," Brady said over her shoulder to CJ as she swiped a banana from the fruit bowl on the counter.

"Out, you," Isabel said, flicking a dish towel at Brady.

"Yes, ma'am."

She led CJ up the wide staircase to the second floor and turned down a hall lined with half-open doors. "Christopher's room, Josh's room and mine," she said, pushing the door open. "My parents have a suite on the other side of the house."

CJ walked in ahead of her, looking around curiously. She had pictured Brady in her bedroom all week, but her imagination hadn't done the room justice. It was bigger than she'd expected, lighter and airier with French doors that opened out onto a brick-tiled balcony overlooking the courtyard. Framed art hung on the striped walls, modern and colorful.

"You gave this up for the Army?"

"What can I say?" Brady shrugged. "Guess I'm just a girl with a star-spangled heart."

CJ snorted. "That recruiting slogan is awful, and you know it."

"As long as you do too." Brady closed the door behind her and approached CJ, her eyes half-lidded. "Would you like to try out my bed? It's very comfortable."

"Nice line." CJ let Brady take her hand and lead her toward the wide canopy bed.

"It appears to have worked on you."

"You know what they say about Wacs."

"That we're easy?" Brady asked, pushing her down on the bed and leaning over her.

"Exactly."

CJ closed her eyes as they kissed. Brady tasted of Spearmint gum and lipstick. But before CJ could register anything else, Brady pulled back.

"Isabel is expecting us," she said, jumping up. "Besides, I need to pack."

"Why? Where are we going?"

Brady smiled mysteriously. "You'll see."

CJ kicked off her shoes and lay back on the bed, watching Brady load her overnight case: magazines, a few phonograph records, swimsuits, underclothes, night clothes and civvies, enough to last the weekend. Meanwhile she left her dress uniform and most of her other service clothes in the closet.

"Do we not need uniforms wherever it is you're taking me?" CJ asked as Brady changed into a white shirtwaist and her summer uniform skirt.

"We do not," she confirmed. "I hope that's okay."

"Fine by me."

Back downstairs, Isabel was putting the final touches on a brimming picnic basket. A wine bottle and glasses poked out the top.

"Aw, you didn't have to do that." Brady hugged her. "But thank you."

"You are welcome." Isabel straightened her apron. "You could use a little amount of joy after what you have been through. Now what do you want me to tell your parents?"

Brady glanced over at CJ. "You can tell them that my best buddy from the Army has made me very *happy* by surprising me for New Year's. Oh, and tell them we're spending the weekend at..." She leaned forward and whispered in Isabel's ear.

The housekeeper brightened. "Your grandpapa would be glad you are using it. I will call Mr. Gardiner to make sure everything is ready."

"Thank you," Brady said. "That would be great, Isabel."

"It was very nice to meet you," the housekeeper said again, nodding at CJ. "You take care of this girl, okay?"

"I will."

A few minutes later they were back in the car, picnic basket and overnight cases secured in the car's small trunk. Brady handed CJ an apple she'd liberated from the fruit bowl. "You're going to need this," she said as she turned the car around and headed back down the driveway. "We've got a bit of a drive ahead of us."

CJ crunched the apple as Brady guided the car west on Route 66, passing parks and more Spanish colonial churches, storefronts and homes along the way. The road took them over a small rise, and she briefly glimpsed the ocean in the distance, winter sun shining on it, before it disappeared again beyond the horizon.

A few blocks later, Brady made a snorting sound.

"What's wrong?"

"Amherst Ave. and Wellesley Ave.," Brady griped, gesturing at a street sign, "but no Smith. Cretins."

As they passed a cemetery with headstones decorated with tiny American flags, CJ remembered what she'd wanted to ask Brady.

"You wanted to tell me something about Nate's sister," she commented, "didn't you?"

Brady hesitated, her relaxed expression fading, and CJ reached over to take her hand. "Amy told me Nate got my letter. *The* letter."

"How does she know?"

"Because he wrote to tell her how relieved he was. Apparently," and here she paused to take a deep breath, releasing CJ's hand to downshift for a red light and then grabbing hold again, "he and Cathy, the girl from New Haven, got back in touch while he was in basic, and he realized he wanted to marry her after all. Amy thought I deserved to know, given the circumstances. She also asked me not to tell their parents. I'm not sure that's the right decision, but it's not mine to make."

CJ held tightly to Brady's hand, only letting go when she had to shift. "I know it's not kind to speak ill of the dead, but he was a spineless idiot who didn't deserve you."

Brady shook her head. "It's okay. Nate is—was a good person, and we did genuinely care about each other. He may not have been strong enough to stand up for what he wanted, but who am I to judge him for that?"

When she put it that way... CJ squeezed her fingers. "Have I told you recently how amazing you are?"

"Yes," Brady said, her smile returning. "But you can say it again. I won't mind."

Soon a white tower appeared in the distance, eventually materializing into an art deco skyscraper as they drew closer. They were almost upon the seashore before CJ realized it. Route 66 ended at Ocean Avenue near a park with an expansive view of the Pacific and signs that pointed the way to the Santa Monica pier. Brady turned in the opposite direction, heading north along the seaside drive.

CJ stared out at the foaming waves as they drove along the wide boulevard. She could hear the thunder of the surf over the hum of the engine and the steady croon of brass instruments on the radio, and it wasn't at all what she'd expected. This was her first time seeing the ocean, any ocean. She'd always thought it would look like Lake Michigan, also too wide to see across. But the Pacific was so much more powerful. It was the largest ocean on Earth, and on the other shore lay Japan, their sworn enemy, as well as China, their ally. Joe had shipped out from this very city across this same body of water. Now he was thousands of miles away in a jungle or on a beach, sleeping or swearing, fighting or holding the hand of a wounded or dying friend. As long as he wasn't wounded or dying himself.

"It's so big," she said, and Brady glanced at her.

"Is this your first time?"

When she nodded, Brady pulled over and guided the car into a parking space at the edge of the road.

"Come on," she said, removing the picnic basket and a Mexican blanket from the trunk. "This is a perfect spot for a picnic."

The sun was warm and the breeze mild, and as they spread the blanket on the grass at the edge of the walkway, CJ almost forgot that it was the last day of the year. While they ate cold chicken and potato salad and shared a glass of wine, Brady told her about the area—how Santa Monica used to be a popular tourist draw but had fallen on hard times during the Depression. Any city that depended on tourism was bound to be in trouble when the bottom fell out of the economy, they agreed.

"And now with the mandatory blackout..."

"There's a blackout in effect here?"

"Ever since the war started. Remember those Japanese subs that shelled the oil fields in Santa Barbara right after Pearl Harbor? They may not have done much structural damage, but the people around here have lived in fear ever since."

CJ looked out at the water, trying to imagine a submarine surfacing and firing tracers at them. She knew that exact thing had happened not far from where they were sitting, but she couldn't get her head around it. The surreal nature of war, once again.

When they were done eating, they kicked off their shoes and strolled down to the water's edge, cool sand squeezing between their toes. CJ looked for stones to skip while Brady waded into the water.

"*Brr*," she said, shivering. "It's freezing!"

CJ waded in beside her and started to laugh. "It's warmer than Lake Michigan in the middle of summer."

"Remind me not to go swimming when we go there," Brady said.

"My father invited you to visit."

"Before Sean's bombshell or after?"

"After. Though I think we'd better give my mother some time," CJ added, watching her. Brady's hair was loose and unruly in the breeze, blonde highlights even whiter in the sunlight.

"It's a date." Brady slipped her arms around CJ's waist, tugging her closer as the waves crashed around their ankles.

"Brady," she said, glancing around nervously.

"Don't worry, no one's around. It's far too cold for the natives." And she kissed her, the sound of the ocean drowning out everything else as their lips met and lingered.

A little while later, Brady checked her watch. "We should probably get back on the road. We have to be in before sunset."

They packed up the remains of the meal and headed north again along the coastal road. Soon they had left the city behind and had only ocean to the left and barren foothills to the right. After a quarter-hour, Brady turned the car east onto a gravel road that switchbacked up the side of a hill to a slight plateau where a small house sat all by itself. There, Brady turned into the driveway and parked.

"We're here," she said, smiling at CJ.

"Yes, but where?"

"My grandfather built this cabin. My brothers and I used to come up here all the time and sleep on the floor like a pile of puppies, as my grandmother liked to say. Since they died, we haven't used it nearly as much."

CJ stepped out of the car and looked around. They were far enough up in the foothills that the road sounds were minimal, the ocean roar more of a dull rumble. It was a clear day, and in the distance she could see two sets of islands rising up out of the ocean.

"Come on," Brady said, leading the way through a split-rail gate and up a gravel path to the front deck. She unlocked the dead bolt on the French doors and threw them open. "Welcome to Brady Manor."

"Brady Manor?"

"My grandmother's maiden name."

Inside, the cabin was one big room, with a sitting area immediately to the left and an updated kitchen on the right with a built-in breakfast nook. A small vase of flowers on the pine table told them that Isabel had managed to reach Mr. Gardiner, the property's caretaker. At the far end of the room was a large brass bed.

"We had the place remodeled about ten years ago," Brady said as she unloaded the picnic basket into the refrigerator. "Before that it was kerosene lamps and a pit toilet out back. Now it's a tad more luxurious."

"Luxurious" seemed a stretch even to CJ, but the cabin was bright and airy and clean, and best of all, it was far from everyone and everything. They could start the new year here together, just the two of them.

"What do you think?" Brady asked, turning to lean against the counter.

"I think it's wonderful." CJ approached her slowly, pulling her tie off as she stepped out of her shoes. "I also think you should close the doors if you don't want anyone passing by to see us naked."

"There won't be anyone passing by. There never is." But she closed and locked the doors and tugged on the cord that held back the blackout blinds.

The room went dark and stayed that way until Brady lit a candle on the wood stove in the corner near the breakfast nook. Then she turned to CJ, her eyes in shadows.

"Would you like to try the bed?" she asked for the second time that afternoon.

"Thought you'd never ask."

* * *

Later, after the sun had set and the temperature began to drop, they lit a fire in the wood stove and sat in bed feeding each other chicken, chips and salsa and finishing off the rest of the wine as they caught each other up on their time apart.

When they'd demolished the food and drink, they took a shower together in the tiny bathroom, giggling as they knocked elbows and knees into the surround and each other. Back in bed, they explored each other's bodies again lazily, lingeringly, each bringing the other to a pinnacle of pleasure that, for once, didn't have to be enjoyed silently. They could voice their passion as loudly as they wanted here, for as long as they wanted, and no one would hear or see. Solitude was an amazing thing, they agreed afterward, snuggling up in each other's arms as the wood fire crackled.

"It's almost the new year," Brady said when their breathing had slowed.

"In the East Indies, it's already January second."

"Are you quoting our dear president?"

"I am. I still say he's the best orator of his generation."

"And I still say he has a very talented speechwriter."

"You're so cynical," CJ said.

"And you're not, which is why we make such a great team."

"Much better than Sean and I were," she agreed. "Although he was a pretty smooth dance partner, I have to say."

"Should I be jealous?"

"Hardly. I feel sorry for him. I don't think I felt for him even a smidgen of what I feel for you."

Brady nodded. "At the memorial service, I kept thinking how tragic that Nate's fiancé didn't love him. But then Amy told me about the letter, and I realized the real tragedy was that he didn't have the courage to go against his family's wishes sooner. I don't want that to happen with us. I don't want to regret anything."

"Neither do I."

Brady slid her hand down CJ's bare arm and entwined their fingers. "I've been thinking—it isn't fair of me to keep you from flying when you obviously love it. It's not your fault that Nate didn't know how to be faithful. You're nothing like him, and besides, I do trust you. The next time Nell or any other pilot offers you a hop, I don't want you to say no because of me, okay?"

CJ bit her lip. "Funny you should mention that—Nell was the copilot on the flight that brought me here. But don't worry. She flew the Lightning back to base today, so we don't have to ride back with her."

Brady closed her eyes and took a breath. Then she looked back at CJ, her gaze clear. "You know what? That's fine."

"Really?"

"Really. They brought you here so you could be with me. For future reference, I can't promise not to be a little envious if you keep flying off into the wild blue yonder with a cute WASP—"

"She's not *that* cute."

Brady pulled her hand away and sat up straighter in bed, the sheet falling away from her. "You're supposed to say she isn't cute at all! But then you would be lying, and that would be worse."

"How do you know what she looks like?"

"I *may* have looked up her service photo."

"Brady!" CJ shook her head, laughing.

"What? Being in the PRO has its perks. But even I have to admit she's attractive, if you go in for that Midwestern natural look."

"Which some people do," CJ said, leaning forward to nuzzle Brady's neck.

She tilted her head to give her more room. "Mmm, some people do."

"I prefer blonde bombshells myself."

"Good. Because you're stuck with this one."

"I wouldn't call it *stuck*."

And then she was pulling Brady on top of her and demonstrating once again how deep her love ran.

A little before midnight, Brady pulled a record from her overnight case and placed it on the phonograph in the sitting room.

"May I have this dance?" she asked, smiling and holding her hand out to CJ as the opening strains of "Begin the Beguine" sounded in the small cabin.

"Of course," CJ said, taking her hand.

Outside the palms swayed and waves crashed and stars turned overhead while inside the cabin the orchestra played, and CJ thought she knew what Cole Porter had meant when he wrote about serene rapture.

"I love you, Brady," she said, holding her girlfriend close as one year ended and another began.

"I love you, CJ. Happy New Year."

And it would be. She could feel it.

CHAPTER TWENTY-FIVE

December 1949

CJ stepped into the hotel room, still shivering from the Michigan wind. "Dang, it's cold out there!"

From where she sat on the bed propped against pillows, Brady smiled. "I believe the South has ruined you, my love."

"You may be right." She set the drugstore bag on a nearby dresser and crossed to the bed. "Everything quiet here?"

"So far so good."

"Feel like company?" She wiggled her eyebrows.

"Absolutely, but only if you help me finish these Christmas cards. It's three days until Christmas and they're still not done."

"Oh, dear, what would the editors of the Smith alumnae magazine think?" CJ teased, snuggling in beside her.

"Late Christmas cards is the least of their worries as far as you and I are concerned."

"Good point. So which friends need a note?"

"Almost your entire stack. Mary and Chris, Sarah and Jack—"

"Aren't we delivering theirs in person?"

"Yes, but I am of the radical opinion it probably shouldn't be blank inside. Also, there's Holly, Nell and Trish, Reggie, and Toby and Ka—I mean, Toby and *Paulina*. Sorry."

"That's okay. I do it sometimes too."

Of all their friends, CJ had assumed Toby and Kate would stay together. But in late 1944, with the end of the war in sight, both the Regular Army and the WAC began issuing blue ticket discharges at the slightest provocation. Janice had managed to protect Brady, CJ and their immediate friends from dismissal, but she hadn't been able to stop Kate from being transferred to Daytona. The previously happy couple had tried to maintain their relationship, but in the end, the separation had proven too much.

Around the same time Kate was transferred, the WASPs were disbanded and Holly left for an instructor position at a flight-training school in San Diego. Shortly after that, she and Reggie had also broken up. Sarah and Jack, on the other hand, had gotten married in El Paso before Jack shipped out to the Pacific. He was one of the lucky ones—he'd been wounded a few months in and sent stateside, where he spent the rest of the war training replacement troops at an AA base in Nevada. Now he worked for his older brother's insurance company in Chicago. Sarah had given birth to their first child a year after the war, a little girl CJ and Brady would meet for the first time at New Year's.

For a while the room was quiet, save for the sound of pen tips scratching against cardstock and distant traffic noise from the street ten stories below. Their flight out of DC had been delayed, and rather than rushing to make the late train, they had decided to stay in Detroit overnight and catch the early train out in the morning.

"Done," CJ said, laying her pen and stack of envelopes on the nearest bedside table.

"Almost there." Brady didn't look up.

"You can finish on the train tomorrow." CJ leaned in to kiss the spot on Brady's neck that she knew would produce the desired result. Beneath her touch, Brady shivered.

"No fair."

"Who said I had to be fair?" CJ pulled her closer, their bodies molding together in a familiar way.

"You and hotel rooms," Brady said, but she was smiling.

CJ touched her lips to Brady's, amazed that kissing her could feel so familiar and yet so thrilling at the same time. As the kiss deepened, she heard a faint sound from the next room, connected to theirs by an open door.

"Dang it," Brady grumbled, pulling away to listen.

CJ leaned back beside her, tilting her head. *Crap.* There it came again.

"Want to wait it out?"

Brady shook her head. "Not here. No need for the neighbors to suffer."

"You're right." She touched Brady's lips with her thumb. "Rain check?"

"I'll add it to all the others."

CJ rose and crossed into the adjoining room. In the dim light from the night lamp they'd brought from home, she could see a small face staring up at her from the hotel crib.

"Mimi," the child said, smiling impishly up at her.

"Mads, why aren't you asleep?"

"Want to snuggle with you and Mama. Pease?"

"All right. But only this once," she said, which they both knew was a lie.

She lifted the child out and carried her into the other room. "Look who I've got."

Brady was already clearing a spot in the middle of the bed. "Come here, sweet girl. Why aren't you sleeping?"

"Want to snuggle," the girl said, as if it were obvious.

CJ smiled at Brady over the ring of dark curls. *Their daughter.* It had been two and a half years since they'd gotten the call from Nell's friend, and she still couldn't quite believe their luck. Despite Brady's prediction, finding a child to adopt had proven difficult after the war, especially for a "single mother." They had already had a potential adoption fall through after the birth mother decided to keep the baby, so when Nell's stunt pilot pal contacted them about the child she had inadvertently conceived with a relative stranger, they had been wary. But everything had gone smoothly, and seven months later, they traveled to New York City to be in town for the birth. Afterward, they went home to North Carolina as a newly christened family of three. Brady was the official mother, but the legal documents were clear—if anything were to happen to her, custody would automatically go to CJ.

"She's lucky she's so cute," Brady said, but she didn't sound irritated. She rose and got ready for bed, and then CJ relinquished the toddler and got ready herself. By the time she slid between the cool sheets, Maddie was curled against Brady's side, asleep with the lights on.

Carefully, CJ smoothed back their daughter's hair, silky from the bath they'd given her earlier. "I keep thinking of her as a baby, but she isn't anymore, is she?"

"I know. It's almost sad. Speaking of which, I forgot to ask—did you find baby powder?"

"Yes, and the sweetest little jumper in maize and blue. I swear, drugstores are more like a civilian PX these days."

"I should have known better than to send you out alone with our spending money."

"I want her to look her best for my parents. Is that so wrong?"

"They're going to love her no matter what she's wearing," Brady said.

"And you. They're going to love you."

"Well, of course. How could they not?"

CJ knew that her girlfriend's confident exterior masked a worry she fully comprehended—she hadn't met Brady's parents yet either. They knew she existed, but as long as Brady remained "discreet" about her alternative lifestyle, they allowed her and Maddie a full role in Buchanan family life, albeit from afar. Almost as importantly, they hadn't cut her off financially. GI benefits were covering the cost of CJ's graduate program at UNC, but supporting two adults and a child on a teaching assistantship would have been much harder without Brady's parents' aid. Fortunately, the Buchanans' friends outwardly accepted the story that Brady was too heartbroken over Nate to consider marrying anyone else. She had adopted the baby to ease some of her pain and to help out a less fortunate friend, and wasn't that just like their generous-to-a-fault daughter?

"It'll be great," CJ said, trying to reassure Brady with her eyes.

"I know."

"Want me to take her back to the crib?"

"I feel better having her in here with us. Is that paranoid?"

"No, I think it's *parenting*. And you're a good little mother."

"You're lucky she's between us or I'd show you who's little, all right."

"I'm shaking in my GI shoes."

"Damn right you are." As CJ's brow lifted, she corrected herself. "*Dang* right, I mean."

"Can you imagine if the first thing she says to my mother is a curse?"

"I don't know. It might take some of the heat off me." As CJ raised a spare pillow, threatening to whack her, she held up a hand. "Shh! You know the rule: Never wake a sleeping baby."

A little while later they turned out the bedside lamps. CJ tried to relax, but her mind busied itself with conjuring up potential disasters for the following day. What if her mother refused to acknowledge Brady or Maddie? What if Pete or Rebecca, both back living at home after college, reacted badly? She and Brady had managed to insulate themselves in Chapel Hill among a community of scholars and liberal intellectuals who barely blinked at the idea of two women raising someone else's illegitimate child together. Why had they felt the need to leave their safe cocoon? It was one thing for airline employees and hotel desk staff to assume they were merely good friends traveling together. Maddie's presence made a man a required accessory to at least one of them in most people's minds, and honestly, it was safer to go along with those assumptions than to challenge them. But Kalamazoo was a whole other ballgame.

Since the war's end, they had dutifully given her mother the space she needed. A week before mustering out of the WAC in late fall of 1945, CJ had called the history department at UNC to find out if they still had a spot for her. The department chair, a decorated veteran of the First World War, had thanked her for her service and offered her a place in the program to begin "as soon as you can get here."

"How's spring semester?" CJ had replied, smiling across the table at the orderly in the Company D day room.

"Wonderful," the aging professor had said in his gravelly voice.

Brady had gotten out three weeks before she had, and they had spent the remaining months of the year traveling to various corners of the United States to visit friends and family, including their brothers, all three of whom had returned unharmed, and their parents— separately. In January, they moved to Chapel Hill to begin a new adventure. Supremely tired of hiding their relationship, CJ had told the department chair about Brady during orientation week, offering him the option of rescinding her acceptance.

He had stared at her across his heavy mahogany desk. "I would be offended if I didn't know the prejudice you are accustomed to encountering in your private life. But it is exactly that, from my perspective—private. I hope you will not trouble yourself further on this matter, Miss Jamieson?"

"No sir," she'd said, and had left his office that afternoon lighter than she'd felt in years.

People could surprise you. That's what she was hoping would happen with her mother tomorrow when they showed up at the house. After her father had suffered a mild heart attack a few months earlier, CJ had flown in to be at his hospital bedside. That day, he had told her he wanted her home for the holidays—*with* Brady and Maddie, this time.

"What about Mom?" she'd asked.

He had shaken his head, looking gray but determined, machines at the bedside measuring his every breath and heartbeat. "Don't worry about her. It's time we met our granddaughter and your—companion. Is that what we should call her?"

CJ had nodded, anxiety already rising. Given that her mother still barely looked at her when she visited, it was hard to imagine she'd appreciate being forced to confront the evidence of CJ's lesbian existence.

Her older brothers had already met Brady and their niece, as they rightfully considered Maddie. She had been afraid to tell them, but Joe had come to visit her shortly before Maddie arrived and she'd decided she ought to tell him before he became an uncle. After the war, he had rejoined the Cubs for a single unhappy season before retiring to become a coach at the minor league level. When his job brought him to North Carolina, she took him out to a bar, bought him a drink and gave him the lowdown.

"You and Brady? As in, your *roommate* Brady?" he'd repeated, eyes momentarily widening.

She'd nodded, peeling the paper from her bottle of beer in a nervous habit she'd picked up from said roommate.

"Holy smokes." He shook his head. "I can't believe a girl as good looking as she is would go out with my little sister."

"What's that supposed to mean?" CJ had shot back, and then she realized he was smiling around the side of his whiskey glass. "Wait, so you don't mind?"

"I'm a little jealous, maybe." His eyes grew serious. "After everything I saw over there, I honestly don't see what the big fuss is. Besides, we were a bunch of young, red-blooded men away from women for months at a time. It doesn't take a genius to figure out what went on in the dark. Of course, if you ever quote me on that, I'll deny it."

Alec was a different case. Joe had offered to tell him about Brady and Maddie, and CJ had let him. She knew Alec didn't approve, but he wasn't overtly rude either. She'd take that over their mother's habit of staring at her when she thought CJ was unaware, her expression more befitting of something in a Shakespearean tragedy than the rare family get-togethers they'd managed since the war.

She was glad Joe would be there tomorrow, along with his wife, Alicia, a Hispanic woman whose brother he had coached in Chicago.

"Thanks for taking the pressure off," CJ had kidded him the night before his very Catholic wedding in a massive church on Chicago's south side.

He had half-hugged her. "What are big brothers for?"

Alec would be there too, with his wife and twin baby boys in tow. Then again, they were always there—he'd bought a nearby farm and didn't plan to leave Michigan ever again. His wife, Angie, had confided to CJ that she had other plans, but that she'd let him stay put for now. Joe had told her that Angie, whom CJ had known since kindergarten, had taken the news about her sister-in-law's proclivities in stride. Apparently she had a favorite unmarried uncle in Chicago who lived with his male "friend."

Friend. Still awake, CJ turned on her side and gazed at the woman whom she thought of as her wife sleeping peacefully beside their daughter. After tomorrow, there would be no more pretending with the Michigan clan. Bringing Brady and Maddie home to the farm was the last major hurdle in CJ's ongoing campaign to blend her pre- and post-war families.

In the years since she and Brady had first found their way, stumbling, to each other, they had become accomplished at being gay. It wasn't easy, of course. Being caught out could land you in prison or a psychiatric ward, and employers could fire you if they discovered your secret life. But lesbians, as CJ had learned to call women like them, and gay men had existed in the shadows of mainstream life for centuries, if not longer. The WAC had taught her how to evaluate potential danger spots—and people. In the aftermath of war, eluding the traps set by the government and conservative cultural factions became second nature.

The country had changed significantly, and not just because the United States was the lone world power that wouldn't have to rebuild. The war had displaced even more Americans than the Depression, bringing young men and women off the farms and out of the small towns and into cities and military units where they were forced to remake themselves far from the watchful eyes of their families and communities. At war's end, those who didn't want to return to their former lives didn't, and the population in military demobilization centers like San Francisco and New York City grew exponentially—as did the gay and lesbian communities in those cities.

Chapel Hill wasn't San Francisco or New York, but as a university town it was home to an intellectual populace who didn't particularly care about the broader culture's view of race or sexuality. They had friends there, both gay and mainstream, and there were even other "roommates" raising children together. When she finished her PhD in the spring, she was sure they'd find a similar community to call home—western Massachusetts, for example. Brady's mentor in Smith's

English department had not only helped get her first feature published in *Scientific American*, but she had also mentioned CJ's dissertation topic to her colleagues, who had shown interest in adding an expert in slave narratives to the faculty. Northampton was a consummate college town where unmarried women were not all that uncommon, as CJ knew from the handful of pilgrimages they'd already made to Brady's alma mater.

Then again, Kalamazoo was a college town, and CJ's mother was an educator. She and Brady couldn't be the only homosexuals she'd ever encountered. After a chilly start, her mother had embraced Alicia and the Chicago in-laws. Was her father right? Was it time?

"Hey."

CJ blinked in the dim light. She hadn't realized Brady was awake. "What?"

"It'll be okay, you'll see."

"I hope so. Guess we'll know tomorrow." She paused. "I told you we'd get here for Christmas one day."

"I think I was the one who told *you* we'd get here, Caroline."

She smiled in the dark. "Don't call me that."

"Just warming up for Kalamazoo. Anyway, it's a term of affection."

CJ reached across Maddie and took Brady's hand. Then she closed her eyes and willed her mind to be quiet.

Shortly before sunrise, she awoke disoriented in the strange room to hear Maddie whimpering. Beside her Brady shifted, consoling the child in a sleepy voice, "It's okay, sweetie. Mimi and Mama are here."

Soon Maddie settled back down, and CJ lay in the semi-dark pondering the moment when, only a few hours from now, she would walk into her childhood home and introduce Brady and their daughter to the rest of her family. Brady's words came back to her, and she decided then and there that no matter what happened in Kalamazoo, it really would be okay.

Thanks to a quirk of fate, she and Brady had found each other on a military base in the wilds of West Texas, and they had made the decision jointly to stick it out through the war and ensuing peace to build a home and a life together. They were lucky, as they often reminded each other—they had Maddie and their friends and the unconditional support of more than a few family members.

In the end, they were each other's family. And that, she knew, would be more than enough to see them through whatever this day—or any other, for that matter—would bring.

Author's Note & References List

When I was in college, I took an American women's history class that changed my world view, and not only because of the course material. During discussion one day, a fellow student called out the instructor for failing to include lesbian history, readily available in the recent (at the time) publication of Lillian Faderman's *Odd Girls and Twilight Lovers: A History of Lesbian Life in Twentieth-Century America*. I promptly went out and found a copy of Faderman's groundbreaking work, set aside any and all homework, and devoured *OGTL*.

Imagine my surprise when I reached the chapter on World War II and read, "During the war years…female independence and love between women were understood and undisturbed and even protected" (Faderman, 119). While the next sentence decries a return to the normalized American societal view of lesbians as "borderline psychotic," I couldn't get the image out of my mind of the Women's Army Corps and other American women's military units as a type of government-sponsored foray into progressive social norms.

Allan Bérubé's seminal history of gays and lesbians in the military during World War II, *Coming Out Under Fire*, further advances the view of the Women's Army Corps as a temporarily safe space in which lesbians could come out and fall in love. This wasn't the case for men in the military, of course, because Americans have always responded differently—and violently—to gay men. Once the war began to wind down, that safe space was quickly revoked. But for a few years, lesbian soldiers enjoyed a sense of freedom and value as they helped defend their nation against the Axis powers roaring across Europe, North Africa, and Asia.

On a personal level, the idea of a same-sex, lesbian-friendly community captured my imagination because I had recently left a homophobic public high school in the socially conservative Midwest and journeyed to a private women's college in liberal western Massachusetts. Like the soldiers in question, I had separated from my family and hometown and been given a chance to explore my same-sex attraction in a tolerant, all-women environment. Not to compare women's colleges of the 1990s to sex-segregated military units of the 1940s or anything.

Later that same year, my girlfriend, a philosophy major, and I both decided to apply to write an honors thesis. But like many philosophers, she was more attracted to discussion than to action. At least, that kind of action. By the end of the academic year, she had left me for a circus clown (really) and also given up on writing a thesis. I, on the other hand, had received a green light from my department to move forward with my proposal: an examination of American women's military participation in WWII. For primary sources, I would rely on the letters of an alumna and the journal of a WAC captain, both of whom had served overseas during the war and later donated their papers to the college archives.

As a senior, I conducted research and wrote my thesis, "Women in Combat Boots." But this was 1993, before the 50th anniversary of the end of WWII renewed interest in the conflict, before the Internet existed as anything more than blinking green hypertext trails, before self-publishing made the memoirs of average people available, and long before Amazon set forth its endless inventory of obscure titles. I relied heavily on the archives collections and the handful of texts that had been written about American women's military units. When I finished, I had one hundred twenty pages of dry description, analysis, and argument that I knew in my heart wasn't the story I wanted to tell. What was? A love story, of course. Only instead of a raven-haired beauty and a handsome young male officer, my story would feature two young women who discovered each other—and themselves—in the WAC.

The first draft of *In the Company of Women* arrived in 1998. But neither my research nor my writing skills were up to par, so I tucked the manuscript away with a promise: *someday*. Twenty-three years after I first read Faderman, the time finally felt right to revisit my WWII tale of lesbian love that was "understood and undisturbed and even protected." Fortunately for me, by now the Internet, Amazon, and self-publishing had all muscled their way into existence. This time when I set out to tell the story of a Michigan farm girl and a California women's college graduate who meet in the WAC and fall in love in the dusty reaches of West Texas, I had more than a dozen first-hand accounts at my disposal—not to mention all of the photos, videos, and letters housed in the National Archives and other online collections. Working at a university with unlimited access to academic titles helped too, and my first draft soon gave way to a second that featured the same characters and settings, but in all other ways appeared new.

As I noted in my dedication, nearly 400,000 American women served in uniform during World War II. The most, by far, served in the Women's Army Corps, so that's where I set my story. Out of those who served in the WAC, a majority served in the Army Air Corps, precursor to the Air Force, so it seemed only natural to make one of my characters an Air Wac. Armed with Aileen Kilgore Henderson's detailed account of life as an airplane mechanic at a Texas airfield and Anne Bosanko Green's beautifully written letters home to Minnesota, as well as a dozen other memoirs and letter collections of those who had served on the home front, I set out to breathe life into my story.

Too much life, or at least too much historical detail, as my editor and wife agreed during the revision process. But with their help, I managed to cut out some of the historical rambling. The result is this novel, set in a brief-lived era that found American women leaving home in droves, joining the military, and coming out with the support of their friends and colleagues. A brief period that Faderman, Bérubé, and other historians agree was critical to the development of the modern women's and gay rights movements.

What ITCOW is—and isn't

As a work of fiction, my book cleaves to a different set of rules than nonfiction works do. There are undoubtedly factual errors, and even times when I purposely conflated events to fit into my story's timeline—for example, the arrival of additional WASPs at Bliss and the B-17 crash in Chapter Ten. While these and other events related in the novel actually occurred, the real-life events took place at different points in the war. Also, while Wacs did serve at Fort Bliss, I have no reason to believe that any female mechanics were assigned to Tow Target, or indeed that any of the Biggs Field WASPs fraternized with enlisted Air Wacs. This part of the story is an example of me taking liberty with the often sketchy accounting that plagues women's history in general and lesbian history—and by extension, lesbian historical fiction—in particular.

On a related subject, my military experience is limited, so if I made errors related to uniforms, unit organization, daily activities, and so on, please accept my apologies.

Reading List

There is no requirement in the field of historical fiction to cite one's references, but I thought I might list some of the works I drew on for the edification of those interested in learning more about the historical context of my characters' lives.

- *Coming Out Under Fire* by Allan Bérubé
- *An Army in Skirts: The World War II Letters of Frances Debra* by Frances Debra Brown
- *Odd Girls and Twilight Lovers: A History of Lesbian Life in Twentieth-Century America* by Lillian Faderman
- *A Secret Place in my Heart: A Diary of a World War II Wac* by Dottie Gill
- *One Woman's War: Letters Home From The Women's Army Corp 1944-1946* by Anne Bosanko Green
- *Stateside Soldier: Life in the Women's Army Corps, 1944-1945* by Aileen Kilgore Henderson
- *Winning My Wings: A Woman Airforce Service Pilot in World War II* by Marion Stegeman Hodgson
- *We're in this War, Too: World War II Letters from American Women in Uniform* by Judy Barrett Litoff & David C. Smith
- *Creating G. I. Jane* by Leisa Meyer
- *Not All Soldiers Wore Pants: A Witty World War II Wac Tells All* by Rose Rosenthal
- *The Women's Army Corps (US Army Green Book)* by Mattie Treadwell
- *We Were WASPS* by Winifred Wood

Thanks for picking up a copy of *In the Company of Women*. Happy reading!

Kate Christie
Western Washington
5/1/2015

About the Author

Kate Christie was born and raised in Kalamazoo, Michigan, and currently makes her home in Western Washington with her wife, three daughters, and the family dog. Recently she moved her writing office from the spare bedroom—requisitioned by her twin toddlers—into a backyard shed that she built from a kit with help from her father and father-in-law. She now enjoys the nightly stroll from the back deck to her new office, accompanied variously by the songs of birds settling in for the night, the flutter of bats taking wing, and the pitter-pat of rain dripping from hundred-foot tall fir and cedar trees.

Bella Books, Inc.

Women. Books. Even Better Together.

P.O. Box 10543
Tallahassee, FL 32302

Phone: 800-729-4992
www.bellabooks.com